Circles in Time

ALSO BY TRILBY PLANTS

Gatekeeper

CIRCLES IN TIME

Trilby Plants

Kay – dream on & make your magic.
Trilby Plants
Oct. 2012

MURRELLS INLET, SC

ISBN-13: 978-1479256709

Pywacket
P·R·E·S·S

pywacketpresssmall.wix.com/pywacketpress

Printed in the United States of America
10 9 8 7 6 5 4 3 2 1

This one's for Mom. She would have liked it.

PROLOGUE

Ireland, 974 A.D.

The druid glared at his daughter. The smoky haze from the peat fire made his eyes water. He resisted the urge to cough.

"You will obey me," he said, his voice low. "The signs – "

"Bah," she said. "I see signs too, Father."

"It must be done my way, Lassariona." He forced power into his words. "No missteps."

She laughed and pushed unruly auburn curls from her face. "Your magic will not work on me, Ceallachan."

Did she use his name to mock him? He could not tell. The flames in the hearth behind her shadowed her face.

"I see true signs of what will be, Lassariona," he said. "We must follow the path the Earth Mother has laid out for us." He fingered his gray-shot beard. "You are but fifteen, child. Where you see events, I see the entire journey. Murchad o'Ruairc must bed the fey one and get her with child before you go to him."

"I do not understand why it must be so complicated." Lassariona's petulant voice carried a hint of anger. "Would it not be simpler for me to go to the o'Ruairc's fortress and slip into his bed?" She smiled seductively. "I do have some charms."

"Every journey is complicated," Ceallachan said. He tried to stay calm, but impatience gave his voice a sharp edge. "The path diverges many times. I know which turns we must take to reach a satisfactory end."

The hearth fire did little to chase the pre-dawn autumn chill from the circular hut's single room. The druid stepped around his daughter, closer to the fire, holding her gaze with his. Her green eyes glowed in the firelight like those of a night creature reflecting a hunter's torch. But her expression remained unreadable. Ceallachan could not tell truth or deception from the girl's face.

Lassariona shivered and looked away from him. She pulled her *brat* around her shoulders. The folded square of tattered wool had been her mother's, who had died birthing her. Ceallachan sat down on a three-legged stool with his back to the hearth. The warmth felt good on his bones.

"Will you see it done?" he said.

"Of course," Lassariona said. "When the bannachs are cooling, I will sprinkle the powder on one." She held up a small square of folded parchment.

"All of it at once."

"All at once," the girl repeated. "But Siobhan's mind is quick."

"Perhaps," Ceallachan said. "But she is young and only half-fey. Her human blood will betray her so the o'Ruairc can bed her."

"Do not worry, Father," Lassariona said. "The scullery girl will deliver the bannachs. But I am certain Siobhan will sense the taint as soon as she swallows the first bite."

"One swallow will annul her magic," said Ceallachan. "It is a powerful potion." He glanced toward the shelf above the hearth where his herbs and equipment were stored. "Not as strong as the other, but adequate when used correctly."

"Father," Lassariona said, sidling closer to him, "does this mean so very much to you?"

"It means everything to *us*, daughter." Ceallachan said. "Murchad o'Ruairc is desperate for a son. Naming some distant cousin as heir will not do. That idiot, Liam, will only squander it foolishly. Stupid boy's only talent seems to be for singing. He would turn the place into a school for bards and lose the land to the first raiders who knock on his gate."

Ceallachan rose from the stool.

"The land is our birthright." Passion made his voice boom. More quietly, he said, "It is only fitting your child should reclaim it. I have cast the runes and read entrails, daughter. The Earth Mother does not lie. Even the star signs point to your child. If he is *not* the first born, he will inherit."

Lassariona sighed. "But the o'Ruairc loathes the fey people. He believes the teachings of the White Christ. The monk says the fey ones are abominations – "

"I do not know if he truly believes. The potion will overcome his aversion. The way is clear." He glared at her. "You must let Murchad bed the fey woman before he comes to you. The child he gets on you must be the second born. The bastard will help us regain what is ours."

Lassariona pulled her *brat* over her head, covering the fiery highlights in her hair.

"Morning will soon fade the stars," she said. "Perhaps they will speak to me before the sun rises."

"Daughter," Ceallachan said. "Never doubt the stars. They say our battle is beginning. We were here before Murchad's people and even before the *Sidhe*. We are the rightful guardians of the Earth Mother's legacy. Those of *Faerie* do not care. They have abandoned the land and gone into their enchanted realm. There are only a few witches like Siobhan who still live in this world. This is our chance to take back the land and be rid of her kind forever."

The young woman turned and unlatched the door.

"Do not go to the fires tonight, Lassariona," Ceallachan said.

Although her face betrayed no dissembling, a spark of rebellion flashed in her green eyes. She must play her part else the rest of his plan go awry.

Lassariona nodded. She clutched her *brat* tighter and slipped into the autumn morning.

The cold wind that swept the last dregs of summer away from the green hills of Eirinn swirled into the room. Mist obscured the opposite shore of the small lough near the cabin. Lassariona quietly closed the door behind her.

Ceallachan held his hands toward the fire. Moments later horses' hooves and men's voices shattered the silence outside the hut. The door slammed open, shaking bits of daub from the walls.

"Murchad," Ceallachan greeted the man who entered. "Closed doors are supposed to mean something."

Murchad o'Ruairc was short and stocky, his hair blue-black like a raven's wing. Although age etched wrinkles on his face, his neatly trimmed beard was dark. An iron pin stuck through a circle of gold held the fabric of his *brat* together. The gold glittered in the firelight as if it possessed power of its own. Beneath the heavy red- and blue-dyed wool Murchad wore leather armor over a linen tunic, and a short sword at his hip. A tracery of scars on the man's forearms attested to his battle experience.

"This is my land, Ceallachan," Murchad said. "I go where I please."

Ceallachan studied the silence between them. Determination showed on the hard lines of Murchad's face. Outside a warrior dressed in homespun and leather sat astride a scruffy chestnut gelding. The man held his reins in one hand and his short sword in the other, along with the reins of the o'Ruairc's bay stallion. Both man and horses blew clouds of breath that hung on the still air.

Perhaps now was not the time to confront the chief of the o'Ruairc clan, with at least one of his warriors at the ready and no doubt others just out of sight.

Ceallachan raised an eyebrow, waiting for Murchad to continue.

"Do you have what I requested?" Murchad said.

Ceallachan did not like this chieftain, nor did he have reason to trust him. He must force the man into following the path.

"Murchad." Ceallachan said, "what you ask is – "

"Do not say it is impossible, Druid," Murchad said. "Everything has a price."

"It is…costly." Ceallachan's gaze did not flinch.

"Then how much?"

"Murchad, it is not a question of payment – "

"It seems to me that it is. If it can be done, and it is costly, then we are merely haggling over the price." Ceallachan did not respond. Murchad continued. "I have silver. Good horses. Some gold – "

"Ah, yes, gold." Ceallachan pointed to Murchad's cloak pin. "'Tis a fair token of craftsmanship."

"Very old," Murchad murmured, glancing down at the brooch. "A birth gift. It is not part of the bargain. I have other pieces to barter."

"Ah, but can gold warm your bed?"

"Do you mock me?" Murchad's expression darkened.

"Not at all," Ceallachan said. "But I have little use for ornaments. My daughter and I do not sell our potions in your fortress merely for silver."

"I have cattle and sheep – "

"Neither do I have time for the care of animals," Ceallachan said. "But," he lowered his voice, "the land – "

"Never." Murchad stepped back. "I will never concede even one parcel of my land."

"Ah." Ceallachan waved the idea away. "But no one truly owns the land. The Earth Mother lets us use her fruits as long as we care for her wisely."

"Do not burden me with your lectures on the old ways." Murchad's voice was tense. "Will you sell me what I require? If not, I'll be on my way. There are others who would do my bidding."

"But they are not as skilled as I," Ceallachan said.

Murchad turned toward the door.

"Wait," Ceallachan said. He had set the hook. This petty ruler would do his bidding. "There will be no payment. I will give it freely. A gift."

"Ha." Murchad whirled. "I know you too well, Ceallachan. Some payment is expected."

"Perhaps my daughter can continue to trade her potions in your fortress."

"Done," Murchad said.

"The elixir requires great enchantment," said Ceallachan. "And full cooperation on your part. I cannot guarantee the results if you do not obey my instructions. You will have but one chance to make it work. And even then – "

Murchad took two steps forward, his left hand on the hilt of the short sword at his hip. Ceallachan watched Murchad's eyes for a sign that he would grasp the weapon cross-handed with his right hand and draw it.

"Unhand your blade, Murchad," Ceallachan said. "Do not threaten me before my own hearth. If you lay iron to me, you will never get what you want, will you?"

Murchad's knuckles on his sword hilt whitened with anger. "Can you give me what I desire?" he growled.

"An heir?" Ceallachan said with a disarming smile. He moved toward the fireplace. Various containers and old tomes cluttered a crudely fashioned cedar shelf that served as a mantelpiece. Bundles of dried herbs and flowers hung from the ceiling.

"An heir is what we are discussing here." Murchad's voice had become husky. "Nothing more."

"Ah, yes, so it is." Ceallachan plucked a tiny vial from amidst the jumble. He raised a container made of a dark, shiny substance. Flames leaped in the hearth fire. The vial glinted red as blood. The burning turf settled back to a flicker, and the impression vanished. Ceallachan moved the vial from side to side, enticing Murchad.

Murchad's gaze followed the movement. He stepped forward, then checked himself. "Will it work?" he said.

"Oh, yes, it will work," Ceallachan whispered. "But you must do exactly as I say. Any deviation will have disastrous results. You must swear. This is powerful enchantment."

"You have my oath I will follow your directions." Murchad snorted. "But this best not be a sham, such as reading entrails or hearing the stars."

"Do not speak of what you do not understand, Murchad," Ceallachan said. He drew himself to his full height – a head taller than the other man. "This is not some trivial medicine my daughter would make to ease a woman's headache, or dull the cramps from her monthly courses. This is different. Older. Notice the container. It is made of a hollow crystal." He held it up.

Murchad reached for it, but Ceallachan held it back.

"It must be destroyed as soon as you have drunk," Ceallachan said. "Shatter it in your hearth with a wood fire blazing. Do not leave even a drop of the liquid – nor a shard of the container – for some hapless person to sample by accident. And carry it on your person until you consume it."

"I will do as you say," Murchad said. Impatience showed in his greedy gaze.

"And," the druid closed his hand over the vial, "you must swallow it tonight – *Samhain* Eve – in your chamber as the last glimmer of sun drops behind the hills. No sooner, no later. I will not vouch for its efficacy if you do not follow these instructions. Do you agree?" Murchad nodded. "There is one more condition."

Murchad rolled his eyes. "There is always a last condition. That way, if it doesn't work, you can deny responsibility."

"I have never denied responsibility for my potions, Murchad. Never before in my life have I made one this powerful. You must understand what is involved."

"All right." Murchad glowered. "What is the condition?"

"It will not work on a mortal woman."

Anger flashed in Murchad's dark eyes. "That is not a condition. It is an absurdity." He turned toward the door. "I can see I am wasting my time," he hurled over his shoulder.

"Nothing is ever wasted," Ceallachan murmured. "Everything is part of the Earth Mother's pattern. You do not understand."

Murchad turned back, his face a mask of rage. Had Ceallachan misjudged him? Murchad must take the potion or the plan would be thwarted.

"I understand better than you seem to," Murchad said. "What good is a fertility potion that will not work on a woman? Do you think me stupid?"

"I said it will not work on a *mortal* woman." Ceallachan kept his voice low.

"Not mortal?"

"It is simple," Ceallachan said. "You must find a woman with fey ancestry. The potion in your blood will call her to you. Bed her tonight, and you will have your heir."

"Fey," Murchad growled. "They are loathsome creatures. Besides, only one of them has come to dance around the fires the last few years. She is addled in the head."

"The one who lives in the wood and comes to your fires is only half fey. She is as human as you." Ceallachan raised the vial. "After you drink the potion go to the Samhain fires. She will dance before the Horned God. Call her, and she will come to you. The full-blooded are too wise, but one such as she, with only a spark of fey heritage, will be bedazzled by you. You are, after all, known for your generosity. You rewarded all three of your lawful wives handsomely for their services."

"The law provides that a man may put aside a barren wife – "

"But poison, Murchad?" Ceallachan said.

Murchad's face reddened. He reached across his body for his sword.

"That was uncalled for," Murchad said, his voice low and menacing. He half drew his blade.

Ceallachan tried not to wince at the hiss of metal sliding across leather.

"Ah, so it was." Ceallachan forced a disarming smile. "Your last wife succumbed from a bad mushroom. An unfortunate accident. My daughter's potion arrived too late to do the unhappy woman any good. At least she did not suffer long."

Murchad's eyes gleamed hard and cold. His gaze pinned Ceallachan's.

"Be that as it may," Ceallachan said. "If you follow my directions you will seduce a fey maiden."

Murchad's hand on his sword relaxed, and the blade whispered back into its sheath. "There will be a child?"

"I know this from the signs," Ceallachan said. "You have my word."

He offered the vial. Murchad hesitated, then snatched it and tucked it into a leather pouch at his waist.

"You are still welcome in my fortress," Murchad said. He squinted through the smoky haze. "Your daughter, too, as long as you are on a medicinal errand. Just do not let the monk see you. It would not do. I cannot justify the old ways with the new teachings. The monk says his God frowns upon magic. Appearances must be kept."

"I thought you did not believe in that."

"I do what must be done to maintain order in my holding. Remember what I have said, Druid. Watch yourself, and no ill will come to you."

"Follow my instructions exactly," Ceallachan said. "And you will be rewarded."

Murchad nodded and left the cottage. Ceallachan closed the door and went to warm his hands by the fire.

His daughter's destiny – and Murchad's – depended upon a few drops of enchanted potion.

1

Siobhan crouched beside a tree at the edge of the forest and watched the humans in the field beyond. Heavy clouds leaked cold mist. She shivered and reinforced her spell of warming.

Young men gathered downed tree limbs from the edge of the *Sidhe* Wood. They did not venture alone into the forest, fearing such as she.

Two men swathed in heavy homespun brats over their shirts and wool leg wrappings approached. Siobhan blended so well with the tree that sheltered her they would not see her.

One man, taller and older than the other, carried an ax over one shoulder. He surveyed the nearby trees and pointed.

"We'll take that one, Cormac," he said. "It's near dead and will burn long."

His youthful companion paused. "Too far in," he said. "I do not plan to never see home again."

"Ach," the other man scoffed. "What can happen to us in sight of our clansmen?"

"If sight there is in such uncanny shadows," the younger man mumbled.

The man with the ax laughed and strode forward. "Just don't eat or drink anything the witch offers you. Besides, our witch is addled." He wiggled his fingers at one temple.

The youth glanced behind him toward the field of broken cornstalks where villagers and clansmen stacked wood into two huge piles. Small boys scurried around stuffing dry bark and cornstalks under the wood where the tinder would stay dry.

Samhain, the druids called the celebration. The end of the year. After the harvest, when the Goddess shed her summer greenery, and autumn stalked the glens and painted leaves gold and crimson. *Samhain* was the one night when the Horned God's spirits roamed the earth searching for fresh souls to torment. Humans appeased the Horned One so he passed over them, and they would see the earth reborn in the spring.

Siobhan leaned back against the rough bark. She centered herself, unmoving, waiting. The humans could walk within arm's length of her and not see her.

The rain let up and afternoon sun cast long, pale shadows. Two women came to the edge of the wood, one bearing a bundle wrapped in a tattered piece of cloth. Urged by the older woman, the younger one stepped cautiously into the near darkness under the trees. After a few paces, the girl set the bundle down and turned and ran from the forest, not pausing for the other woman to catch up to her.

Siobhan waited and watched and listened. Silence surrounded her. The oaty aroma of fresh-baked bannachs wafted from the bundle. They were much tastier than the flat cakes she made with acorn flour. The village women left offerings for her. In exchange Siobhan sometimes put a small spell on the early lambs to keep them warm, or on a kitchen garden that it would produce well.

Her senses alert, her mind questing for danger, Siobhan crept to the bundle and grabbed it up. She scampered back into the deeper shadows carrying her supper. Preoccupied with thoughts of dancing around the fires, Siobhan had eaten nothing all day. She devoured a bannach, barely tasting it, and then spent a few moments savoring the next one. The last bun she carried with her to the edge of the forest where she resumed her watch.

Twilight deepened, and darkness came early. Many humans gathered in the field. Young men kindled the bonfires. Great pyramids of flames crackled and licked the low clouds with blood-red tongues.

The fires consumed vast piles of wood and refuse and a few large, rough-woven baskets that held straw effigies of humans. Sacrifices meant to please the Horned God and his minions. Before the coming of the monks who built the abbey, Siobhan had heard the cries of living creatures – animals and men – when the fires were lit. Now, the bloodless reminders of older days burned in silence.

People drank to the fruitful harvest and a mild winter. Maidens danced like living flames around the fires. Youths in various stages of drunkenness leered at them, and old men cast covetous glances at the lithe bodies. Men and women linked by marriage pledges vanished into the night. One by one the unmarried women chose men and left the fires in their company – warriors and craftsmen, highborn and peasant – to couple in the fields and along the edges of the forest.

The babies born of these unions were welcomed and revered, but only the first son of a couple united by a marriage bond inherited a man's property. Siobhan knew from her dealings with humans that the land from the forest toward the rising sun was ruled by Murchad o'Ruairc.

The chief of the o'Ruairc clan was childless. Gossips whispered the land would be wrested from him by some cousin when the o'Ruairc grew too old to fight. As if humans could truly own the Earth Mother.

Siobhan often went about in the village, unseen by others, and had overheard the whispers that she was a bit mad because she was neither human nor fey. She did not believe she was addled, but the other was true. Her father had been *Sidhe*, her mother human. Siobhan never knew her father. Ostracized by humans, she and her mother had lived apart from the settlement as long as Siobhan could remember. Her mother was long dead, succumbing to her human mortality.

Siobhan often observed the humans, knowing they shunned her, yet she longed to be part of their community. Her only contacts with them were begging oat cakes and selling trinkets and charms to the women.

When the fires burned low, she would dance and tease the humans. Some might follow her, but none were alluring enough to take to her bed.

Still hungry, Siobhan bit into the last bannach. It tasted peculiar. Bitter. She swallowed the mouthful and peered at the rest of the bun. The top crust was greeenish, as if it had sat too long. But it still held a faint warmth from the hearth. Another bite. There was definitely something wrong with it. She spit out the mouthful and tossed the rest into the brush.

Both bonfires had burned to half their original height. Time had somehow gotten away from her.

She glided from the forest, wanting to be seen. Some of the humans looked away quickly, lest they be enticed to follow her into the forest. Going into the Wood might mean abduction into the fey realm, never to be seen again by the living. A fate nearly as loathsome as going to the Horned God's demesne.

Siobhan paused under the eaves of a great tree. A few younger girls, not yet of an age to lie with a man, still danced, ogled by toothless oldsters who tipped their mead cups and nodded knowingly to each other in memory of their lost youth.

A solitary harper's melody trembled on the cool night air. The music warmed Siobhan and drew her to the smoldering coals. Music echoed in her mind. Her vision blurred. Her body moved to the rhythm of the harper's fingers.

She snatched a cup of mead from a one-armed warrior and downed it in two gulps. Then she flung herself into a dance with wild abandon. She felt a strange urge to offer this intimate gift to the Horned One in defiance of her *Sidhe* father's prohibition. The Horned One was enemy to those of *Faerie*, inimical to the Earth Mother's mercy and goodness.

She had never come so close to the fires before. Unfamiliar excitement pulsed through her veins, and she reveled in her youth and vitality. She peered into the faces of each man she passed looking for…what? Something she lacked? She lacked for nothing. Except….

Siobhan paused in her dance. The bannach. The one with the green crust. There *had* been something in it. Some potion that made her mind fuzzy and kept her thoughts whirling. Who would do such a thing?

Hands groped at Siobhan's legs. An old man, his eyes clouded. She danced away from him. Youngsters mooned after her with lustful eyes. Her feet barely touched the ground. Her body moved sensually, reflecting an unnatural need inside her. Her restless gaze passed over elders, over warriors too maimed to be of interest to maidens, over callow youths whose cheeks flushed red with burgeoning desire. Instead, she listened for something beyond the music.

"Shhh…."

Her feet faltered. Her name? But called as if from a great distance. A little girl with a gap-toothed smile nearly collided with her, but Siobhan avoided her and skipped away from the fires toward whatever beckoned her.

"Siobhan…."

From the forest. As if of their own volition, her feet carried her into the shadows under the trees. Was the sound only wind-rustled leaves? A movement drew her attention. A shadow darted between two trees.

She felt light-headed, more than the result of the mead she had drunk. Her fingers formed the sigil for a spell that would put her body in order, but she couldn't seem to trace the right path. She giggled at her forgetfulness and stepped deeper into the shadows. She felt breathless and giddy.

What was happening to her? She was not an unwary human, foolish enough to be seduced into *Faerie*. Her heritage gave her the power to refuse.

A footfall crackled. A drunken youth, perhaps, seeking a conquest among the fey folk? He would present no difficulty for her. She would cast a spell of confusion upon him.

She stopped, her arms gently waving, keeping time to the distant music. "Siobhan…." A whisper of sound.

She strained to hear with the fey part of her mind. Only silence. Dread prickled along her bare arms, but an odd eagerness quickened her heart. Her gauzy shift fluttered against her skin. She felt a wanton sensuality she had never before experienced.

Where had these thoughts come from? She had never come to the *Samhain* fires seeking a man. She only came to dance and tease and then fade into the forest. The humans would talk about one of the fey folk who had beguiled them and then vanished. What had led her away from the fires into the woods?

Another footfall disturbed the leaves.

Curiosity drew her further into the forest. There could be no danger here at the edge of the *Sidhe* Wood. This was her home. Her magic kept her safe here.

A man stepped from behind a tree, a darker shape among the shadows. Some harmless human made brave by drink. An easy game. She would have fun with this one.

But the mead must have made her tipsy. She wanted to see better, but she could not remember the spell for light. As if at her bidding, the moon's silver face peeked through the tree branches.

"Murchad," she cried. She knew him, this leader of the o'Ruairc clan. She had seen him from the shadows when he had presided over the fires of the *Bealtain* festival in the spring.

"You surprise me," she said.

A half-smile played across his lean, angular face. He pulled his *brat* over his head and let it fall to the ground. Siobhan caught a gleam of gold and the whiff of the iron shank that secured the brooch to his *brat*. He folded his arms across his leather-armored chest. His hair was a cap as dark as ravens' wings.

"Is it possible to sneak up on one of your kind?" he taunted.

"Only if we allow it." Best to put him off guard with scorn in her voice. But what came from her mouth was soft, not stern, as if she were teasing him. She probed his thoughts, finding only fragments of a bard's silly rhyming song for children. The words threaded through his mind, obscuring his deeper thoughts.

He stepped toward her.

"No closer," Siobhan warned. She tried to feel angry, but her resolve melted into warmth.

"What," he said. "Will you turn me into a spider?"

Shape shifting was beyond Siobhan's powers. Her mortal mother had diluted her magic. The part of her that was human overwhelmed some of her *Sidhe* abilities. Perhaps if she conjured a rush of spiders that dropped down on him from the trees, he would be frightened and leave. She raised her hands. She did not feel the rise of magic. Puzzled, she looked at her hands. Murchad stepped forward again. She should leave.

She felt his gaze upon her. Her cheeks burned with frustration that she could not cast a spell or turn and run.

"You are beautiful," he said, his voice husky. He unfastened his armor. The pieces of leather fell to the ground.

From his mind she caught the image of a tiny vial of liquid he had drunk. Puzzled, she probed deeper, only to find again an echo of the harper's song that masked…something…an undercurrent of deception. But she could go no further. Her enchantment failed her.

He was not ugly. By human standards, his face was handsome and his body pleasing. Lust burned in his dark eyes. Heat flushed up Siobhan's body. Desire warmed her cheeks. She shook away these thoughts and tried to make her voice cold.

"Come no closer," she said, "or I will – "

"You will what?" he said. Another step. "I am unarmed as you can see. No iron. Tonight we are equals, woman."

That was why she had not sensed him. His iron sword would have warned her. Siobhan's mind swirled with conflicting ideas, like bees swarming inside her head. She recalled drinking a cup of mead. Had she drunk more than she remembered?

"Equals?" She laughed. As soon as she took the first step toward him, she knew she was lost.

Something in her food….

She could not turn away from Murchad. He untied his tunic and let it fall. Unbidden desire coursed through Siobhan's veins when she saw him naked. She gestured toward her shift, but the spell of unclothing failed.

This should not happen. Magic should not desert her. Her head spun, and her knees felt watery.

Murchad knelt beside her, his face close to hers. His hands caressed her arms. His lips moved, but she heard no sound. How had she come to be lying on the ground on his *brat*? Jumbled images flooded her mind, and the question flitted from her grasp.

Murchad fingered a strand of her unbound hair.

"So pretty," he breathed. "Like gold."

Siobhan wanted to push him away, but she could not summon the strength. Although she did not direct them, her arms raised. Her fingers touched the dark hair of Murchad's chest. A thrill coursed through her.

"Why have I not seen you before?" he said softly.

Siobhan tried to answer that she had come to the fires before, but she heard her voice whispering, "Yes, yes," while her mind cried "no." Something was wrong, but she could not muster the energy to run away. There was something she had eaten…something he had drunk….

He pulled up her gown. Her flesh tingled at his touch. She moaned, not sure where the response came from. He cupped one breast with a calloused hand. His breathing grew ragged, and his hands became more insistent.

She tried to say, "No," but a moan of pleasure came from her throat.

Murchad's lips were on her neck, her breasts, and his weight pressed her hips into the soft forest loam. His hands and mouth became urgent and forceful.

He raised himself above her. Against her will Siobhan lifted her arms and welcomed his body to hers, even while she fought against the desire. He pushed her arms above her head, holding her wrists down. His weight smothered her. He hurt her, a sharp, breathless pain that made her want to pull away, but she could not. She squeezed her eyes shut against the giddiness in her mind and the unwelcome invasion of her body. But she was powerless to resist.

His hot breath blew on her face. His hands – too rough – bruised her. He thrust into her again and again.

Why did she not have the will to refuse? In that moment Siobhan felt shame for the first time in her life. She endured. Without magic she could not push Murchad away. Finally his body convulsed, and he collapsed upon her, driving her breath away.

Night faded to true darkness.

Siobhan opened her eyes, only to find she was still lost in gloom. She blinked, felt tears. Why had she cried in her sleep? There had been an awful dream.

Oh, Goddess, why had the dream seemed so real? There had been a mortal…and she was willing….

Memories flooded her mind. It was not a dream. It was real. She remembered Murchad's face, felt his heavy body, felt pain. And shame. What had stolen her magic? It was gone. Her human legacy.

Confusion clamored inside her head. Tears filled her eyes. She lay still, husbanding her strength. Her mind slowly cleared. Time would heal her body. Her magic would return when her human emotions calmed.

Murchad had shamed her. She would not have given her maidenhead to him by choice. There was enchantment involved. But he alone was not capable of stealing her will and her magic. Someone must have given him the means. Someone powerful. The tainted bannach? Someone from the village? No. The humans feared her, but they would not deliberately harm her. She searched her memories, but could not discover how the deception had been wrought.

Murchad probably reveled in his Great Hall, drinking and laughing and recounting how he had bedded her. Siobhan knew the truth. He had not bedded her; he had violated her. There was no passion in what he had done, just deceit.

Her revenge would be sweet, knowing what she knew about Murchad o'Ruairc: he could not get an heir on several wives, so he had turned to forcing one of the fey. It would not bode well with his people that he had debased her – in their minds not quite human. He would be ridiculed and perhaps ostracized.

Cold anger replaced her feelings of helplessness and gave strength to her resolve. She could not remain here. Murchad might regret what he had done and realize the only way to cover his crime would be to see her dead. In her depleted state she would be easy prey.

She would discover the one who had betrayed her. But first she must recover both in body and mind. Revenge would only be possible if she lived. She must be well enough to eavesdrop at mortals' doors, to go to the village on market days and listen to idle gossip.

She pushed herself to a sitting position. Murchad's *brat* lay across her bare legs. He must have thrown it over her before he left her. In the darkness her fingers felt the texture of the rough woven wool. She felt Murchad's cloak pin, heavy in her lap. The shank was missing.

Siobhan unfolded the fabric and pulled it around her, grateful for the warmth. She picked up the pin and flinched, but the metal did not burn her. The pin was gold, which could not hurt her. Her chilled fingers traced the outline of the brooch and discovered an intricate design. Craftsmen of Murchad's holdings were incapable of such fine workmanship. Perhaps the stories about the old smith who vanished into the Wood were true, after all. Siobhan had been a child at the time, secluded by her mother away from the village. According to the stories, he had been a true artisan with silver and gold.

Siobhan hoped Murchad realized its worth and regretted its loss. Even a rich chieftain could not afford to lose his treasure. She found her purse on the ground beside her, its braided string intact. She put the golden circle in the pouch and tied it around her waist.

She rose, and the forest spun around her. She stood a long moment, steadying herself. Above her, through the nearly bare branches, stars swirled in giddy patterns she did not recognize. She could not hear their music. Without their music they could not guide her.

She searched her mind for the magical path to her own private world away from time, but her enchantment was disrupted, and she could not find the way. She must go somewhere. Away from where she was. Away from human retribution. Someplace safe. Into the heart of the *Sidhe* Wood where mortals feared to travel, and even her kind seldom went.

Her sandaled feet stumbled on the uneven ground. A dry branch cracked, stilling the voices of the forest. Streamers of mist snaked between the trees, wrapping her in chilly dampness. The forest grew thicker, until she squeezed between tree trunks set so close together there was little space for moonlight. Twigs and old leaves littered the ground and crunched under her feet.

Curiously, stars descended and fluttered close to her and brushed her skin with a warm breath of comfort that drew her anguish away, but rattled her concentration. She must remember why it was important to find a safe haven. She must avenge herself, first on Murchad, and then on the one who had betrayed her.

She tried not to think beyond the moment, tried to keep her feet moving. Mist cocooned her, and the firefly lights guided her steps and gave her warmth.

Weariness overcame her. Her knees buckled, and she sank to the ground.

Get up, Siobhan....

She could not rise and meet the speaker, for in doing so, she would have to face her humiliation.

Siobhan, get up....

A voice in the forest? Another mortal?

Siobhan....

Someone had spoken her name thrice and thus invoked power over her.

Siobhan struggled to her feet and was once more wrapped in a swirling radiance of lights. The lights quieted her mind into a profound silence that quieted the myriad tiny voices and rustlings of the forest and the turmoil of her thoughts.

"Where am I going?" she whispered. No one answered. Perhaps this was only a fever dream.

Siobhan followed the lights. After awhile the trees opened into a meadow where the mist thinned and some starlight penetrated. The lights danced over the dry brown grass like butterflies on a summer day. She stumbled across the meadow. Again she stepped into the tree shadows. The fog grew thicker, and the lights drew closer to her.

This was not the way home. She should not be here. Humans and her kind avoided the deep places of the Wood, for the heart of the forest belonged to the ancient ones. Those of her father's ancestry, whose magic was far beyond her understanding, those of *Faerie*. She whose blood was tainted by the mortal who had lain with her father could never aspire to such power.

But the lights compelled her to follow and numbed her shame. She was powerless to resist.

The fog rolled away. The lights grew more agitated, fluttering and blinking around her. She stumbled up a slight incline and stopped. An ancient, twisted oak loomed above her, darker against the sky, blotting out the stars. The firefly lights retreated and faded, leaving her alone.

"No," she murmured. "Do not go. Stay – "

The world went dark, and she fell a long way, but there was no sensation of rushing wind. After a time she stopped falling, knew she was lying on a soft surface, but the darkness was so complete she could not even see herself. Was this, then, death?

No. She could think. She breathed. Thoughts and breath meant life.

A vague glow grew in the darkness and coalesced in front of her. The luminescence drew together and resolved into eyes, nose, lips and nearly white hair. The face belonged to someone she thought she should know. But she could not find the name for the pale woman who leaned over her.

"Poor girl," the woman whispered.

"Help me," Siobhan tried to say. She was not sure she had spoken. Her throat felt dry and scratchy.

Cool hands fluttered over her face, brushed her body like the fall of snowflakes, barely felt. She tried to shrink away from the touch, but she could not move. Immobilized by magic more potent than hers would ever be, Siobhan submitted and gazed into icy blue eyes.

"Siobhan…." The voice was liquid melody. "Listen, child, I will send you away."

"Where?" Siobhan said, or did she only think it?

"Far away, child. You will be safe. Someone will help you. But you must not leave the place I send you to." Siobhan nodded. "Speak it," the Lady of Light said.

"I will stay where you send me," Siobhan whispered. "Why – ?"

"Rest. You will mend." The woman's smile was radiant. She held out a goblet encrusted with bits of shiny stone. "Drink, child. It will ease you."

"Do not make me drink," Siobhan whispered. If she partook of the enchanted drink she would be bound forever to the land of *Faerie*.

"Hush, child," the woman said. "It is the only way I can help you. It will not harm you or bind you. You have my word. You must drink."

Perhaps it was best that she give in. She could spend the rest of her days dreaming, away from the mortal world, never to know anger, discomfort, longing or any other human emotion.

Siobhan could not resist the hypnotic command in the ageless eyes. She reached for the goblet and drank. The elixir was sweet and warming. She drained the cup, felt it leave her hand, and then sank back on soft cushions.

The Lady's hands fumbled at Siobhan's purse. Siobhan tried to push her away, but she could not overcome the numbness that spread through her body.

The cloak pin in the Lady's hand filled Siobhan's vision with a golden circle of light.

"Siobhan." The Lady's voice came from a great distance. "This must stay with me. The brooch is an endless circle. Remember this, what will happen is what must be. Sleep, child." The Lady's hands traced a feathery touch on Siobhan's forehead. "Sleep…."

Once again the lights hovered over her. Siobhan tried to raise an arm to touch them, to welcome them, but her muscles refused to obey. Her eyelids grew heavy. The Lady's pale face floated over her. Hands clasped a band around her neck.

"This will bring you back, child," the Lady said.

Where am I going? Siobhan wanted to protest, but dizziness overtook her. She lurched forward into damp mist. The lights faded into the mist.

"Help me," Siobhan cried, but it was only a whisper that the fog flung back at her.

A soft glow brightened the haze. There was no going back, nothing behind her, so she stumbled forward.

Snow swirled around her. It covered her feet. Cold nipped her toes, but there was no help from her magic. Her power was depleted. Only rest and time would bring it back.

Ahead, indistinct in the fog, a mound shone from within brighter than the firefly lights. She stepped toward the promised sanctuary. But the reek of iron repelled her. The mound was an iron turtle taller than she was, the metal worked to a fineness she had never encountered.

A man leaned into the turtle's shimmering mouth. The monstrous creature's yawning jaws were about to swallow him.

She had not escaped at all. The man rushed to her. She surrendered to darkness that closed around her.

2

Portland, Oregon
Present Day

B rant Edwards held the sketchbook in the crook of his left arm, trying to keep it together. Extra pages he'd torn from other books threatened to spill. He dug his key from his jeans pocket and got it in the lock.

He hesitated. Again he had a feeling he had forgotten something. On the drive home from the cabin he had been plagued by thoughts that distracted him from the road. What the hell was he supposed to remember?

He twisted the key and opened the door. He balanced the overflowing sketchbook and pocketed his lucky key. If what he had forgotten were important, it would eventually come to him. He hoisted his battered leather duffel with his free hand, entered the loft apartment and nudged the door shut behind him with one foot.

He shivered. The loft was cold and empty. Although he had only been gone a couple of days, he felt tired, as if it had been weeks since he'd last stepped through the door. He dropped the duffel and tapped the thermostat up to 70, thankful to be home.

Home. His cabin in Washington was a rustic tranquility – a retreat from the stresses of everyday life – but this loft in a huge old warehouse was part of the material world, Brant's idea of success. Now that he had lived in the loft for a year and had everything almost the way he wanted it, it was home.

He stepped to the writing desk behind the sofa and dumped the sketchbook on it. Papers scattered and fluttered to the floor.

"Shit," he muttered. "Typical." He kicked his way through the papers toward his bedroom.

A hot shower would wake him up and rinse away the clinging odor of wood smoke from the cabin's fireplace. He toed off his sneakers and draped his jacket over the back of a chair.

He headed for the bedroom, unbuttoning his flannel shirt as he went. The shirt slipped off his shoulders. The door opened. The setting sun from the bedroom window silhouetted a tall, willowy figure. Feminine.

"Who – ?" he started.

"Brant." The woman's voice was sharp. She stepped into the living room, stark surprise on her face. "Where the hell have you been?"

Freckles sprinkled her nose and cheeks. Dark hair pulled back in a clamp accented her fair complexion. She wore blue jeans and a white turtleneck.

Brant felt as though he knew her from somewhere, but couldn't place her.

Before he could think of a response, she flung herself at him. She burst into tears and clung to him. He wasn't about to embrace a stranger. And besides, what was she doing in his apartment? Unsure what to do, he patted her shoulders.

"Oh, God," she said breathlessly. "We thought you might be dead."

"Dead?" We?

"I've been frantic." Her words tumbled out. "So many people have been looking for you – "

"Whoa," he finally managed. "What are you talking about? What are you doing here?"

"I came to water the damned plants," she said.

He glanced at the jungle of green in the corner of the living room by a bank of windows. His little jungle.

He pushed her away.

"How'd you get in here?" he said.

"What?" She rolled her eyes. "I used my key."

"Key?" He didn't remember giving anybody a key to his place, least of all a stranger. He would have remembered her.

"Key," she said. "You gave me and Rich a key when you moved in here."

"What key?" A dull ache throbbed in his left temple.

"This key," she said. She reached in her jeans pocket and pulled out a single key on a give-away ring from a local auto repair shop. She held it out. "*My* key."

Brant snatched it and closed his fist on it.

"How'd you get this?" he snapped.

"Oh, for crying out loud, Brant. You gave it to me – "

"Why would I give a key to somebody I don't know?"

"What?" She stared at him, clearly at a loss.

His head hurt. For an instant he almost felt he should know her name. How could he?

"Who the hell are you," he said slowly, "and what are you doing here?"

"What do you mean?" She backed away from him, her gaze flickering away from him toward the doorway.

"An introduction would be nice since you're trespassing in my home," he said.

"What's going on, Brant?" Patient, as if she were speaking to a little child.

"Damn it, nothing's going on," he said. "I want to know who you are and what you're doing here."

"Stop it, Brant," she said. "You're scaring me."

He moved toward her, and she side-stepped, angling around him. She kept her gaze on the door.

"I'm calling the cops," he said. "And you'd better have a good reason for being here."

"You're joking." She raised her chin in defiance.

If she was a burglar, she was a damn cool one.

"I'm dead serious," he said.

He slapped his pockets. No cell phone. That must be what he'd forgotten. It was in the car. He moved toward the phone. What if she had a weapon? A gun? She bolted past him, yanked the door open and fled.

Brant hadn't seen anything in her hands. But that didn't mean she hadn't taken something of value from him. The throbbing in his head became a full-fledged headache. He glanced around, checking to see if anything obvious was missing. Television, CD player, appliances in the kitchen. Everything seemed to be in place. He opened his studio door and turned on the light. All appeared to be as he had left it, neatly organized, three unfinished canvasses on easels. He went to buzz Hank Mitchell at the security desk.

Maeve Edwards Gordon ran down the hall to the elevator. This time her brother's practical jokes had gone too far. By the time the elevator opened on the lobby she had cooled down enough to wonder what she should do. Her purse hung on a hook in Brant's coat closet. If she had cab fare in her jeans, she'd go home. Her pockets yielded only a single dollar bill and some change.

Brant had been so…odd. Should she just go back up and demand an answer? Brant had been so…odd. He could never keep a straight face when he joked with her. Something else was at play.

"Evening again, Maeve," the security guard greeted her. He was hanging up the phone. There was a quizzical expression on his face.

"Hello, Hank," Maeve said.

Hank Mitchell looked at her with concern in his rheumy eyes. "Everything all right?"

"I don't know, Hank," Maeve said.

"That was Brant on the phone." Hank frowned at her. "He said there was a prowler in his place. A woman. Looked just like you. Wanted me to stop you until the cops got here. I didn't see him go up. Musta parked in the garage and didn't even stop. He okay? Is this a joke or something?"

Maeve shook her head.

"You two have an argument?" Hank said.

"No," Maeve said. "Not really. I don't know what happened. We had a…disagreement. Sort of. And I left my purse upstairs so I don't have any money – "

"Want me to call you a cab?" Hank's voice held genuine kindness.

"I don't know….Could I use the phone?" she said. "My cell's in my purse, and I'd rather not go back up alone." The understatement of the century. "I'll just call Rich."

"Sure." Hank handed her the phone. "Just dial nine and then your number."

She punched nine, waited for the tone, then entered Rich's cell number.

"Detective Gordon." Rich's calm, matter-of-fact voice.

"Rich," Maeve said. "It's me."

"How are ya, honey? Hangin in there?" His voice changed to reassuring, normal. He chewed something crunchy. He must be eating dinner at his desk again. Some high fat takeout they both tried to avoid.

"Rich," she said, "you're not going to believe this, but you'd better come over here. I'm in the lobby of Brant's building. It's – " Her voice stuck in her throat.

"Maeve, what's wrong?" He swallowed audibly. "Are you all right? Is Brant—?"

"I'm fine," she said. "But *he* just walked in." She surprised herself by feeling angry at Brant.

The phone was silent a long moment. She listened to the faint hum in the receiver.

"I was watering plants," Maeve said, "and he just...walked in as if nothing was wrong."

"Really," Rich said.

She imagined him hunched over his messy desk, his elbows resting on the papers, one hand kneading his forehead in concentration.

"And Rich," Maeve said. "He was...it was weird...he told me to leave."

"Why?"

"I have no idea. It was as if he...as if he didn't know me. He told me I was trespassing and he was calling the cops." She felt her control slipping. "Maybe he's been hurt." She dropped her voice to a whisper. "Or he's on something."

"I'll be right there," Rich said. "Stay put. Don't go back up."

"Don't worry," Maeve said. "No way I'm going up there alone. He scared the shit out of me, Rich. Please hurry."

"Lights and siren, Maeve," he said. "You sit tight. Love you. Bye."

He broke the connection. Maeve set the receiver back on its cradle.

She gasped and flinched when something touched her shoulder. She turned and saw Hank's startled face.

"Sorry Maeve," he said. "Didn't mean to scare you." He tipped his baseball cap at her, a holdover from a more chivalrous age, a gesture she found comforting.

"Oh, Hank," she said. "It's not your fault. Rich is coming to get me."

"If you'd like to wait in my office, you're welcome," said Hank. "There's a pot of hot water for tea. I've got different kinds of tea. Some real, some herbal. There's milk in the fridge and sugar on the counter. Help yourself. I'll let you know when he gets here."

"Thank you," she said, managing a thin smile.

Thinking was always easier when your hands felt warm. Tea reminded Maeve of her mother. When she was little, her mother made tea when she or Brant was sick, or hurt or heartsick. Tea cured almost everything, and it comforted. Maeve missed her mother, even after so long. She followed Hank across the lobby to the office.

Ten minutes later, Detective Richard Gordon strode into the lobby of the Willamette Towers Co-op, open raincoat flapping around his knees. He tucked the right side of his shirt back into his trousers. Rich always felt slightly rumpled, and now, after a long day investigating a murder committed during an armed robbery, he felt frazzled.

He found Maeve in the security office, slumped in a chair, her hands wrapped around a cup of steaming tea. Rich worried about her. Since her brother's disappearance two weeks ago, he had heard her puttering around the apartment during the nights, despite trying to work during the day. She hadn't been eating regularly. At his insistence she had called in sick again that morning. In the last two weeks she had missed at least four days of work – more than she had missed in five years of teaching sixth grade.

"Maeve, honey." He held out his arms. She rose and hugged him, laid her head against his chest. He stroked her hair.

"You've been crying," he chided, immediately sorry for sounding like a peevish parent.

"I thought I'd run the well dry," she said. "But – "

"Come on." He turned toward the door. "Let's go up. I'm sure Brant'll clear this up. He's just pulling another prank." His voice took on a grim tone. "This time it isn't funny."

"No way." Maeve shook her head. "I'm not going up there till we find out what's going on, Rich. I think he was really serious. His eyes were so strange…."

"At least he's home."

"Is he?" Maeve said. "You didn't see him. It's like he's not even the same person. Please, Rich, you go. Maybe you can make sense of it. And get my jacket and purse? They're on the peg in the hall closet."

"All right." Rich sighed. "I'll be the heavy."

He tried not to let anger override his professional duty. How could a man drop off the face of the earth for two weeks, and then walk in as if nothing had happened? If the bum had gone off on a drug binge, Rich vowed he'd come back when he was off-duty and make hash of Brant, despite his being family.

"Trust me," Rich said. He released Maeve and left the cubbyhole office.

"Want me to call up?" Hank called. "Or come up with you?"

There was nothing more frightening than being backed up by a hired security guard. But Hank had been on the job, a career beat cop who loved his job, and wasn't willing to give it up when he retired. Rich liked Hank, and Maeve got on well with his wife. The two couples had spent time together.

"Nah, thanks, Hank," he said. Keep it in the family. "I'll just go up unannounced."

Hank nodded and returned to his security monitors and magazines.

In the elevator Rich could not avoid his image in the burnished brass surface where the buttons were set. A strand of dark hair hung in his face. He needed a haircut. Maeve reminded him of such things, but lately she had been too preoccupied to notice. She had begun to think the unthinkable – that her brother was dead, his body somewhere waiting to be stumbled upon. Or perhaps never found.

Rich loosened his tie. At 29 he was still fit, still wore the same size as when he'd graduated from the Police Academy after graduating Oregon State. But lately he felt tired and worried he was headed for burnout. He liked his job, and he was good at it, but he wasn't sure he could stick it out like Hank until he hit retirement. He and Maeve had talked about buying a restaurant or some little business, but it was only wishing. He was just going through a phase. Sometimes the job got him down, but he always came back.

He'd never drawn his weapon on the job, or been shot. Life could be worse.

Rich stepped from the elevator mentally toting up the hours he had spent trying to find Brant. He'd used official department resources and even pulled some strings in the local FBI office. How would he explain to his captain that the subject of a three-state search just came home?

He punched the doorbell. In seconds the door opened, and Brant, his curly hair damp from the shower, stood there. A pale blue sweater made his eyes look cold as winter sky. A pang of concern washed over Rich when he saw the blank look in Brant's eyes.

"Yes?" Brant said. No recognition in his expression. He usually greeted Rich with a hug.

"I'd like to talk to you," Rich said. He pulled aside one overcoat lapel and pointed to his badge stuck in the breast pocket of his sports jacket. It made this interview a formal police matter. It also gave him an uncomfortable sensation in the pit of his stomach.

"Hey," Brant's eyes narrowed. "Hank must've called you. You got here quick. When I came home, there was a woman here. Said she got in with a key."

"Hank didn't send me," Rich said. "Could I come in?"

"Why?" Suspicion clouded Brant's eyes.

"Just like to ask you a couple of questions. Routine. Do you mind?"

Brant hesitated. He looked pale and drawn, and there were dark circles under his eyes. But then, Rich rationalized, it was dim in the apartment. The curtains were drawn.

Rich brushed past him. A pile of papers – sketches – on the desk had spilled onto the floor. Brant was usually fussy about his personal space.

"Since you're the police," Brant said, "I guess you can come in. Want a cup of coffee?"

"Yeah, thanks." Rich went to the sofa and sat. How many times he and Maeve had sat here after dinner, drinking wine, laughing, talking about life, the universe and everything. A momentary pang of guilt assailed Rich when he saw the worn spot on the edge of the old trunk Brant used as a coffee table. Rich always propped his feet there.

In moments Brant returned from the kitchen with two steaming mugs. He handed one to Rich. "You use anything in it?"

Why would he ask that? Rich had always taken his coffee black.

"No, this is fine," Rich said. "Thanks." He took the mug and sipped. For a moment he felt normal, just sharing a cup of joe with family. Then questions flooded his thoughts. He set the mug on the old trunk and extracted his notebook and pen from his jacket pocket.

Brant sank into a chair facing him. He leaned back and dug into a pocket of his jeans. He extracted three white pills, popped them in his mouth, and washed them down with a gulp of milk cooled coffee.

"Ibuprofen," he said. "Got a pounding headache."

Rich wondered if the pills were really Ibuprofen. He waited with his ballpoint poised over a blank page.

Brant leaned forward. "Did you see a woman wearing jeans and a white turtleneck on your way up here?" he said. "Dark hair, attractive. You know, the kind you stare at?"

"No," Rich said. What was going on? Brant was talking about his sister as if he didn't know her. His expression betrayed no emotion, no sign he was lying or joking. "Didn't see her."

"Hank was supposed to hang onto her," Brant said. "Like I said, when I came in, she was here. I don't know how she got past Hank. Carried on like I was her long lost brother." He frowned, pinched the bridge of his nose. "I think maybe I've seen her somewhere before, but I can't place her. I'll have to get my lock changed. What if she's some crazy?"

Anger goaded Rich. Maeve was perfectly rational. Which was more than he could say for Brant Edwards. He studied the man carefully. There were subtle differences. His face looked drawn, and he'd lost some weight. His eyes…his eyes looked strange, not quite focused.

One of Rich's favorite science fiction movies rose in his mind: *Invasion of the Body Snatchers.* But this was real. He tried to keep his voice neutral. "Sure you don't know her?"

Brant frowned and shook his head. For a moment Rich thought he might say something, but he remained silent, as if he were listening to something Rich couldn't hear. Rich waited. The silence grew uncomfortable.

Finally Brant cleared his throat.

"You have some questions?" he said.

Brant hadn't once called Rich by name. Maybe the direct approach would elicit some response.

"You can start by telling me where you've been. I'll keep it to myself if you want."

"At the cabin," Brant said. "Up in Washington."

"Why didn't you call?" Rich said. "Let us know. Or let Hank know where you went."

Brant frowned. "I just wanted to get away for a few days."

Rich kept his gaze on Brant's eyes, looking for some clue to the other man's veracity. "The Lewis County Sheriff and I went up there last week looking for you. The cabin was empty. No tracks in the snow."

"How do you know where it is?"

"I've been there, Brant," Rich said.

"I don't remember taking you there."

"I've been fishing with you."

"I don't know what to say." Brant shrugged. "That's where I was. I went up Thursday evening and came back just a little while ago."

"So why'd you go there?" Rich glanced down, jotted a brief note in the notebook. *Drugs?*

"I needed some time alone," Brant said. "I'm an artist." As if Rich didn't know.

"There's a problem with my exhibition," Brant went on. "The gallery owner's getting antsy. I thought if I got away for a few days, the whole thing might work itself out. Inspiration might hit me. I didn't do a damned thing." He stopped and looked as if he were trying to remember something that had slipped his mind. "Oh yeah, I did some sketches."

Rich studied Brant a long moment and underlined the word he'd written in his notebook.

"Okay," Rich said, grasping for a different approach, "you didn't answer your cell. I must have left 50 messages."

"No service up there." Brant looked genuinely puzzled. "I think the phone's down in the car. I'll check it later…." He shook his head. "Anyway, Nate knows where the cabin is if there was a dire emergency."

The family attorney.

"Feldman's in Africa or something." Rich said. He tried to keep his voice patient. "No phones. Nobody else in the office knows where the cabin is."

"Not my fault," Brant said with a note of insolence.

"Christ, Brant, you could've let us know."

"Let you know?" Anger sparked in Brant's eyes. "Why? What's so goddamned important about a couple of days?" He rose and paced to the windows, then back and stood beside the chair.

Apprehension knotted Rich's stomach. Maybe he was getting an ulcer. Drugs. That was the only logical explanation. Brant had to be on *something*.

"A few days?" Rich said. "Brant, people don't disappear without a word, without – "

"Disappear?" Brant rubbed his eyes and muttered, "What do you – let's see…Friday was Halloween. Saturday, Sunday…this is Monday – " He threw his hands up. "What difference does a few days make?"

Rich went through what he knew about street drugs, trying to sort out what Brant might have taken. If it was a bad mix, it could be dangerous. Brant might be having a psychotic break or something.

"What's the date, Brant?"

"Shit, I don't know. Must be November third or fourth."

"Today's the seventeenth."

"No fucking way." Brant stood up straight. "I haven't been gone two weeks."

"Look at my phone," Rich said and pulled it from his coat pocket. He held it out toward Brant.

Brant shook his head and paced back to the sliding door that opened to the balcony. He pulled a curtain aside and looked into the darkness outside. Finally he turned.

"Look," Brant said. "I don't know what you're trying to pull, what kind of a con you're working here, but I want you to leave. For all I know, you and that crazy woman are in this together. I'm not some senile old guy who'll fall for a scam and hand over my life's savings. And you'd better believe I'm going to check you out, Detective – what'd you say your name was?"

Rich rose. "Come on, you sonofabitch," he said. "The joke's gone far enough. If you're on the outs with Maeve, just tell her and have it over with. She's been a basket case worrying about you, thinking maybe you were hurt.

Or worse. So don't do it this way. Talk to her, for chrissakes. She's your sister. If you were on an alcohol or drug binge – "

"That's it," Brant said and pointed at the door. "Out, or I'll call security. And don't come back unless you've got a search warrant or something." His face was flushed, his eyebrows nearly scrunched together with his frown.

Rich jammed the notebook and pen in his coat pocket, stomped to the closet, yanked it open and grabbed Maeve's belongings. He stuck the jacket under his arm, clutched the purse and stalked to the door.

"I'm not done with you, Edwards," Rich said over his shoulder. "Don't leave town. I'll be in touch. You oughtta read a newspaper. They've had a field day over you."

He slammed the door.

"Stay the fuck away from me," Brant yelled after him.

This was no joke. It was damned strange. Rich ran through ways he could have Brant picked up. He might convince a judge it was necessary for the man's welfare. Rich could trump up some suspicion of criminal activity. Maybe suspected drug trafficking. Judge Harry Belding might write a commitment order as a favor. Brant could be held for a few days for observation, longer if a competency hearing showed it was necessary. They might at least identify the substance involved.

Rich imagined movie credits rolling. Some maudlin film from the Forties where the hero just walks away into the fog. He almost laughed aloud at the old cliché, then sobered at the thought that the whole thing didn't make any sense at all. He didn't feel like a hero, and something was very wrong with Brant.

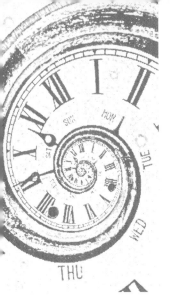

3

Siobhan awakened in the night. Darkness filled every corner of the cabin. She had dreamed, but the details were hazy. She pushed back the quilt and sat up. Brant slept peacefully beside her. His eyes moved under his lids. Dreaming.

Careful not to disturb him, she swung her feet onto the floor. The floor planks felt cold even through the man's wool socks on her feet. She went around the bed and stood beside him, brushed a fingertip along one of his stubbled cheeks. He twitched, but did not wake.

She had spent fourteen nights with him. It seemed an eternity. And yet it was just an instant. For a long moment she watched him sleep. Her home and time were far away, as were the memories of what had happened to her there. If only her magic had been stronger.

What had awakened her? The cabin was silent. She heard the man breathing, heard the low-pitched, mournful call of an owl outside. An answering call. A tingle began in the back of her mind. A bothersome tickle that quickly became a certainty. A calling. The gold torque around her neck seemed uncomfortably tight.

Siobhan....

"No," she murmured. "Not yet. I need time."

Siobhan...

The Lady of Light called her home.

Siobhan....

She could not resist. Magic far more powerful than hers had brought her to this time, and now it summoned her home.

Siobhan pulled off the socks and slipped her feet into her own scuffed shoes – shoes made of bark and scraps of linen. She removed the shirt he had given her, held it to her face and inhaled the fragrance of him. Then she spread the shirt over the sleeping man, gently tucking it around him. He did not stir.

Her wool shift hung on a peg, shabby and torn, but washed clean in the sink. She pulled it over her head and smoothed it down her body. There were a few tears, but otherwise it would suffice. She pulled her *brat* around her shoulders.

In the little room the man called a bathroom she traced a sigil with her hands and whispered the words of a spell. Blue light gathered around her fingers and lit the space. She looked longingly at the razor on the shelf. Such a wickedly sharp tool could be useful. But it contained iron. She looked over all the articles. Finally, she took one item: a comb made of some neutral substance, rich with the man's memories.

Once more in the cabin's main room, she let her mind drift outward. Saw the man's dream. Saw her in his dream, her image sharp and clear as if she were there with him. She felt his longing for her, felt the depth of his love for her. Down deep an elusive image lurked: stars…blue fire….

Siobhan withdrew from his mind. A terrible decision trembled in her thoughts. Whether fey or mortal, another's mind was inviolate. Even those of tainted blood such as she must follow this imperative, a rule that must never be ignored.

But she had no other choice. She loved him, hopelessly, without reservation. The kind of love that transcended her inhuman heritage and was part of her heart forever. And *he* loved her. She had not won his love by magic or deceit.

She did not want to abandon him. But she had to protect him. She knew what would happen to him if he went home and spoke of his encounter with her. He had told her what people thought of fairies. And magic. There was no real magic in this world. People had forgotten about fairies. Loving him made what she must do even more abhorrent.

The summoning drummed louder in her mind. She had very little time left. She took a deep breath and focused her energy. She plunged in, floating down through the layers of his mind. Down, past the dream, past language, past his childhood to his deepest hopes and fears, and then to the old parts of his mind. Still she sank to where old memories were stored and new ones waited to be sorted.

It was easy to find his thoughts of her. He saw her in a magical light, much more beautiful then she thought she was. That would facilitate her task. But it would not make it any more palatable.

Although she had tampered with emotions, she had never altered someone's memories. She knew how it was done. It seemed so easy now that she was inside his mind.

Her power flowed easily, rising with a strength that surprised her. All she had to do was gather his memories of her and sever them from his consciousness. Days gone from his life would not be missed. If he could not explain them, if they were never there, they would not exist for him. She must take the time she had spent with him – the images, the emotions that had burgeoned between them – and destroy them.

His memories tumbled through her thoughts. She saw events as he saw them. Not once did he blame her for what Murchad had done. His tenderness toward her never wavered. Tenderness became fondness and in only a few days fondness turned to love. He was surprised and delighted at his feelings for her.

Brant could not believe he had ever been truly alive before she came into his life. Siobhan knew before Brant was aware of his desire for her. She had wished that she could tell him how she felt, too. But he'd kept a distance between them, mindful of her feelings of betrayal and reluctance for intimacy.

Four evenings after Siobhan walked into Brant's time and life, she made an advance. She confessed to him that she had fallen in love with him.

"I cannot help what I am," Siobhan had said, "and I know not how long we have together. I love you with all my heart and mind."

"I thought you'd never get around to it," Brant said.

They were sitting on the couch in front of the fire after eating supper. Brant had made a delicious vegetable stew from ingredients that came from containers. Corn and peas and beans that seemed almost as fresh as if they had come from the field that morning.

He leaned toward her. "I love you," he whispered. "I want to be with you forever."

Siobhan kissed his lips, a light, lingering touch that sparked fire inside her.

Brant groaned. His reluctance to hurt her held his arms still. He resisted a hot passion that urged him to wrap her in an embrace and keep her safe beside him.

She gazed into his eyes. "We may only have a few days," she said. "I must go soon." She put her hands on either side of his face. "You would never hurt me."

Brant's arms went around her and crushed her against him. His lips on hers were hungry. She melted against him and shut her mind to his, allowing only physical sensations to flood her body.

Together they rose from the couch. His hands on her back ignited a primal lust inside her. She fumbled with the fastening on his pants. His desire was obvious. She could not manage the strange closure. Brant undressed, and she shed a shirt he had given her and her shift.

They made love slowly on the floor in front of the fireplace, each giving pleasure and taking it as a gift.

Afterwards, they sealed their bond with a bottle of drink Brant kept in a cupboard. Siobhan transformed two cups into goblets, and whispered a spell over the bottle. Brant poured a sparkling stream of aqua liquid that burst into bubbles that twinkled on the surface of the alcohol. Sated from lovemaking, they both got pleasantly drunk. They had slept together in the bed, nestled side by side until morning.

But now Siobhan must return to her own time without the man she loved. She rose above his memories of her, watching them swirl below her. She sent her will out and pulled the memories to her. But something curious occurred. The golden mornings, the aching cold of the air when they walked in the shadows of the towering trees, the physical sensations he experienced with her, the fragrance in her hair – all the details he remembered – slipped away from her mental grasp. It should have been easy to gather the memories, but each time she tried, thoughts scattered like butterflies kicked up from a meadow…like butterflies….

Siobhan. An urgent command in her mind. *It is time*. The torque around her neck grew warm.

Desperate, not understanding why the man's mind behaved so unpredictably, she did the only thing she could. Instead of taking away his memories of her, she shut them off. She wondered about the strangeness in his mind, but there was no time to search for answers. Time…time tugged at her like a puppy pulling its master's pant leg. Time….

Carefully, with painful awareness of the wrong she did, Siobhan set traps in his mind. Mirrors to deflect his probing thoughts, mirrors that would lead him away from the memories of her. Loops to confuse. Doors that would open endlessly onto other memories, leading him away from the time he had spent with her.

When she finished, she felt confident she had altered his thoughts enough that if he tried to think of the time he'd spent with her, she would be a long-ago acquaintance, perhaps only a dream. She compressed this down to a brief encounter and made to leave when she stumbled over her name. It was too cruel to take even her name from him. She left him that, hidden among the clutter in his mind, behind doors and mirrors. Someone he had once met, but dimly remembered.

Stealthy as a stalking cat, feeling the Lady of Light's beckoning magic, she withdrew from the man's mind. Her heart fluttered. She felt slightly queasy and guilty over her willful invasion.

The fire had died to embers, casting only a pale glow. She blinked away tears and motioned toward the hearth. She murmured a few words, and blue flames leapt from the ashes, burning steady and warm. It would last until the man awoke, then fade as if it had never been.

She gazed at his face and touched his dark hair. If only –

Siobhan. The calling was urgent. *Now.*

"Farewell, my love," she whispered in her own language, so softly it might have been but a breeze.

If only he could know. She would never love another as she loved him. Never. She wished there could be a returning for him, but once back in her own time – the man's past – he would be forever beyond her reach.

She turned and glided out of the cabin into the night. The door sighed shut behind her.

She levitated herself a hand span above the new fallen snow and floated away from the cabin. She paused and looked back. Her hands traced a powerful spell of protection. The words trembled on her lips. Blue sparks followed her hands. A brief flare of azure radiance chased the shadows into the forest. Then the brightness faded, and darkness once more filled the clearing. The house would now be safe from invasion for as long as the man owned it. The spell removed the one that had created the other cabin, identical in every way, set away from this one, empty, so that anyone who came to look at it would see only a deserted dwelling.

Siobhan looked at her hands, marveled at the power of her magic, then steeled herself to leave.

"Keep well, love," she whispered.

She turned away, blinded by tears, and followed the urging to the place that would take her to her own time. She stopped between two huge Douglas firs, feeling small and alone. Little golden lights gathered around her, but they could not draw the pain from her heart.

Resigned, she bowed her head. Tears sparkled like crystals when they hit the snow. She surrendered to darkness that wrapped its cloak around her. Siobhan plunged into silence. Tiny lights winked before her eyes, but without perspective she could not tell if they were close or as far away as the stars. Despair gripped her. Cold numbed her. After a long while she heard a faint, rhythmic sound: her heart beating.

Warmth rushed back into her body, and she felt flushed and breathless. She found herself standing in a room suffused with a soft golden glow. Polished wood walls marked the room's perimeter. Simple wooden furnishings filled the space. The friendly lights that had borne her to this place faded.

"You look well, child." A melodious voice. Light danced in the air and gathered into a woman's face. The Lady of Light.

"Yes," Siobhan said. She kept her voice steady, not ready to face her sorrow. "My body and my mind are whole. I owe you more thanks than I can say. I cannot repay you."

"No payment is necessary, lass," the Lady said.

The woman floated closer. Moonlight shimmered in her gown. Her eyes reflected a radiance and an agelessness that made Siobhan feel young and naive. A memory from her childhood surfaced.

"I know you," Siobhan whispered. "You are of the ancient ones. Older even than my father's people. You are Orghlaith. The Golden Lady." The woman nodded. "Why did you help me?"

"I was nearby," Orghlaith said, "and one of my kind was in need of aid." Her smile warmed Siobhan's heart. "I could not prevent what happened to you. For that I am sorry."

"It was not my fault." Siobhan spoke with quiet conviction. The man had told her that. The fault lay with the one who had given Murchad the potion that had stolen her will.

"No, it was not your fault." Orghlaith peered at her. "You are different, lass." She extended her hand to touch Siobhan's cheek. Siobhan did not flinch.

"You have learned much," Orghlaith said.

"Why could I not stay?" Siobhan said. "I was happy there. There is nothing here for me."

Orghlaith shook her head. "The spell was self-limiting. You did not belong in that time. Things must be as fate decrees them. That is why I could not prevent Murchad's treachery. What happens is what must be." She sighed. "It cost me dearly to send you there."

Siobhan thought the powers of the Old Ones were beyond measure.

"Yes," the Lady said, "my powers have limits."

"How can I live with what I have lost?" Siobhan whispered.

"Think of what you have gained, lass."

"Gained?" Siobhan grew bold. "I have gained pain. A deeper pain than that of the body."

"Pain of the heart is a human trait, lass," Orghlaith said. "One that my people would like to feel. But, alas, we have been out of the tide of human events for a long time. I have forgotten much, child. I think time will heal you and diminish the shame."

If not for Orghlaith, Siobhan would feel only shame, not the terrible loss that gnawed at her heart. She wanted to say angry, hurtful words to the woman, but words would change nothing. What was done could not be changed.

What happens is what must be.

Siobhan fumbled at her throat for the torque. It slipped into her hands, and she offered it to the Lady. The band formed an unbroken circle. Orghlaith accepted it with delicate fingers and tucked it away somewhere in the folds of her gown. She held out a hand. A bit of gold glittered in it.

"This is yours," Orghlaith said.

Murchad's cloak pin. Siobhan shook her head.

"I do not want it."

"You must take it. It is a thing of beauty and power, not to be flung away thoughtlessly. It was made by one of my people when this land was younger and wilder. It has old magic in it. I took it from you before I sent you to the other time. It could not be in two different times. Its past and its future are separate."

"If you know what will be, why not just tell me what I should do?" Anger rose in Siobhan, warming her cheeks.

"Ah." Orghlaith said. "Life is not that easy. Only *some* events that will come to pass are clear. The rest I see as through a veil, distorted by things that *are*. But know, Siobhan of the *Sidhe*, that the brooch is important. It is part of your destiny, and it must follow where you go."

"Why do you call me *Sidhe*?" Siobhan looked away. "All my life I have been an outcast. Because of my human blood, I was never accepted by your people, and humans shun me for a mad woman."

"Fate," Orghlaith said, her gaze unwavering, "is a fickle thing. The *Druii* see patterns in stars and destiny in the entrails of animals. They believe fate cannot be changed. But my people know that what we see in the future is only a possibility. Your actions, Siobhan, can alter what might be."

Siobhan accepted the golden ornament and put it in her purse with the comb. She tugged the knot of her *brat* tighter and bowed to the other's superiority.

"You must have great magic, my Lady," she said. "I truly thank you. I do have one question if you would favor me with an answer." Orghlaith nodded. "I know your enchantment far exceeds mine," Siobhan continued. "But while I was…away…the spells came easily. They were never that effortless. I always had to overcome my human reluctance to make them work."

"Look within yourself, Siobhan," Orghlaith said. "You will find the answer. Use well what you discover."

The Lady of Light began to fade. As she grew transparent, she spoke again, a thin whisper in the quiet room.

"Go through my door, child. You will find yourself beside the oldest oak in the heart of the forest. If you ever have need of me again, come into the wood and seek my tree. You will pass safely. Knock three times on the trunk to summon me, and if your need is great enough, I will answer. Remember, child, I do not interfere in outside events for inconsequential matters."

Siobhan nodded.

"And remember this, Siobhan of the Forest: life is a circle. Endless circles draw together, Sought by three who find them. Once made whole, the circles close. Eternity will bind them."

An effervescent shower of golden light bloomed around Orghlaith's form and lingered a moment on the still air before it faded. Orghlaith had vanished. Her absence chilled the room.

Siobhan turned to the door. As she reached for the latch, she closed her eyes. She would not betray one who had given her so much. If she did not know where she stepped from the oak, she could never be forced to tell the secret. She pushed the heavy, carved door and stepped through the opening into her haven, the insubstantial place she had created away from the real world, a place out of time, apart from mortal eyes.

She built the safe place and discarded it at will, without questioning how she did it. It did not exist in the real world, but while she was there, everything she made was tangible. Only she could make changes. Each object she created remained just as she left it until she altered it with a flicker of thought.

No one else could enter Siobhan's special place, so she would be safe. She needed time to think. Time away from the course of mortal events.

The door closed, and Siobhan was alone in utter silence.

4

Somewhere a door slammed. Murchad o'Ruairc flinched. The boy whose hands hovered over him paused in his task.

Murchad took a long drink from his flagon of mead and thumped it noisily on the table.

"Ha," he said. "Some strong-willed lad impatient with his mother's discipline." But the sound lingered in his mind, a disquieting echo.

He perched on a wooden stool with a deer hide draped over his knees and an old *brat* hugged around his shoulders. Wind-blown gusts of rain stalked the hills. The infernal dampness crept through the windows, around the heavy tapestries and penetrated to his bones. It reminded him that, like the season, he was in the autumn of his years.

He fidgeted impatiently while his cousin Maella's youngest son, Liam, trimmed his beard. He'd decided to keep it shorter when he'd heard from a traveling bard about a man who had lost his eldest son to a Norse invader's blade. The boy had been unhorsed in a skirmish and might have rolled free to get his sword, but the Northman grabbed his beard, pulled him up and slit his throat, easy as slaughtering a pig.

Liam went back to his trimming.

Murchad jerked his head back.

"Ouch, you oaf," he thundered. "That's the last time, by God, that you'll pull my hair out by the roots."

Liam stepped back and lowered his small dagger. He was tall for twelve, and slender, with long, delicate fingers, more fit for harping than hair cutting. He was apprenticed to the bard Teague Mac Lochlainn who lived in the village closest to the o'Ruairc's stronghold.

Murchad's guards stepped from their posts at the open doorway, hands on their sword hilts. Liam looked stricken. He ran shaking fingers through his sandy hair and licked his lips.

"My lord" – his voice cracked – "I am truly sorry. I am much more skilled with a harp than a knife. And besides, your beard would defy a *Sidhe* blade."

Murchad gestured dismissively to his warriors. Still, they stood ready to protect him. He would not have it said that an apprentice bard was threatened in his holding, even if the boy was an incompetent barber. Had the boy heard rumors of what Murchad had done?

"A *Sidhe* blade. Bah!" Murchad laughed uneasily. "Nothing forged of moonlight could cut a man's beard. The witch knives cannot even cut flesh." His voice turned bitter. "They only wound the heart."

"It was only a jest, my lord," Liam said, looking down at his feet. "I meant nothing."

Murchad studied the boy. Of course he could know nothing of Murchad's shame. *Samhain* Eve, after the madness of the druid's potion had left him, he took two trusted warriors back to the edge of the wood. But the witch was gone. Probably carried away by one of her own. Or better, he hoped at the time, eaten by some wild animal.

Now Murchad regretted wishing her dead. A fortnight had passed, and she was nowhere to be found. The druid said she would give him an heir. No mortal woman had been able to do that. If she were truly dead, Murchad's hope for an heir could be dead, too.

Murchad did not want it whispered that he had forced a woman. Even a witch. Damn the druid. To think that a few heartbeats of time could make such a difference.

"I know you meant naught, lad." Murchad cuffed the boy playfully. "But you have much to learn about trimming my beard. Perhaps you should practice on your own."

"Naught to practice on, my lord." Liam rubbed his smooth jaw and grinned.

"If you knew what it feels like having your hair pulled out," Murchad said. "You would be more careful." The guards unhanded their swords and dropped back to their places by the door. It was good that his warriors were vigilant. A man's life could depend on his guards' alertness, even within the walls of his own fortress.

Liam brightened.

"If I am to practice on myself," he said. "I will have to see Master Conall in the village about sharpening the knife."

"You tell Conall that if he was the one sharpened it in the first place, he will be justly rewarded," Murchad said. "I will use the damned knife on *his* beard."

"I will tell him, lord." Liam bowed and turned to leave.

"Come back, lad," Murchad called after him, "when the blade is sharp and you can use it properly."

Liam stopped, turned and bowed elaborately.

"I shall, lord. And I am certain Master Teague will sing of this. I will suggest he call it 'The Cutting of Murchad's Beard.'" He grinned at his bold wit.

"Leave, boy, before I lose my temper." Murchad wanted to add a stinging invective, but he caught himself.

He had no doubt that Liam's well-known ear for parody was already busy composing a song that incorporated Murchad's words, twisted into meanings that would make him look silly, while not being offensive enough to incur his wrath. Besides, who would be foolish enough to bridle a bard's mouth? If a bard could not pursue his avocation, the news and family histories of entire clans could be lost.

Traveling bards used their music to carry news about the countryside. They sang of births, marriage alliances, deaths and other events important to a clan's history. Their easy melodies and rhyming lyrics recorded the triumphs and sorrows of the clan that protected them.

Mac Lochlainn's songs documented in detail five generations of o'Ruaircs and their wives and children, cousins and other family members. Every chieftain endured songs that recounted unflattering personal stories. Every chieftain would defend his bard with his life to protect the family histories the bards passed on to their apprentices.

Murchad could hear Liam humming a tune as he trotted from the room.

Damn. A few nights hence Murchad would no doubt be subjected to the wily Mac Lochlainn's song. Teague would smile as he sang, and Murchad would have to swallow his pride and laugh with the rest of his clansmen.

He stared after Liam. The air in the doorway shimmered like heat waves rising from a meadow on a hot summer day. An icy draft swept the room. Not given to premonitions, Murchad felt a frisson of foreboding.

Something was going to happen, he thought. Soon. Something unpleasant.

He pulled his *brat* around him and rose. The deer hide slipped off his knees. He kicked it aside. In a fluid motion he grabbed his sword from where it leaned against the table. Blade in hand, he faced whatever came to meet him.

A tall figure entered the room. He was clothed in a long robe of coarse wool, his face hidden by a hood. Murchad's guards scrambled to flank the intruder, leveling their swords at the man's throat.

Murchad smelled the rich scent of forest loam, moldy leaves and cold rain. He advanced and raised his blade until it pointed at the robed man's heart.

"Ceallachan," he spat. "How did you get in? I left orders at the gate –"

"I heed no man's orders," the other man said.

The voice issued from within the shadows of his hood. Murchad had the irrational feeling that there would be two glowing eyes in the darkness where the man's face should be. Nothing more. Just two eyes. He crossed himself, dismissing the superstitious idea. The holy man from the abbey had said the ritual gesture would ward off evil. A young warrior who had recently come across the channel from Britannia made the sign frequently and claimed he had never been wounded in battle.

Ceallachan chuckled.

"Your orders and gestures are amusing, but harmless, Murchad," he said. "I come and go as I please."

Ceallachan's use of Murchad's name irritated him. He calculated that the druid would not be foolish enough to attack him and waved his guards away. They lowered their swords and moved back. The druid stepped forward until his chest touched the point of Murchad's blade.

"You are a fool, Murchad o'Ruairc," Ceallachan said.

Murchad's sword did not waver. The druid's body remained still against the tip of the blade.

"No man calls me a fool within my own walls, Druid." Murchad spoke in a low, menacing voice. "Bide your tongue if you value it."

The druid laughed. His hood slipped down, and Ceallachan stood wreathed in a wildness of auburn hair and beard. A prickly warning again crawled across the back of Murchad's neck. He held his sword steady.

Ceallachan slowly raised his hands, held them out palm up.

"If you would lay steel to an unarmed man," Ceallachan said, "one of the Earth Mother's children – then you are twice the fool, Murchad. Stay your sword and hear me. I expected you to follow my instructions. *Samhain* is more than a fortnight past, and still you have no fey woman in your bed."

Murchad forced himself to hold his gaze steady.

"What I did with the potion is no one's business but mine."

"Ah," sighed Ceallachan. "It is my business when the efficacy of my preparation is in doubt."

Murchad winced.

"Oh, it worked," he said. Too well. He pushed the idea away in case Ceallachan could truly hear his thoughts. He had heard rumors....

A preternatural gleam shone from the watery depths of Ceallachan's eyes.

"If you followed my directions, Murchad, then where is the woman?" His voice was very soft, and he glanced pointedly at the rumpled sleeping pallet on the other side of the chamber.

Murchad ignored him. To his guards he said, "Wait outside. What business we conduct is between us only."

"Lord?" one man said. He was very young with only a shadow of a beard.

Youth and virility were important. Murchad's virility was in question.

"Go," he insisted. "The druid is unarmed. His illusions are no use against steel." He tipped his sword up, and then lowered the point to the floor. He stood, casually at ease, but the corded muscles in his arms were prepared to sweep the blade up in an instant.

"Yes," Ceallachan said. "Go." A slight smile tugged the corners of his mouth. "What profit to me if I sliced your lord's throat? My daughter would lose a good market for her medicines."

Murchad glared at Ceallachan. The second guard, a seasoned warrior, glanced from Murchad to the druid.

"If you have need, lord," he said, "just call."

Murchad waited until the door was latched.

"Now, Druid," he said. "Say naught that would tempt me to spit you on my blade like a piglet."

"If you think to frighten me, the threat is useless," Ceallachan said, the faint smile gone from his lips. "I am old enough that death holds no fear. If you spill my blood, there are those of my brothers who would look ill upon it. You might find the blade that trims your beard instead at your throat."

Murchad started, then realized that Ceallachan must have seen the hair on the floor.

"Why did you come here?" Murchad said. "State your business and be gone."

"Did the potion do what you required?" Ceallachan's gaze remained steady, not defiant, but not acceding.

Murchad studied the other man. Was there genuine curiosity in the druid's eyes?

"Not exactly," Murchad said.

Ceallachan crossed his arms over his chest.

"If it did not work," he said, "I will give you another. I am an honest man. I will not have it rumored that my preparations have no power."

"You must sell many potions," Murchad said. "Why are you so interested in the outcome of one?"

"Your clansmen and women do not gossip about a woman in your company. I did not see you at the *Samhain* fires. One of the village lads is said to have been seduced by a *Sidhe* maiden. I heard he left the fire with her and wandered into the forest. His mother weeps for him still."

Murchad snorted.

"If you want to talk about a fool – "

"And what was wrong with my potion?" Ceallachan said.

Murchad looked away, focused his gaze on a flowered tapestry.

"Nothing," he said. "Perhaps I did not use it."

"Oh, you used it, all right. You cannot lie to me. Not only was there powerful magic in it, I used a compulsion to force you to drink it."

Murchad blanched and tried to maintain an even expression while the druid studied him.

"Did you take it down in one gulp?" Murchad nodded. "Ah, then it should have worked. That was no ordinary love potion. It should have brought you a fey lass – " He stopped and stared at Murchad, his gaze piercing into the chieftain's soul.

Murchad felt his mind laid bare. He recalled the song he had used to mask his thoughts from the witch woman.

"You used it," Ceallachan said. "But you could not wait. You drank it moments too soon, before the sun sank below the hills. You let your lust consume you. You used me – by the Earth Mother, Murchad, what have you done?"

Apprehension gnawed in Murchad's stomach. Perhaps the man could indeed hear his thoughts.

"What I have done is my own doing," Murchad said. "But I did not receive what I was promised. I bedded the witch, but she is gone. Perhaps dead. That is what your damned potion has gotten me.

"Leave me." Murchad pointed to the door with his sword. "And do not try to give me anything again. I'd rather traffic with a witch than deal with you."

Ceallachan assessed Murchad with eyes the color of storm clouds. Although Murchad had faced certain death many times in battle, he suddenly felt stripped of his defenses.

"You defied my instructions," Ceallachan said softly. He started to say more, then must have seen the murderous intent in Murchad's eyes, for he closed his mouth and turned to leave.

At the doorway he paused and turned.

"Murchad," he said, "you are worse than a fool if you think this is your business only. The branches of the oak affect all that grows around it. If the leaves are healthy, the tree grows. If the leaves are sickly, the tree will be barren. The last wife you put aside because she did not conceive was the lucky one. Her suffering ended quickly. Mark my words. Those living and those yet to come will rue the day you were born."

"I did not have Ciara killed, you pile of dung," Murchad growled. "A woman? By the gods, I would not stoop to assassinate a woman." Ceallachan's accusation had finally goaded him to anger. "Truth be told, she ended her own life with the death mushroom."

"That's the pity of it," Ceallachan retorted. "That she felt so soiled, she would never give herself to another man."

The druid turned and strode from the room. With a howl of rage Murchad loosed his hold on his *brat* and lunged across the chamber, his sword raised. He ran headlong through the opening and fetched up short in the corridor. The guards, who had been leaning against the opposite wall, sprang to attention.

"Where is he?" Murchad demanded.

"Who?" they said in unison, frowning at each other.

"That bastard, Ceallachan."

"No one passed, my lord," the younger man said.

Murchad slumped.

"Let it be known among your company," he said, "that if a stone should fall on the druid's head, or a noxious poison appear in his water, there will be a prize for the man who claims the act. But only within my walls. I will not pay someone to ride out against him."

The two warriors shuffled their feet and were silent.

"Do you understand?" Murchad voice grated in his throat.

"Yes, lord," they said together.

Ignoring the questioning glances they cast at each other, Murchad spun and went back into his chamber. He threw his sword on his bed, grabbed his *brat* from the floor and pulled it tight around him to quell the shivers that chattered his teeth. Damn Ceallachan. And damn that witch to whatever hell accepted her kind. He fervently hoped she was dead. If she lived she could torment him with the reminder of his folly.

Murchad slammed the heavy oak door. He remembered his premonition. The important thing had not been the druid's visit. There was something else waiting for him. He was certain he would not like it.

5

L ook inside, Orghlaith had said. *Look inside....*

Siobhan looked within herself. Recoiled. Had Orghlaith known? Of course she had.

How could it have happened? The potion in her food must have disrupted more than her magic. It must have affected her command over her body.

A child grew inside Siobhan, a child conceived of Murchad's scheming.

Her human heritage could not mask the truth of her fey sight. She felt the unformed thoughts of the babe – human, with no hint of magic. The child would be feared and hated by mortals because of its potential, and shunned by the *Sidhe* because of its humanness. Outcast. Part of neither world. Just as Siobhan was.

Despair washed over her, and she wept futile tears for what had been and what could never be.

Eventually, despair ran its course. The tears stopped, and Siobhan was left to contemplate her dilemma. The child was precious. New life must be nurtured. Of this there was no question. But, despite her mistake in not detecting the potion in her food, perhaps she could find legitimacy for her child. Not among the *Sidhe*. If the child were mortal, it would never belong. And what did it matter that she would have to sacrifice her own integrity and a brief span of her long life to give her child what she never had?

There was a small chance the child would be fey. It would be subtle but sweet revenge to see an obviously human child raised and accepted by mortals, only to come into its heritage during adolescence, as occasionally happened. If she stood by the child, she could guide and protect. And manipulate.

Murchad o'Ruairc was growing old by human standards. Three wives and a succession of women had come to his bed. They lasted only long enough to prove barren. And when they were safely married to another man – except the one who died – and with child, rumors ran unquenched about whose fault it was. She had heard the druid's daughter laughing about it.

Druid...potion....

Siobhan saw in a flash of insight what Murchad had done. Someone had given him a potion to make him fertile. The only one capable of such magic was Ceallachan.

Damn him. But she immediately repented her curse, believing in her heart that the man was twice damned for trafficking with the dark forces of magic.

There must be something Siobhan could salvage from her circumstances. If she presented Murchad with an heir it would cement an alliance – if only temporary – between mortal and *Sidhe*. If the true *Sidhe* saw such an affiliation perhaps they might not retreat so quickly from the mortal world, but grace it for a while longer. Their benevolent presence would ensure good harvests and mild winters. With abundance of the land, perhaps the mortals would leave the *Sidhe* in peace.

Siobhan knew she could never bow to Murchad's dominance. But perhaps there was a bargain to be made. If he desired an heir half as much as Siobhan had heard, he would accept the prohibitions she laid upon him.

She traced a simple pattern with one hand and clothed herself in a gown that would glitter in the rush lights and dazzle mortal eyes. If she could find courage, she could save her child.

With resolve a tight knot in her stomach, Siobhan left her safe place and materialized in Eirinn. Late afternoon sunlight filtered through the forest canopy. She peered through the shadows across a wide tract of open land.

A trampled, rutted road led up a slope. Atop the hill, surrounded by a wall made of stones and sharpened trees twice the height of a man, squatted the ugly blemish that was Murchad's refuge. Within the walls were scattered the huts and outbuildings necessary for the comfort and defense of a congregation of humans. Smoke wafted upward from cook fires and drifted on the lazy breeze. The central dwelling reared its massive stone bulk above the other buildings, thrusting a tower into the air. On the lofty parapet a guard paced his way around. He stopped from time to time to look out over Murchad's fields and outlying hamlets.

Some stone structures Siobhan had seen were not so atrocious. The abbey the monks had built was not unsightly. Its rough stone walls soared upward in a gentle curve, topped by a simple wooden cross. But Murchad's fortification had been built by one whose eye had little appreciation for style or for the intrinsic beauty of the native stone. The ugliness of this place, built strictly for defense, repelled her.

She took a deep breath and settled her mind. She glided over the deserted road and stopped a little way from the gated arch that gave entrance to Murchad's lair.

Two leather-helmeted men huddled beside a small fire, their *brats* held close around them. One squatted and warmed his hands, his naked sword on the ground before him. One sat slouched with his back against the stone wall, his chin almost on his chest, his sword across his thighs. Neither stirred at Siobhan's silent approach.

"You there!" she called to the guards.

Both men scrambled to their feet, fumbling their swords to point at her. The one who had been sitting blinked sleep from his eyes. The man by the fire touched his forehead, chest and shoulders. Siobhan felt the burning emanations of forge-tempered iron.

"You have no need for weapons or charms," she said. "I bear a message of urgency for your chieftain."

One man – the older one by the fire – stood his ground. His thoughts told Siobhan he held fast from duty, not from courage. Had she been a human invader, he would have charged her with his sword. The other man leaned his back against the unyielding oak of the gate. She saw in his mind his unwillingness to use his blade against a woman, even one of her kind.

"Come no closer," the man beside the fire said, pointing his sword toward her.

"I will not steal you away to the land of the *Sidhe*," she said. "Truly, I bring a message for your chieftain."

"No closer," the man repeated.

Siobhan tried to ignore the burning iron and held out her hand with the brooch.

"Give this to Murchad o'Ruairc," she said. "Tell him I ask safe passage to speak to him."

The man stepped forward, snatched the brooch from her fingers and retreated quickly.

"Your name, girl?"

"The trinket will speak for me," Siobhan said. "I will wait until the sun sets." She glanced up at the sky where the sun sat just over the treetops. "If Murchad does not answer in that time, I will be gone, taking something he would value as much as his life. Tell him that."

"Wait here," the guard said.

Siobhan nodded. The man went to the gate and strained against it. Creaking in protest, the heavy doors gave a little, and he squeezed through. The other guard stood with his back against the gate as if to draw strength from the wood. Confused thoughts raced through his mind. She watched him. A confused mortal could be dangerous.

Would Murchad answer? If he did not, then she would leave as she had come, silent as ashes, and he would never know what he had missed.

Impatience, then indecision assailed her. She could not force him to acquiesce. Her feelings swung between resolve and terror. She could have misjudged him.

The sun disappeared behind the trees. She turned to go.

"Wait!"

Turning back, Siobhan saw a fair-haired youth slip through the open gate, followed by the guard who had gone inside. The boy approached her, his thoughts reflecting open curiosity at her dazzling image in the lowering twilight.

"I am Liam, the bard's apprentice," he said. "My master bids you enter. He grants you safe passage. But within the walls you must not use magic." The boy spat the last word derisively. He did not believe.

Siobhan stepped close to him and held out her hand. He dropped the cloak pin into her palm. She pulled a portion of the fabric of her gown through the ring of gold and made a small knot to secure it. The boy watched her. His thoughts told her he was bright and quick of wit. Already he composed a song about her.

"The o'Ruairc awaits you," the boy said. "You are to come with me. If you choose not to come, then he said to tell you to be on your way." Despite his youth, his voice was firm, and Siobhan saw in his mind the words were truly spoken.

She hesitated.

"My master promises not to harm you," the boy said. "He swears no one will lay a hand upon you as long as you use no treachery."

Siobhan put little trust in Murchad's word, and she would not give up her only defense. "I will come inside," she finally said. "Upon my word as

Sidhe, I will not turn my sorcery upon any who do not hinder me."

The boy must have been given some authority in this matter, because he nodded.

"That will suit the o'Ruairc," he said.

Siobhan raised her chin, walked past the staring guards and through the open gate. The boy caught up with her and took a slight lead. He edged away from her, casting occasional cautious glances back at her. His surface thoughts showed he was curious, but sensible.

Never before had Siobhan been inside a stone building. She followed the boy across the open area between the outer wall and the keep, marveling at the workmanship.

But she dreaded leaving the open air. Inside the monstrous structure, the weight of the rock pressed down on her, an almost tangible burden. Dampness oozed from the walls. Discreetly, she flicked one hand to conjure a spell against the cold, deciding that her comfort would not violate the terms of her meeting.

There must be many stories hidden in the stones. A shiver coursed up her back. Some stories were perhaps best left unremembered.

The youth wore a clean tunic of eggshell-white wool that hung loosely from his shoulders to his knees, with linen leggings and a dark wool *brat* wrapped around his shoulders. A bronze brooch secured his *brat*. His soft leather boots padded silently across the flagstones.

The fine quality of the fabrics indicated he was the first-born in a noble family. Humans valued birth order. First-born ruled, while other siblings fought for their places in the hierarchy. Mortal women were nothing more than chattel. In the world of the *Sidhe*, all children were equals and must earn their places.

But Siobhan's child would be the only child of a mortal chieftain, heir to his holdings. He would inherit all Murchad's possessions and land. If Murchad agreed to her terms.

They passed through a large hall lit with flickering rush lights. People sat at long tables laden with platters of meat and vegetables. The smell of cooked meat sickened Siobhan, who consumed only fish, plants – and eggs and milk when she could obtain them. Several scruffy hounds sprawled under the tables gnawing on bones and tidbits dropped by careless and deliberate fingers. The dogs raised their heads and sniffed the air. Their glassy eyes followed her progress.

Voices stilled. People turned to look at Siobhan, but she avoided their gazes. Ladies clutched metal crosses that hung from their girdles and touched their foreheads, chests and shoulders, believing the gestures would ward off Siobhan's evil powers.

The ritual was a symbol of faith. Siobhan, too, needed faith: confidence in her ability to convince Murchad. She raised her chin and followed the boy through the hall, conscious of the effect she created with her glittering gown and sun-pale hair. Abiding by her oath, she used no spell to make people forget her.

In another, smaller hall, metal braziers festooned the walls. But in the dark corridors the gloom was broken only at far intervals by flickering rush-lights. She found herself wanting to see around the next turn, or into the rooms past closed doors. *Sidhe* lights would chase away unwholesome shadows.

She glanced behind her and sent out a stealthy mind probe. People went about their business, and servants attended to the needs of others. She sensed curiosity, wonderment. No one meant her harm.

After making many turns and going up a flight of wide stone steps, the boy stopped before a door where two sentries sat upon low stools. Their drawn swords rested across their thighs. The bitter scent of iron brought a queasy flutter in Siobhan's stomach. Both men nodded to the lad. Siobhan sidled by them, trying not to flinch from the poison, and entered the room. The boy withdrew quietly and pulled the heavy door shut behind her.

Humans must indeed be foolish if they thought a closed door could contain her. But iron was another matter.

Murchad slouched in a chair at a low table with the remnants of his evening meal spread before him. There was some metal here: an iron sword near him and an iron knife on the table next to a drinking vessel of some gray metal – neutral, not poisonous.

He pushed away from the table, but made no effort to rise. Crossing one leg over the other, he raised his flagon to his lips. He took a quick gulp and wiped the back of one hand across his mouth. The muzziness of too much mead sparkled in his bloodshot eyes.

Siobhan dared a glance around the tapestry-hung room, her keen eyes and mind searching the shadows for movement that would signal betrayal. She found no one else. An oppressive stillness hung in the air. Could she endure living within stone walls?

"So," Murchad finally said in a level voice that surprised her with its control. "You live."

"Yes. I live." she said. She gazed at him, willed her racing heart to slow.

Siobhan resisted the impulse to probe behind his dark eyes. Fear was evident in the furrows of his brow and the twitching muscles of his jaw.

He was pleasing to the eye, and she had no doubt that mortals saw in him a charisma that inspired them to follow in his service and women to fawn over him. He rubbed a hand over his neatly trimmed beard.

"What is your message?" The hand on his jaw trembled.

"You are childless, Murchad," she began and was totally unprepared for the effect of her words. He heaved himself up, swaying from the mead. His chair toppled over backward, the crash echoing in the stillness.

"Damn you," he shouted. His rough voice cut through her composure. He strode unsteadily across the room to within an arm's length of her, drunken anger replacing his fear. "Damn you, woman."

She flinched at the vehemence of his words, wondering if he had the nerve to attack her. She held a spell of protection in her hand, ready to defend herself and her unborn child.

"You came to taunt me?" He glowered at her. "Do you not have enough to occupy your time? The druid was right. You and your kind are nothing but trouble."

Siobhan delved into his thoughts. She had guessed right. Ceallachan had given Murchad a potion. A few drops of a liquid imbued with some powerful spell. There was more to the druid than Siobhan had thought. She forced herself to remain calm.

"I did not come to mock you," she said. "You desire an heir."

"Can your magic make one, witch?" He clenched his fists.

"Sorcery does not create children," she said gently. "The child I carry is yours."

Her words fell on silence, a silence that stretched into a long, incredulous moment.

"There truly is a child?" he whispered.

She nodded, wondering if she should have given him more time to absorb the reality of it. She stepped back, ready for a violent outburst.

"After all these years," he breathed. He looked at her with unexpected keenness. "How can you be certain it is mine?"

"I give you my word it is. I am *Sidhe,* and that is how I know. My oath binds me. Hear me, Murchad. I will grant you the child you have fathered. But there are conditions."

"Conditions?" His gaze was steady and appraising. The effects of the mead had vanished. His eyes looked clear and calculating. He was thinking he could get around conditions. There were always ways.

"I will be wife to you in name only," Siobhan said. "I will exact no promises of fidelity, or of commitment. Who you take to your bed is your business. But you must be discreet and honor me. My conduct will be above reproach, and you will not put me aside. Ever. As long as the child lives. In exchange I agree you may raise the child with me. But during the summers the child will go where I go."

"I might agree." His guarded expression softened. His triumphant thoughts held barely concealed joy.

"I will have your answer now," she said. "If I leave I will never return, and you will never see the child."

"I must consult my...advisors," he said. "There are politics you do not understand."

"I care nothing for politics." She turned to go. Pausing, she looked back. "The child is a boy."

"A son," he murmured.

She put her hand on the door latch.

"How do you know?" Murchad said, stepping toward her. "It has been only fourteen nights. Not enough time for you to miss your monthly courses –"

"I know because I am *Sidhe*. I understand my body. The child is male, and he is yours."

He stood scarcely a dagger's length from her.

"There is another condition," she said, forcing herself not to move away from him.

"If I agree," Murchad said, "the boy will inherit my lands, my power and my liege men."

"You must never touch me."

"Are you serious?" His eyebrows raised.

"Even accidentally," she said. "If your bare skin ever touches mine I will vanish into the night mist, taking the boy with me, and you will never see your son again, or hear of him. He will be dead as far as you are concerned. I can do it. There are many of my kind who would shelter us. There are places we can go where you cannot follow."

Murchad looked at her for a long moment. If she had underestimated him....

She turned again to leave.

"I agree," he said.

She stopped.

"Speak it louder," she said. "Loud enough for the stones to witness."

"I agree, damn you!" he roared. "Damn you to hell."

"I cannot be damned to a hell I do not believe in," she said. Before he could respond she added, "I will be at your front gate at sunset three days hence with my belongings."

"Who will give you in marriage?" He ran a hand over his beard, thoughtfully stroking it.

"I am my own guardian," she said. "My people do not give each other to anyone. We are responsible for ourselves. I will give myself of my own free will. There are none who can gainsay it. If you wish, you may arrange a ceremony in keeping with your belief."

"But I thought – "

"You thought wrong," she snapped. "The altar will not crumble at sight of me. Nor will I cower before a cross. My faith in the Earth Mother is not so different from your beliefs. I have no claim to land, but I will bring a suitable dowry of silver and gold. And my promise that as long as you honor me, your holding will prosper. It matters not what you tell your people of me. Truth or lie will not affect me. They will accept me or not, as they choose."

"I will not allow treachery." She lowered her voice. "My powers have grown. I am not playing a child's game, Murchad. I will protect myself and the babe." She tugged on the door latch. "Do not follow me. I will put a spell of closing on your door. If you try to open it you may be injured. In a few moments the spell will fade."

"You gave your oath – "

"This is for my protection," she said. "I agreed not to harm any person."

She pushed the heavy door open and glided out between the startled guards. She turned and raised her hands. Blue sparks flew from her fingertips and splattered against the door. The flames writhed over the surface of the wood and sank into it. The guards shaded their eyes and backed away.

Siobhan strode down the hall and turned a corner where she slipped into her special world apart from mortal time. The stone walls vanished, and her safe place formed about her. Murchad was desperate, pliable. He had bent once. He would bend again until he broke.

6

Morgan and Associates, Attorneys at Law, occupied the top three floors of a recently renovated ten-story glass building in downtown Portland. On the tenth floor Kirk Morgan glared at the receptionist. She was the only employee in evidence. Despite Morgan's medium stature and spare frame, he projected confident authority. Apparently it was wasted on this woman.

He drew a breath and spoke slowly. "Get someone in here who can deal with this." There was no excuse not to have an attorney or at the least a paralegal available. Lawyers existed on billable hours. He expected even his senior partners to work 60-hour weeks.

He glanced at his Rolex. Five minutes after five. Twilight darkened the panorama outside, obscuring Mt. Hood. Kirk Morgan had always liked this office. On a clear day the windows afforded a magnificent view. Photographers often used the roof to take pictures for postcards and travel brochures.

He hadn't actually worked in the building, which he owned, for more than a decade, but he closely oversaw the general operations. And every employee from senior partner to secretary reported directly to him. Supposedly.

A painting hung on the wall behind the woman's desk. Morgan had placed it there almost thirty years before when he had bought the building and opened the firm. He decided the painting had to go.

Then there was the woman. He didn't remember hiring her. Lately he found himself losing track of minor things. Not often, and, he hoped, only trivial matters. There was so much to remember, so much crammed into his mind, that he wondered if it were possible to reach a point at which the mind would be full, incapable of storing any more information. Thank the gods for Blackberries and iPhones. Every piece of information on the Internet at the touch of his finger.

He tried to recall this woman. She must have been hired recently. Or perhaps last year when they had expanded down to take over the eighth floor. The firm was prosperous and practiced all the various branches of law from civil litigation to criminal defense.

She looked steadily at him, her mouth set in thin-lipped stubbornness. She was young, but apparently well trained to deal with unannounced visitors. He glanced sideways at the windows. Dark clouds heralded a November storm that was blowing in from the Pacific.

Damned weather. It rained too much here. Everything always smelled of mildew. He gave the woman one more lingering appraisal.

"Do you know who I am?" He leaned toward her and rested his hands on the edge of her desk.

"No sir, I don't." There was obvious vexation in her tone. She had been adamant that Mr. Feldman was out of the country, and she would not let anyone past her. She had her hand on the phone, ready to summon security. Perhaps she had already pressed the panic button beneath her desk. "Everyone is busy. You'll simply have to wait."

She was doing her job. But he was angry. First for having to come into town, and then finding everybody gone to an early dinner.

"May I suggest, Ms. Leigh Burton" – he read the nameplate on her desk – "that you call somebody who can help me. Now." He deliberately kept his voice low.

He didn't have time for this. He had never learned patience.

The woman stared at him. He was keenly aware of his casual clothes: slacks and a sweater over his shirt. Expensive, but well used. He hoped his eyes did not betray old secrets. Where had that thought come from? This woman rattled him. She was pretty. Dark hair. Young. Long ago, a woman had told him there were old secrets in his eyes. The memory of her mocking laughter had surfaced more than once lately.

Leigh Burton punched a button on the phone.

After a moment she said, "Mr. Harper? This is Leigh. Could you please come out here? There's a man here who insists that I let him into Mr. Feldman's office. A Kirk Morgan – "

"Shit. Let him in."

Morgan heard the expletive clearly through the phone. The woman flinched. Harper was probably taking a nap and got caught.

With great aplomb she set the receiver back in its cradle and looked directly at him. "Mr. Harper will see you."

He turned toward Harper's office and met the other man as he was coming through the door. Robert Harper, senior partner, was a dapper man of about 40 with thinning hair. He pushed his wire-rimmed glasses up his nose, smiled disarmingly and extended his hand. "Mr. Morgan, you're looking good."

Morgan declined Harper's hand. "Nice to see somebody remembers me here, Rob."

"Uh, Leigh" – Harper turned – "this is Mr. Kirk Morgan, of Morgan and Associates – but of course you've met…." He seemed to just run out of breath.

A flush rose in the woman's face. "Oh, Mr. Morgan, I'm so sorry – I – nobody told me. I've only been here a week – "

"Don't worry about it." Perhaps the woman had some use after all. Her regret sounded genuine. People could be bought. She would have a price. She had nice breasts, judging by what her top revealed. He relished the thought of negotiating.

"At least now I know there is protocol here," Morgan said. "And you know who I am. I'm sure it won't happen again."

"Yes sir." She twisted her hands nervously.

Morgan turned to Harper. "Rob, Nate seems to have lost one of our clients. An important one at that."

"I told him Mr. Feldman was out of the country," Leigh said.

Morgan had never liked women who spoke out of turn.

Harper glanced at her as though willing her to silence. "What seems to be the problem?"

Morgan inhaled, telling himself to hold his temper. Nothing was solved in the modern world of law by physical might. Everything was finesse. He put his hand on the other man's shoulder, ushered him into his office and closed the door behind them. "We have a client named Brant Edwards."

"Oh yes." Harper nodded. "I've met him. He's an artist. Quite successful but – "

"Well, Rob, I was a bit embarrassed that you couldn't find his cabin when the police asked. After all, that's a matter of public record." Morgan looked intently into the other man's eyes. Harper blinked several times and pushed his glasses up again.

"It's a bit of a problem," Morgan said. "Police commissioner Matson is a friend of mine. We play chess every Monday night. I didn't realize Edwards has been gone for two fucking weeks. Why didn't someone notify me?"

Harper's face paled, and he stabbed at his glasses again. "Well, yes, he has, but, well, there was nothing to report. He just left, and, well, nobody's seen him. We searched Nate's files, but didn't find anything about the cabin. When Edwards' father died, apparently the cabin wasn't part of the estate. They must have owned it jointly."

Harper paused, and when Morgan didn't speak, he went on, "Someone from the police department was here about it. A Detective Gordon, I believe. He said he had someone check it, but there was nobody there. He didn't say where the cabin is. Said it was none of our business. You know the mother's been out of the picture since Brant and his sister were – "

"The mother died when Maeve was 10. Brant was 19. That's old news, Rob."

"We haven't had any luck yet. Unfortunate mix-up."

"Unfortunate." Morgan snorted, allowed a steely edge to creep into his voice. "My firm doesn't lose things. Or clients. There must be an explanation."

"Sorry, Mr. Morgan." Harper fidgeted. "I mean, we'll get right back on it. We have a few local Private Investigators on retainer, but they haven't turned up anything. Edwards just vanished. There's been no activity on his credit cards or his bank account – "

Morgan turned away and sauntered to the window, gathering his thoughts. This was one of those times he wished things could be done as he had done them as a young man.

"Lovely view, don't you think?" he said.

"Oh, sure." Harper sounded hesitant.

"Rob," Morgan said quietly, "have the cabin located and checked."

Harper pushed up his glasses, an annoying habit. "That'll take some time."

Anger heated Morgan's face. It was a pity the law of the sword had been replaced by rhetoric. "I don't care if the bastard is on the fucking moon, Rob." He felt his speech reverting to the old accent he had worked so hard to eradicate. He spoke more slowly, "I want that fucking cabin found. And I want it found now. I don't care how it affects the bottom line." The media had accused Morgan of having more money than God. It was close to true.

Harper blanched. "Yes sir."

Morgan glanced at his watch. "I'm leaving now." At the door he looked back. "I expect to get a phone call in my car on the way home telling me you've found the cabin. And I don't give a flying fuck how you do it."

"Yes, sir."

"And, Rob."

"Yes?"

"Take down that painting over Ms. Burton's desk. I don't like it. I'll call Park's Gallery for something more appropriate. Maybe one of Edwards'."

"Yes, sir," Harper said.

Before Morgan left, he had the satisfaction of seeing a sheen of sweat on Harper's forehead. He wished for a moment he could be a fly on the wall in that office. He'd like to see the activity that would begin as soon as he was gone. To become a fly would take witchcraft. Witchcraft was a sham, just an illusion. Revenge was the only thing that endured. And wealth had given him the resources to exact his revenge. Wealth had its advantages.

He had barely driven ten blocks when the phone in his limo rang. He answered it, leaving the driver to his duty.

"Morgan."

"Rob Harper here."

Good. Not some flunky.

"You're going to be surprised."

"You found the cabin."

"No, we found him. Well, that is, he found himself. He came home about an hour ago. He's okay, but there seems to be some problem. The detective who called said he may be on drugs. He said he'd keep us informed."

Morgan sighed. The prodigal returned. Good. One burden eased. Keeping track of Edwards was turning into a full time job. Perhaps it was time to deal with the sister.

The painting arrived at Morgan's home the next morning. He carefully cut the canvas from the frame and burned it in the fireplace. Flames exploded in the old paint.

It wasn't a very good painting. A Dublin street scene painted in the 1850s. Indistinguishable from hundreds of others. The artist had been Brant Edwards' four times great-grandfather. Most likely the one who had contributed the artistic talent to Edwards' gene pool. The artist had died young. Murdered in his prime.

Despite being somewhat impressionistic, the painting showed one thing clearly. Standing beside a woman on a street corner was a man who bore a striking resemblance to Kirk Morgan.

"Al," Maeve Gordon said as she sat down on the couch beside her friend in the deserted faculty lounge. Maeve had left her sixth grade classroom in charge of the teacher next door. She glanced at her watch. 10:21. She couldn't be gone long. She figured she had about 10 minutes or so before Jason would get antsy and realize she hadn't just gone down the hall to the bathroom.

"Hi, Mevvie," chirped the plump blond woman who sat with her feet propped on a battered coffee table. "It's good to see you back. Tracked me down, huh?" Her expression changed to one of alarm. "Any news?"

"I'm sorry. I heard you had a rough time with that parent, but I had to talk to you."

"Never a dull moment in public education."

Alison Reed was a loyal friend. The two women had met in college and had gravitated to diverse professions – Alison as a social worker, Maeve as a middle school English teacher. They had begun and continued their careers in the same school system. xxx

"What can I do for you?" Alison's face lit up with an easy smile.

"Al, I've got a problem," Maeve began.

"I should be so lucky," Alison sighed. "Brant came home safe and sound."

Maeve shook her head. "Can't beat the old teacher to teacher grapevine. I simply could not call you last night. But…well…I don't know what to do. I need some advice – "

"What's wrong? Oh. My. God. Maeve, are you and Rich pregnant? That'd be peachy."

Tears formed in Maeve's eyes. "Oh, Al, no. It's not that."

Alison leaned against Maeve's shoulder, sincerity softening her eyes. "I didn't mean to be flippant, Maeve. I'm sorry. What's wrong? Did you and Rich have a fight? I thought everything was good – "

"Yes," Maeve interrupted. "I mean no, we didn't argue. Rich and I are doing great. Kids are a little way off. But, well, I don't know what's going on with Brant." She told Alison how he had treated her as a stranger. She stumbled over words, reluctant to verbalize what she found inconceivable.

"You really think he could have been high on something?"

"I honestly don't know, Al. He disappeared for two weeks. Rich checked the cabin, and he wasn't there, although he says he was. Where could he have gone? He looked so strange, and he didn't know who I was – or said he didn't. After I ran out Rich talked to him and said he was almost incoherent and complained of a headache. He rambled and didn't really make sense.

"Rich called him later and he talked about a girl in the woods. There weren't any accidents – you know, plane crashes, that sort of thing. Three law enforcement divisions have been up at the cabin for two days with dogs and searchers and can't find anybody. The judge ordered an involuntary commitment to see if he's dangerous to himself or others. They're picking him up today, but they can only hold him for 72 hours."

"For heaven's sake, why are you here? You have sick days. Take some time off."

"I know," Maeve said. "It's easier to work. That way I don't have to think about it."

"Is he dangerous, Maeve?" Alison's expression was solemn.

"I honestly don't know," Maeve said softly. "It's like he's a different person."

Alison pursed her lips and pulled a pad of paper from her blazer pocket. "It does sound peculiar. I have a suggestion. If the cops haul Brant in, they'll take him to the psych ward at Portland General. Nothing against the hospital, but I know a better place. Especially since the State has to pay." She scrawled on the top sheet of the pad, tore it off and handed it to Maeve. It was the name of a clinic in Milwaukie, a Portland suburb, with a phone number.

"See if they can take Brant there. Ask for Elizabeth Barrett. My brother's dating her. He's all gaga. I think he's about to pop the question. But that's a story for another time. Anyway, Brant might be more cooperative with someone he knows. She was at the staff party last spring – ash blond, pretty and thin."

"I remember her. I'm glad for Mark."

"Yeah, maybe a spring wedding. Anyway, I'll call her and talk to her. It'll be way better than a city hospital."

Maeve tried to smile, but she knew it came across as a feeble effort. "Thanks, Al. I really appreciate it."

Alison hugged her. "Well, as they say, 'It isn't *what* you know, it's *who* you know.'"

Maeve rose. "Thanks again, Al."

Alison waved. "Try not to worry."

Maeve did smile. "I know. It doesn't solve anything." She headed for the door.

"Good luck," Alison called. "Call for a substitute to take your classes. Go home and rest or watch a movie or read a book."

"I will, for the rest of the week. I'll let you know what happens."

Maeve headed back to her classroom. She used her cell to call a sub and then pushed the button that speed dialed Rich.

Judge Harvey had issued the order to have Brant held for evaluation, but Rich wanted a couple of uniforms with him. Nobody at the precinct could lend him some time until the morning shift arrived. He would make the arrangements with the clinic in Milwaukie.

Maeve slept fitfully that night. She kept waking and not finding Rich in bed beside her. When he finally rolled in after two o'clock, he told her everything was set. He'd be at Brant's place at 9:00 a.m. with two uniforms and papers in hand.

Maeve muttered a sleepy, "Thanks," and curled up against his warmth. She didn't think she would sleep well and didn't.

In the morning Maeve's alarm went off at 6:00 a.m. Damn. She had forgotten to cancel the alarm. She punched it off and was lying back on her pillow when Rich came into the bedroom wearing only boxers, still damp from the shower. He put his arms around her and nuzzled her neck.

"Don't worry, honey," he murmured. "It'll be all right."

She looked into his eyes. "Are you sure?"

Rich sighed. "Okay, I'm not so sure. But now he's had a couple of days to sleep it off, he'll be okay, babe."

Maeve pulled away from him and threw an old bathrobe on. She scrambled eggs and made toast. After Rich left she did the dishes and puttered around the apartment, beginning many tasks, finishing none, trying not to worry – about either Rich or Brant.

She tried to watch something on TV, and surfed through hundreds of digital cable channels, unable to focus on anything. By two o'clock she was reduced to pacing.

Maeve glanced at her watch for the hundredth time in an hour. It was only a few minutes later than the last time she had looked: 2:13. Brant had given her the watch for her last birthday – a milestone. They had always joked that being 25 was halfway to 50. Right now Maeve felt more like 50.

She had forgotten lunch, couldn't remember what she'd had for breakfast.

She found herself in front of the refrigerator nervously gulping another diet Pepsi – she'd lost count. She wondered which was worse: her constant diet soda or Brant's high-octane coffee habit.

Dangerous path, she chided herself. Don't think about him. That only led to more worry. Don't wonder about what is happening to him, what they're doing to him, what drugs they suspect –

Stop it, she told herself, brushing away tears.

When the phone rang a few moments later, she dived on it. "Hello?"

"Maeve?"

"Rich, what happened? I've been – "

"Everything's fine. He's in the hospital. He came quietly, Maeve. Seemed a little dazed at first, but he was cooperative. I think he realizes he's in trouble."

"It's so late I thought something had gone wrong."

"No, nothing's wrong. He was just like the other day – kind of confused. He said he didn't know me, but the other cops intimidated him into coming quietly. They're running some tests, tox screens and such. I talked to Alison's doctor friend. She seems okay. Said in addition to the physical tests she'd do a full psychological workup on him. It's all set up."

"Thanks, Rich." Maeve sighed. "I love you."

Rich must have sensed the defeat she felt. "He'll be all right, honey. Don't worry. It's a lot nicer than Portland General. He's got his own room, and they don't take the really dangerous cases. He'll be fine. Don't wait up. I've got to go back to the precinct and follow up on a few cases. And I've got paperwork. We made an arrest in the Hanson killing. It'll be on the news tonight."

"Good," she said. A woman in a nearby neighborhood had been killed in a carjacking in broad daylight. Now the streets would be safer. "I'll put a dinner plate in the fridge for you. Wake me when you come in."

"I will, Maeve. Try to get some sleep."

She was still awake, trying to read and worrying, when he came home just after midnight.

7

"You must not marry this…this woman," Ceallachan hissed.

Startled by the unexpected sound of Ceallachan' voice, Murchad's hand jumped. The bronze brooch he had been trying to secure to his *brat* flew from his fingers and landed with a clink somewhere to his left.

The druid had appeared, seeming to materialize from the oaken door in Murchad's chamber, as the chief of the o'Ruairc clan made a final adjustment to his wedding garments.

Murchad's hand went to his sword as he whirled. He froze when he saw the druid. The *brat* slipped from his shoulders and landed on the flagstones in a splash of maroon and hunter green plaid.

Ceallachan's long robe blended with the color and texture of the door behind him, making him seem part of the wood.

"I said," he repeated, his heavy beard masking the movements of his lips, "you must not marry this woman, Murchad."

"Why not?"

The man's effrontery galled Murchad. He would not lower himself and order him to call him lord. If the druid was capable of more than clever deception, if he indeed controlled some dark sorcery, this was not the time to test the man's power.

The druid crossed his arms in stoic defiance.

"She carries my child," Murchad said. "A son."

"I am aware of the child. He will be born under inauspicious stars,

Murchad, because you did not heed my instructions and drank my potion early. Mark me well. No happiness will come of this union. You could have legitimized the boy without taking the witch to wife. She is not human." Ceallachan's quiet voice filled the chamber with ominous echoes.

"Your potion worked too well, Druid," Murchad flung at him.

"Do not blame me for your weakness. It was a fertility potion, Murchad, nothing more. What you did by drinking it a few moments early was your doing, not mine."

Ceallachan stood still as water in a deep lough. But there were currents under the man's facade that kept Murchad at a distance. He finally looked away from the druid's intense appraisal, picked up his *brat* and adjusted it around his shoulders.

"I got what I desired, Druid," he said. "That was the bargain."

Ceallachan nodded. "Mayhap you got more than you bargained for."

"It is done," Murchad said and turned to look for the brooch. It lay on a flagstone near his bed, almost hidden by the edge of a blanket. Toeing it out, he picked it up and slipped the long shank through the layers of the *brat*, securing it high on his left shoulder.

"It is done badly," Ceallachan murmured.

"What do you mean?" Murchad faced the druid, feeling slightly uncomfortable looking directly into the taller man's watery eyes.

"The stars...."

"What about the stars?" Siobhan had spoken of the stars. Foolish woman claimed the stars made music. "The stars are not part of your Earth Mother."

"The stars are part of the whole pattern, Murchad, and the stars do not bode well for either the marriage or the child. Neither do the entrails of several goats."

"Bah," Murchad spat. "How can you speak for the child, Druid, when he is not yet born?"

Ceallachan raised his arms, extending them outward. "Earth spells speak true, Murchad. My ways were old when Siobhan's people came to this land in their shining ships. The signs speak to those who heed them. They tell me the child will be born into your world, but he will never truly belong. He will live in the shadow of still another world that will draw him all the days of his life. The stars also say that eternity will not heal the grief that will follow your son."

Murchad laughed deep in his throat. "You do not frighten me, Druid. Eternity does not affect me. Your enchantment is little more than illusion.

You cannot even be sure you have read the signs aright. The only true sorcery is *Sidhe* magic, and with the witch woman as my wife I will have that at my fingertips."

"Do not be too certain, Murchad," Ceallachan muttered.

"You vowed there would be no payment for the potion," Murchad said. "So there is no debt between us. Now begone before I lose my temper. I have no wish to spill your blood on my wedding day." His hand closed tighter on the hilt of his sword.

Ceallachan waved a hand as if shooing away a fly. His voice was low and steady. "Your threats are as rain on my hair, Murchad. I do not fear you. I seek only to warn you. You are a foolish man not to heed the star signs and those the Earth Mother shows us. Blood will be spilled because of this day. And blood will follow you all of your days."

He raised his arms again and chanted softly. A cloud of mist gathered about him, obscuring his form. The vapors faded, and the druid was gone. The door swung ajar.

Murchad drew his blade and stepped through the doorway.

A company of guards waited to escort him to the ceremony. Even on his wedding day he must be cautious. There were those who would depose an heirless king. Murchad did not see the druid in the hallway and did not ask his guards about him.

Siobhan paused at the entrance to the Great Hall. People crowded the space. Women were clad in fine muslin and wool dresses, men in tunics of wool and some in rich velvet. All wore linen leg wrappings against the chill. Sunlight streamed through the window holes high up in the stone walls illuminating the colors, heightening the shades of indigo and magenta clothing. Unlike some of the dank rooms and twisting corridors she had seen in Murchad's dwelling, this room was light and airy. A cool draft brushed her face as she assessed the crowd. She shivered, whispered a spell that surrounded her with warmth.

She picked up stray thoughts:

...pretty....

...she is a child...

My daughter's face is more fair...Murchad should have....

So fragile...not accustomed to the hard work of running a household.

My niece...more suitable wife than this pale wench.

Siobhan stepped forward, chin held high. People moved aside, forming an aisle through which she walked to the far end of the room. Murchad stood beside his holy man. A golden goblet rested on a table behind them. The workmanship of the goblet was exquisite. It was adorned with shiny stones, and there were intricate patterns in the gold. Perhaps the village smith had made it. He was much renowned for his work with precious metal, as was his father and grandfather before him.

Behind the table on the wall, hung a cross with a nearly naked man on it. Siobhan did not like the image of the man on the cross, crucified, his head drooping, eyes closed in death. She moved her gaze away from the cruel icon.

A ripple of surreptitious movement passed among the gathering. Dainty hands and calloused fingers pressed against crosses made of wood and pewter and bronze. But she felt the presence of much iron in the room. Its cold scent repelled her.

A flutter of impatience rippled among the people.

Beautiful...she is beautiful....

A thought washed over her mind, clear as the call of a song bird.

A shame she will lie in another man's arms....

A man's thoughts, vivid with lusty images.

She paused, turned her head slightly, encountered intense eyes the color of a bright summer sky. The thoughts had come from him, a tall man clad in the simple garments of a knight from across the sea. His lack of beard branded him a foreigner.

A handsome face. His strong jaw and blue eyes stood out in the crowd. She judged him to be about nineteen or twenty mortal years. So young, but his eyes knew sorrow. Dark hair curled around his ears, in need of a tie to hold it back.

He stared at Siobhan with open curiosity and undisguised longing. She sensed he was at the ceremony for another reason, but she did not probe beyond the surface of his mind. Many came to Murchad's land from the great island across the channel, questing for some Great Cause, or running from trouble. She wondered what his story was. And why there was such sadness in his eyes.

Color rose to his cheeks as if he knew she had caught his thoughts, but his gaze did not waver. He smiled, revealing even white teeth and a dimple in one cheek. His name was Gareth Spencer. He had come a great distance and never expected to meet one of Siobhan's kind.

Beautiful...men would kill for you....

Siobhan closed her mind to all distractions.

She strode forward until she stood only an arm's length from Murchad. Behind him was another man, tall, with auburn hair and beard. Probing gently, she directed her mind to him and recoiled. His mind was blocked. Pushing more aggressively, she met an almost tangible wall of resistance that gave slightly, then fortified itself with a practiced blankness, rebuffing her attempt to get in. He was protected by a powerful block, perhaps penetrable, but only with a great strain on her energy. Only her kind could do that…and *Druii*. Ancient professors of earth magic. Illusionists. Purveyors of the future they claimed could be found in the entrails of slaughtered animals. His dark eyes stared at her, annoyed her with their directness.

She turned back to Murchad, clenched her fists, willed her voice to sound controlled, and said quietly, only for Murchad's ears, "The druid must go."

Startled, Murchad glanced around.

"What?" he said.

"The druid will go," she said. "Or I will."

"He is merely a guest, woman," Murchad said.

"He will leave," she repeated.

"Murchad," the druid whispered, "you should heed my warning."

Murchad glanced from one to the other, then to the monk, but he found no answer in the holy man's puzzled expression.

Finally Murchad sighed. "Go, Ceallachan."

"She has bewitched you, Murchad," the druid said, his gaze still on Siobhan. She felt he peered into her very soul even though she knew he could not. The barrier she had erected in her own mind could only be broken by death.

"He is free to do as he wills," Siobhan said. "As *you* are, Druid. But I will not share my wedding day with one of false sorcery."

Ceallachan's expression remained implacable. "My enchantment comes from the Earth Mother, *Sidhe* woman," he said. "Old even by your measurements. I will leave of my own choosing, but I will have my say." He lowered his voice. "The child you carry will not inherit what you expect. All the days of his life he will be torn between your heritage and that of mortal man.

"We who are doomed to die before your kind even attains adulthood, will judge your kind in the end. What I say is true. The Earth Mother speaks not in perceptions, but in eternal truths. Another world will follow the child, just as it does you – another world or another time…a time of darkness will pull your family apart as surely as lightning sunders a storm cloud. Dark…the child will be dark…dark like his father, but not like his father." He stopped.

Before Siobhan could prevent the intrusion, unaware that Ceallachan's ilk could even accomplish the feat, she felt the ripples of the druid's mind on the surface of her thoughts.

There is another, Siobhan, the man's mental voice spoke directly in her mind. *Another whose claim on you will endure after I am ashes. And one other still who will influence all that you and the child do, but who cannot speak of his devotion for you.*

She centered herself and drove the druid out like a whipped dog. He laughed softly, turned on his heel and strode from the Great Hall, his long robe swishing around his ankles. Silence lingered in his wake.

Siobhan stepped up beside Murchad to receive the holy man's blessing. Murchad glanced after Ceallachan several times. His eyes held not fear, but expectancy. Siobhan was not rid of the druid. He had tested her mind once. He would try again to judge the depth of her power and perhaps the strength of his own. She must always be on her guard.

Later at the banquet, nobody spoke to Siobhan. She nibbled a few bites of bread and retired to her chamber. She wore only her undergarment, a simple linen shift, savoring the fresh, cold air that swirled in despite the tapestries that covered the window holes. The ceremony had seemed endless, but she had made all the necessary responses, even to pledging her fidelity and handing over her dowry – a few pieces of silver and the golden brooch the *Faerie* Queen had returned to her. It greatly pleased Murchad to get the brooch back.

The stars wheeled slowly in their passages, negligible movements even to her senses. She wished the man she had left could hear the star music and take comfort as she did in their timeless melodies. But he was part of another world, a time yet to happen. He was lost to her. It was best to forget him. For the sake of the child she would forget. She turned from the faraway music to the bed.

The door slammed open. Murchad strode into the room accompanied by the odors of food and drink, a bronze goblet held carelessly in one hand. She had not thought he would enter her chamber without permission.

He closed the door and barred it. For a fleeting moment Siobhan felt a pang of apprehension. Could he have learned something that might negate her spells again? But no, he was merely mortal, and now that she was aware of the druid's animosity toward her, she was prepared. His illusion could not prevail against true enchantment.

"You enter without my permission," she said.

She spoke to him as one of equal station. It irritated him that she did not address him as lord.

He stopped and gestured vaguely. "This is mine," he said, his voice slurred by too much mead and wine. He spread his arms, slopping wine on the floor. "I have no need to ask anything. I command."

"Why have you come here?"

"I have come for what is mine by marriage right." He swaggered across the wide room to stand at the foot of her bed. She held his gaze.

"Have you forgotten your bargain?" she said quietly.

"Bargain?"

"You agreed not to touch me. Ever."

He laughed. "Oh, that. Surely you do not intend to hold me to it."

"Did you think I entered into this arrangement without careful thought?" Siobhan said. "I agreed to your terms, and you agreed to mine. If you wish to see your son, you will honor the bargain. Otherwise...." She let her voice trail off.

His eyes narrowed. "Damn it, woman, you are my wife." He threw the goblet on the floor. The cup clattered into a dark corner leaving red wine splattered on the stones. With a quick gesture Siobhan clothed herself in a spell of protection. Enchantment sparked over her body, making a blue glow in the room. With another gesture she extinguished the rush lights, replacing them with tiny, glowing *Sidhe* lights that hugged the corners near the ceiling. Either she had underestimated Murchad's courage, or he was too drunk to be impressed by her sorcery, because he didn't seem to notice the change in the light.

"I am your wife in name only, Murchad. That is all I will ever be. I will honor the bargain only for the sake of the child."

Reaching out, he took a step toward her. But he encountered the resistance of the spell and drew back quickly, shaking his hand as if he had been burned.

"You can be killed," he said.

"Did your druid not tell you?"

"Tell me what?" Murchad said, his tone sullen. He rubbed his fingers.

Siobhan scanned the surface of his mind. He truly did not know. "Your advisor is remiss, Murchad," she said. "When women of my people are with child, our enchantment is much enhanced. We become invulnerable. It is the way of my kind. It ensures our perpetuation. You cannot hurt me, and I will never allow harm to come to the child."

Understanding dawned in his dark eyes. He shook his head, trying to clear it, but the drink had taken its toll.

"The servants will see the linens in the morning," he said. "I will lose face."

"What? What do I care?"

"There must be blood on the bed linens to prove the consummation of our marriage. Our union will not be recognized until the serving girls take the bloodstained sheet to the monk. If there is no blood, the child will be a bastard."

"Blood should not be difficult to obtain for one such as you." The instant the words were out, Siobhan regretted giving into her emotions.

Menacing and angry, Murchad stepped toward her again. "Ceallachan was right. You are not human." The barely controlled fury in his voice was apparent even to one who could not hear his thoughts.

"No, Murchad, I am not quite human."

He fumbled for the brooch and yanked out the shank.

"Here, witch," Murchad said. "Take it back. I have no wish to be sullied by something that was probably made by your kind. I will settle for a trinket crafted by a loyal smith from the silver you have given me."

He flung the gold brooch at Siobhan. It glittered in the light, tumbling end over end. Knowing his intention, nonchalant in the certainty of her power, Siobhan flicked a hand, expecting to see the golden circle stop in midair and fall to the floor. To her astonishment, the object did not obey her spell. There was no time to duck. The edge of the brooch grazed her cheek and landed in the middle of the bed where she had turned down the heavy covers. Murchad gazed at her open-mouthed.

Siobhan raised her hands again and sent an immobilizing spell to hold him where he stood.

Pain radiated along her jaw. With hesitant fingers she touched her cheek. Blood on her fingers. She shook the dark drops onto the bedclothes and stepped backward, away from Murchad and the bed.

Why had the brooch passed unhindered through her spell? Indeed it must be an object of power. Orghlaith was right. The craftsman who fashioned the pin had endowed it with enchantment.

"Here," she spat at him, letting anger into her words. "Here is blood.

As long as it is mine, the customs are satisfied. Consider this marriage consummated."

She brought up the *Sidhe* lights by thinking them brighter. The room blazed in sudden brilliance. Murchad's face paled. She didn't care whether it was fear or anger that gripped his thoughts.

"You may go, Murchad. The holy man will have his proof in the morning. But know that there will always be a warding spell on every room in this fortress. Whoever deigns to cross the threshold of any chamber containing me or my son with mayhem in their minds will pay an instant and severe penalty." She released him from her spell.

He staggered backward, keeping his balance only by sheer force of will. "I will keep my bargain," he said through clenched teeth. "Nobody will ever touch you in this house. *Nobody.* The druid was right. You do not possess even a hint of humanity."

"Go," she flung at him, pointing to the door.

He blinked blear-eyed and backed away from her. She flipped up the bar with a thought and opened the door as if a great wind had blown through the room. Dust swirled, making Murchad blink. Siobhan was not affected. The dust stopped against an invisible barrier that created a place apart in which she stood. Murchad stared for an instant, and without another word he stumbled out, grasping his *brat* around his shoulders. She gave in to her anger and slammed the door hard enough to jar loose fragments of mud from the ceiling. A shower of particles rained down in the chamber, sliding over the barrier of Siobhan's protective spell.

She ran her fingers over her cheek. Blood. She used the sheet to clean herself.

Orghlaith had known. The ornament *was* a part of her life. She pulled a corner of the light tapestry that hung behind her bed and threaded it through the circle. She could not use the iron shank, but a knot of fabric would secure it. Such then was fate. She would carry the pin always, if only to infuriate Murchad.

Using a scrap of linen meant to be a drying cloth for her morning toilet, she picked up the brooch shank and threw it out the window where the raw emanations of the iron would not bother her.

Murchad stumbled into the noisy celebration in his Great Hall. Smoke from the fireplaces and the rush lights created a haze that blurred the far end of the room. Looking around at the revelers, he realized none of them missed the newly wed couple. Most of the guests had come only to eat and drink at his table.

Damn. Damn her to hell. But for the moment there was nothing to do but enjoy the festivities. He gazed around. His glance paused on a vague shape at one of the tables. He blinked, trying to clear away the alcohol that blurred his vision. The shape solidified into Ceallachan's auburn hair and beard. Murchad felt the druid's gaze locked on his, probing into him. Ceallachan raised a goblet, saluted him. Murchad swallowed.

Ceallachan vanished, and in his place sat a woman whose fiery hair reflected the light in a halo of soft curls. Murchad's feet moved. He wanted to stop, to talk to some of his guests, but the woman's presence drew him like a lodestone. He stopped in front of her, still riveted by her green eyes. Eyes whose depths held a promise. A thrill of danger raised goose bumps on his arms.

The woman rose. "My name is Lassariona," she said. "The druid's daughter. I have been watching you." Her husky voice caressed him, and her smile sobered him for an instant. "May your marriage be blessed with an heir."

Unable to speak or look away, Murchad gazed into her eyes. He wanted to tell her not to blink because her long lashes hid the mystery in her eyes.

She held out a cup. "Drink, Murchad. The *Sidhe* woman will not begrudge you a drink."

Murchad took the cup, raised it to his lips, and drank. Wine and… something bitter. He drank anyway, not caring if the wine had gone to vinegar, and set the cup down. The woman rose, her hair a fiery halo around her face. Her creamy skin was flawless and glowed with the vitality of youth.

He leered at her. "You are too young, child."

"Come with me, Murchad," she whispered, beckoning. "I will show you I am old enough."

He wanted to walk away, but he was powerless to resist. He stumbled after her. She grasped his arm. She smelled like flowers. Spring flowers.

"There was something…." he started.

"Yes?"

"The wine. Something in the wine…." Poison?

She laughed. "There was nothing."

Her teeth gleamed in the far spaced lights of the corridor. How had they gotten to the hallway? His vision wavered. They stopped before a door. No guards. They must all be drunk on his mead.

The door opened. He found himself in his own chamber, Lassariona standing beside his bed. Her beauty paled the tapestries and ornaments of his private residence.

"Murchad." Her voice excited him, stripped him of his instinctive warrior's caution.

He mumbled, "Wine…something…." The wine. He couldn't concentrate. There was….

"Murchad." She undid the ties that bound her gown. The linen rustled softly as the garment fluttered down around her ankles. There was a sharp sound as the latch dropped in the door behind him. Nobody else was there. How had the door locked? But he couldn't hold the thought. Curiously light-headed, he moved toward the child-woman.

She stood like a statue, beautifully proportioned. Her green eyes flashed. He touched her shoulder – milky skin, soft as rain – ran his fingers down to her breasts, her belly. His whole body tingled, the same thrill he felt before a battle.

She unbuckled his sword belt. It clattered on the floor. With deft fingers she unfastened his garments until he too stood naked before her.

Her arms encircled his neck. He drew a deep breath, drowned in her eyes. Eyes as deep as the sea he had once seen. He pulled her against him, smelled a flowery scent in her hair: sweet and elusive. Hair the shade of a summer sunset.

He felt her surrender, welcome him, and he pushed her back onto the furs of his bed. Something tugged at his thoughts.

"Lassariona?" He had trouble forming the word.

"What?" she said. Green eyes drew him into their bottomless depths. Forest-green shadows invited him.

"I – " He shook his head.

"Come, Murchad," she said, her breasts pressing against his bare chest.

He spread her legs roughly, and pushed himself into her. She gasped, whether from pain or pleasure, he cared not. Her nails scratched fiery paths down his back.

Lassariona laughed deep in her throat.

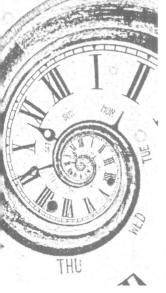

8

B rant Edwards had waited in the doctor's office long enough to be impatient. He grabbed a pen from the desk and sketched a woman's face on the open calendar. He stared at the incomplete drawing. She did not seem familiar, and yet he knew she was fair with sunlit hair and pale eyes.

A woman entered the room. She moved with an athletic grace that made Brant feel awkward as he rose from the chair. She was slender, dressed in black slacks and a pale gray sweater that had the soft look of cashmere. Her ash blond hair was pulled back with a comb clip that allowed wispy ends to escape. No rings. Just small gold knot earrings.

Her clear hazel eyes appraised him. She looked young, maybe his age.

"Mr. Edwards?" she said. "I'm Elizabeth Barrett."

He rose. "Brant, please. Mister is what people called my dad." He wondered what psychological conclusion she would draw from that comment.

"Brant," she said. "I'm a staff psychiatrist here at Maywood. I'll be your primary physician." She set a folder on her desk and held out her hand. He shook it. She had a strong, confident grip.

"Call me Liz, please. We met last spring at a cookout for the staff at your sister's school. I'm dating Alison Reed's brother, Mark."

"I don't have a sister," Brant said automatically. She raised her eyebrows. "But I remember you. I know Alison and Mark from – " He stopped. He didn't remember how he knew the Reeds, but he had known them for some time. Maybe from his college days. His stomach fluttered, and a twinge of pain bloomed behind his eyes.

She smiled with a genuine warmth that calmed the nervous fidgets in his stomach.

She motioned for him to sit, and he sank back into the chair. She seated herself in a leather executive chair behind the desk and opened the folder. Probably Brant's life history.

"I'm sorry I didn't get a chance to meet you when you came in," she said. "The last few days have been pretty hectic for you. I want to thank you for cooperating. I know this is uncomfortable."

"I just want to get out of here."

"I bet you do. Are you sleeping well?"

"Not really."

"We'll release you this evening, so you can sleep in your own bed."

He nodded, suspicion gnawing at the back of his mind. This woman was too pleasant. If he could look into her mind, he thought he would find she held a great deal under the surface. The pain in his head throbbed once and subsided.

She leaned back and crossed her legs.

"Well, Doc," Brant said.

"Liz, please."

"Liz. My big question is, will I be able to play the piano?"

"Not if you couldn't before."

"Damn. I always wanted to learn."

She looked directly into his eyes. "Uncomfortable, are you?"

He nodded. Honesty couldn't hurt. "I never saw a psychiatrist before. And all the tests were tiresome. I've never been sick before. Never even had a cold."

"Ever?"

"Not that I remember."

She jotted a note in the folder.

"Don't worry," she said. "This is only a routine evaluation. I hope you don't feel like we've invaded your mind. The personality test is standard, and the interview with the psychologist was designed to put you at ease and get you to talk about yourself." She folded her hands on her lap. "I didn't get to talk to you long at the cookout. But I love your work. I have one of your early pieces. It's called *Fairy Wood*. The forest on the Olympia Peninsula. It looks like another world with the mist – "

"When did I meet you?"

"Your sister – "

"I don't have a sister."

She looked at him, silence stretching out like a ribbon of emptiness.

"Maeve Gordon," she said.

He shook his head. "I *don't* have a sister."

Liz drew a breath. "Well, then, what happened to her?"

"She – maybe I had one once, but, I don't know, maybe she died when I was little." Who the hell was the woman claiming to be his sister?

Liz's expression was noncommittal. "We'll explore that later. Right now I'd like to go over the results of your tests."

Brant couldn't think of a joking remark.

Liz looked down at her clipboard, flipped up a few sheets. "The drug tests were negative. You said you'd taken Ibuprofen – "

"Headache. I had a horrible headache." He felt sheepish, like a child admitting he had done something wrong. "Maybe I took more than I should have."

"Maybe you did. Your blood sugar was a little low, and you were slightly anemic. You said you'd lost some weight, but couldn't account for it. It looks like maybe you haven't eaten right for a while. You seem to be eating well here."

"Yeah. Can't seem to get enough."

She nodded. "Your nurses say you've been requesting double portions of main dishes."

"The food here's good."

"It is. We're a private facility with good funding," she said. "I did find something interesting."

What could be *interesting* about him?

"The personality test session with the psychologist – I understand at first you didn't want to do it."

"I didn't see the point."

"You interrupted the test session halfway through. What was bothering you?"

"How do you mean?"

"Did you feel threatened by it? Were the questions too personal?"

"No." Brant kneaded his temples. "My head hurt. I couldn't concentrate."

"You showed some degree of stress. There was an indication of PTSD."

"That's what troops have when they come home from the war."

"Post Traumatic Stress Disorder," she said. "Did something happen at the cabin, Brant?"

He tried to think about the time. The ache became a full-blown headache. "Nothing...something...shit, I don't know." He rubbed his temples. "Nothing happened. Except I thought I was there a weekend and it was two weeks."

"Brant, the psychologist who did the tests with you left me a note."

"'Not cooperative'," Brant said. "'Exhibits signs of PTS. Complains of headache'."

Liz stared at him.

"What?" he said.

"Did my colleague show you this?" She peeled off a bright green Sticky note and held it up. "He said he wrote it after you left."

Scrawled on the paper were the words Brant had spoken.

"I didn't – " he started.

Mind reading…ESP.…

He didn't *hear* the words, but saw them in her thoughts as if the letters were written in the air over her head. He shook his head, felt the ache in his head intensify.

"It's impossible," he said.

"What's impossible?" She looked up at him, her eyes startled.

"Mind reading." It wasn't that he heard the words so much as saw them in his mind. It was what she was thinking. What she was reading from the chart on her desk.

"I didn't say – " She glanced down at the paper again. Didn't speak for the length of time it took her to draw a deep breath. "I'm looking at another note the tester left for me." She peeled off another bright green note, held it over the wastebasket beside her desk and let it go. It fluttered into oblivion.

Brant *knew* what was written on that piece of paper. As if he had read it himself. Yet he was certain he hadn't seen the man – whose name he couldn't remember – write that note. It said: Further eval needed. The words were underlined.

"Oh, God." Brant leaned back in the chair, trying to relax the headache away. He knew it wouldn't work.

"I was tired," he said, "and my head felt like little guys inside were hammering to get out, and they were about to break through."

She appraised him for a long moment.

"How often do you get headaches?" she said.

"Never."

"Never?" She frowned at him.

"I mean I never had them before."

"Before?"

"Before I…before I came home from the cabin."

She flipped some sheets on the folder. "Your MRI was perfect." She wrote something on one of the sheets.

He sighed. Deep down, he'd wondered if he had something seriously wrong with his brain.

"But," she continued, "the EEG showed some anomalies."

So there *was* something wrong. "EEG?"

"Electroencephalogram. It tests electrical activity in the brain. There are Alpha wave spikes we couldn't account for. The technician attributed it to your being nervous. Have you ever had a head injury, even a minor one?"

He shook his head. "No. Why?"

"Epilepsy is a remote possibility. But the EEG doesn't fit the pattern. I'm just asking for the record. Don't worry. I'm sure it's nothing. Maybe a technical error." She made another notation on his file.

Brant stared at her. The planes of her face made interesting shadows. She would be a good portrait subject. He could visualize her sitting on a bench in a garden with sunlight on her hair, surrounded by greenery, her hazel eyes almost golden –

"Brant? Head injury?"

"No."

"Okay then. Tell me about your stay at the cabin."

The direct question caught him off guard. He knew she would ask about it, but he thought she would work up to it.

"I went up there for the weekend. I was there for two weeks, although I don't remember it. I thought I stayed a couple of days. It's as if the time just disappeared." He frowned, trying to remember. A dream. "There was a girl who came out of the woods...." Only a dream. "The cops searched. Didn't find anything."

"That's all?" she said. Her eyes probed his.

"Yeah. Weird, huh?"

"Why did you go up there?"

He sighed. "To get away for a couple of days. I've got an exhibition at Park's gallery just before Christmas. I had an argument with the owner – my agent – about how to hang some of the paintings. It was really minor. A couple of the bigger pieces I'm working on aren't done." He shifted in the chair. "It was really nothing. I realize now that I should have just let it go. After all, the man has made me famous. Not to mention selling my work."

"Detective Gordon went to the cabin, and it was empty. Your car wasn't there."

"I don't know how to explain that. I was there for the weekend."

"Two weeks," she corrected him.

How could he forget that many days? "That's what that detective and the newspapers say happened."

"You mean the stories about alien abduction?"

"No. The dates. I lost two weeks of my life. That's a hell of a lot of time. Usually abductions are minutes or hours." He snorted. "Alleged abductions." He remembered one unusual story. "Except for that guy who was snatched from some mountain in Arizona right in front of his friends. He showed up a few days later claiming he'd been inside an alien spacecraft. His friends backed up the disappearance part. And he still swears that it happened. There was a movie about it."

When she didn't speak, he said, "Hey, I don't believe that 'abducted by aliens' shit."

"Is it possible you were somewhere else besides the cabin?"

He tried to remember. "I don't think so. I only remember driving up there and – "

"What?"

"And then I walked back into my loft and found that woman there who claimed to be my sister."

"What were you wearing ?" Liz said.

"Why? What difference does it make?"

"Professional curiosity," she said. "I'd like to hear some details. So far you've told me only the barest outline. In almost the same words that are in the police report. I'd like to hear the little things. If you truly don't remember what happened, it's possible that some traumatic event occurred that your mind is blocking because it can't face it. Maybe focusing on the details will free up other memories."

"I – "

"Close your eyes if it helps you remember."

He tried to picture himself in the cabin.

"Jeans. I was wearing jeans."

"How do you know?"

"I'd been painting when I decided to drive up there. There was paint on my jeans. I hated to get rid of them. You know how you get attached to something that's comfortable."

He shifted in his chair, eyes still closed. Images formed. "I guess I had a duffel with a few changes of underwear, another pair of jeans and a couple of shirts. I always take that. Oh, I took an extra sweater and a winter jacket. We've had snow up there on Halloween before."

"Okay, so you drove up on Halloween wearing jeans and...."

"A turtleneck. It was cold and raining. I remember looking at the car thermometer. It said 35 degrees."

"When was that?"

He thought a long moment. "Maybe later." He didn't remember.

"What route did you take?"

He didn't hesitate. He could visualize the road because he'd been over it so many times. "I-5 to the Spirit Lake Highway exit. It was foggy. And raining. And getting colder. I went through Toutle – couldn't see much because of the fog. My mom used to say the fog was so thick you could sew buttons on it. It was like that. Then I turned north up the Toledo cut-off."

An echo of childish laughter rang in his mind. Not his voice. A dark haired little girl giggling and singing, *Sewing buttons on the fog*. The memory faded.

"A car came around a corner on my side of the road," Brant said. "He almost hit me. I swerved. Banged my knee on the steering wheel. You know how it hurts when you hit your funny bone?" He rubbed his knee, reminded of the pins and needles that shot up his leg.

"Yes," Liz said. "Was it raining when you arrived at the cabin?"

"Yeah. Drizzle. And still foggy. It was almost midnight. I was exhausted. I'd brought a new bottle of Canadian Club. It was the first thing I took inside. Figured I'd drown my sorrows, wake up Saturday with a hell of a hangover and then be fine by Sunday. It was cold, so I started a fire. Oh. I went out to the car to get my bag. I wanted the other sweater." He stopped, remembering. "The fog curled around me. Rain....I was wet. I didn't have the power company turn on the electricity so I used a battery lantern. I left it on the porch so I could see – "

The almost-ache manifested itself again in his right temple.

"Go on." Liz's voice was quiet, gentle. He shook his head. She prompted, "The fog."

"I opened the back of the Explorer, got my bag. Started to close the back. I told the cops this. There was a girl, a small woman who looked like a girl... she came out of the fog. Shimmery. There were little lights like...like fireflies. There was a glow – " He shook his head again, trying to remember.

"I dreamed...." He swallowed, trying to focus on the memory. "It seemed real. Suddenly she was there. She glowed....it was the lantern light. Her face was bruised, and her dress was torn. Someone had been rough with her. I have no idea why I dreamt that. She was so vivid, like someone I remember meeting somewhere." He stopped, saw the blank expression on Liz's face. "There might have been a car accident or…or maybe a small plane went down. It happens. Every once in awhile you read about some hikers discovering the remains of a plane in a glacier on Mt. Adams or Rainier."

"But the authorities searched," Liz said.

"I know. There was nothing. I told them it was only a dream."

"Sometimes when our minds can't deal with the reality of an event, we block it, or change it into something else, something we *can* deal with."

"It was a dream." He snorted. "Or I was drunk."

"All right, Brant, in your *dream*, or your drunken vision, when you saw her come out of the woods, what did you do?"

"I felt sorry for her. She looked awful. I – " He concentrated. His head felt like it was expanding and contracting in time to the pain that pounded through it. "I'm not sure. Talked to her. I was angry…."

"At the girl?"

"No…later I was angry…." He hesitated, trying to remember where his anger had been directed. "I don't know."

"What happened to her?"

He spread his hands. "She just disappeared. You know, like things in dreams have a habit of doing." The ache behind his forehead expanded.

"Why did you let her leave if she was hurt?"

"It was a dream, dammit. There was nobody else there…I don't know." His head hurt worse, if that was possible.

"This is more than you told Lieutenant Gordon."

"Once I started talking about it, I seemed to remember more. Like I just woke up from a nap and was telling you my dream."

Liz was taking notes.

"Don't you tape your sessions?" he said.

"Usually, but this really isn't a therapy session, so I didn't start the tape. What about after the girl disappeared?"

"After the dream? I stayed until Monday afternoon and then came home."

Liz looked at him sharply. "But that only accounts for three nights. You were gone two weeks. What happened to the rest of the time?"

Brant was silent a long moment. "I still can't believe it was that long. I just can't remember. But every time I look at a calendar, I wonder where the hell the time went."

"Do you think it was real, Brant? That there really was a girl?"

"No. It was a dream. Only a dream. I can't imagine why I told it to the cops."

"Did the girl have a name?"

"In my dream? I don't know. Sh-h-h – "

"What?"

It felt like his brains were rolling around inside his skull. "I don't know what I was going to say."

"Why didn't you call 9-1-1?"

He tried to will the pain away, but it battered him. "No cell service up there." He paused. "She – I don't know. Shit. I sound like a broken record. Can you give me anything for this damnable headache? Nothing I take seems to touch it."

"Yes," Liz said, "I can. Do things look funny? Do you feel sick to your stomach?"

"No."

"Good. Then it's probably not a migraine. The tests showed no evidence of that."

He rubbed his forehead, but it still felt as if the pounding inside would shatter his skull like glass…

…a mirror…a reflection of a memory…shadows in a mirror….

"A mirror…." he murmured.

"What?" Liz looked up from writing a prescription.

He ran his hand through his curly hair. He needed a trim.

"Nothing," he said.

"I'll have the nurse bring you one right away. You can fill this scrip" – she handed it to him – "at the pharmacy on your way out. Don't drive while you're taking this. And don't drink." She rose from her chair and held out her hand.

He shook it, feeling weak.

"My professional advice," she said, "is that you check yourself in for a while so we can find out what's going on in your head. Even though nothing showed up on our tests, we can help."

"I'll think about it," he said. He didn't need some shrink prying around in his head, probing how he felt about his mother and father and grandparents. He caught himself. Best not to go there. The happy memories always gave way to sadness and guilt.

"Yeah. Thanks," he said. "Do you mind if I go back to my room and lie down for a few minutes before I leave?"

"Not at all," she said. "I'll sign the discharge papers. When you're ready to go, stop at the front desk. I'll leave the papers there. You'll have to sign some forms to get yourself out. Official stuff. Oh. And have someone come get you. The medication will make you feel better, a little mellow."

"That's fine. I came in a police car. I'll go home in a cab. I ought to hire myself a chauffeur."

"Brant," Liz said, "my report to the judge will say you are competent and not dangerous, but I recommend counseling. You should find out if there's a reason for the blank in your life. Especially since your mind seems to have blotted out your relationship with your sister and her husband." She laid her pen on the desk. "Brant, do you know what a fugue is? Medically."

He shook his head.

"Sometimes," she said, "people blank out. They don't remember their lives at all. A sort of amnesia. It's a little understood psychological phenomenon. People can be perfectly functional during these episodes. They've been known to start new lives, become other people."

"Do they ever wake up or come back?"

"Yes. It can be hours, days – there are cases in which the fugue state lasted years. Something happens, and they suddenly remember their real lives. They have no idea how they got where they are."

"Is it caused by something like a brain tumor?"

"No," Liz said. "I told you there's nothing physically wrong with you. People who experience a fugue are otherwise healthy. Sometimes severe emotional trauma is suspected, but most of the time it just seems to happen. But I've searched the case studies and I can't find a single case like yours of *selective* amnesia." She leaned toward him. The fluorescent lights gleamed on her gold earrings. "Brant, I'd be happy to admit you here for a short time for intensive therapy."

He spread his hands. "I don't have time for that. I have a lot to do for my opening. A couple of paintings still to finish."

"If you reconsider give us a call." She handed him a paper with names and phone numbers on it. "Here are a couple of psychiatrists in the city. If you call one of them, tell them I referred you. And please, take it easy for a few days."

He rose and followed her to her office door. She turned and said, "Good luck with your art."

"Thanks," he mumbled, desperately wanting the conversation to end so he could rest.

When he got back to his room, a nurse was waiting for him with a pill. He didn't even ask what it was, just swallowed it and stumbled to the bed. He laid down, not bothering to take off his shoes, and closed his eyes, trying to wall himself off from the pain. He drifted off into restless sleep.

Liz Barrett looked up when Rich entered her office. She sat at her desk, behind a litter of open textbooks whose pages were marked with dozens of Sticky notes.

"I'm sorry I dragged you out here on such a nasty night, Lieutenant," Liz said. "I just didn't want to say this over the phone, and I thought it best to wait until Brant went home."

"Part of the job, Dr. Barrett." Rich brushed raindrops from the front of his raincoat.

"Liz, please. We met at a party last spring at your wife's school. I'm dating Alison's Reed's brother."

"Oh, yeah, I remember you. Liz."

"I realize you're the investigating officer, but you're also Brant's brother-in-law. There's a matter of doctor-patient confidentiality. This is strictly off the record."

"Brant's in trouble." Rich rubbed the back of his neck. It was wet where the rain had leaked inside his coat. His throat was scratchy, and his nose felt tingly. Shit. He hoped he wasn't catching a goddamned cold. He had too much to do to get sick. He was trying to clear three murders, not to mention this thing with Brant.

Liz nodded. "I think so."

Rich sighed. "Well, I just have a couple of basic questions. Is he cracking up, Doc?"

"He does have headaches – "

"Never knew him to have headaches."

"He told me that," she said. "Is he still your friend?"

Rich considered a moment. "Yeah," he said. "I like the guy."

"I can tell you a little," Liz said, "but I'll deny I said it. It's pretty close to the line. It's not in my report." She handed him a folder. "I don't have much to go on. Just a hunch. The memory gap might be due to a traumatic incident. Either something he witnessed, or something he did."

"Something criminal?"

She shook her head. "I really can't say – not because I don't want to violate ethics. I really don't know. I didn't have time to get into it with him."

"Is he dangerous?"

"You mean psychotic? No. I think he needs help. I suggested counseling, psychotherapy. Other than the memory loss, he seems like a nice guy."

Ted Bundy seemed like a nice guy. People liked him. Rich wished she would get to the point and ethics be damned. Edwards wasn't just an ordinary patient. He was family.

"What *would* you say about him?" he said.

"My gut feeling?" Liz drew a deep breath. "I think something terrible happened to him. I don't know what. Something has changed him."

"But, is he *dangerous*?" She didn't answer. She put her pen in her mouth and clicked her teeth on it. Rich felt a chill of apprehension. "Is he?"

"He presents a baffling case," she said. "Without a definitive diagnosis...." She shook her head. "His judgment is impaired, and I'm not sure if he can distinguish between reality and fantasy. Look at the dream he related. He talks about it as if it's real, but says it's a dream. He knows right from wrong, but he doesn't seem to be able to choose the right thing to do. He seems confused and has difficulty making inconsequential decisions. It's almost as if he's turned off part of his life and doesn't want to tune back into it. It happens to people. It's called a fugue state. The patient clicks out for a period of time – sometimes years. They don't remember their old lives at all." She was silent a moment. "I'd like to see him get inpatient counseling. Find out what he wants so desperately to forget, and yet tries to remember."

Rich dropped the big one. "Could he commit murder?"

"Murder?" Her brows arched up.

"Could he kill someone?"

"If you're asking if he's capable, I'd have to say yes. Everyone is capable. But he doesn't seem like the type."

Rich could almost hear the gears moving in her mind. He wondered where her thoughts were taking her.

"He appears unstable," she said, "perhaps delusional."

"Did he talk about a hitchhiker?"

"No," she said, "nothing about hitchhikers. Is he a suspect in a crime?"

"No," Rich admitted. "Personally, I don't see him as violent. He's always been a gentle guy."

She pursed her lips. "If you have reason to suspect him of a crime then you'll do what you must. His mental state is fragile. He may have made a wrong judgment that his mind cannot accept without completely coming apart. The mind is amazingly self-protective, you know. But murder...."

"Well," Rich said. He stepped back from the desk, hating to go back into the cold rain. Liz rose and came around the desk. He held out his hand. "Thank you," he said. "You've been some help."

"Not really," she said, shaking hands firmly. She had a nice smile.

It surprised Rich that she was slender and petite. Her dynamic personality made her seem tall and strong.

"I think you should keep an eye on him," she said. "Something's going on. He could be unpredictable. Please urge him to check himself in here – or somewhere. He has insurance. It should pay almost all of the bill. Perhaps you and your wife could do an intervention. I'd be glad to help, as a doctor and a friend. I've managed several situations where family members confronted somebody with the facts and got them into therapy."

"He won't talk to us," Rich said. "Says he doesn't know Maeve."

"That's a strange thing," Liz said. "Not remembering his own sister. He says he had one when he was little, but can't remember what happened to her. Do you think there's a possibility there really was a girl up there?"

"We searched the cabin and the woods. Nothing. No car wrecks, no planes down, nobody reported missing." Rich shrugged. "Farfetched, but possible. We're still checking. Look at that character, D.B. Cooper, who parachuted from the jetliner in the 70s with all that money. Some of the money's been found, but no trace of Cooper. That's desolate country. Someone could get lost."

"Watch out for him, will you?" she said. Her smile was genuine. "I'm concerned about him." She handed him an envelope. "I emailed this to the judge."

"Thanks, Liz," he said, tucking the envelope inside his coat.

Rich left her office and strode down the corridor. A word kept echoing in his mind.

Dangerous....

He pushed open the lobby door and sprinted for his car. The rain was heavier and seemed colder than it had been.

Dangerous....

The word echoed in his mind. Rich wished she hadn't said it. Saying it made it real, endowed Brant with a quality used to label those who committed violent crimes.

9

Siobhan stumbled to her serving woman's chamber.

"Bebhinn," she said, her voice barely a whisper, strangled by the cramp in her swollen belly. The child inside her strained to be born. Breathless, she stopped at the threshold of Bebhinn's room. She clutched her belly until the pain eased.

"Bebhinn," she called, "come quickly."

Fear washed over Siobhan. While in child-bed she lost her enchantment. She could not summon even a small *Sidhe* light to push back the darkness. She could not defend herself or the child until he drew his first breath. Had she not been in the fortress she would be deep in the forest, protected by the trees and woodland animals until she delivered.

She had never felt so vulnerable.

Bebhinn sat up in her bed. Starlight shone on her plump, rosy face, and accentuated the worry in her eyes.

"It is time," Siobhan whispered.

Futile tears threatened to spill, and she shivered. During the long hours she had endured the pains alone, she had been unable to use her sorcery to ward off the damp chill that pervaded the stone dwelling at night, even now in midsummer.

Bebhinn rose and stumbled toward her. She wrapped her *brat* around Siobhan's shoulders and put an arm around her. She was the only human Siobhan allowed to touch her.

"I am here, lady," Bebhinn said, rubbing sleep from her eyes. "The babe is early."

"Only half a moon cycle. He is strong and ready."

Bebhinn guided Siobhan back into her room. Siobhan hugged her belly and moved awkwardly, the child insistent. The only light came from the dying peat fire and the cold stars shining through the open window slit. Perhaps it was better without the *Sidhe* light. Darkness would hide her fear. Siobhan had not confided her weakness to Bebhinn. She sank into the welcome softness of her bed.

"Are you certain I cannot send for one of your own?" Bebhinn said.

Siobhan shook her head. It was better for the child to be brought forth by one of his own kind. Bebhinn was the logical choice. She delivered many babies in the fortress and the surrounding countryside. Of all the servants in Murchad's household, she was the only one who was at ease with Siobhan. All the others, if not in outright fear, stood away in awe. Bebhinn had become her only human friend and confidante in the months she had lived in the o'Ruairc stronghold.

The only other midwife was the druid's daughter, Lassariona. Siobhan shuddered at the thought. She had glimpsed the red-haired woman from afar and had heard veiled rumors of her injurious practices. The woman, like her redoubtable father, inspired only horror in Siobhan. Besides, the girl was about to be brought to child-bed herself with a bastard. She would not name the babe's father, not even to the holy man from the abbey.

"Lie back, lady," Bebhinn said.

Siobhan obeyed. With a few deft motions Bebhinn plaited her long, graying hair into a single braid.

"How long have you been thus?" Bebhinn said. Her hands were gentle on Siobhan's belly.

"Most of the night," Siobhan said. "I did not wish to disturb you if it was not true labor."

"You should have called me. I would have sat with you."

Siobhan saw, with only intuition, the depth of Bebhinn's kindness.

"I know," Siobhan said and grasped Bebhinn's hand. "But *you* at least got some sleep."

"So even you do not know all things," Bebhinn said, not unkindly.

"I never professed to."

Another contraction began in her belly, the birthing push that would force the o'Ruairc heir into the world. Siobhan gritted her teeth and, bereft of her sorcery, tried to force the pain from her mind. It did not work.

The contraction finally subsided, leaving her gasping for air.

"I cannot banish the pain, Bebhinn," she said. "I cannot control it."

Bebhinn's face filled with genuine compassion. "I have heard many women say that, lady. I will stay with you. Tell me your wishes."

"I truly need nothing more than any other woman," Siobhan whispered.

"We are all alike in this, are we not?" Bebhinn's eyes twinkled. "Childbirth is woman's lot. Men could never endure it."

Another contraction seized Siobhan. When it passed, she was aware that Bebhinn held her hand fiercely, as if to assume some of the anguish herself.

"Bebhinn," said Siobhan, "why have you never had children of your own?"

The woman shook her head, smiled a little sadly. She was missing a few teeth, although she was only in her third decade of life.

"I was married," Bebhinn said. "A long time ago. But the fever took him...Connor was a good man."

"You are a good woman, Bebhinn."

"Thank you, lady. Besides, I have the joy of many children I brought into the world."

"Get your things," Siobhan whispered. "The child will come soon."

Her son would be born in the hour before dawn under a new moon, the darkest time, when wild things prowled the night and vented their anger at being dispelled by the light.

Bebhinn bustled around the chamber. She lit a precious beeswax candle and set it beside the bed and threw a chunk of peat and a few sticks of split wood on the fire.

Siobhan wondered if the monk's White Christ would help her if she asked. She doubted it. This new God would disdain her just as humans did.

She wondered why Gareth Spencer, the man from across the sea, spent much time kneeling in front of the cross in the Great Hall praying to the crucified Christ. Murchad had little time for such ceremony, and of all the men who supped at Murchad's table, only Gareth made the signs over his food that warded off evil, suffering in stoic silence the chides of the other men.

Siobhan imagined Gareth's handsome face, his clear blue eyes. Gareth's faith was strong. Siobhan envied him his certainty that his God would watch over him. The Earth Mother seldom interfered in the lives of humans and *Sidhe* alike. Interference was the province of the druids.

Within moments Bebhinn was back by Siobhan's side. The woman's presence comforted her. Siobhan neither needed nor wanted anyone else present. Bebhinn had even convinced Murchad to absent himself, consenting to allow Bebhinn to witness the birth as long as he could see his child immediately.

"I sent for Murchad," Bebhinn said. "He waits by the door."

Siobhan closed her eyes and tried to relax as Bebhinn moved around her, humming softly. The woman had a fine voice. In the evenings her sweet soprano lifted above the quiet fortress, calming all who heard it. Now it soothed Siobhan, drew away some of the pain.

Siobhan allowed Bebhinn's hands on her body, helping her push, assisting the child. Bebhinn pulled the head and then the whole wet, pink form into the world.

He drew a shuddering breath and squalled, thin and hiccuping.

"It is a boy, lady, you were right. A boy," Bebhinn said.

Siobhan's enchantment flooded through her, strong and sure, and embraced the child in an impenetrable spell of protection. She touched his face, smoothed back his damp, dark hair.

Bebhinn wrapped the baby in a *brat* softened from years of washing, and then allowed Murchad into the chamber. His eyes that seldom laughed were smiling and proud. He kept his distance from Siobhan. Bebhinn held the infant out to him. Murchad unwrapped him and gazed at his progeny.

"It is a fine boy," Murchad said. "Do you have a name, lady?"

"I – " Siobhan started. "I thought you would – "

"You may name the child," Murchad said, stroking his son's dark tangle of hair.

Siobhan thought it was a male right in the mortal world to name boy children. "I – " She looked at the baby, still wet from the birthing. He looked tiny in Murchad's hands.

Siobhan was surprised Murchad had so readily acquiesced. Did he think to curry her favor?

"His hair is dark," she said. "Dark like the raven…His name will be Bran. Raven."

Murchad nodded. "Bran o'Ruairc. So it shall." He handed the child back to Bebhinn and left quietly.

Siobhan dozed, vaguely aware that Bebhinn sat beside her. The servant's eyes were tired, but Siobhan knew with the certainty of friendship – not magic – the woman would maintain her vigil while Siobhan slept. The child slept beside her, warmed by her body, making little sucking sounds with his mouth.

Sometime later Siobhan roused.

"Is he all right, really, Bebhinn?" she said.

"He is a fine boy," Bebhinn said. "You will be proud of him when he is a man."

Siobhan's pain dissolved into hopes and dreams for her child, for the man he would someday become. There were images during the healing sleep, and Bebhinn's quiet ministrations. When Siobhan awoke, her enhanced magic awaited her command.

As for Murchad – despite his giving her the honor of naming his son – all she had to do to exact revenge upon him was wait. She had more patience than he. Infinitely more.

10

B rant left the clinic in a cab and arrived home just as the local late news was starting. He flopped on the couch and tried to watch, but dozed and awoke after a few minutes, remembering nothing of what he had seen. He stumbled to the bathroom, downed one of the pills Liz had prescribed, and then fell into bed.

He awoke to sunlight pouring through the window, warm on his face. He'd been so exhausted he had forgotten to lower the shades. His iPhone said 10:27. He couldn't remember sleeping past 8:00 since he'd been in college. It must be the pills. The headache was totally gone, and he didn't regret sleeping in. In the bathroom he ignored the prescription bottle on the vanity. He wanted to work clear-headed.

He showered, shaved, and with a mug of coffee and a slightly burnt bagel slathered with cream cheese, he went to his studio. Three unfinished canvasses confronted him. They had sat on easels for weeks, taunting him: his trademark landscapes of the Northwest. One showed the mist rising from Spirit Lake before Mount St. Helens altered the terrain. The other depicted the cliffs at the Oregon shore, rocks battered by a stormy sea.

Another canvas – finished and framed – leaned against the counter. He liked the light in this forest scene, the way the canopy of firs filtered the sun into myriad tiny beams that didn't quite dispel the shadows along a path that disappeared into the trees. Something about the picture set off fragmented images in his mind. Memories or dreams? He wasn't sure.

He set the half-eaten bagel on the counter and went to the living room. The sketchbook and drawings were still scattered, bright against the old pine floor. He bent to pick them up and sloshed coffee over several of them.

"Shit."

Brant stared at the splash of brown liquid. It reminded him of something, some memory that refused to come to the surface. He scooped up the sketch pad, wiped it on his t-shirt.

Back in his studio he swept the unfinished paintings off their perches and leaned them haphazardly in a corner, substituting two new, sized canvasses.

He tore the sketches from the pad and spread them across the work counter. From an upper cupboard he took a disposable palette and began pulling tubes of paint from drawers. Colors filled his mind: the luminescent quality of moonlight on fog; old growth Douglas fir trunks, gray in uncertain light; a woman's face, elusive as moonlight, with eyes as blue as the sea.

When he'd covered a palette with blobs of color, he docked his iPhone in speakers and pressed play. Binaural music filled the sunlit studio. Music meant to stimulate the creative part of his brain.

Brant studied the first canvas a moment, and then loaded a brush with paint.

The first stroke was fog. Successive strokes became a forest with mist curling in the shadows. There was a face in the mist, not quite focused, but recognizable if he could get the light just right.

His hand flew from the palette to the canvas, mental images taking shape, becoming real. When the canvas was covered and the palette was empty, he reloaded, wiped the brushes haphazardly on a rag and moved to the next easel.

He was unaware of time passing until the light faded. He put what he thought might be the last brush stroke to a canvas and stepped back, not really seeing what he had done, lost in ideas that swirled in his mind's eye.

By the time he cleaned his brushes it was almost dark. He never studied a finished painting right away. The next day when he looked at it, he hoped he would be pleasantly surprised at what his mind and hands had created.

Tomorrow, if the paintings were good, he'd have them sent to the gallery. Maybe then Pollard would get off his back. The gallery owner could be snippy. Although Brant had worked with Pollard Smythe for almost five years, he still wasn't sure if his brusque manner was real or just an affectation to inspire – or intimidate – his artists into producing.

Brant's stomach rumbled. Disgusted by what little there was in the refrigerator, he left the building, hailed a cab and directed the driver to a tavern near the waterfront that made great burgers. On the way he stopped at an ATM.

Sailors and merchant seamen of various nationalities filled the space. Despite the statewide smoking ban, the odor of cigarettes lingered. Brant settled himself on one of three empty stools. He ordered a cheeseburger, fries and a Canadian Club, neat.

Brant bent over his drink, brooding, until his meal arrived. He ordered another CC and gobbled the greasy food, vaguely aware of desultory conversations around him in foreign languages.

His hunger sated, he dropped his napkin on the empty plate and pushed it toward the back of the bar. He raised his empty glass and signaled the bartender who sauntered over to him and laid down a check.

"Yeah?" the bartender said.

He was a tall, African American man. Hands on the counter, he leaned toward Brant. Hard muscles rippled under his black t-shirt. He probably lifted weights and ate people, spitting out only the teeth and shoelaces.

"Gimme another," Brant said.

The bartender shook his head. "You don't need another, man."

"Why not?"

"I gotta cut you off."

Brant glared at him. "One more won't hurt."

"This is my place, and I can't let you go out of here unconscious. I don't want no trouble."

Brant picked up the check. It reflected a great deal more than the meal and a couple of drinks.

He held up the slip. "How come I owe you so much?"

"You drank a lot."

"That much?"

"Yeah. That much." The barkeeper stood his ground. "I don't take plastic. Cash only."

Brant reached in a pocket of his jeans. He glanced at the clock over the bar. After midnight. Lost time again? At least it was only a couple hours and not two weeks.

"Awright, awright," Brant mumbled. He pulled out a wad of money, unfolded it, peeled off several bills and handed them to the bartender.

"Too much." The bartender dropped two bills on the counter. "I'll get change." He headed for the cash register down the bar.

Brant looked at the two bills. The were fifties. He went to fold them back into the wad from his pocket and saw they were all fifties. He thumbed through them. Ten. Where the hell had he gotten that much money? He thought he'd taken maybe $200 from the ATM. He never carried much cash, relying on plastic for almost everything. Before he could puzzle it out, the bartender returned and laid a twenty on the bar.

"Keep it." Brant said.

"You sure?"

"Yeah." Brant stuffed the rest of the bills back into his pocket.

The bartender grinned. "You be careful, man. It's dark on this street."

Brant nodded, nearly fell off the stool and aimed himself at the front door.

"Hey," the bartender called. "You're not driving, are you, pal?"

"Nah," Brant said. "Can't walk, either. Too wasted." He was vaguely aware that his mouth didn't seem to work right. His teeth felt numb.

"Want me to call you a cab?"

"Nah, get one on the Boulevard," Brant mumbled.

He threaded his way unsteadily between the scattered tables, nodding at people he passed.

He fumbled with the door, then realized it didn't latch like the cabin door. Where had that thought come from? He pushed, but the door remained closed. Finally, he pulled it open. When all else failed, read the sign.

He staggered into cold fog that nearly obscured the buildings down the block. A chill crawled up his spine. He pulled his light jacket together against the raw air, but the zipper refused to work.

The streetlight in front of the bar wasn't lit. The light from the bar's stuttering neon sign gave the fog a reddish tinge.

Brant looked toward Willamette Boulevard. Car lights streamed by, their headlights softened by the mist. Almost at the corner a streetlight fluttered, but didn't quite stay lit. The dark warehouses and a few small businesses shrouded in mist, were silent and eerie, washed gray, not unlike a monochromatic watercolor might be.

Two nondescript, beat-up vehicles languished in front of the tavern. Where was his Explorer? How had he gotten here? He didn't remember driving.

Which way was home? Just beyond the last flickering streetlight, the fog was lighter.

Where the hell had the money in his pocket come from? Why couldn't he remember how much he had drunk? Some memories from his childhood were sharp, but the immediate past seemed hazy.

Brant took a few steps toward the brighter street. Voices behind him. He glanced back. Two men came from the bar. They looked up and down the street. Searching for their cars, probably. He wondered how they would drive if they were as drunk as he was. He turned and concentrated on walking.

"Hey." A man's voice.

Brant stopped and looked back. The world spun for a moment. He would have closed his eyes to steady himself, but he knew if he did, he might fall down. Dammit, he shouldn't have drunk so much.

"Yeah?" he said.

The two men came toward him.

"You dropped this," the shorter man said and held out a hand.

"No," Brant said, "I didn't drop any – "

"Yeah, you did," the taller man growled. "Look here." He held his hands low in front of him, a small pistol in one hand. "Y'see, man?"

"Yeah, I see." Brant sighed. "Whaddya want?"

"You know, pal," the shorter man said. The nasal quality of his voice irritated Brant. The other man, the one with the gun, kept darting quick glances up and down the street.

Pal? Not likely. Shit. Why him? He'd never even been in a fist fight.

Brant knew he should do what they wanted, but the sight of the gun aroused a bitter anger in him. His thoughts cleared. The men's faces steadied, slid into focus.

"The money," the taller man said. "The roll you was flashin like you was royalty."

"Money?" Brant echoed. It was *his* money. Why should he give it to these strangers? The man with the pistol stepped closer. Long, dark hair shadowed his face. The weapon seemed to grow bigger.

"The money," the man growled. "Now." Nicotine-stained teeth.

If the man hadn't smiled Brant might have handed over his money, but the grin infuriated him. He swung. The gun flew from the man's grasp and clattered in the street. The man grunted, clutching his wrist, his eyes wide, the grin gone.

"Aw, shit," he whined. "The fuckin gun wasn't even loaded."

Surprised at his sudden success, Brant raised his fists. He would not go down easily. Not like his father had, taken unawares on the street one afternoon in front of the bank. Brant's slight hesitation lost his advantage.

The other mugger had worked his way behind him and pinned his arms. The gunman leaped and delivered a sharp jab to Brant's jaw. His vision darkened.

The shorter man, holding Brant's arms, growled, "You could've made it easy, man. You shouldn't've done that. Makes me mad. Hit 'im, Nick."

Pain exploded in Brant's gut. Air rushed from his lungs, and he doubled over. The man behind him jerked him upright, wrenching his arms. It felt like a hot poker driven through his left shoulder. Was this what his father had felt when he'd been knifed and his life bled away?

Was this how Brant would die? He should run, but couldn't force his legs to move. Lost in a haze of pain, he couldn't find the strength to fight. He should have given up the money.

The taller man came at Brant again. Brant managed to lift one knee up hard into the man's groin. The man squealed and clutched himself.

The man holding Brant flung him away with a grunt. Brant stumbled and tried to stay on his feet, but his shoulder and stomach hurt like hell, and the world tilted. The sidewalk heaved up at him, and he heard a thud as his head hit.

Brant's thoughts were disjointed and fuzzy. Darkness sucked him down. He fought the descending blackness and rolled, looking for his attackers. The man he had kneed knelt on the ground, bent over, his head almost on the cracked sidewalk.

The other leaned over him, hand on the injured man's shoulder. "Y'all right, man?"

Brant felt a surge of satisfaction.

"Fuck, Artie," the man groaned, hands still at his groin. "He got me good."

The smaller man rose and started toward Brant. "He's gonna be sorry,"

Even in the near darkness and his semi-conscious state, Brant sensed the angry determination in the man's expression. He tried to get up, but his body refused. Pain slammed against his ribs and then his back as he rolled, trying to get away.

Each breath was torture. A booted foot pushed him onto his back, kicked him in the ribs again. He drew a shallow, painful breath, waiting for the next blow, but none came. He opened his eyes. His attacker straddled him, held him down with a knee on his chest.

"You could've made it easy," the man hissed, his face livid, murderous rage in his eyes. "Nobody hadda get hurt." His grimace showed a broken tooth. "You're gonna pay, shithead."

With a peculiar detachment Brant felt blows land on his face and torso. The man was going to kill him, but he was powerless to move. The alcohol, the knock on his head and the pain in his ribs and back combined to anesthetize him and sap his will. Why didn't somebody stop this? Maybe it was time...his fate...he spit blood at his attacker....

Brant spiraled down into a dark abyss from which he knew he would not escape.

Listen. Listen to the stars. You can hear the music if you listen.

Someone spoke to him from a great distance, a voice from a dream. Someone he should recognize. He had to fight back, before the man beat out the last spark of his life. He didn't want to die.

With every shred of his fast-fading will, Brant gathered his energy. He opened his eyes a crack. The man stood over him breathing raggedly. A knife blade flashed.

Though he knew he couldn't move a muscle, Brant struck out. He visualized throwing a baseball, flung it with all his strength, all his anger, his bitterness. Blue fire flashed, blinding him.

Voices, far away:

"What –"

"Fire! Artie, help!"

"Burning –"

Two shrieks split the air, cut short by a flash of light so intense Brant saw it through closed eyes. A tremendous crash jolted him and rattled buildings. In an instant the radiance disappeared.

Brant opened his eyes to utter darkness. The streetlights must have gone out.

A face floated over him, African-American. The man from the bar, his dark skin shiny.

The man's mouth moved. "...ambulance...."

There was more, but Brant couldn't make it out.

Darkness sucked him down. A siren wailed in the distance. Too late... too late....

11

Awareness came – a siren screamed, a horn blared – and slipped away from Brant's grasp. He drifted up to consciousness and was surprised he felt no pain. White- and green-garbed medical personnel examined him and muttered. They asked him questions he couldn't comprehend, nor could he muster energy to speak.

He faded out only to awaken to a mind-wrenching agony that stabbed into his side when he breathed. A dull ache had settled in his lower back, and his body throbbed from numerous pains. A vague shape in white jabbed a needle ignominiously into his hip even though he tried to protest. He could not speak. His throat was blocked.

He slept, a long dreamless, timeless sleep.

Brant vaguely marked the rhythms that ebbed and flowed around him. Each time he surfaced from sleep, he wondered why he didn't hurt any more. Routines occupied people who moved ghostlike in and out of his vision: the doctors who mumbled to each other; the nurses with soothing voices who appeared, adjusted the tubes and machines that surrounded him, and vanished quietly. Occasionally he glimpsed the woman who claimed to be his sister and the husband, but they did not enter his little room.

Electrodes itched the shaved skin on his chest and an IV protruded from his arm. Sometimes a machine beeped, and a nurse changed the bag of clear fluid suspended from a stand beside his bed. Out of the corner of his eyes he read the label on the bag. Saline solution. There were other letters and numbers, but they were blurred. His eyelids dragged down....

Whispers…whispers he couldn't quite hear.…

Beep…beep…far away.…

Someone ran on soft soled shoes…sleep…no dreams.…

A woman leaned over him, a glowing vision of white. She was a ghost, a wraith clothed in pale light.…

"What the – " He came awake suddenly, no demarcation between nothingness and wakefulness. His throat felt raw and dry.

"It's all right, Mr. Edwards." The voice floated down to him from a great distance. "You're in a hospital. We just removed your breathing tube."

"How long?" he croaked.

"You've been here three days. You were pretty badly beaten, but you're going to be all right. A doctor will speak with you in a little bit. There's a policeman who wants to ask you some questions. Doctor says he can have five minutes. No more."

Another fuzzy shape appeared beside his bed.

"How are you, Brant?"

It was the man who had taken him to that other hospital. Gordon. That was the man's name. Lieutenant Rich Gordon. The detective who claimed to be his brother-in-law, the one who thought Brant was nuts. Maybe he was right.

"Just a few questions, Brant. Then I'll go. Can you talk?"

Brant nodded slightly. It took great effort to swallow.

"You in pain?" Rich said.

"No," he mumbled, amazed he could talk. His tongue scraped the roof of his mouth like sandpaper.

"You're going to be here awhile, Brant. I don't know what they've told you. You got broken ribs and a bruised kidney. And you've got a few stitches in your forehead and chin. They tell me you'll be okay. I got you in a private room after they let you out of ICU."

"Thanks," Brant said. He meant it. This must be what it was like to die, hooked up to all those machines, not able to say he didn't want any more –

"What happened, Brant?"

"Two guys…beat me up.…"

"Yeah, they did. But what happened?"

Brant tried to focus on the man's face, but his eyelids were so heavy they kept closing, and Gordon's features kept slipping away. He gave up, kept his eyes closed.

"Brant, what happened?"

"Don' know…what…what you mean…."

"The two men, Brant. What happened to them?"

"Don' know," Brant mumbled. All he wanted to do was sleep away the pains and confusion. If only he could sleep….

"You'll have to go now, Officer." A female voice.

Brant didn't open his eyes to see who it was. The voice reassured him into forgetful sleep.

There were dreams this time, but when he swam up from the darkness, he couldn't remember any of them. He just knew he had dreamed, and they didn't leave an afterimage of uneasiness.

"Brant?" a nurse said, another face in a succession of hazy faces. He didn't want to talk. All he wanted to do was sleep.

"Yeah?"

"Dr. Norman's here. He wants to speak to you."

"Oh, yeah…." He let it trail off. Maybe if he feigned sleep they would leave him alone.

"Hi, Brant." Brant remembered the voice from before. He opened his eyes. Glasses. Graying hair. Expensive suit. "Mr. Edwards, this is Cam Schultz," the doctor said. "Dr. Schultz has been evaluating your case. He thinks you may need surgery on your kidney."

"Why?"

"We think your left kidney is hemorrhaging. So I asked Cam for a consult. He's a fine surgeon."

The face that came into view was younger, perhaps Brant's age. Athletic build. The man exercised regularly to keep in shape like that.

"Hi," the man chirped.

Too cheerful. Doctors should be more formal. He couldn't tell the nurses from the doctors. They dressed alike. Nothing to worry about. He closed his eyes. It was easier to sleep than talk….

"Dr. Norman here tells me you're stubborn," the new man said.

"Stubborn?" Brant said, not opening his eyes.

"He says you won't take the medication he's prescribed – "

"I know my rights," Brant said, opening his eyes wide. His voice felt stronger.

"It's not a matter of rights. It's your life, Brant. We're doing what we can to help you get better, but you must cooperate. The medication will ease your pain and we want you to rest and – "

"I don't hurt," Brant cut in. "Why should I take all that stuff?"

"It'll help you relax. Help you heal." The doctor's voice was calm, professional.

Nothing hurt. He just felt tired.

"Do you mind if I look at you, Brant?"

"Go ahead," Brant said. "I'm a captive audience."

The nurse moved to undo the hospital gown and expose his torso. Warm hands. She was plump, matronly.

The doctor sat carefully on the edge of the bed. He didn't look old enough to be a surgeon. The man leaned over, his cold fingers probing first gently, then more insistently. Brant winced, expecting it to hurt, but it didn't.

"Hurt?"

"No," Brant said, "ticklish."

The doctor gently rolled Brant to one side, examining his back, pressing here and there. "Are you in any pain at all?"

Brant shook his head.

The doctor peeled back the bandage on Brant's chin and the larger one on his forehead. He turned Brant's face from side to side. The doctor's smile turned to a frown. Muscles flexed in the man's jaw.

"Well," the doctor said. "Things look better. We'll schedule some tests, check your kidney function. I'll come by in the morning."

"Steak," Brant said. "I'd like a steak. Rare. I'm hungry."

The doctor glanced at his older colleague. "I'll see what I can do." He stood up. "Nurse. You can remove the dressings from Mr. Edwards' cuts. And have someone remove the sutures. He doesn't seem to need them anymore. Be seeing you, Brant."

"Bye," Brant said and closed his eyes. Sleep. Sleep brought relief.

He heard two sets of footsteps recede into the hall. Then the younger man's voice, angry. "What the hell is going on, Fred?"

"What do you mean?" Sharp.

"You saw him. There are no bruises, not even on his face. There are no cuts on his face. Why the hell would somebody suture him? What's going on down in the ER? His ribs are fine. Fractures. Ha. You set me up, Fred. I haven't had one of these since med school. I wasted time coming all the way over here. I only came as a favor to you. It's not funny."

"This isn't a joke, Cam," the older man said. "I saw him three days ago when the ER docs finished with him. He was in bad shape. Drunk and beaten, fractured ribs, probably a punctured lung, contusions, concussion. The MRI clearly showed the damage to one kidney. You saw that."

"I saw *someone's* kidney."

"I can't explain it, Cam. The bruises have just vanished. And I swear to God his kidney was hemorrhaging."

"That's impossible."

"I don't know what to say, Cam. I'm telling you…."

The voices faded. Brant slept.

He was discharged the next morning with instructions to go home and take it easy for a few days. The hospital had given him a scrub top. His bloody shirt was ruined when they cut it off at the scene. He was coming out of the cashier's office when he saw Rich Gordon leaning against the wall.

"What are you doing here?" Brant said.

"I thought you might appreciate a ride home. Besides, I have some questions. Police stuff. You look tired." Rich ran a hand through his tousled hair, but it refused to lay flat.

Brant spread his hands. "I've felt better," he said. "But I think I'll live." Fatigue crept up his body. It had been a long walk from his room down here to settle his bill. He had flatly refused the wheelchair and had accepted the escort only because she insisted. He waved the woman away.

"Thanks for seeing me out," he said.

"You take care now, Mr. Edwards." She turned to the cop. "You taking him home?"

Rich nodded. "Sure. He's in good hands."

The woman hurried away.

"My car's parked at the entrance," Rich said. "I figured I could justify police business." He fell in beside Brant, his longer stride adjusting to Brant's slower steps. "Thought you might like to know there's also a small crowd of media people."

"Why?"

"You're news. I'll run you interference, but I don't think you should try to sneak out the back. I'll answer questions if you want."

Brant turned to the detective. "Why would you do that?"

"I was rough on you before when you came home from your… ah… disappearance," Rich said. He tucked in his shirt. Smoothed his hair. Adjusted his tie.

"You don't owe me a thing – "

Rich grasped Brant's elbow and stopped him. "Listen. I knew there was something wrong with you when I took you to that clinic. You've changed.

You're – different. I should have seen you were headed for trouble. I like you. Admire you. For chrissakes, you're my wife's brother. You could just let me do this for you without looking for some hidden meaning."

Brant pulled his arm away from the other man's grip. "All right," he said. "You can drive me home. But I'm not talking to those fu – "

A nurse walked toward him, smiling at him. Blond, petite and attractive. He didn't finish the word, but nodded to her and watched her back after she passed. She reminded him of someone....

Reluctantly, he turned back to Rich. "I'm not talking to those reporters and television people. I'm exhausted. I can barely keep my eyes open. I just want to crawl into a hole somewhere and sleep for the rest of my life. I can't deal with them."

"Great," Rich said. "All you do is say, 'No comment.'"

"Are they going to buy that? Remember, I joked with a reporter who called, and that cheesy tabloid said I'd been abducted by aliens."

"Probably. If you say you'll release a statement later."

"Why – ?"

"You're going to have to say something eventually, Brant. First you disappear, and then you get beaten up on the street, and your assailants die in rather gruesome circumstances. You're going to have to talk about it to someone." He straightened his badge where it was clipped to the pocket of his coat. "Just be cool, and I'll field the questions. There's my car. Not far to walk. Just don't get angry with them. They're only trying to do their jobs."

"Yeah. Prying into other people's lives."

"It's a living," Rich said and pushed the door open for Brant.

Brant stepped through the door into the chilly sunshine. His knees felt wobbly. He should have accepted the wheelchair instead of insisting he wasn't going out in one unless his life depended on it. He stumbled over an uneven place in the cement. Rich took his arm and steadied him. It seemed like a long, steep descent down the sloped concrete to Rich's unmarked car.

He stopped, and the dozen or so reporters and camera operators rushed toward him. For a moment he wanted to run, but he knew he wouldn't get more than five feet before he'd collapse and make an even bigger fool of himself.

"Mr. Edwards," a dark-haired aggressive young woman said, cramming a microphone in front of his face. "Is it true that you set your assailants on fire?" She was dressed in a conservative dark business suit with a white top under it that showed a lot of cleavage. A cameraman moved around to record her.

The woman's face blurred. Dizzy….

Rich came to his rescue. "No, it isn't true. Mr. Edwards is going home after a three-day stay in the hospital. He's tired and just wants to leave in peace."

"Mr. Edwards." A young man stepped forward with a microphone, held it under Brant's nose. "Are you going to explain what happened to you when you disappeared for two weeks?"

Brant shook his head. Dizziness washed over him, leaving him weak and nauseated.

Rich held out his badge. "Back off, people."

A reporter shouted from behind Brant, "Officer, are you taking Mr. Edwards in? Is he under arrest for something?"

Rich held up his hands. "It's Lieutenant. And no, and no. I'm his brother-in-law, and I'm just taking him home. I'm sure Mr. Edwards will release a statement to the press tomorrow or the next day when he feels better." Brant nodded. "Now can you let us through? He just wants to go home."

Brant felt Rich's grip firm on his arm steering him through the little knot of people. One, two, three – he counted the steps. It took tremendous effort to raise his feet. Four, five, six. He was almost to the car. A few more steps, and he could collapse in relative safety. Seven, eight, nine –

His foot snagged on a crack in the cement, and he felt himself stumble – couldn't stop – dizzy – couldn't catch his balance. He put his hands up in front of him, contacted something, then regained his balance. A crash brought him back to reality.

"Shit!" The expletive came from a cameraman sprawled on the pavement, indignant surprise etched on his face. His camera was beside him in pieces.

Brant looked down at his hands. He hadn't shoved the man – hadn't touched him. He was sure of it.

The man rolled over, rubbing one hip, and said, "You're gonna fuckin be sorry you did that."

"Hey," Brant began, "I'm really sorry. I – "

"Sorry?" The man exploded to his feet. "Sorry? That won't fix the goddamned camera. You hit me. You deliberately hit me." He raised his fists and charged Brant.

Somebody stepped in front of the man, making a black silhouette against the sun. The angry look on the cameraman's face intensified to rage. Then Brant realized the shadowy figure was Rich. Confused, Brant backed away.

"You'll hear from my lawyer, Edwards." The man raised a fist, peered around Rich who moved to keep himself lined up between him and Brant. "You don't hit the media and get away with it. You're news, buddy, and you're not getting off so easy. You'll be hearing from me."

The man bent and picked up the broken camera, sorting through the pieces.

"Just send me a bill," Brant offered. "I'll pay for damages – "

"You're goddamn right you'll pay," the man said. He kicked away a broken part, spun and stalked off, followed by the pretty woman with the great cleavage.

Brant would have gone after him, if Rich hadn't put a hand on his shoulder.

"Don't, Brant," Rich said. "It isn't worth it. The guy's just mad. When he cools off, he'll realize it was an accident. Don't make it worse."

"I'll pay for what I broke," Brant insisted, "but I don't think it was my fault." Fatigue drained him. He swayed, willed himself to remain standing.

"Come on," Rich said and ushered him toward the waiting car. "It'll keep."

Brant looked over his shoulder at the little crowd of reporters milling around. They were silent, staring at him. Cleavage talked to her colleague, gesturing expansively. The man looked to Brant and nodded. Brant turned away and let Rich push him to the car.

"It was an accident," Brant insisted.

Rich opened the door for him. "Of course it was, Brant. You had the shit kicked out of you a few days ago. You should have taken the wheelchair."

Brant nodded. "Yeah." He sank into the seat. "Take me home, will you? I just want to crash."

Rich started the car. Brant leaned back in the seat and said, "Thanks."

Rich didn't look at him, eased the car out into the traffic. "That's what family's for."

But Brant had no recollection of Rich as family. Did not remember the woman who claimed to be his sister. He kept staring at his hands. They looked blue, probably from the chill. And he was certain he hadn't hit that man.

12

Siobhan stood on the watchman's walk looking out over the o'Ruairc's holdings. Above her the blue sky was cloudless. She luxuriated in the warm spring sunlight. It seemed only yesterday that little Bran had been a babe at her breast. From here she had showed him the wonders of birds in flight. And at night, above the rush lights, she had told him about the stars and their eternal music.

How quickly the years had flown. Now four-year-old Bran walked with Bebhinn near the walls of the fortress. Two guards followed discreetly, swords always ready to defend the o'Ruairc heir. Far beyond the field, where the hills rose higher, she could see the darker green of her beloved forest.

"The child is handsome, my lady, and quick of mind." A deep, quiet voice behind her. Gareth Spencer. Over the years she had only caught glimpses of him in the fortress. She knew from his surface thoughts that he actively avoided her. He deliberately left a room when she entered. Allowing him his privacy, she assumed he held some special revulsion for her kind.

The summer before Siobhan had married Murchad, Gareth had come from the island across the sea – Britannia, the monk from the abbey called it. Gareth was a man with a cause. A man who once had killed for his liege lord and run away from his duty. Coward, some called him.

Siobhan heard all the gossip from Bebhinn. Gareth had spilled blood because the northern men would not pledge their fealty to Gareth's lord. And Gareth had been part of an avenging army that marched to put down the highland upstarts. All in his God's name. Siobhan wondered again why such a God would allow the men He created the liberty to slaughter each other with such wanton cruelty.

But Gareth had thrown down his weapons and fled the battleground to find his way to Eirinn and Murchad. He stood before Siobhan, weaponless but for the dirk at his belt he used for eating, his clothing that of a simple scribe.

An educated, personable man, Gareth had taken over the keeping of Murchad's accounts: the records of grain and livestock transactions for all the o'Ruairc's holdings, including several tiny settlements scattered around the fortress.

"Thank you, sir," she responded. "He is a fine child."

She turned back and watched Bebhinn as she strolled outside the ramparts with Bran's trusting hand in hers. Bebhinn paused from time to time to bend and pluck a wildflower or other plant. With consummate patience she showed each flower and herb to the little boy, explaining its uses. Siobhan marveled at the woman's forbearance of the child. Bebhinn really loved him, and Siobhan knew she would protect the o'Ruairc heir with her life if need be.

Gareth cleared his throat. Siobhan turned again to him. It eluded her comprehension why a grown man should be so nervous in front of her. She hadn't displayed any sort of enchantment in public in a long time. At least nothing that could be visibly linked to her. She had learned to be surreptitious with her spells to calm colicky babes, ease the passing of oldsters, spells for good harvests and sound livestock. He twisted what had once been a quill in his hands. Now it was limp and bedraggled, no longer usable as a writing instrument.

"Yes?" she said with ill-concealed temper. She immediately regretted the sharpness of her voice when his face betrayed his chagrin.

"I – I – would – " he stammered, took a quick breath and said, "Would you like to ride?"

She knitted her brows in question.

He drew a deep breath. "Would you like to ride with me?" he said. "It is said at the stable that you ride. I have business at a farm, and I would be honored if you would accompany me. They told me you haven't been out in a few days, and the Kerry mare is fat with foal and restless. The stable lads are afraid of her bold manner. She wants exercise. Murchad suggested I speak to you." He put his left hand on his hip, fumbled to rest his hand on a sword that wasn't there, and then let his fingers worry the quill again.

Siobhan was delighted with the request. She often rode by herself, declining servants or guards. Murchad, although attentive to his son, never offered to accompany her. In fact, he rarely communicated with her other than on routine matters. He left the ordering of the household to her, making no requests or demands, other than to inform her from time to time that he would be entertaining visitors, or that he would be traveling away from the fortress for a few days. Loneliness was not an easy burden.

"Yes," she said. "I would like to go."

"Fine. I will meet you in the courtyard." Gareth turned and strode away.

He was so young. Barely twenty-five. And yet he had taken many lives.

Gareth was fair where the other is – *was*, Siobhan reminded herself – dark. She had to think of him in the past, although his time was yet to come. Thinking of him in her past made it easier to put him away from her thoughts. And yet he was there every day, while she was awake and often in her dreams. His face, his laughter, his quick and witty mind – she missed that. She missed his touch and his lips and his passion. Her heart skipped with longing, an all too human emotion.

She was pulled back to the present by the memory of Gareth's clear blue eyes. Eyes that held no malice, only duty and compassion. But under the kindness was sorrow. While they rode, she would probe his mind a bit. Perhaps she could understand him better, discover his motives, learn why he had fled the battlefield and abandoned his pledge to his lord. She wondered if he was, as the serving girls whispered, just another coward come to hide.

She hurried to the stable.

The horses were saddled, and a short time later they left the fortress behind and rode through warm spring sunshine. It had been cold and wet for so long Siobhan had despaired of ever seeing summer before she and the boy left the fortress for her bargained time in the forests and glens of the hill country. With the greening fields and the bright sun on her back, she found it easy to forget the stifling confines of the stone dwelling.

Gareth sat his rangy roan gelding with a litheness that surprised her. His hands were gentle on the reins, and he guided the horse with his knees. Siobhan's gray Kerry mare had been a gift from Murchad at the birth of her son. A passing harper had ridden her to the fortress. How a poor bard came to possess such a fine horse was a mystery. He said she was payment for services. Siobhan knew it was the truth; besides, a dishonest bard would find no place in a chieftain's stronghold.

The mare had been great with foal and unable to travel. Murchad haggled, finally paying a winter's lodging, a riding horse and pack animal of much lesser breeding, and some trinkets and tools the man required. It was a better bargain for Murchad. She was a fine mare. She had produced two handsome colts, and the foal she carried swelled her sides. The sire was Murchad's finest stallion.

Gareth talked little, only pointing out an occasional landmark or a farm worked by one of the o'Ruairc clan. His keen eyes spotted a pair of hawks circling above an open meadow. A flock of cranes took clumsy flight from a swampy pond as the two horses passed.

Gareth settled his sidestepping mount with quiet words, while Siobhan soothed the mare's mind with images of grain when they returned. Siobhan's hands had no need for the reins that rested on the mare's withers. She guided the animal with thoughts she sent into the beast's mind, needing only to pat her neck from time to time to reassure her. Ordinarily nasty tempered with the stable boys, with Siobhan the mare was tranquil and obedient. The creature's mind projected only an eagerness for exercise and a curiosity of its surroundings.

"Can you truly command enchantment?" Gareth's voice interrupted Siobhan's mental meanderings. "It is said, my lady, that you are a sorceress."

"It is?" She meant only to tease him, but his face showed a sincerity that surprised her.

"Yes, lady. Is it true?" he said.

"That I am a sorceress?"

He nodded, looked away from her, flicked an imaginary fly off his gelding's mane. The gelding was a big raw-boned, plodding horse, capable of nothing but a stolid placidity and an occasional shying from sudden noises. Siobhan had to slow her mount to match his pace.

"Are you?" he persisted.

"Every living thing has a bit of enchantment of its own," she said. "Even ordinary people can do mighty things if they put their minds to it. People often call this sorcery."

"It is said that you are one of the *Daoine Sidhe* – the Fair Folk. That you can truly do magic and that" – he swallowed – "that you traffic with Satan." The word carried a caustic inflection.

"I know not this...Satan."

A flush spread across his face. He looked down. Long lashes brushed his cheeks.

"Would you like me to show you some magic?" She sent a tendril of her mind into his, a whisper of a probe.

She must not know...important...if she knew...he would....

"I would give a bit of gold to know your thoughts." She tried to keep it casual, bantering.

He looked startled. "It is also said that you hear the thoughts of others as if they speak them aloud."

Must not know...I could not live with it....

Could it be, Siobhan wondered, that there was something portentous hatching in this young man's mind that she should know? Something that perhaps Murchad had dreamed up that might adversely affect her or her son?

Siobhan reassured herself that no harm could come to Bran as long as she was around.

"No," she said, withdrawing from his mind. "It requires some effort to hear the thoughts of others. I do not just eavesdrop at will. It is not right to invade the privacy of another mind."

He reined in his horse. "It is true that you are not human?" Did his voice hold a hint of revulsion?

She halted the mare with a thought.

"I am as human as you," she countered.

"Then you are capable of great evil." His conviction chilled Siobhan.

"Capable, yes," she said. "As capable as anybody. But even though I was born into this limited form, I may use it as I choose in unlimited ways. I do not choose the path of evil."

"Sometimes, my lady, we embark on a path with the best of intentions. God gave us the capacity for evil when He created us."

"As one of your God's creatures," she reasoned, "isn't it possible I was just granted slightly different abilities than humans? Would your God deliberately make me evil? Wouldn't he instill in me the ability to choose my own path? Can't you see I am just as human as you?"

He looked into her eyes. "Oh, yes, I see that," he said.

"Sometimes," she said, "I wish I were not quite so human."

"Why do you stay?" It was unexpected. She should have held her mind receptive to his thoughts so as not to be taken unawares. "With the o'Ruairc," he said. And then the words came tumbling out. "Why do you stay and allow him to treat you the way he does? He has women, many of them. He almost flaunts them in front of you. The whole fortress is buzzing with nothing but gossip. And you are above reproach. You are kind and fair to all and unstinting in your attention to the servants and guests. And you love the boy. That is plain to see – "

"So does Murchad," Siobhan interrupted. "We all do what we must do.

You murdered in the name of your God. In many respects I am more human than some. I am subject to the same emotions, the same corruptions – "

"Never, my lady! You are – Oh, God, I – " He stopped, flustered. "If only you could know what is in my heart." He turned his face away.

She shut her eyes and plunged into the easily accessible thought paths of his mind. She recoiled at the raw emotion and lusty images she found there.

He loved her. Desperately and without reservation. Just as she loved another. He would never love another woman as he loved her, without wanting anything in return. He loved her in spite of his disgust that she practiced what he considered to be witchcraft.

What made Siobhan feel such compassion toward him was his conviction that he could never speak of his love, could never reveal his true desires, never acknowledge the depth of his devotion. He knew with a profound intuition, that she loved another, so his affection for her was hopeless. Worse than hopeless.

"I do know what is in your mind, Gareth," she said softly. "I do know."

Gareth's blue eyes filled with painful sorrow.

"Then you know I cannot speak of that which burdens my heart," he said.

She nodded. "But I know how you feel. Will you allow me to accept your offer of friendship?"

"For all my life, my lady," he said. "I will be your truest friend. If ever you have need of me, just call and I will ride to the ends of the earth if I must. I – I would take up my sword to defend you and the boy." He stopped, suddenly aware of what he had promised. He kicked his horse into a fast walk. Siobhan's mare followed, keeping pace until the gelding dropped back to its usual lazy amble.

"Why did you lay down your sword?" she said. She was afraid to find the answer in his mind.

He sighed. "It is a painful story."

"Tell me."

"My brother was to have fought for King Edgar. My father had sworn allegiance to our king who tried to unify all our land in the name of God and the Church. Those who would not accept the church of the king, perished. My brother was three years older than I. He…he died. Not in battle. There is no glory in a drunken fall from your horse. My mother and father were shattered. He was the firstborn. I tried to stop him from riding off. He said I was too young for him to fight, too young for him to bother with. And off he went. I hoped to redeem myself by going in his place, but when I saw the killing…such a senseless waste. They say I was a coward. If it is cowardice to turn my back on such useless slaughter, then so I am one. I vowed I would never take up a weapon again."

"You have no wife. Many of the girls would be glad to share your bed. It would ease your loneliness."

"Chastity is small penance for my sins. Until I become a worthy servant of God, I will lie with no woman. You are the first soul I have even spoken to in true fellowship."

"How did you come here?" Siobhan said.

"That tale, my lady, is best left for a rainy evening's entertainment after supper with the men." He flushed again, looked down at the ground.

"You are a good man, Gareth, and no coward."

"True or not," he said, "your faith uplifts me and makes my loneliness bearable. Bran is a wealthy child to claim you as mother."

"Bran benefits much from your guidance, Gareth."

"He learns quickly. He can repeat some of my simpler tales. He asks about how I keep the records for the o'Ruairc."

Siobhan urged the mare closer to Gareth's bigger horse. "Could you find some little time to tutor Bran and teach him to read and figure?"

He looked startled by her request.

"Murchad seems bound to make a warrior of him," she said. "I think you could temper Murchad's influence with some education. I would consider it an honor if you would take the time. The boy likes you. You have an easy way with the children in the holding. I would see that you are rewarded for your time."

"No payment. I will do it for friendship, my lady." Gareth bowed his head slightly.

"I accept your friendship," Siobhan said gazing directly into Gareth's blue eyes, "but I insist on some small compensation for your efforts. My powers can at least add to your comforts. I can warm your room and cool it with an effortless spell – "

"No, my lady, thank you. I am quite happy. I want for little."

She vowed at least to protect his chamber with a warding spell.

"Perhaps a word to the stable master?" he said. "A better horse would suit me. This nag is almost beyond my endurance."

She laughed. "Done."

"Thank you mightily," he said. "I will do my best with the boy."

Siobhan stopped her mare and restrained Gareth's gelding with a mental command. She put a hand on his shirted arm and felt muscles flex beneath her fingers. It was an innocent gesture, but he drew away. Siobhan saw the anguish of unreturned love behind his watery blue eyes.

She spoke softly. "Know this, Gareth Spencer. If I had met you under other circumstances I could fancy you. You are a good man with a kind heart. But I, too, have lost my heart to another. One who is so far away he is not within my reach. As long as I draw breath I will love him. But I can give part of myself to you in comradeship. I am truly sorry that I cannot offer you more. It would be cruel to deceive you."

Some of the pain in Gareth's young-old eyes faded.

"Your friendship," he said, "is the greatest prize a man could possess. Murchad is poorer for rejecting it. I will not put you in jeopardy by speaking my feelings again. But if you ever have need of me, I will be there."

"Thank you, Gareth, for all you have given me," Siobhan said. "Now may we continue? I neglected to eat, and I am hungry. There is a farm up ahead beyond that stand of beeches. The wife bakes excellent bread and will feed us for the small price of a spell of protection for her lambs."

Gareth laughed and urged his gelding into a swinging trot. Delighting in the wind in her hair and the minor challenge, Siobhan let the mare surge forward, and despite her near term foal, her better breeding won the race for lunch.

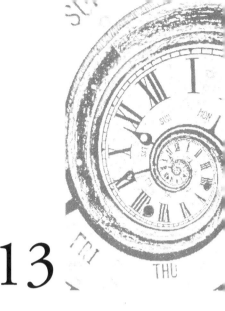

13

Brant fidgeted in the overstuffed chair. The television studio stage was small and enclosed with a low ceiling, and he felt claustrophobic. Jessica Thomas tugged her jacket down a bit, exposing more cleavage. Nice breasts.

"Beauty wins audiences before brains," she said and flashed a genuine grin.

"Are you sure we haven't met somewhere before?" Brant said.

The director and producer conferred in quiet tones and gave a few last minute instructions to the television crew. Technicians jockeyed cameras and lights into position. A young woman wearing a headset fiddled with the microphone clipped to his denim jacket, adjusting the wire so it was hidden inside.

Jessica shook her head and peered at him over reading glasses.

"No, Mr. Edwards – "

"Brant," he insisted.

Her blond hair was smoothed back into a professional style that flattered her softly rounded features. A tailored red shirt under a charcoal gray jacket revealed a hint of nicely shaped breasts. He forced himself to look into her eyes.

"All right, Brant," she said. "The first time I saw you was last week when you left the hospital – "

"I'm really sorry your guy's camera got broken."

"Not a problem. Greg stumbled. Our insurance covered it. No hard feelings." She removed the glasses and tucked them into a jacket pocket.

"Then when I met you at your place."

"Not very friendly, was I?" He'd been downright nasty to her.

"Friendly? Hardly."

"I wasn't feeling too great," he said.

Brant had felt rotten for reasons other than the beating. He'd promised the doctor he would take it easy, but as soon as he got home, he broke out a new bottle of whiskey and drank half of it before he fell asleep – or passed out – on the couch.

Jessica Thomas had knocked on Brant's door at 7:00 the next morning. She used her press creds and told Hank she had an appointment. He let her up.

"You're persistent," Brant said.

Dressed in t-shirt and jeans, with her shoulder length fair hair loose, she could have been anybody off the street trying to get a look at the local celebrity.

She introduced herself. "You won't answer your cell, and you haven't returned the 12 messages I left."

"Not interested," Brant said. His stomach felt queasy, and his hands shook. "No interviews."

He wasn't about to live in a public fish bowl. It would be easy to like it, to be seduced by the glamor and publicity. He relied on word of mouth to sell his paintings. Being reclusive gave him an aura of mystery.

"Don't you have an agent, Mr. Edwards?" Thomas said in a silky voice.

He stood there in the rumpled jeans and polo shirt he'd worn the previous day and wished she would leave.

"You really should get someone to handle your publicity. They don't have temper tantrums," she said. Her voice dripped honeyed sarcasm.

"Get lost," he snapped and slammed the door.

Later that morning the phone rang.

Brant answered it, about to utter an obscenity when Pollard Smythe's crisp English accent cut him short.

"Brant, old chum. I know you guard your privacy, but you need help." After years in America he still pronounced privacy with a short i.

Brant didn't respond.

"You have a big show in less than a month," Pollard said. "There will be a lot of very rich people here, and since you haven't come through on a few paintings you promised, you could use some positive publicity. Being on the telly would help."

Brant snorted. "If I died my stuff would skyrocket. You'd love that. More commission in your coffers."

Pollard was silent for a long beat. "I don't wish you dead, Brant," he said quietly. "I just wish you luck. I like you – at least I did before this disappearance thing. You're…different. I don't know why you're so angry, but as a friend, I'm asking you to do the talk show. Some of your lesser pieces are quite affordable, and getting the word out might sell some of them and push up the pricier ones. Can I call Ms. Thomas and set it up?"

Brant sighed. "I suppose."

"That's the spirit. I'll do it right off. Ta-ta." He broke the connection.

Brant imagined the Englishman's round face beaming and his thoughts calculating how much his commission would be if all Brant's paintings sold.

Thomas called a half hour later. Brant halfheartedly apologized for his behavior that morning and agreed to be on her show.

"Can you come tomorrow morning?" she said. "You *are* news, and we'd like to air your segment the day after tomorrow."

"Sure," he said.

"Here are the ground rules," she said. "Besides talking about your art, I'm going to mention your recent disappearance and the mugging. Just giving you heads up. I won't supply the exact questions ahead of time, but I thought you might want some time to think about your responses. My show is honest, and I don't pull any punches."

"Yeah, all right," he agreed.

Except for the hangover, Brant was fully recovered from the beating. The doctors must have been mistaken. He couldn't have been hurt as badly as they had told him.

After getting the details of the interview from Thomas he'd worked in his studio all day. He paused for bathroom breaks and made himself a sandwich for dinner, which he ate while putting the finishing strokes on a painting. He worked until well after midnight, cleaned brushes, left the studio in some disarray, and fell into bed fully clothed. His alarm went off at 6:00 – a mere four and a half hours later.

He had made it to the television studio by 7:30, and at 8:00 he sat in the guest chair of Portland's popular afternoon talk show, *Lunch with Jessica*.

Jessica Thomas smoothed her hair back and gave him a quick glance.

"You're looking much better," she said.

Brant tried to decide whether her voice held a sarcastic undertone, then concluded she meant it.

"I clean up okay," he said. He'd forgotten breakfast and had gulped down a large Frappuccino – some exotic flavor of the day – at a Starbucks by the studio. Someone had given him a cup of bad coffee while he sat impatiently for makeup. Unease fluttered in his stomach.

He glanced around. "We're not on the air yet, are we?"

She chuckled. "No. I always inform guests when they're on camera. I really don't intend to put people in awkward positions. But I can be intense. You nervous?"

He nodded. "I suppose you're used to all this. But I've never been on TV before."

"Oh, I'm used to it, but I'm always a little nervous. My mother used to tell me if you aren't nervous at all, you won't do well. Never go into any performance feeling cocky. You need that little adrenaline rush to sharpen your mind. Try a deep breath and let it out slowly. Just look at me, and don't worry about which camera is on you. It's the operators' jobs to make sure you're in the picture."

"Okay." He would be acutely aware of every camera and light in the studio when they started.

"Oh," Thomas continued, "you're the last guest on the program, but we're taping you first. So when we begin I'll give the welcome back routine after a commercial." She smiled. "And relax. I'm not out to uncover anything scandalous in your past or anything like that. This show is purely entertainment. Honest entertainment."

A thin, balding man peered around a camera and pointed at her. "Ready, Jess," he called, counting down on his fingers. She straightened in her chair.

"Break a leg," she whispered.

When the man pointed at her, she said, "Welcome back," in her well-modulated on-camera voice. "Today's last guest is Portland's – and the West Coast's – hottest artist, Brant Edwards. Mr. Edwards will be having a one man show at the Park Gallery on Milwaukie Avenue on December fifth." She held a print of one of Brant's paintings.

"This picture," Thomas said, "hangs in our lobby. It shows Mt. Rainier. In the foreground a man and a woman holding hands are gazing up at the white expanse of glacier. Seen from the back, they're both carrying climbers' packs, and ropes are draped across their shoulders.

"Imagine what these two are thinking. Are they looking forward to the spectacular view from the summit, or facing their fear of disaster if something goes wrong while they're climbing? Now we can ask the artist."

She turned to Brant. "Welcome, Mr. Edwards. It's nice to have you here."

"Thanks," Brant said. "Glad to be here." He tried to look at Jessica, but his peripheral vision was cluttered with lights and partial images.

"I've always liked this painting," Jessica said. "I've always wanted to ask you about the story behind it."

"Well," Brant said. His voice sounded weak. He cleared his throat. "Actually, those are real people. I met them when I had my first paintings accepted at the gallery. They were amateur climbers, and they told me an incredible story."

Thomas leaned forward slightly. "Will you share it with our viewers?"

"Sure," he said. "They climbed alone. I tried to show that in the painting. Two small people against the hugeness of Nature. They'd been doing it for several years. Most of Rainier is a fairly easy climb. Even amateurs can make it to the top. Anyway, they had promised each other that if anything ever happened, that if either of them ever fell, the other would cut loose so there would be one to go for help."

"What an awful decision to have to make," Thomas said.

Brant nodded. "One of them fell."

"Oh my. What happened? Were they okay?"

"They were going down about a 50 foot cliff at the end of a climb. He was above and she was below, and one of those rings you drive into the rock came loose, and he started to fall. She made the decision in about a half a second flat and cut him loose. She said it was the longest few seconds of her life watching him go down. He landed in some brush. She was sure he was badly injured, maybe dead. She got out her cell phone and called the Park Service to send help."

He took a deep breath. The distractions around him faded. "She got down as fast as she could, probably a half hour. She couldn't decide whether to go look at him or wait for someone. She finally got up her courage to see if he was all right, and he was lying on his back on a huge snow bank, his face bloody. He was alert and joked with her. The branches broke his fall, and he landed in snow. One cheek was cut, and he needed a couple of stitches, but otherwise he was fine. He was just bruised and scratched. By the time help got there he was sitting in the car and apologized for causing such a ruckus."

"Do all your paintings have stories behind them?" Jessica said.

"Oh, yes. Although some I'd rather keep to myself." He remembered a portrait he'd done for a woman who had more than posing on her mind.

"Then there's honesty in your art, isn't there?"

"Yes, I suppose there is." He felt relaxed talking about his work. She had a way of drawing him out. No wonder her show was so popular.

Jessica turned away from Brant and faced a camera. "This is the quality of work you can expect from this rising artist, whom the art world has dubbed Painter of the Northwest. I think he should be called the Honest Artist. His work can be seen around town and at the Park Gallery on Milwaukie Avenue."

She turned back to him. "Life seemed pretty great for you, until recent events. A week ago you were assaulted."

She laid the print on the table beside her.

"Mr. Edwards," she said, "what happened that night?"

The activity behind the cameras blurred. "I guess I got mugged."

"Did the muggers take your money?" she pressed.

"Uh, no. I was foolish. One of them had a gun and...I really don't know what made me do it. It wasn't bravery. It was stupid, really. I knocked the gun out of his hand. I know you're supposed to cooperate in a robbery. I just...it made me mad."

"Sometimes you just react in an emergency." Jessica's voice was kind. Maybe she didn't think he had acted like a jerk. Everybody else he knew, including that detective, had told him he was lucky to be alive.

"Mr. Edwards, what happened to your assailants?"

"I...."

He must have been silent too long, as Thomas prompted, "Go on. What happened after you knocked the gun away?"

"I really don't know," he said. "I remember hearing it hit the pavement, and the man who'd had the gun told me it wasn't loaded. As if that made it all right. They jumped me and knocked me down. I hit my head on the sidewalk."

"Than what happened?" she persisted.

"I was woozy. One of the men had a knife. I remember thinking I was going to die. Then there was a bright light. Lightning, I guess. Then a...an explosion. I guess I was lucky."

"Police theorize there was a gas explosion, or a freak lightning bolt." Thomas leaned forward in her chair. "What do you think?"

"It seems to me that if it had been one of those, I would have been injured. I heard the thunder. I was only half conscious. And in a lot of pain."

"Do you know how the muggers died?"

He nodded. "The police told me."

"They were burned. Incinerated. You were exonerated. There was no evidence you had done anything to cause a fire. The remains were difficult to identify as human beings, and yet the sidewalk was barely scorched. Strange, isn't it?"

He shuddered. "It was horrible. Most of it's pretty much a blur. I do remember a man bending over me asking me if I was all right. I knew I wasn't, but I couldn't say anything."

"Yes," Jessica said, "the bartender. He called the police. I'm happy to see you fully recovered."

"I was lucky," he said again lamely. "I wasn't as bad off as they thought."

"On a more optimistic note, Mr. Edwards, the inevitable question. Where do you get your ideas?"

"Ideas?" he repeated. He had never really thought about it. He avoided media interviews, not wanting his private life available for public scrutiny.

"Ideas? When I was a youngster, I was always sketching things. It drove my teachers nuts. I was pretty good at caricaturing people. I did political cartoons for the school newspaper in college, then later for some West Coast papers. After Mom died I supported myself doing portraits of people and pets. But my real love has always been landscapes. Even in the most idyllic setting, there's always something honest. My friends used to think I was nuts to think I could actually make a living with my artwork. They're not laughing now."

"No, I don't suppose so," she said.

"You know, I have the ideal job."

"How's that?"

"I work pretty regular hours, except sometimes when I'm on a roll, I'll stay up half the night to finish something. I really love my job. I can make a living and have free time to do other things."

"Interesting point, Mr. Edwards," Thomas said with a smile.

Brant tried to look directly into Thomas' eyes, but the camera behind her had a blinking light that drew his attention. He was keenly aware that the camera was focused on him, and his palms grew moist. He wiped them on his jeans and shifted slightly in his chair.

Thomas spoke again. As if she sensed his distress, her voice was reassuringly calm. "I understand you had another unnerving experience, Mr. Edwards."

He looked at her, the cameras fading to the edge of his perception.

"The 'Strange Disappearance of Local Artist' the papers called it."

"Oh, that." Damn. Pain bored into his head. He had left the pills at home. He'd wanted his mind clear.

"According to my information," she said, "you left the city on Halloween evening to go to your cabin in Washington. You say you were gone for the weekend, only when you came home you had lost two weeks. How do you account for it?"

"I…I don't know."

Brant's thoughts whirled. He remembered the prescription bottle on the vanity in his bathroom, wished he had a pill.

"I really don't know," he said again, trying to push the headache away. "I just went up there for a few days to think and work on some sketches."

"Where is the cabin?"

"Oh, come on, I want *some* privacy."

"Well," she said, "then where is it generally?"

"Up near Mossy Rock, Washington," he said. "Out in the middle of nowhere. Surrounded by thousands of acres of Weyerhauser timberland. It used to be private land. My grandfather bought a few acres when he first came to this country from Ireland and built a hunting cabin. The guy he bought the land from sold the rest to the lumber company and got rich. My dad made improvements to the cabin. It has all the comforts of home, but quiet. And the light is good. It's a relaxing place to work. When my grandfather died, my dad inherited the place. My mom never cared much for it. Too isolated. I love it up there. Especially in the summer."

"What do you suppose happened to you, Mr. Edwards?" Thomas smiled for the camera. "Were you in fact abducted by aliens?" She winked.

"Aliens?" Brant laughed. "I did say that. Some reporter called and asked where I'd been for two weeks, and I was ticked off and said that maybe I was kidnapped by aliens. I didn't think he'd print it."

"Nobody else did, Mr. Edwards," she said gently. "But the fact remains that you did vanish for days. People aren't just magicked away." Her smile showed white, even teeth.

Magic? *Magic…magic….*

An image stirred in his mind.

Jessica Thomas reminded him of somebody. Somebody in a dream. A tiny figure whose sun-flecked hair framed a face pale as a trillium blossom.

"Magic," Thomas said. "Illusion."

"There are many illusions in our lives, many truths," Brant said. "Maybe if we stopped to look at the…stars, we'd – "

The stars made music…magic. Someone had told him that. Stars made music in their passing. The music never changed. The music was constant… *magic*….

"Mr. Edwards?"

A voice called him, the sound far away. He wanted to tell her not to go, but he couldn't see her. Then the ghostly figure faded into the stars and was gone.

"Mr. Edwards?"

"What?"

"Brant? Are you all right?"

Jessica leaned over him, staring at him with frightened eyes. A door slammed somewhere, making him start. His head throbbed.

"What – ?" he started.

"You were…were gone. You just blinked out for a few moments."

"Are the cameras still on?" he said.

"No," she said. "You were a million miles away for at least a minute. You didn't answer. We were worried. Would you like a doctor?"

He shook his head. "I'm okay. Just a little tired, I guess. Got a splitting headache. It's better now." He was aware of people moving back to their positions.

Thomas straightened up. "Why don't you go on home? I can do the wind-up without you on camera. You know, the 'So long and good luck, Portland' bit. The director says we can eliminate the last couple of minutes about alien abduction. It was just a wild tangent."

"Thanks," he said.

"Thank *you*," she responded, offering her hand.

He raised his hand to shake hers and discovered he was clenching a headache pill in his fist. Where the hell had it come from? He must have stuck one in his pocket in case he needed it. He palmed the pill into his left hand and dropped it in his jacket pocket.

Brant shook her hand, and then the others on the set who wished him well with his painting. He avoided Jessica's eyes, knew he would find concern and curiosity in their blue-gray depths. Rumors had her looking for a job as an investigative reporter when her talk show popularity had run its course.

A few minutes later he settled into a cab. He swallowed the pill without water and leaned back. The afternoon had turned rainy, and a bitter wind blew late November cold inland from the Pacific.

The next morning in Jessica Thomas' tiny office the argument between her and the show's producer had gone on for ten minutes.

"We can't rerecord the show." Jessica regretted her impatient tone.

Laura Miller sighed. "I know."

Miller was perhaps 10 years older than Jessica, had produced successful local cable shows in Portland and Los Angeles for 15 years.

Laura rose from the chair she occupied across from Jessica's. "I know we can't," she said. "And it's not your fault, kiddo."

Jessica had always taken the other woman's use of "kiddo" as an affectionate nickname.

"There's something wrong with the recording," Laura said. "Tomorrow we're going with your other two guests: the psychic and the girl high school football kicker. The only thing to do is to take out the Edwards part, Jess, and use what we have on the other two guests to fill the half hour."

Jessica rose.

"Lloyd wants you in the viewing studio pronto," Laura said. "Says there's something you have to see."

Jessica fumed with impotent anger in the elevator on the way up and stormed into the office that opened into the viewing room. Lloyd McDonald sat at his littered desk in front of an open laptop. His face was buried in his hands. Half consumed cups of coffee and sandwich crusts were scattered across the papers that overflowed onto the floor of the cubbyhole office. He was a short, slender man, probably thirtyish, with round features and receding hair. Thick glasses perched on top of his head.

"Lloyd," Jessica said, "you all right?"

"Oh. Yeah. Hi, Jess. Just tired. Worked almost all night." He replaced the glasses on his nose and peered at her through seriously myopic eyes.

"I'm sorry to bother you, Lloyd, but Laura says the Edwards tape is screwed up. What happened?"

"Weird, Jess," McDonald said. "Look at it. Everything's fine, sharp, no problems of any kind. Remember the time we had a bad microchip in a camera and everything came out a funny color? The cameras are in perfect condition. I checked them all. Edwards' image is blurred on all of them. Got a bluish halo around it like interference. Nothing else is hinky. We recorded more than an hour with the other two, and they're fine. You're fine. Everything else in perfect focus. I never saw anything like it before, and the technicians can't get rid of it. Want to see?"

"Yes," she said. "I would."

Jessica rarely viewed uncut recordings. She discovered early in her career the attraction of wanting to edit and edit, never quite attaining perfection. Now she fooled with the show as little as possible. Let the director, producer, camera operators and others do their jobs. If it wasn't quite to her liking, that was okay. She was the talent. Viewers watched *her*, not the nuances of editing.

It all boiled down to the fans. They loved her show. So the people who made the decisions about what to cut and what to keep must be doing a good job.

A short while later Jessica left Lloyd's office with an uneasiness deep in the pit of her stomach. There was nothing wrong with the digital recording. Perfect audio. Perfect video. Except that Edwards was blurred, bluish around the edges, like static. His image was the only thing affected. Everything else – background, her likeness, even the print of Edwards' painting she'd held up to the camera – everything was crystal clear.

Lloyd had consulted everybody in the technical department. He'd even called someone at one of the local colleges who was a whiz at computer enhancement. Nobody had ever seen anything like it.

After she left Lloyd, Jessica called an acquaintance across town at KPTV, a Fox affiliate, and a short cab ride later arrived at their viewing studio. Jane Barrett, a news reporter she had met once at a media event, greeted her. Jane was a handsome, middle-aged woman who looked ten years younger on camera.

"Hi, Jane," Jessica said. "I really appreciate this."

"Jessica," Jane said. "You going to tell me what this is all about? I don't usually get calls to dig up week-old news recordings. But you sounded mysterious. You know me. I love mysteries."

"I'm just interested in a story," Jessica said. "I'd like to see the original. It's not the same on television as it is raw." She really didn't have a concrete idea. Just an uneasy feeling in the back of her mind. Reporter's hunch.

The other woman's face took on a crafty expression. "Are you doing a story about that guy Edwards knocked down? Edwards didn't touch him."

"Well," Jessica lied, "let's say I'm working on it."

"All right," Jane said. "But you'll see. It wasn't assault. Edwards just had an attack of the klutzies, and he stumbled. But he didn't touch that man. He wasn't close enough. If it was intentional, it was cleverly done. And the tape isn't clear anyway. We used it on the evening news, but it doesn't show much. You can see space between the two of them, but…well, why don't you look at it and then tell me what you think."

The footage prior to the incident was clear. Jessica saw the piece that aired on the news and the cameraman being knocked backwards. Jane could provide no explanation as to why Brant's image was slightly out of focus and surrounded by a faint blue glow. The station had run the piece anyway, because it was the only one available of the entire incident. The technicians had tried to improve the focus, but nothing could be done to make Brant's image sharper.

Jessica thanked Jane, telling her if she ever needed a favor, Jess owed her one. But she wouldn't – *couldn't* – tell the other woman what she was working on. Something didn't quite fit together. She couldn't articulate it, but her gut told her something was wrong. Something didn't match.

Or rather two somethings *did* match. Two images of the same man blurred on two different recordings, when everything else was perfect. It didn't make sense.

Jessica's intuition told her it might be worth following up if she could find the time in the next few days. Edwards had come across well. At least his personality had. Besides, he was a fascinating story. People in the modern world didn't disappear for two weeks and show up as if nothing had happened. Over the weekend she would call in a few debts from local contacts and check into the life of Brant Edwards.

14

The forest canopy above Siobhan smoldered with the beginnings of autumn. A few stray leaves drifted down.

"Why do we return early, Mother?" Bran o'Ruairc said. He gazed at Siobhan, his dark eyes were so much like his father's. "We always stay until the leaves fall."

"I truly do not know, little one." Siobhan sighed. "Sometimes I feel that something should be done. I do not question my senses, child. Perhaps it is an accidental glimpse of what will be. I feel in my heart we must go."

She stacked the wooden plates and cups neatly on the shelf and set the shelter in order. Siobhan had made the dwelling from tree branches held together with vines and magic. She and little Bran spent the summers practicing the spells she tried to teach him and making oddments from bits of wood and leaves. He enjoyed summers in the forest with all its adventures.

"We went home early last year, too," Bran said, pouting. "The time gets shorter as I grow up."

"No," she said and laughed. "You just grow more impatient."

Ten years old and Bran was nearly as tall as Siobhan. His face bore the delicate features of the *Sidhe*: wide eyes, high cheekbones, narrow, straight nose. His hair, dark like his father's, reflected blue highlights in the diffused sunlight.

He played with a small cup he had woven from a strip of bark. He had learned the skill Siobhan taught him and refined it until he could weave a cup no larger than his thumbnail. Its miniature detail was perfect, and it held a tiny drop of water. He was proud he could better his mother at something. But he could not cast even a simple spell.

"Your father misses you, child," she said. "And Gareth needs your help with the accounts."

"Gareth likes me, Mother," he said with a child's honesty.

"Yes, Bran." She urged him outside the dwelling and laid a hawthorn branch across the opening, protection from intrusion. "Gareth likes you very much."

A surreptitious flick of one hand reinforced the spell of protection on the summer shelter. It wasn't inviolable like the dwellings of the true *Sidhe*, but humans could and did pass within arm's length and not notice it.

Bran drew himself up to his full height. "I want to be like Gareth when I grow up, Mother," he said.

"You would be a fine man indeed if you were like either Gareth or your father," she assured him.

There was truth in her statement. Since Bran had grown old enough to notice, Murchad seemed to live a celibate life. And Gareth – it was better not to think about him.

"Duncan says my father was not such a fine man when he was younger – "

"Your father has done well by you," Siobhan said. "You will not malign him. It does nothing but demean you if you engage in idle gossip. The past is past."

"But Gareth likes me. He tells me stories. And he listens to me."

"Gareth and his stories," Siobhan said, ruffling her son's hair. He grinned and ducked away from her.

"Gareth's stories are wonderful," Bran said.

She nodded. "Yes, child, they are."

Siobhan took Bran's hand and walked with him into the forest shadows. She sighed, glanced at Bran, hoped he had not heard her heavy breath. She could find no enchantment in the boy. Often she facilitated his efforts. His delight at success made her happy. But during the past summer it had become increasingly apparent to Siobhan that Bran had not inherited any fey powers. Perhaps when he grew older he might develop some minor enchantments.

Bran's talent seemed to be at figures. When he was five, Gareth began teaching him how to record accounts. After watching and listening to Gareth's dealing with an angry farmer, little Bran suggested Gareth appoint a trusted clansman or two to make the collections, then follow up in person, thanking the farmers for their generosity.

It was a simple and effective solution. Gareth was amazed nobody had thought of it. Impressed by Bran's perception, Gareth intensified his instructions, making good on his promise to Siobhan. Bran learned how to figure and inscribe the sheets of parchment that kept the permanent records. With writing came the knowledge of reading. Bran read letters and quoted figures to Gareth and Murchad. It made the scribe's job much easier, especially since Murchad was often absent, being much occupied with the direct supervision and safety of his holdings and people.

Being a scribe was honest work, but Siobhan had hoped the boy would have some fey sense, perhaps an affinity for animals, mind touch, or only empathy.

Eventually she would have to tell Bran he had no aptitude for enchantment at all. Perhaps next year, or the year after....If puberty did not bring a transition, he was destined to live a mortal lifetime. She would see him grow old and die, and his children and grandchildren....

Lost in gloomy thoughts, Siobhan barely noticed Bran's dialogue about the properties of plants he had learned from Bebhinn and his observations of birds and nature.

"What?" Siobhan said. She stopped in the last copse of alders before the rutted road leading to the o'Ruairc's fortress.

"Why can't we see stars in the day?" said Bran. "It seems – "

Siobhan held up a hand to silence him. From the fortress came shouts and the clang of iron against iron. A woman's scream rent the air, but was cut off with an abruptness that chilled her.

She grabbed Bran's arm, hushed him with a finger to her lips and pulled him into the shadows of the trees.

"Mother, look," Bran whispered, peeking through the branches.

"I see," she said.

The stone and timber wall surrounding the fortress and its outbuildings had been breached in several places, and the great front gate hung askew on its massive iron hinges. Men fought with swords and daggers and axes. A few buildings blazed with greedy flames that threatened to engulf the entire compound.

There must have been ten of the enemy warriors to every one of Murchad's. Dead and dying men, women and children, lay scattered – bloody and broken. Some of the women and older children brandished knives and garden tools, but there was little hope of survival.

Siobhan's alarm became anger. She turned to Bran.

"Remain here under my spell," she said. "Do not move. The spell takes much effort to maintain. When my attention is distracted it will be little more than illusion and will not protect you from the harm that iron will do you. Do not move." The little boy nodded gravely. "Do not leave this spot until someone you know well and trust comes for you." Again he nodded.

Siobhan clothed herself in dazzling light. Mortal eyes would not see her face clearly, but would perceive instead a magical creature, radiant and otherworldly.

She ran to the front gate, a streak of light on a sunny day. Within moments she stood inside the wall. In the center of the courtyard Murchad, surrounded by his men, battled enemy warriors who pressed in with bloodied swords and axes. Murchad stood, feet apart, his great sword swinging in deadly arcs. Siobhan thought how much grayer his hair had grown, but there was no time for useless sentimentality.

These attackers were not the rough troops of a neighboring clan bent on avenging some minor misdeed. These men were taller of stature than Murchad's people, muscular, fair-haired men with wild blue eyes. Northmen. She had heard of these ravening hordes – heathens, Bebhinn called them – who crossed the northern sea. They came from the land of ice and snow to conquer Eirinn's fertile lands. Instead of living peacefully and farming, they attacked mercilessly, driving the people off the land they had nurtured for centuries. Some had joined them, rebelling against Brian Boru, their own heroic leader. She thought the attacks ended years ago. Perhaps some invading chieftain wished to expand his holdings at the expense of the o'Ruairc.

With mounting horror, Siobhan took in the carnage in the compound. A few bodies littered the open spaces – people she lived with, people she had grown to like. She could not let this slaughter continue.

She raised her arms. Scintillations of light flowed from her and illuminated the courtyard. The fires in the compound died as if snuffed by a giant hand. A few men stopped, turned and stared. Others followed until all the Northmen, Murchad and his men and a boy Bran's age who held a pitchfork, gazed at her, silenced by the brightness.

Sorcery blazed around her. "Who is the Northman who dares attack this place?" she said.

For a moment she wasn't certain the leader would acknowledge her challenge, or perhaps he had been injured or killed in the melee and could not come forward.

"I do, woman." A giant of a man stepped away from Murchad and his inner guards. Sweat and blood dripped down his face. "Who are you to interfere in my battle?" he roared. He glanced back to his own men and Murchad's who held their weapons ready.

"Your battle is over," Siobhan said. "This dwelling and the lands that surround it are protected by one of the *Sidhe*. You may leave now with your lives, or stay and die."

"And how would a woman do me harm?" The man's long blond beard, braided in two tails, wagged as he spoke. He raised his broad sword to shield his eyes from the splendor of Siobhan's countenance and stepped toward her.

She did not allow herself a look within his mind. She did not care to learn his motives.

"I tell you one last time," she said. "This land and all who dwell here are under my protection. You and your men may leave now with your lives, or your bodies will be burned here."

The giant threw back his head and roared with laughter. He waved his wicked sword over his head. Drops of blood flew off, shining crimson in the late sun.

"*You* leave," he snorted. "This is not woman's work. If you are still here when we have dispatched this old warrior, then you will belong to me."

"I belong to no mortal," Siobhan said.

"You will be mine, sure enough," the man growled. "When I finish with you, no other man will want you." He leered at her, and made a thrusting gesture with his hips and sword. She heard a few snickers from his men.

A red haze of anger rose in Siobhan's mind. She forced her fury down. Anger would defeat her enchantment. She gazed at the murdered bodies around her, men, women and children slaughtered. She coerced her mind into calmness, tried to shut out the acrid scent of iron and sent her humanity into a distant corner.

"You would do well to heed the *Sidhe* woman's warning," Murchad said.

The blond man laughed again. "I heed no woman."

He stepped toward Siobhan and whipped his sword up in front of him, not to shield his eyes, Siobhan realized, but to bring it into striking position.

He was slightly out of her reach, but she felt the burn of iron, worked and beaten into honed perfection. Heard the metal cut the air. She smelled the currents of fear that emanated from the people around her, even from those who knew her. But the big man before her feared her not. He knew only the joy of battle and the thrill of killing that surged through him. The blood lust. She read in his eyes his intentions an instant before his muscles responded.

"Foolish man," Siobhan whispered. She had no power over the sword, but she could hurt the man. She unleashed a spell. Blue fire flew from her fingers, splattered against him. The sword fell from his hands as if it had scalded him, and blue flames seethed over his body. His agonized scream was cut short by a thunderclap that resounded throughout the courtyard.

When the echoes died away, nothing remained of the Northmen's leader but a charred spot on the ground and the man's sword lying in the dust. She regretted that iron was beyond her power. She would have melted it on the spot. Even though it contained other alloys, it contained too much pure iron to submit to her spells.

"Put down your weapons and flee while there is still breath in your bodies," she commanded in a voice amplified by a small spell. If she didn't use enchantment, her voice would quake. "I grant you safe passage through the o'Ruairc's lands.

"But despoil naught and take no other life, or for every bloody body you leave behind, twenty of your Northmen will die the way your leader did. Never return. I will not bargain with you, and the o'Ruairc will not confer even the smallest amnesty to any of you for what you have done here today. Let it be known through all of Eirinn that this land is protected by the *Sidhe*."

The attackers pelted from the courtyard like terrified chickens before a fox. One of Murchad's men raised a sword at a fleeing man, only to have Murchad's own hand turn his aside.

After the last of the Northman had fled, dragging their wounded with them, Siobhan strode to Murchad. A tall man in the dress of a household servant stood beside her husband. Weary from the power she had expended on her spells, she glanced into Murchad's face, then to his defender. Gareth held one of Murchad's swords, tip down. Blood dripped down its length into the trampled dirt. He too was spattered with blood.

"You returned in time," Murchad said.

Siobhan looked into Gareth's mind. She sensed Gareth's humiliation that he had killed not to protect his chieftain, but for love of her. A small spell of comfort made Gareth blink and stand straighter.

"Gareth," she said, "the child awaits at the edge of the road where the alders stand. He hides under a spell of invisibility, but with my exertions the spell has worn thin. If you would walk along the road and call to him, he will move, and you will see him. I am too weary to go for him."

"I will fetch him, my lady," Gareth replied.

He handed his bloody sword to Murchad and strode away, his shoulders slumped with fatigue. Siobhan knew some of the blood on Gareth's garments was his own, but his wounds were superficial. She would tend to him later, accompanied by Bebhinn.

Siobhan turned to Murchad. "I would speak with you," she said. "When you have washed your hands, you may come to my chamber." She turned and walked to the dwelling. At the threshold the glory faded from her.

In a short while Murchad knocked on Siobhan's door. She opened the door and admitted him. He had cleaned up and changed his garments. But still he appeared fatigued and sorrowful. He did not speak

Finally, Siobhan broke the silence. "The boy should go to the holy place."

Murchad raised his eyebrows and ran a hand thoughtfully along his bearded jaw. Gray flecked his hair and peppered his beard.

"Why?" he said.

"He must learn skills that will help him be a leader after you are gone," she replied. "Gareth says Bran is quick and compassionate to the landholders, and he assures me Bran can learn what is taught by the holy men. If he is to be educated, the time is now before he develops other interests. Besides, the man who comes from the abbey to minister to your family is good and kind."

Murchad sighed. "I will never make a warrior of him, Siobhan," he said. "He has no aptitude for killing. He cannot stab the practice figures because he refuses to comprehend the reason for it. He says he feels sorry that the art of the craftsman is destroyed for sport. He hunts with me, but his arrows always miss. He does not even think to defend himself when Duncan and the other boys tease him. He sees no reason to fight and even less to kill." He chuckled ruefully. "He has not grown to suit either of us, has he?"

"No, Murchad, he has not. But I see now that he should grow to suit himself. He is quick of wit and truly happy with his figuring. Sending him to the abbey will give him the education he requires."

"Gareth will take him," said Murchad. "I will assign guards to ride with them and watch over him. He will want for nothing."

She nodded in agreement.

He looked searchingly at her. "No conditions?" he said.

"None."

"It is settled then. We should both talk to him, explain." Murchad stepped toward her. Stopped.

Siobhan stood her ground. Would he put his hands on her, forgetting his oath not to touch her? But he did not. His arms hung at his sides, unmoving.

"Bran understands much, Murchad," Siobhan said. "He spoke of it while we were in the forest. He is proud that Gareth thought so much of him and disappointed that he could not live up to either of our expectations."

"It is not too late for the boy," Murchad said, gazing directly into Siobhan's eyes.

"Thank you," she said. "See to the dead, Murchad. I will help tend the wounded. But I will not have the druid witch inside the fortress." She turned away.

"Done," he said softly and closed the door as he left.

15

Maeve made spaghetti sauce from scratch to occupy her mind. Rich made a salad and opened a bottle of good Chianti. Loading carbs was comforting. Probably better for them in the long run than filling up on high fat food like ice cream. But she didn't eat much, just chased the spaghetti around her plate. Her salad was virtually untouched. She drank most of the wine.

"Maeve." Rich's voice seemed flat.

Not babe, not honey like he usually said.

"Hm?" she said.

Rich pushed his empty plate aside and settled his elbows on the table.

"Maeve," he said. "Please don't freak out. I need to tell you something. It's really weird. Well, not weird, strange, well – "

"What?" She wasn't at all given to premonitions, but tension knotted her stomach.

"Yesterday Jessica Thomas called me."

"That woman who does the TV talk show? Brant was on yesterday, but I forgot to record it."

"He wasn't on the show. She called me and told me they couldn't use the recording for some reason. She also asked some odd questions."

"Like what?"

Rich drained the last swallow of his wine. "She asked about your family. Said she was doing some background research. Wanted to know where Kirk Morgan had come from."

"The family lawyer." A prickle of tension ran up Maeve's back. "I never liked him. His eyes…well, his eyes are predatory. When I was little I thought he looked at me like he was a hawk and I was a rabbit." She hiccuped. Too much Chianti?

"I had a funny feeling about the guy," Rich said. "You know how when you meet someone and they just rub you the wrong way? When I called him the other day to tell him Brant showed up, he sounded…strange."

"You've always said you inherited a batch of intuition. That's what makes you a good detective."

"Something about him just didn't sit right with me," Rich said. "Call it a hunch. Morgan seemed *too* relieved when I told him. Wanted to know all the particulars, where he'd been, what he'd done. I told him I couldn't say anything, that it was an active investigation." Rich shook his head and pushed his empty plate aside.

"He tried to be casual about it," he continued, "but he was just too eager. And then Thomas called with her questions. I got curious. So I ran a background check on Morgan. A few things didn't add up, so I dug deeper. He doesn't seem to have been born."

"What?" Maeve set her fork down, her meal forgotten. "What's the punchline?"

Rich fished his notebook from his back pocket and riffled pages. He stopped and folded the cover back. "Morgan got his undergrad degree in 1968 from University of Washington," he said. "No photos available. Started law school in 1971 at Oregon Law in Eugene, graduated middle of his class in '73. Again, no photos. No draft record."

"The Vietnam War," Maeve mused. "Student deferment?"

Rich shook his head. "No record."

Maeve thought a moment, waited for Rich to continue.

"Morgan passed the bar in Washington and Oregon. He moved to Portland, bought a building and opened the law firm of Morgan and Associates. Guy's got more money than God. He must be worth a hundred million. Most of it pretty well hidden by holding companies and covers. All very legal. But strange."

"Lots of people have money, Rich."

Rich flipped a page back in his notes. "I dug some more," he said. "He came to America in 1951 from Ireland, became a naturalized citizen. Before that? Nothing."

"Nothing?" Maeve repeated.

"Morgan's got no family, no parents. Nothing. He just appeared." Rich looked up at her, his hazel eyes intense. "Now, listen to this. His citizenship application lists his age as 19. So that means he was born in 1932. No way he's 80 years old. He looks like he's maybe 45 or 50. How is that possible?"

Maeve's mind spun with the inconsistency. "A good plastic surgeon?" she finally said. "You said he has money."

Rich took a breath. "Now, babe, please don't be angry with me. I looked into your family, too."

"Why?"

"When I hit the wall on Morgan, I started to wonder about your parents. The only connection I could find with Morgan was to your family. Do you remember your grandfather at all? Your mom's father."

Grandda, her mother and Brant had called him. Patrick O'Reilly. She shook her head. "He died when I was only a year old. But Brant remembers him. He told me that when he was in kindergarten, he was scolded at school for saying 'Oh, Jaysus' in front of the teacher. He claimed he was just repeating what grandpa said and didn't know it was naughty. I've heard him say it."

"How did he die, Maeve?" Rich's voice was soft.

"Mom and Brant told me he died when he was deer hunting up in the mountains. Maybe a heart attack?"

"He was killed, Maeve."

"How?" she whispered.

"Another hunter found him. He'd been shot. The case is still open." Rich leaned toward her and asked, "How did your father die?"

"I was 13. I don't like to think about it – "

"How?"

Tears started in Maeve's eyes. "He was killed by a mugger in Longview. We lived in Toutle, Washington. He was a teacher at the high school. Home of the Toutle Ducks." When she was in grade school she'd had a shirt that said Toutle Ducklings.

"Up toward Mount St. Helens," Rich said.

"Yes. Brant told me when I was older that Dad came out of the credit union, and a man stabbed him for no reason. All the robber got was $25 Dad had taken out for spending money." Why would Rich open these old wounds? "I remember Mom was depressed after that. She never really seemed to be happy. Then – " She stopped, remembering what happened two years later.

"What?" Rich gently probed.

"I was 15. Mom died."

He nodded. "The Cowlitz County sheriff's department had a file on the accident."

Maeve nodded. "They investigated, along with the Highway Patrol."

"Your brother pushed for more. Apparently he didn't believe it was an accident."

"What?"

Maeve sipped her wine. If she swallowed, she would have to focus on that and wouldn't cry.

"Your family has suddenly become complicated, honey."

"It was a car accident," Maeve said and pushed her plate away. She put her elbows on the table and rested her chin on her hands. "Mom ran off the road on the way home from the library where she worked in Castle Rock. She was killed instantly. They said she hit the brakes to avoid a deer or a dog or something. It was raining. Icy."

"Brant thought there was another explanation."

"Oh, come on, Rich. Dredging up old grief isn't going to help Brant now."

Rich held up his hands. "Bear with me. I had someone I know in the coroner's office look at the autopsy results. He said some of the injuries were inconsistent."

She stared at him. What did this have to do with anything?

"In his opinion," Rich said, "your mother was dead before the car hit that tree."

"Oh, God."

"Maeve, she was probably murdered and the accident staged. It was done well. Professional."

Maeve felt stunned. Both her parents *murdered*? A grandfather *accidentally* shot? The coincidence boggled her mind.

"There's more," Rich said.

What more could there be?

"I called someone I know who works for the *Longview Herald*. He dug through the morgue files and came up with a couple of articles about your other grandfather, your father's father – George Edwards."

"An obit?"

"He was killed, Maeve. In 1978."

"Before I was born."

"He was a longshoreman," Rich said. "He worked at the Longview docks when it was a thriving seaport. There was a bar fight. Someone stabbed your grandfather. He died the following day."

She needed an antacid, or maybe a dozen. "I remember Mom talking about her dad," she said. "She was 14 or so. She said his death was sad. I always thought she meant that he was really sick. What happened to the man who did it?"

"He was arrested. Stood trial for murder."

"Good. I'm glad justice was done. Mom never told me that."

"He should have gotten life. He pled to manslaughter. Got five years, was out in three."

"Not much for a life, is it?"

Rich shook his head. "It gets weirder."

"How can it get weirder? Three people in my family were probably murdered, one maybe *not* accidentally shot."

"Guess who defended the man who killed your grandfather?" She shook her head. "Someone from Morgan and Associates."

"Why would – ?"

"Not Morgan himself. One of the junior partners. They took the case *pro bono*. The murderer, Victor Pallini, was shot to death in a drug dispute in Portland. The dealer wasn't prosecuted. Insufficient evidence."

"What about my grandmother, his wife?" Maeve dug in her memories for the name. "Martha."

Rich drew in a deep breath and looked down at his notes. "She died a few years before your grandfather. In 1976. Brant would have been two. She drowned."

"How?" Maeve's hands felt cold. She fought a shiver.

"All the paper ran was a small article, more like an obituary you'd find in a local paper where they carry stories like 'Mr. Carson went to town yesterday for groceries.' That sort of thing. The article said she drowned in Spirit Lake. A family there on a picnic found her body. There was only a cursory investigation because the sheriff didn't suspect foul play. There was an autopsy that apparently got buried. I found a copy of it. There was no water in her lungs."

"She didn't drown?"

He shook his head. "She was most likely strangled, then dumped in the lake."

"What about Mom's mother? I vaguely remember her. I think I was four or five when she died. She was really sick."

Rich shook his head. "I'm still checking on that. It's possible she was poisoned."

Maeve's whole body went cold. "Six people – "

"Died under suspicious circumstances, probably murdered."

"What is going on, Rich?" The wine she had drunk suddenly evaporated, leaving her senses acute: she smelled garlic, the rich aroma of the spaghetti sauce, Rich's faint aftershave, heard the clock above the stove ticking, felt a sinking feeling in the pit of her stomach.

"I don't know." He reached across the table and took her hands in his. "But I'm going to find out. This is a pattern, Maeve. Someone is killing your family. That means you and Brant – "

"Are in danger." she finished.

"Yes."

Her hands trembled. Rich held them tighter. "I can protect you, babe. I'm a cop," he said,

"Oh, God, this is like some bad TV cop show. Who is doing this to us?"

"I'm going to find out. Can you take some more time off work?"

"Well...."

"I mean it. It's hard to keep you safe on your way to and from work. It's too routine, too easy for someone to chart your movements. You stop at the same Starbucks every morning at the same time within a few minutes. If you can stay home for maybe a week, I'll make sure you're protected. There'll be a patrol car out in front of the apartment. By then I can get a handle on what's going on."

She nodded, thinking how much work that put on her colleague, Jason Thatcher. He had the classroom next door to hers, and they always made sure things ran smoothly when either of them had a substitute.

"I could take off another week," she said. "It comes under the family emergency provision."

"No offense, honey, but you're not indispensable."

"I know," she said. "But teachers like to think they are. I have so many sick days saved up, I'll never use them all."

"Make the call."

"Oh," she said. "I almost forgot. Maybe now, with all this, it isn't important. Pollard Smythe called me this morning."

"Brant's agent," Rich said.

"Yes. He offered me a job."

"In the gallery?"

"No. He says Brant told him he has paintings done that should go to the gallery. But Brant won't let any of his delivery people come get them. Pollard wants me to go to Brant's and take care of it."

"What'd you say?"

"I told him I had a job. And Brant might not let me in either." She sighed. "But since I'm taking time off, I could try."

Rich looked searchingly at her. "You sure?"

"If Brant really doesn't have a clue who I am, he might let me in if I represent the gallery. At least I'd get to see him. And maybe seeing me will jog his memory. It's worth a try. Pollard said he'd call Brant and set it up. He won't tell him it'll be me."

"All right," Rich said. "But you are not to leave this apartment until the uniform shows up."

"You mean I get a police escort?"

Rich grinned. "Absolutely."

"Everywhere?"

Rich nodded. "And don't argue. You don't have a choice here."

"It seems like a lot of fuss."

Rich rose from his chair and came around the table. He stood behind Maeve and put his arms around her, his hands gentle.

"I love you, Maeve," he said close to her ear. "I don't want to lose you. I think five people, maybe six, in your family were murdered. I just want you to be safe."

She looked up, and he bent down and kissed her.

"I love you, too, Rich."

"Come to bed, babe," Rich whispered, his voice husky and his breath warm on her ear.

Heat spread throughout Maeve's body. Intimacy was a bulwark against trouble. It would hold back the emotional turmoil that battered her. She could think about all he had told her tomorrow. She rose, took his hand and led him to the bedroom.

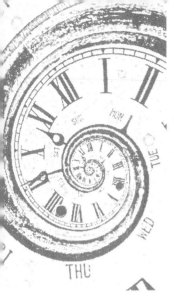

16

Maeve stood in the doorway while Brant studied her. He was shirtless and barefoot. His jeans were smeared with paint, and he smelled of turpentine.

"The burglar," he finally said.

She sighed. "I was here to water your plants."

"Whatever."

He started to close the door.

"Wait," she said.

"What do you want?" he growled. He rubbed his forehead, his thumb and forefinger kneading his temples. "Christ. It's not even seven in the morning."

"I'm from the gallery," Maeve said.

"I thought you were a teacher."

"I'm taking some time off. Pollard asked me to come and have your paintings sent over. You do remember Pollard, don't you?" She crossed her arms, both hands balled into tight fists. Anger would accomplish nothing.

"If you don't get the paintings there," she said, "Pollard may back out of the show. I'm sure you need the money, Brant. An artist's income isn't like a paycheck. I know you've put all your efforts for the last six months into this show. You turned down a lot of portrait jobs."

"Yeah, Pollard called," Brant said.

Brant hesitated. His eyes were bloodshot, and his beard had grown enough that it looked reddish. He obviously hadn't shaved in a couple of days.

After a long moment he gestured. "Come in then," he said. "Sorry about the mess."

She looked around, appalled. Brant had always been almost compulsively neat, even when he moved back home after Mom died. His artist's eye didn't allow for disorganized clutter. The loft was a disaster. There were clothes and newspapers and dirty dishes everywhere. A sheaf of papers from the sofa table had spilled onto the floor. They must have been there some time, as they had footprints on them. Some were stained with dark splashes.

Maeve picked up one of the sheets. It smelled of coffee. Under the brownish stain was a rough sketch of a woman with no facial features.

"I – " Where would she start? What should she say?

"I've done more than three canvasses," he said. "Sit down. I've been up all night. Need a shower." He swiped a pile of newspapers off a corner of the couch.

Maeve sat gingerly on the edge. She mapped out the shortest route to the door. This time she was prepared with her wallet in her pocket.

"God, my head hurts," Brant said to no one in particular. He scratched his chest and headed for the bedroom.

"Have you eaten?"

"Yesterday, maybe."

"Can I fix something?"

"Suit yourself."

He shut the bedroom door behind him. The lock turned with an audible click.

She started in the kitchen clearing counter space. By the time Brant wandered into the living room, damp and wearing fresh jeans – still paint spattered – and a clean t-shirt, the dishwasher hummed, and the kitchen was orderly. She cut a large cheese and onion omelet into two sections and slid them onto plates, giving Brant the bigger portion.

"Breakfast," she said and poured him a mug of coffee.

He sat on a stool at the counter. "How'd you know I like these?"

"Because I – " She wanted to say "because I'm your sister." Instead she said, "I like them myself. I'm the chef here, so you eat what I cook." She set the plates on the counter, got herself a cup of coffee, and sat on the other stool. Without looking at him she forked omelet into her mouth.

He dug into his. "Good," he said. "I like my eggs well done."

"Thank you. About the paintings…."

He nodded, kept eating. A few bites later he said, "There are a few more than Pollard bargained for. I hope he likes them. They're…different. You'll see when you go in there. You must be a gift from whatever Gods watch over starving artists. I couldn't seem to get up the ambition to get the courier service over here."

He nodded at the kitchen. "Thanks for cleaning up. I didn't make dinner last night because there weren't any clean dishes. Didn't have the energy to order pizza. Maeve? Is that your name?" She nodded. "Is that what you'd like me to call you? No nicknames?" Again she nodded. "You that detective's wife?"

"Yes." She ignored his faulty memory and shoved her deep sense of loss to the back of her mind. She glanced at him and caught him staring at her.

"What do you do for fun? I mean when you're not babysitting me?"

"I'm not babysitting you," she said. "I'm just going to call the courier and get the paintings over to the gallery, make sure they arrive all right. In real life I teach sixth grade English. I read. I knit."

She felt weird telling him things he already knew. She couldn't tell him what Rich had told her about their family and the danger they might be in. He wouldn't believe it.

"Pollard called me," she said. "I took a few days off to help you out."

"Do I sense a conspiracy?" he said. He finished the last bite of omelet, drained the coffee and rubbed his forehead, grimacing.

"Headache?" she said.

Brant had never been sick. Never a cold, or the flu, or even a headache. Seemed odd, looking back on all the things she'd picked up from other kids.

"Hurts like a bitch," he said. "I took a pill that doctor at the clinic gave me, but they don't help much. I'm going to bed. When you rang the bell, I'd been in the studio all night. But I got a lot done." He rose from the stool. "Do me a favor, will you? Tell anyone who calls I'm not in." He started for the bedroom.

"I'll take your calls and get the paintings sent."

"Thanks," he said. "And again for breakfast."

The bedroom door closed and locked behind him.

Maeve hoped Brant's civility was genuine. If he had been polite because he was exhausted, he'd probably revert to being nasty to her when he awoke.

Maeve spent two hours straightening up. She filled three garbage sacks with trash. Both recycling bins were overflowing. One trash bag was too full to fit through the chute in the hallway, so she had to re-bag it into two. She ran the vacuum over the large area rug in the living room and dusted surfaces.

A lick and a promise as her mother said. The place looked presentable. Finally, she headed for the studio.

Maeve opened the door and froze. She hardly saw the clutter and disorganization in what was Brant's usually neat domain. What drew her attention were the paintings. She counted 12 of various sizes, leaning against the walls, the tall cupboards that made up one wall of the room, and sitting on easels.

These were not Brant's signature landscapes. They were impressionistic, with splashes of bright color and hazy images. Every one seemed to be of the same woman in varying poses. She was young and beautiful in an ethereal way, with delicate, pale features, big blue eyes and pouty lips. She was dressed in a flowing garment so sheer it seemed to be made of moonlight. The paintings were powerfully sensual, some bordering on erotic, some faintly disturbing. All compelled her to look at them, to contemplate the artist's intent.

She recognized Brant's talent in all the canvasses. And his signature, more embellished, but his. It was as if his talent had been magnified, transformed into art that transcended his former work. From her contact with the art world, Maeve recognized true genius.

Her practical mind finally overrode her amazement. Brant's large canvasses usually sold for between two and four thousand. If these were as good as she thought, they might go for three times that. Even conservatively, that meant she was looking a great deal of money. And he had done them all in three days.

She pulled her cell phone from her pocket and punched the button that speed dialed the gallery.

"Pollard," she said when he answered, "you're not going to believe this."

Brant woke to gray twilight with the uneasy feeling that something he had dreamed was real. He couldn't remember details, only that it seemed important. He sat on the edge of the bed, then went to the window and drew back the drapes.

He had slept the day away. The sun was setting behind piled-up clouds, beyond the city over the Pacific, painting the sky red and pink and orange. Four stories down in the glow of streetlights people returned home from work. It must be almost five o'clock. From the living room he heard the strains of binaural music, the kind he believed stimulated the creative part of the brain.

He vaguely remembered watching television yesterday – or was it the day before? – and hearing something about an Arctic low pressure system taking aim at the Northwest. It would mean cold rain in the city and sleet and snow in the mountains.

Brant pulled on a sweater from his dresser without looking at it, used the bathroom and then stumbled into the brightly lit living room. Maeve was curled up on the couch, asleep. He cleared his throat. Her eyes flew open. She sat up, her sunny smile fading to a perfunctory one.

"You look better," she said, lowering her gaze.

"Yeah. Thanks. Did you get the stuff sent?"

She nodded. "All 12 of them."

He frowned. "I thought there were three big ones and a couple of smaller ones."

"No. Twelve all together. Pollard's amazed. Brant, it's the best work you've done. He's putting the new ones up front. He says they're going to set the art world on fire."

"Good," he said. "The money'll be great."

She rose from the couch, pulling her sweatshirt down. "Who was the model?"

"Model?"

"It's the same girl in all of them," Maeve said. "When I picked up the stuff in here, the floor was littered with sketches of her. I stacked them on the counter. Your studio was pretty disorganized, so I put things away. I put the tops back on paint tubes, cleaned the brushes, that sort of thing."

"I left brushes?" Damned things were expensive. He always cleaned them.

"They're okay," she said. "They hadn't been sitting long."

"I worked all last night," he said. "Night before, too. And yesterday."

"Brant," she said, "did you understand what I said about the paintings?"

"Yeah. I can pay some bills. Guess I got lucky." He looked around. "You did a great job on this place."

"Magic fingers." She wiggled her fingers at him.

Something nagged at his thoughts. "What?" He stared at her.

"Magic fingers," she repeated.

Magic...an image rose in his mind...flames...blue fire...a woman dressed in oversized clothes...a ghostly form hovering over him, but when he reached out for her, she evaded him.

Like a silent movie, a scene played in his mind's eye:

He shows her how to work a hand held can opener. a simple task made complex by explaining it.

"Why is this metal so light?" A musical voice.

"It's aluminum," he says. "Close it hard so the wheel goes into the can top."

It slips from her hands, clatters on the floor. Laughter.

He looks up, trying to remember her face, but she is only a blur.

Her name. He remembers her name. If he calls her, names her, he will see her face.

"Siobhan – "

The image fades, and Brant falls into darkness.

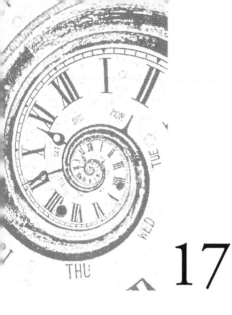

17

Hours later Maeve walked the corridor in the Maywood Clinic. The lobby wasn't large enough to pace, and the other people waiting there had looked at her as if afraid she was a patient about to go berserk. So she had retreated to the hallway off the lobby.

The officer assigned to protect her peered around the corner occasionally, taking his assignment seriously. She didn't know him. He was young, only a year or so on the job. She threatened to have him fired if he called Rich, so he reluctantly agreed and, with her in his squad car, followed the ambulance that took Brant to the clinic.

She glanced at her watch again. After eight. She had been here three hours.

The paramedics said he was catatonic. It was such an awful word. They asked her if he had taken drugs. She didn't know. Brant just stared off into another world, not responding to any of their questions.

Maeve insisted they take him to the Maywood Clinic even though Portland General was closer. She finally said to the driver, "Oh, for God's sake. If it's money, I'll pay for the damned ride." She took out her wallet and handed him her MasterCard.

Her assigned officer glared the man down until he agreed to drive the 15 miles to the Clinic.

Maeve looked at her watch for the thousandth time. Liz Barrett strode through the No Admittance doors from the emergency room. She appeared calm.

"What in God's name is wrong with him, Liz?" Maeve said.

She was now convinced that things would never be the same again. The Brant she had known – the man who was her brother, who had taken care of her after their mother died – was gone.

Liz shook her head. "We might have to transfer him to General, Maeve. He's totally unresponsive. Perhaps a seizure of some sort. We really don't know. If it is a seizure, it's massive, and we don't have the facilities here to treat him. He needs a neurologist. I have to tell you it could be a…."

"What?"

"A stroke, but – "

"Oh, God." Maeve's legs felt rubbery. She leaned back against the wall.

Liz put a hand on Maeve's shoulder. "Or it could be something minor," Liz said. "We won't know for a while. General has a helicopter. They're just waiting for me to tell them to come."

Maeve hugged her arms across her chest, acutely aware of the medicinal smell of the place. People stepped around her and Liz, not looking at them.

"I know I should have had the ambulance take him there," Maeve said. "But I wanted him here. I didn't know what else to do – "

"We're waiting on the tox screen. His vitals are good. You did the right thing, Maeve."

Maeve nodded, tears filling her eyes.

Liz took her arm. "Why don't you come to the cafeteria with me and get a cup of coffee or something? You look beat, and I never had dinner."

Maeve shook her head. "Neither did I." It was a long time since breakfast with Brant.

She turned and beckoned to the young officer who followed close behind them down the hall.

Maeve was conscious of her tousled hair and dirt-spotted jeans and t-shirt beside Liz's crisp doctor whites and ash blond hair neatly pulled back with a clip.

A few minutes later, seated with Liz and the officer, Maeve sipped a cup of strong coffee, staring at a stale vending machine sandwich. Liz's pager beeped. She glanced at it and said, "Come on." She rose, ignoring the debris on the table. "Let's go."

Maeve hurried after Liz. Her heart pounded, and a sour feeling flared in her gut. She tried telling herself things would be all right.

At the door through which Maeve could not pass, Liz turned and touched her arm. "I'll let you know as soon as I can." She swiped her ID card and stepped through the door when it opened just enough to admit her.

Helplessness flooded through Maeve. She leaned against the wall, trembling. She stared at the door, willed it to open, afraid that it would.

Her bodyguard looked nervous. "Can I do anything, ma'am?" he said.

Maeve shook her head.

"We need to call your husband, Ms. Gordon," he said. "I'm already in a lot of trouble."

"Don't call," Maeve said. "Wait and see what's going on." Although she felt a desperate need to have Rich beside her, she did not want to cause the rookie any grief.

The door moved toward her. Startled, Maeve stepped back. Liz grinned and beckoned. "Come on," she said. "Damnedest thing I ever saw. He's awake and talking. Like nothing happened."

"Siobhan – "

Brant calls her name. Her face is indistinct, her whole form is fading. Like a dream. He tries to hold on to the memory, but it eludes him. Finally, the face grows so insubstantial he sees the interior of the cabin right through her.

But he was not at the cabin. He was home.

Magic....

"Siobhan," he calls to her dimming form. He wants to cling to her, keep her from leaving....

"Brant. Brant."

He followed the sound of his name. Opened his eyes to harsh light. Blank white ceiling. Medical apparatus lined the walls. A face haloed by white light.

"Brant."

"What?" he said. He did not want whoever it was to see how disappointed he was that it wasn't the face from his dream. It was a doctor. He couldn't remember her name.

The face vanished, another appeared.

"Brant. Are you all right?" The alleged sister.

"Yeah. Only when I laugh."

"What?" Maeve frowned.

"You know," he said, "it only hurts when I laugh."

She stared at him.

"I'm tired," he said.

The doctor's face again. "Could we have a moment, Maeve? I'd like to talk to him."

Maeve nodded and left.

"How'd I get here?" he demanded. "I was home – "

"We think you may have had some sort of seizure," the doctor said. "I'd like you to stay at least overnight. Remember what we talked about when you were here before?"

Her name was Liz. Liz Barrett. She had told him it would be a good idea to check himself in for treatment. He didn't want the shrink in his mind.

– anathema to invade someone's mind –

A soft, musical voice. Where the hell had it come from? Didn't schizophrenics hear voices? Do terrible things? Van Gogh –

"Do you remember, Brant?" Liz's voice was insistent, sharp.

He nodded. Hell, maybe he *was* coming apart. "Yeah," he said. "I worked hard for a nervous breakdown. I deserve it – "

"We don't call them that anymore. Well, what about it?"

"I'll stay," he conceded and tried to grin. "I'm too freaking tired to go home."

"Longer than last time?"

He nodded, acquiescent. Too tired even to play the game. She was pretty. Nice eyes. Hair like –

"I'll stay." He sighed and closed his eyes.

It was after ten when Rich waved at the young officer in the patrol car in front of his apartment building. The officer waved back and pulled away. Shift change. Now he was the one on duty. He didn't know how much longer he could justify the guard on his wife. He had gotten no closer to answers about Kirk Morgan during his shift. He had more questions.

He unlocked the security door. Clean and well kept, the building was located in a neighborhood that had once been fashionable, but was now quietly decaying. During the day children played outside, old women walked their poodles, and men sat on lawn chairs on the sidewalk playing chess and checkers. Not fashionable, but respectable. It was a diverse population, but still safe.

He and Maeve had talked not long ago – before Brant disappeared – about having a baby, moving to the burbs. They liked this neighborhood, but a child would need more space. A house. They could afford it.

Rich opened the apartment door, wood worn smooth and darkened from decades of use. Living here since they were married had made it possible to sock away most of Maeve's salary into savings and investments. They'd been lucky during the stock market downturn. Their accounts were conservative, making maybe four percent, while others he knew had lost 30 percent of their savings. A small gain, or staying even, was better than a loss.

"Hey, babe," he called. Silence and darkness greeted him.

"Maeve?" The stillness was disconcerting. He flipped on a light.

She sat at the table in the dark kitchen with her hands around a cup of tea, head bent over, long dark hair loose, nearly trailing into the cup. She looked up. Her eyes were red and puffy.

"What's wrong, honey?" he said.

Tears trickled down her cheeks, and her lips trembled. He was not accustomed to a weepy Maeve. It seemed lately she was always on the verge of tears. He put his arms around her and held her against his chest until the sobs let up.

"Now can you tell me what happened?" He grabbed a couple of tissues from the box in front of her and gently wiped her eyes.

She told him about the day's events.

"And then," she said, "he was fine and agreed to stay at the clinic."

"Why didn't you call me, or let the uniform call me?"

"I made him promise not to. You didn't need another crisis on your plate. He was with me and brought me home, so I was perfectly safe."

"Oh, honey." He hugged her. "You know I'm here for you."

"I know. I should have told you."

"Is there anything I can do now?"

She shook her head. "This is way beyond him forgetting us. It's downright creepy. I just hope the doctors figure out what the hell happened to him. Something is very wrong with him, Rich. He's not the brother I've known all my life."

Rich cradled her face in both hands. "Look at me, Maeve," he said. "I know this is hard. You just have to have a little faith in him. Somewhere inside him is the Brant we used to know. I'm convinced something happened at that cabin. Maybe it has something to do with your mother and father and your grandparents. Maybe not. But I'm not giving up on him, and you shouldn't either. Just give him a little time. I'm still working on some stuff. Still trying to track down Morgan's story. I think there's a connection somehow between him and your family – other than attorney-client. I think he did a hell of a lot more than just prepare your parents' wills." He squeezed her arms. "Do you trust me?"

She nodded. "I love you, Rich."

He gathered her close and said softly into her hair. "I love you, too."

She spoke into his shirt, her voice muffled. "Thanks for being here."

"Not to change the subject, but when did you last eat?"

"Breakfast – "

"Okay," he said, helping her up from the stool. "We're going to get some dinner." Food alleviated a multitude of problems. "Some of the gang from the precinct are going to the Mexican place. Their kitchen is open till midnight. You could do with a change. And you have to eat."

"Sure," she said. "Why not."

They might not be able to help Brant right now, but if Rich dug deep enough he might find some answers to his questions about Kirk Morgan's involvement with his wife's family.

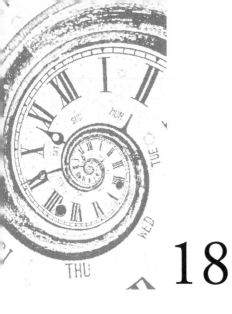

18

Siobhan heard a rhythmic pounding that reverberated through her mind and made her head hurt. She stood in a meadow surrounded by forest. Beside her Bran sat on the grass, picking wildflowers. He was very young, barely walking. A breeze that smelled of fresh grass and clover ruffled his dark baby curls. Birds gossiped in the trees. The pounding was not a pony's hooves, but the thud, thud-thud of a heavy steed laboring under a load. A horse burst from the forest, headed straight for Bran.

The beast was huge and black as a starless night. It galloped closer. Its form was indistinct, wrapped in shadows, an oily darkness that writhed and eddied around it.

Bran looked up and held out his chubby arms. Siobhan reached for him. The horse thundered toward her son, and Siobhan knew she would not be able to pull him to safety in time.

Astride the dark horse sat a figure clothed in deeper darkness. She could not see his face, if indeed he had one. Siobhan's only hope of saving her precious Bran was to snatch him away to her safe place. But she must be touching him. He was too far away. Her arms would not reach far enough. She stretched, and Bran was further away.

The pounding grew louder....

Siobhan opened her eyes, and the dream fell away like wet snow sluiced from the hills by spring rain.

"Siobhan!" Someone called her name and pounded on her chamber door.

"Yes?" She struggled upright.

"Unbar the door, Lady Siobhan."

Gareth. His words filled Siobhan with dread. Had her spells of protection for Bran been overcome by some devious act? Had the druid done something terrible?

The fire had long since gone out. The room was cold. She stumbled out of bed and summoned a warming spell. Why was it that human emergencies so often happened in the dark of night? Calling up a *Sidhe* light, she set it to follow above her to guide her way.

She banished the spell on the door and pulled it open. Gareth's face bore haggard lines of grief.

"What is it, Gareth?" Siobhan used his given name without regard for propriety.

"My lady," he said, his voice breathless, "it is the lady Bebhinn. Please come."

Siobhan's heart thumped. "What has happened?"

"Bebhinn is ill, and the druid's daughter refuses the aid of all who offer."

"Of course I will come," Siobhan said. Her knowledge of healing was limited to herbal concoctions that eased pain and gave comfort. But she would not have the druid witch near someone she loved. She stepped into the corridor wearing only her nightdress.

Gareth looked at her bare feet. "Will you not be cold?"

"No. Fear not," Siobhan said.

He would have said more, she knew from his thoughts, but he stayed his tongue.

"What is wrong with Bebhinn?" she said.

"Nobody knows for certain. I heard one of the serving girls say she should not have dealt with the druid's daughter – "

"Why would she treat with the witch?"

"Bebhinn is old. Her heart has been ailing. She has dizzy spells."

"She said nothing."

"That is her way," Gareth said, maintaining the distance between them. "I gave her my oath I would not reveal her weakness."

Siobhan quailed at the idea of the druidess treating Bebhinn. Many women of the o'Ruairc compound bought potions from Lassariona. Some of the herbal preparations had little efficacy, but most had no properties whatever, or simply covered the symptoms they were supposed to treat. Some had no basis in herb lore and were downright harmful.

Siobhan walked with Gareth in silence, keeping her mind within itself. Bebhinn lay on her bed, unmoving, swathed in furs and homespun wool, only her face showing. Several women gathered around, showing their respect and giving what comfort they could. A peat fire glowed on the hearth, augmented with a few sticks of wood, but the room was still damp and cold.

Bran stood near the hearth, his eyes wide. At twelve years of age he had seen death numerous times. Siobhan saw from the maelstrom of his thoughts that Bebhinn's impending death affected him much more than even when his cousin, Liam the Harper, had died in Bran's arms after a fall from his horse.

Bran hurried to Siobhan. "Mother. Is there nothing to be done?" His eyes were teary.

Siobhan shook her head. "Hold, child. I do not know." She approached the bed. Bebhinn barely breathed. The only sounds in the room were women's sniffling.

A tall figure in a rough-woven robe rose from a stool beside the sleeping pallet. A slender hand threw back the hood, revealing fiery red hair.

The druidess glared at Siobhan.

"Lassariona." Siobhan gazed into the sea-green eyes and spoke quietly. "You do not belong here."

"I have as much right to be here as one of the *Sidhe*." Lassariona's head tilted back in arrogant defiance.

"You will leave," Siobhan said.

Lassariona raised her eyebrows. She assessed Siobhan with an intensity that would force mortals to look away.

"You will leave," Siobhan repeated, "or I will turn my power on you. You know that is not an idle threat."

Lassariona glowered at Siobhan. Siobhan glanced around at the stony faces of the now silent women. She opened her mind to them and found that, although they feared Lassariona, there was little support for the druidess. She gazed at Lassariona, her eyes unwavering. Finally, the other woman gave a slight shrug and looked away.

"I will go," Lassariona said. "But you cannot keep me from treating the women who request my services."

"No," Siobhan said, "but I can set a spell on the gate that will prevent you from entering. I doubt that many would take advantage of your arts if they had to trudge through the cold rain to your cottage."

"You would not –"

"I would." Siobhan said.

Lassariona glanced around. No one spoke for her. She pulled the hood up over her hair and stomped haughtily to the door.

Siobhan had won only a minor skirmish. Lassariona would not give up easily. Her sales of herbal elixirs and poultices were lucrative. No other large steading was near enough to afford her the opportunity the o'Ruairc holding did. Siobhan watched the druid woman leave. Even in defeat Lassariona commanded the attention of every person in the room. Gareth watched her with a soft sigh of longing.

Siobhan bent to Bebhinn. An unnatural pallor marked the woman's skin. Death would claim her before dawn.

"Bran," Siobhan said quietly. "Bring my herb pouch from my bedchamber. And do not dawdle."

Without a word Bran hurried from the room. Siobhan motioned for Gareth. He followed her to stand beside the hearth. The tension within him was plain to see by his furrowed brow. His eyes reflected the fire's glow.

"Bebhinn will die," she stated. "There is little I can do for her other than to ease the way."

"Is it not within your powers to heal her?" Gareth said.

"It is not. Her heart fails. Lassariona did the poor woman more harm than good. Her potions only hid the symptoms. If I had known of Bebhinn's ill health sooner I might have been able to seek help for her."

"Can you not do *anything*?" Gareth said.

"Gareth," Siobhan said and surreptitiously summoned a small spell of comfort for his distressed thoughts, "healing others is beyond my skill. Each of my people has special gifts. Would that mine was curing the ills of another's body. I know about certain herbs, how to alleviate some pains. I can help a troubled mind, but I can heal aught besides myself. And that without my active participation. There is nothing I can do for Bebhinn. It is too late. But if you will sit with me and help me with the herbs, I can make her way into the other world less painful, less bewildering."

Gareth nodded. Siobhan wished with all her heart that healing had been her gift. But wishing could not make it so. Bebhinn was beyond even an accomplished healer's arts, too far into the next world to be brought back.

Bran returned with Siobhan's herb pouch, and she and Gareth dispersed the others.

Siobhan directed Gareth in the making of a strong tea from a mixture of herbs. It would only dull the pain and ease the mind. She spooned it into Bebhinn's mouth, blowing on each spoonful. The old woman swallowed convulsively a few times and then was still. Siobhan drank the dregs of the tea and sat on the floor beside the bed.

Bran and Gareth stood indecisively by the doorway as if to guard it from Death's intrusion.

"No matter what you see," Siobhan said to them, "do not interfere. If you do you could endanger not only me and Bebhinn, but both of you as well. The journey to and from the Land of the Dead is not an easy one."

They both nodded. Bran suddenly looked more grown up than his 12 years. Gareth put a comforting hand on the boy's shoulder. Siobhan wished she could offer them a sleeping spell, but she would need all her energy for the voyage with Bebhinn.

"Gareth," Siobhan said. "You must tell Murchad that Bebhinn is dying. He will wish to prepare a burial in keeping with his Christian belief."

Gareth nodded and left the chamber.

Siobhan smiled sadly at Bran. "Come closer, child," she said. "All of us die one way or another. It is nothing to fear. The fear comes from being unprepared for the journey."

The boy hesitated and then approached and sat at the foot of the bed. His gaze never left his mother. She fought the urge to send him a spell. She had already used some precious strength to warm herself and summon light. The spell that eased Gareth's mind was further energy lost. But Siobhan owed Bebhinn, her truest friend, the comfort only she could give. It would require much of her strength.

Siobhan closed her eyes, pushed away all sensory stimuli, forced her mind outward, questing for the spark of Bebhinn's awareness.

There. Far away, almost lost in the vast darkness.

"Bebhinn," she called in her mind. No answer. She floated closer to the glow. Shadowy shapes fluttered around her, brushed against her as they passed. She could not waste time on them. "Bebhinn, Bebhinn." Speaking the name thrice invoked the enchantment.

"Lady...." Bebhinn's mind was faint.

"I am glad I have found you," Siobhan said.

"Why are you looking for me?"

"I have come to take you across," Siobhan said.

"It is dark."

"I know," Siobhan said. "But beyond, the light awaits you. I will guide you to it."

"I have been searching for a long time, lady, but all I see is darkness. Perhaps the light is not there to find."

"Oh, it is. You do not know where to look." The little glow that marked Bebhinn's being faded away, and Siobhan glided in the direction she thought it had gone. It seemed she went a long distance before she found it again.

"Do not be afraid, Bebhinn."

"Afraid?" Bebhinn's mental voice was confused. "I just wish I could find the way back."

Siobhan reached out an insubstantial hand, groped for Bebhinn's, found it. The hand was cold, and it trembled. "You cannot go back. Come with me. You have served me long and well. It is time to go."

"I cannot leave you," the woman protested. "What of Bran?"

"Bran is nearly a man. He has little need of a nurse," Siobhan reassured her. She gently pulled the woman along.

Siobhan led her friend through stormy darkness, through unseen winds that howled and tore at them, trying to rip Bebhinn's hand from Siobhan's grip. She clothed herself in glamor and held fast to the other woman. Finally, after a long time, they arrived at the edge of a chasm of even deeper darkness.

Siobhan stopped and turned to Bebhinn. "I can go no further. I can only offer comfort and some protection. The perils you will face as you cross the void are very real indeed, but if you cling to the memory of my spells, you will cross uninjured. If you give in to the terrors that beset you and lose the image of my face, you will be lost. You will not arrive at the light on the other side."

"Will it be enough?" Bebhinn's voice was tremulous.

"I took you safely this far," Siobhan said. "Will you trust me?"

"It is so wide. How will I cross?"

"Look into my face, Bebhinn. You will cross on a memory. Remember the Kerry mare? The one that carried me faithfully for so many years? She was sturdy and sure-footed and willing. Remember how sleek her sides were and how fleet she was?"

Bebhinn nodded. "I remember you loved her, lady."

"Hold fast to the memory," Siobhan said. She invoked the spell that would aid and comfort Bebhinn on the way. She could not go further. Even *Sidhe* enchantment could not overcome death itself. Using all her strength, Siobhan sent the spell to Bebhinn.

Azure fire swirled beside the other woman's light, then coalesced into the shape of the Kerry mare, just as Siobhan remembered her. The horse pranced and pawed, its hoofs striking sparks. Starlight glinted in her flowing mane and tail. Her sleek brown flanks glistened as though sprinkled with moonlight.

"Mount, Bebhinn," Siobhan said, "before it is too late."

The small glow leaped to the mare's back. For a moment Siobhan saw the outline of Bebhinn's form, not old and bent, but young and vital, her long, dark hair blowing in an unseen breeze.

The mare tossed her head and stamped impatiently. Its ears pricked and it lowered its muzzle to Siobhan's gentle hand.

"Remember," Siobhan impressed upon the other woman.

"Will I see Connor like the holy man from the abbey says?"

Siobhan nodded, remembering the husband Bebhinn often spoke of. "Yes. He is waiting on the other side."

"I will remember," Bebhinn said.

Siobhan reached up and squeezed the other woman's hand while the memory-horse danced in place.

"Fare you well, Bebhinn," Siobhan said. She hoped the darkness hid her tears.

"Fare you well, woman of the *Sidhe*," the tiny spark that was Bebhinn said. "Thank you for your friendship."

"Thank you for being my friend," Siobhan whispered. She slapped the horse's flank. "Fly, horse. Carry her safely."

With a shower of light the mare leaped into the void. In a moment the glow that was Bebhinn faded into darkness.

Siobhan stood on the precipice, knowing that every moment she tarried used more of her energy. She peered into the darkness until her eyes burned and her head ached. Finally she was rewarded by a distant flash that signaled Bebhinn's arrival on the further shore.

Siobhan drifted back to her body, wishing the invisible currents would wash her mind clean of grief.

"Lady. Lady." Gareth's voice. "Siobhan." The sound rushed through her head, pounded inside with an angry pain.

Siobhan slumped beside Bebhinn's lifeless form. Raw grief and exhaustion stole her breath away. At the foot of the bed Bran sobbed. Siobhan stroked his hair, smooth and dark as a raven's wing.

"Lady?" Gareth said. Concern trembled in his voice.

"See to the boy, will you?" Siobhan said. "Get one of the women to put him to bed. He needs to vent his sorrow." Gareth left and returned shortly with one of the household women who led Bran away.

Gareth assisted Siobhan to her feet.

"Thank you," Siobhan said. His hands were strong on her arms.

"I did little enough."

"You are here as you once promised me you would be," she said. "It is enough."

Siobhan drew away from Gareth. She felt an echo of his touch on her skin.

The monk from the abbey entered the room, moving quietly, his tonsured head bowed. William was the monk's given name. He had wed Siobhan and Murchad. Brother William never hung back in awe of Siobhan, but approached her.

He looked directly into her eyes. "Are you finished, lady?" She nodded. The monk continued, "Thank you for doing what I could not. I gave Bebhinn the Sacraments, but I could not offer her the physical comfort you did."

"You do not fear me."

The monk shook his head. "It has been my experience these many years that your powers are benevolent. They could only have come from the God I believe in. You are blessed with a unique gift and have chosen to use it wisely, my lady. I thank you again."

He moved toward Bebhinn and softly directed the women who would prepare her body for burial.

Drained of her powers, Siobhan allowed Gareth to guide her to her own bedchamber. Grief was a raw ache inside her. Neither she nor Gareth broke the silence during the slow journey. Gareth opened Siobhan's door. A wail filled with terrible sadness echoed throughout the dwelling. Siobhan shivered in spite of the warming spell that still lingered in the room.

"Bainsidhe," she explained, seeing the puzzlement on his face. "Once it was *Sidhe*, but for some reason it gave up its enchanted life. Perhaps it had lived so long immortality held no attraction. Now but a disembodied spirit, it wanders the night when death's darkness is close to the mortal world. When someone dies, it howls, hoping to capture the dead spirit and mesh with it for a few brief moments of living in the real world. It will find no prey in this dwelling tonight.

"Fear not. It cannot hurt the living. Bebhinn is safely gone and away. The *bainsidhe* may wail and moan all it likes. It will depart empty-handed with the morning light."

"Sleep well," Gareth said and closed Siobhan's door.

She collapsed into bed and fell into a dark, dreamless sleep.

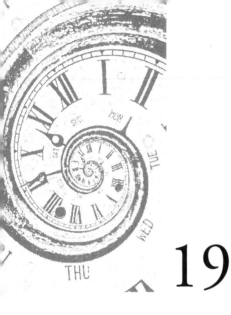

19

A A scream of mortal agony in Brant's dream. It could not be real. It had to be a dream. The wail went on and on. He wanted to wake up, and yet the dream sucked him in, tantalized him with a promise of some great secret about to be revealed.

Paralysis gripped him. He could not move. Blue light glowed, barely lighting a woman's face that floated over him. He smelled flowers and damp fog. Warm fingers brushed his cheek. The woman's lips moved, but he heard nothing, only the silence of the wilderness outside the cabin.

He felt warmth in his groin, the beginning of an erection. Besides a visceral lust, he was overwhelmed by a fierce protectiveness for this woman whose face he could not quite see. If only he could take her hand and hold on to her forever.

He tried to reach out for her, but could not move. Her features blurred, like a reflected image broken by ripples on a pond's surface. She became more insubstantial, ghost-like, and then evaporated like mist.

He threw off the down comforter and put his feet on the cold floor. There was nobody else in the cabin. She could not have vanished. She had to be somewhere. An azure glow emanated from the bathroom. It reminded him of the sky on a warm summer day when not even a cloud or jet contrail marred the blueness. He went to the bathroom door and peered in. Empty. A bluish spark like static flickered along the shelf above the sink, fading as he watched. He was left with a feeling of utter emptiness.

Brant blinked –

– and awoke in a dark room, his head pounding. The clock radio beside the bed read 4:52. He looked for the familiar outlines of his bedroom: the old armoire he'd bought at an auction, his mother's quilt stand – where his father used to hang his sport coat when he came home from work. The quilt stand had been his maternal grandmother's – who had died when Brant was 14. She had brought it with her on the boat from Ireland.

His eyes adjusted to the dimness of his hospital room. He had checked himself in, admitted he needed help. Suddenly he wanted to leave, go somewhere far away. But where could he go? The dream place? The cabin was real, but the woman was just a dream. It seemed authentic, more like a memory. Even now he was awake the images remained vivid and his physical reaction was tangible.

He rose from the bed with its sweaty, knotted sheet and blanket and padded to an overstuffed chair in one corner. He sat there and stared into the darkness. It was the first time since his return from the cabin that he had tried to sort out what was happening to him. How could he connect his present state to a past where he had supposedly forgotten he had a sister and a brother-in-law?

He remembered that Pollard gushed over his new paintings – two had already sold for twice as much as Brant's best landscapes. But he didn't remember painting them. His memories could account for a few sketches and a few canvasses. Then that woman had taken care of the delivery of the paintings and – nothing. He didn't remember anything after that. He'd come to in the emergency room of the Maywood Clinic hours later.

He must face reality: something had gone very wrong in his life. He had to put it right. So he'd agreed to stay. At least it would get that cop, Detective Whatever-his-name-was off his case for a few days.

After awhile his eyelids grew heavy, and he leaned back in the chair.

"Brant?"

Startled, Brant opened his eyes to sunlight. There was a kink in his neck. He rolled his head, trying to stretch the muscles.

"Sorry I barged in." Liz Barrett stood in the doorway. "But the door was open. Bad night?"

"I forgot how early hospitals get you up," Brant said.

"Hey," she said, smiling, "it's 7:00. The best part of the morning. How about I give you an hour to shower, get dressed and eat something?" She gestured to his breakfast tray on the table beside the bed.

He nodded.

"Okay," she said. "Meet me in my office."

"Sure. Haven't got anyplace else to go."

Fifty-four minutes later, another cup of coffee in hand, Brant rapped lightly on Liz's office door.

"Come in," she said.

He entered, and she waved to one of the chairs in front of her desk. She sat in the other one beside him and turned slightly toward him.

"So," she said, "how are you, Brant?"

"Headaches. They're really bad. Mentally....Maybe I'm ready for the rubber room."

Liz laughed. "We don't do that much anymore."

The furnishings in the office were comfortable, two wing back chairs facing her dark wood desk, a leather executive chair behind the desk, a recliner and an armless couch with one end slightly raised. Soft shades of greens and blues. Exactly what he pictured a shrink's office would look like.

She had a disconcerting way of looking him straight in the eye. She said nothing. Perhaps it was a technique to get him to speak.

Finally he sighed. "I guess I'm in trouble," he said.

"Want to talk about it?"

"I'm not sure," he started. "It's weird. It's...." A twinge of pain behind his left eye.

"Go ahead. It might seem less weird if you tell me."

"Christ," he said. "I think I'm having a middle age crisis or something." He rose and paced across the room. "I remember looking out this window before. Doesn't seem like it was only a week ago. Those picnic tables out there under the trees? I remember thinking they looked pathetic in the rain with nobody sitting at them."

"What's wrong, Brant?"

He didn't turn. "Dreams...."

"Dreams?" she prompted.

"Nightmares. They're pretty confused. I dream about being at the cabin. There's a woman there. Someone I know, but I can't quite see her face. She's blurry, as if I see her through a camera lens that's out of focus. Nothing makes sense, and I'm...well, scared as hell."

"Does that bother you?

"What?"

"Being scared?"

"God, yes."

"What are you afraid of?"

"I don't know. But I don't want to see what happens in the next scene of the dream. It's like something terrible is about to happen. It's always the same thing." He told her about the woman bending over him. "It's in vivid color, and I can hear her talking, but I don't understand the words, as if she's speaking some other language. And I can feel her fingers on my face and smell her – "

He turned back to the window, spoke softly. "I can smell her. I've got a hard-on – sorry, an erection – but it's more than that. More than just a wet dream. It's a longing so powerful I think I'll die. But she floats away from me, and when I get out of bed, wanting her more than anything in my life, she's gone."

He went to the couch and sat on the edge. "I think I'm going nuts."

He told her about spending three days and nights painting and not remembering most of it and having no idea why he'd painted impressionistic, erotic angels clothed in diaphanous gowns whose faces weren't quite in focus.

"But," he finished, "two of the paintings have sold. Pollard – my agent at the gallery – thinks I might be the new Picasso or something."

He clasped his hands together. "I thought it didn't matter," he said. "I thought I could function without those two missing weeks. I was wrong. Something happened to me, Liz. The goddamned dreams are driving me nuts. The headaches are awful. Every time I try to think about that time, my head hurts so much I think it'll fall off in my lap."

"You *want* to get to the bottom of this, Brant?" Her gentle smile reassured him. Her words were welcome. They took responsibility away from him. He didn't have to make a conscious decision.

"Yeah, I do," he said. "I've got to know. No matter what."

"Even if there are things you won't like?"

He thought for a moment, then nodded. "I'm sure there will be." A spark of interest flashed in her eyes.

"Okay, then," Liz said. "I'll get the paperwork started. You can sign it later. Detective Gordon brought you some clothes and things this morning."

"I just want to know why I lost two weeks of my life."

He winced as a sharp pain sliced across his head from temple to temple.

"Does your head hurt now?" She rose from the chair.

"Christ," he said. "Hurt isn't the word. I think you give me a pain in the head." When she didn't respond, he said, "Levity, Doc. Humor."

"I seem to have that effect on some people. Does the pain suggest anything to you, Brant?" Her voice was quiet.

"What should it suggest?" he snapped. His head throbbed. He had to think between throbs. Disjointed thoughts. He couldn't focus on anything in particular.

"Well," she said, "I've noticed that when you talk about the missing time, you get a headache."

"What's it mean?"

"You tell me, Brant."

"You're the shrink, you're supposed to tell me – oh, shit." He sighed. "I don't know. The pills you gave me don't do much. They just make me a little goofy, but don't take away the pain." He rubbed his temples, but it brought no relief.

"Maybe your subconscious doesn't want to remember. Perhaps something happened that your mind can't face, and your subconscious has blocked it. The mind is devious, Brant, and amazingly self-protective."

"So what do we do? You're the expert."

"I called a colleague who suggests hypnosis. There isn't an organic reason for the pain."

"Psychosomatic?" He groaned. "It hurts like hell."

"Oh, the pain is very real. It could be your mind shying away from remembering something traumatic. Would you submit to hypnosis?"

He raised his eyebrows. "What if something horrible did happen?"

"No guarantees," she said. "That's a chance you take. But if it was something bad, your mind might come to terms with it if it were out in the open. Maybe it's not something you did, but something you saw, or *thought* you saw."

"Will I know what's happening?" he said. She shook her head. "Will I remember what I say?"

"Only if your subconscious wants your conscious mind to deal with it," she said. "Do you want some time to think about it?"

"Hell no," he said. "I'll do it. But I've got to go lie down. My head's about to split." He rose. This headache was the all-time worst.

"After lunch?" she said, rising too. She moved toward him. "I think we should get right on this."

He nodded. "Assuming the headache goes away by then, I'm willing." He opened the door.

"Would you like to get out of here for awhile?" Liz said. "Go to a movie or out to dinner with friends?"

He shook his head. "I don't think I have any friends at the moment. Except that cop's wife who says she's my sister."

"You could go out anytime, Brant. We're not a prison, you know."

Brant turned to go.

"Brant," she said, "don't be afraid of what hypnosis will tell us. People don't do things that violate their value system unless there's an overriding reason – at least not sane people. And you're sane, Brant, if that's what's bothering you. You're not schizophrenic. Get some rest. I'll see you after lunch."

"Thanks," he said over his shoulder. The pounding in his head let up a bit.

Dr. David Carson, PhD, the hypnotherapist, was a rotund man with graying hair. When he smiled his entire face lit up. He assured Brant the procedure would be painless. Brant reclined on the couch in Liz's office. The clock on the wall said 1:30. Carson told him to watch a penlight. Brant tracked it back and forth, back and forth, and then suddenly, it was a few minutes after three.

"Where'd the time go?" Brant said.

"You were an easy subject," Carson said. "Very suggestible." The man's expression was unreadable.

Brant eyed him skeptically. "I won't start quacking like a duck, will I, Dr. Carson?"

Carson laughed, a deep chuckle that shook his belly. "I'm not a stage magician. There should be no aftereffects whatsoever."

"What happened?" Brant said. Did he really want to know?

"Liz will talk to you about it later."

"Why don't I remember anything?"

"Perhaps it'll take some time," Carson said. "We shall see."

"I feel wired," Brant said. Then to Liz: "Is it all right if I go for a walk?"

"Of course. Have a nice time. Just check out at the desk so security doesn't think they've lost you."

"Thanks, I think, Doc." Brant shook Carson's hand. The hand was damp and warm.

"Perhaps we'll have another session," Carson said.

Brant waved over his shoulder on his way out. He would love to be invisible and listen to the conversation after he left. But there was the niggling thought that he didn't want to know what had happened. When he got outside he put his questions aside and lost himself in exercise.

The day was chilly and bright. Clouds built to the west and might mean a cold, wet night. He walked for more than an hour, first exploring the park-like acres surrounding the hospital complex, then down the street to a small neighborhood commercial district. An independent bookstore advertised newspapers, free wi-fi and pastries and specialty coffees. He bought a newspaper and a large cappuccino and sat and drank and read until he realized it would dark by 4:30.

After dinner, Brant sat in Liz's office finishing the latest of too many coffees. Outside cold rain misted down, prelude to a storm the weather forecasts said would cover most of western Oregon and Washington. The National Weather Service had posted winter storm warnings for the Cascades. The cabin would be beautiful in the snow, nestled beneath old growth Douglas firs. A small throb of discomfort tugged at one temple. He switched his memory to a time he'd been at the cabin with his father. The time Dad had shown him the papers making Brant and his mother co-owners with him.

"That way," his father said, "when I'm gone, it doesn't have to be probated. It'll be Mom's, and then yours when she's gone."

Had his father known that the following spring, he'd be dead? That less than two years later, his wife would die when her car hit a tree?

Brant remembered that time at the cabin clearly: the smell of the wood they had chopped, smoke from the fireplace, his father's aftershave, a slightly citrus fragrance.

"You feel all right?" Liz said. She sat in the chair beside him.

"Thinking about my dad," he said. "And being with him at the cabin when it snowed. It was beautiful. Before Weyerhauser clear cut most of the land around ours. I still have about 20 acres of virgin timber. I used to go and cut a Christmas tree for – " He wasn't sure what he was going to say. He didn't understand the image in his mind.

"What?" Liz prompted.

"I remember cutting a small tree and putting it in a truck. I remember unloading it at home, decorating it, and putting presents under it for somebody. But I can't remember who."

"How old were you?"

"It was after Mom died, so I must have been 24 or so. It happened in my parents' house before I sold it. But I can't for the life of me remember who else was there."

"Does your head hurt now, Brant?"

"No."

"Good," she said. "I'd like you to take this." She handed him a pill and a paper cup of water.

He eyed it suspiciously. "What is it?"

"A mild sedative. It'll only last a few hours."

"Why?"

"I'm going to let you listen to the tape of your hypnosis session this afternoon. That's why I called you in so late. Dr. Carson and a couple of other staff psychiatrists and I had a long discussion about this. We decided you should hear it. The pill isn't strong. Doctors prescribe it for fearful fliers. You won't feel woozy or have a hangover. It'll just take the edge off your anxiety."

"I don't remember feeling anxious."

"No, you wouldn't. And nothing may happen. It's just a precaution."

"Well," he said, "*Sláinte*," and he downed the pill with a gulp of water.

"Brant," Liz said, "remember, our minds sometimes perceive things as we *think* they are, not as they *really* are. Like sometimes when you see something out of the corner of your eye and you think it's one thing, but when you look at it a half second later, you realize it's something else entirely."

He nodded.

Liz set the recorder on the desk and pressed play.

Carson's voice gave the date and time and named himself, and Brant's voice did the same, and then Liz identified herself as a witness. Then Carson's voice telling Brant to watch the light. He droned on for several minutes, and then, silence.

After a few seconds Dr. Carson: "Brant, can you hear me?"

"Yes." His voice, curiously flat, lacking its usual timbre.

Carson: "Brant, I want you to go back in time with me."

"All right."

"Back to the last time you were at your cabin. You went there to get away."

"Yes."

"Tell me how you got there."

"It was Halloween. I'd had an argument with my agent. I was pissed. He was pressuring me for two additional paintings that weren't done yet. By the time I got on the road it was almost dark. Foggy. Pea soup. My mother used to call it the kind you can sew buttons on."

"Good, Brant. Tell me what happened after you got to the cabin."

20

The cabin was cold and damp. Brant turned on a battery powered lantern and went to the fireplace where he always left kindling and small, split logs. He touched a match to a twist of newspaper and stuffed it under the grate.

He took the lantern to the porch, but the light didn't penetrate far into the fog. Damn. He should have had the electric turned on. He had thought about it on the drive up, but decided it was wasteful for just a weekend. He opened the back of the Escape and leaned in to get the duffel. A wild thought went through his mind: it must look like he was being swallowed by some gigantic metal beast.

The fog unnerved him. He'd read somewhere that humans' fear of the dark was instinctual. It came from the days when what lay beyond the firelight was unseeable and dangerous.

Brant swung the duffel up and cracked his elbow on the edge of the door opening.

"Shit," he said. The fog flung the sound back at him.

Numbness spread down his arm. The bag slipped from his grip. He straightened and banged the top of his head on the hatch. He rubbed his head, ran his fingers over his scalp. He'd probably have a lump, but there was no blood. He backed away from the car.

Driving up here was a stupid idea. He should have stayed in the city and worked. He never should have gone to the gallery that morning and vented at Pollard.

"Be reasonable," he'd yelled. "I need some down time. I'm an artist, not a nine to fiver who produces a quantifiable product."

He slammed his hand on Pollard's desk, in hindsight a childish temper tantrum. He'd been holding his lucky key ring. The plastic split the skin on his palm and left a drop of blood on the desk. Pollard calmly handed him a tissue and used another to wipe his desk.

"Come back when you're more rational," Pollard said.

Brant had stomped away and slammed the door behind him.

When he got home, still angry, he threw some things in a bag and headed for the cabin. It was quiet, a good place to think. He'd done all the thinking he needed to do on the drive up. He realized he was angry at himself for not finishing the last three paintings.

There wasn't a cell tower for miles. In the morning he would drive far enough to get in a signal and call – who? A crazy woman who claimed to be his sister?

Brant reached in a jeans pocket for his keys to close the hatch. He studied the key ring: a half circle of gold encased in plastic. It was about two inches long and looked like it had been broken from a larger piece. There were designs in the gold, age-worn and barely visible. Brant's mother had given it to him. She said it had been passed to the first-born son for nobody knew how many generations. Her mother had given it to her shortly before she died.

Brant wanted to preserve the artifact, so he had it sealed in plastic. His lucky charm.

A cold draft prickled the back of his neck.

Something moved at the edge of the lantern light in front of the car, barely visible.

"Who's there?" he called.

A girl stood just beyond the front of the car. Brant stepped toward her, his mind awash in conflicting thoughts. She stumbled backward, raised one hand in a defensive stance. Her fingertips were blue. For a second she glowed, but it had to be an illusion, a trick of the light.

She wore a dress of some flimsy material that barely covered her knees. It was stained with mud and…blood? A piece of dark fabric was knotted around her shoulders. Her eyes were dark shadows against her pale skin.

She spoke. It didn't sound like English. She moved back and looked around. There was a wildness in her eyes that disturbed him.

"Are you okay?" Brant said. Hunters sometimes found years-old crashed planes in the wilderness. Had it happened again?

She backed up another step.

He wanted to reach out to her, but she seemed little more than illusion, an apparition in the snow.

She repeated a few words. Definitely not English.

"Was there an accident?" he said. "A plane crash? Car? Are there others?"

If there were more victims, he would have to go for help.

The girl shook her head like a wild creature. Her hair fanned out like gold. Her body went limp. He caught her before she hit the ground.

She felt light and warm in his arms. Dirt and blood smudged her face.

"It's all right," he reassured her. "I'm taking you inside."

She did not open her eyes. He laid her on the bed and went back out for his bag and the lantern. Would the fog have swallowed the sound of a plane? He couldn't see further than the nearest tree branches. Again the back of his neck prickled. His skin crawled. He retreated inside and locked the door.

Brant set the lantern on the bedside stand. The light revealed bruises on the girl's neck and her bare arms. Her lower lip was split and oozing blood. Dirt smudged her skin and dress.

The hospital was 30 miles away. A long drive on twisting roads in the mist that was probably freezing on the paved roads.

Why was she out here in the middle of nowhere? Could she have wandered away from home? The nearest houses had to be eight miles away over mountainous terrain. She was unconscious on his bed. His responsibility.

From habit he dug the cell phone from his pocket and checked again. No service.

Oh, Jesus, what was he going to do?

His grandfather used to say that in his Irish brogue. "Oh, Jaysus."

His mother had scolded him about profanity in front of a child, but Grandda winked at Brant and said it anyway. Brant's kindergarten teacher told him that just because his grandfather said it didn't make it appropriate.

When Grandda had said it, the words rolled off the his tongue, mixed in with his ramblings about the little people and the Deeny Shee – the Fair Folk – and banshees and the green hills of Ireland.

"Oh, Jaysus," Brant said aloud.

Maybe this girl had gotten away from an attacker. Someone who picked up young girls and murdered them. It had happened before. There could be a killer in the woods.

The girl's eyes fluttered. She mumbled, "Murkan." It sounded guttural, like German. A name? Place?

Her eyes widened in panic, and she skittered to the far edge of the bed.

"I won't hurt you," he said.

Her eyes were very blue, disturbingly blue. Unsettling eyes.

A extraneous image filled his mind: the emergency room at Longview Memorial: he had been there twice in his life. Once when he was 12 when his father was shot, and again when his mother died in the car crash. Both times he had gone to the hospital hopefully, but it was too late.

"No, no," the girl said, recognizable English.

"You should see a doctor," he said. "I'll take you." He imagined the headline: *Local Man Finds Lost Child.* "But Officer, I found her in the woods."

The cop would hook his thumbs in his belt and say, "Sure you did, son."

She crouched in the corner of the bed, knees drawn up. One eye was bruised.

"Where did you come from?" he said.

She stared at him.

"Who are you?" he said. "What's your name?" It was a waste of time. She didn't understand English. Or was she deaf?

"Siobhan," she whispered. "I…am…Siobhan…."

So she wasn't deaf.

"I'm Brant Edwards," he said, pointing at himself. "Are you hurt? Where did you come from? Was there an accident – do you speak English?"

She shook her head and reached out to him. He took her hand. A small shock coursed through him, and a faint blue spark of static flickered on his arm.

Her eyes were ice-blue, like a glacial lake. He thought he could drown in them, drown in her lovely eyes until there was no hope of rescue….

"Do not…be…afraid, Brant Edwards." She spoke slowly, forming each word separately. "I…won't hurt…you."

"That's my line."

"Line?" she said. "I not know line. You…helped…me."

"I did, but I think you need medical help."

"No," she said, her voice soft and musical. "I must…get up. I do not think…I can do it alone."

Something was wrong. He should try to convince her to let him take her into town, but he could not think beyond the moment. He helped her stand beside the bed. She swayed and trembled.

"I have to…go…you know." She touched her lower abdomen.

Bathroom. She had to use the bathroom.

"Oh. Yes," he said. "There." He pointed. What if he had to help her?

She stared at him a moment. "Yes, I understand. A bath room." She said it as two distinct words.

Brant held her hand and guided her across the room. In the bathroom he dropped a liner into the bowl of the incinerating toilet.

"If you need help," he said, "call me."

"I am all right." She rolled the r slightly, and her words were precisely enunciated, but they were faster, less uncertain. She touched her forehead and leaned against the door frame. "I feel…dizzy…."

Had she been hurt badly, something that didn't show? He waited a moment, holding her arm. She trembled.

After a moment she stood straighter. "I can do this," she said.

Brant left and shut the door.

After a few moments she called.

He opened the door. She leaned against the sink.

"I'll take care of it," he said.

He closed the toilet lid, stepped on the pedal and pressed the button. The heater and fan came on with a soft whoosh. The toilet was wired separately from the main cabin, always on, and burned propane from a small canister.

The girl jumped back to the doorway, her eyes wide and scared.

"What is this?" she said.

"Don't you have indoor plumbing?"

He remembered his father telling him there were families who lived up near Mount St. Helens years ago who had no modern amenities. How could that happen?

"Why are you unhappy?" she said.

"Me unhappy? You're lost out here in the middle of nowhere, and you ask me why *I'm* unhappy?"

Brant got the quilt from the bed and wrapped it around the girl. He led her to the couch and gestured for her to sit. He sank into the soft cushion, and she sat on the arm at the other end and stared at him. Her gaze unnerved him.

"What happened to you?" Brant said. "Are there others?"

"I…I am not sure."

"Where did you come from?"

She shook her head. "I do not know where I am. I do not think this is Erin."

"Erin?" She'd said that word before. Grandda had used the word for Ireland.

"Ireland," she said, as if she heard his thoughts.

She leaned forward, her eyes intense. "There is another language," she said. "We are different. I am different. I am what you call the Fair Folk. *Faerie*. Language is a gift. I took it from you."

"Fairy – what do you mean you took it from me?" Brant rose from the couch and backed away from her. The girl was obviously a nut case. He had to get away. His hand went for his keys.

She waved one hand. His panic subsided. He had questions, but couldn't voice them.

"Later I will tell you," she said.

It made perfect sense. Later....

She hugged her knees. Her body seemed small, child-like barely taking up space on the arm of the couch.

"It was autumn," she said, her voice soft and musical. "The end of the year. Sah-win." The word sounded foreign. "The fields had been harvested. The fires burned for the god of the dead lands. The spirits were close. The ancient ones hovered around, but did not join the dance."

Her eyes were hypnotic, blue as a summer sky. Brant could not look away.

"I danced around the fires," Siobhan said. Tears filled her eyes.

Brant put a hand on one of her shoulders, but she flinched away.

"Sorry," he said and pulled his hand back. "I didn't mean to hurt you."

"Hurt," she said. "It is I who am sorry, Brant Edwards. You did me no harm. You are not like...him. You are different...." She brushed tears from her cheeks.

Her hair hung over her face, a golden fall. He touched it. It felt like tangled, dewy cobwebs.

"You said another name," he said. "It sounded like Murkan."

"He...he...came with no iron," she whispered. "He said we were equals. Someone put something in my food. I did not wish to, but I could not refuse...." Her voice trailed off.

"What?" he prompted.

"I let a mortal bed me," she finally said. "He forced me. I could not refuse him. There was something in my food – a – potion – "

"A drug? How could somebody – ?"

"I was not careful enough. I am to blame."

"It wasn't your fault."

"The fault *was* mine," Siobhan said. "I could have – "

Brant put both hands on her shoulders. She did not look up at him.

"Listen to me," he said. "There was nothing you could have done. It wasn't your fault that someone drugged you."

"He deceived me. He wanted me, but on his terms. Only to brag of another conquest. He does not believe in us. He is not like my people."

"What do you mean, not like your people?"

"He is...like you. Not like me – "

"You mean you're not like me?"

"No."

A remembered word echoed in Brant's mind. Fairy....He was stuck in the wilderness with a nutcase.

"Do not be afraid." She reached for his hand. Her fingers touched his. A faint blue spark lit his skin. Static again that tingled.

Brant's apprehension became curiosity. He wondered if he should instead be afraid.

Pain crossed her face. "I am the one who is lost," she said. "I do not know how to get back. The Lady of Light sent me here. I did not do it myself. I have not the power."

She touched a thin gold band around her neck. "The Lady gave me this. It must be important. The Lady...nobody believed in her any more. Even my people did not think her kind still lived. This is not Erin."

"No. This is Washington."

"Wash-ing-ton?"

"State."

She looked blank.

"United States," Brant said. She shook her head. "You know. Land of the free, home of the brave. Twenty-first century. It's October – no, November first – "

"Twenty-first – " She stopped and whispered, "two thousand and – "

"Eleven."

"So long," she said.

Weirder and weirder.

"Brant, I am tired," she said. "If you will give me a drink of water and let me rest, we will talk. I will explain."

There were questions in his thoughts, but he couldn't bring himself to voice them. He got her a drink from the pump and handed it to her.

"What?" he said. "Explain what?"

She studied the plastic cup a long moment before she drank, a long gulp.

"The world," she said. "Changes…things are different – I am afraid I know the truth, and you will not believe me."

"Try me."

She gazed at him over the rim of the cup. Her eyes were magnets, drawing him into their secret depths.

"Brant," she said, "when this happened to me, when that man did this to me, it was Sah-win – what you call…Halloween – the end of the year."

The back of Brant's neck prickled.

Ghoulies and ghosties and things that go bump in the night….

"I know how men count years," Siobhan said. "When I danced around the fires, and the Lady of Light sent me here, it was a long time ago. A thousand years."

That didn't make sense. People didn't appear out of the mist from the past. Brant was drowning. He'd only wanted to help her, take her to the hospital, but he could not form a coherent thought.

He yawned. He needed rest, so he left the questions unvoiced and stretched out on the couch. Sleep took him in seconds.

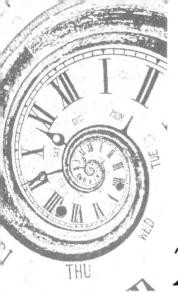

21

Liz punched the Stop button on the recorder. It was his voice, but Brant didn't connect with any of it.

"Well," he said. "Now what?"

"You don't remember this?"

"No. Obviously, I made it up."

Liz shook her head. "Dr. Carson doesn't think so. He says it could be what you *think* happened. There's more on the tape. At that point you became agitated and either couldn't or wouldn't go on, so Dr. Carson asked about the muggers." She punched the Fast Forward, let it run for a few seconds, and then hit Stop.

"Did I do something awful?" Brant said.

"No," she said. "Well, not intentionally, if what you say has even a shred of truth in it. This is where it gets really strange. It's difficult to explain in the normal sense."

"What do you mean?"

"Have you ever read anything about spontaneous combustion?"

"Fires that start by themselves?"

"Yes, but fires that burn people?"

"Not much evidence of that, is there? Just tabloid crap."

"Brant, keep in mind that what you talked about is the way you saw it, your perception of the event. It's very subjective, and there's a completely logical explanation. Do you remember when you asked me if I believed in ESP?"

"Mind over matter and all that?"

"Yes."

"Yeah," he said. He thought a moment. "When I was little, Mom told me Grandda – her father – believed in leprechauns. He came from County Cork, Ireland, in 1950 with his wife and a few personal possessions and started a new life in this country. My grandmother died when I was in high school. Mom said she had the second sight. Knew things would happen, when people far away died, that sort of thing. I never saw it."

He fished his key ring from his jeans pocket. "This came from him." He held up the encased arc of gold. "He gave it to my mother and she gave it to me when I turned 21. Family treasure. Just a lump of gold, but really old." He returned the keys to his pocket. "ESP? Only in books and movies."

"All my life I've been fascinated by research into extrasensory phenomena," Liz said. "I volunteered for some ESP experiments when I was in college. I never amounted to anything, but I saw some of the test results on others. I think ESP may exist, but it's coincidental, not something we can control."

He chuckled. "That's not very scientific of you, Liz. And anyway, I'm feeling pretty mellow from the pill."

"Even scientists accept subjective data, Brant. The mind is a marvelous mechanism, fully 90 percent unexplored. Who knows what lies over the edge of the world, so to speak?"

"'The Shadow knows'," he said. "My dad used to say that. Came from an old radio show."

"Before my time, but I've heard that. You ready?" Liz said.

He drew a deep breath, settled back in the chair and crossed his legs. "Let her rip."

"Here goes," she said. "If I think you're in trouble I'll stop the tape, and you can listen to it another time."

His words on the recording were slurred. Even though he had been wasted, the memories of that night spilled into his mind, vivid sounds and smells.

The tavern was dimly lit and smelled of old beer, smoke and sweat. The black man behind the bar was the owner. He was big. Didn't need a bouncer. His teeth looked bright against his dark skin. Brant ordered a drink and a burger. He ate the food and had a few more drinks. When he got up to leave, it seemed like a long way down from the bar stool. The tables were an obstacle course. He stumbled over some guy's foot. The man said something in a foreign language. Something obscene, judging from the laughter of the man's buddies.

Brant ignored he jeers, made it outside.

The street was dark. He couldn't find his car, then realized he had come in a cab. He looked left. Fog made the street seem darker than it should have been. To the right, far away, lights shone through the fog. The Boulevard. Taxies.

Two men came out of the bar behind him. One was tall, one short. Sneaky. They looked up and down the street. One of them had a gun. Brant thought he was going to die like his dad had.

Brant swung at the gunman. The gun landed in the street, too far away to reach. They came at him. One grabbed him, yanked his arms behind him. His shoulder snapped, and pain shot across his back and down his arm.

Brant's head hit the sidewalk. Everything went dark for a second, and then it hurt like hell. The muggers would kill him unless he fought back.

Siobhan couldn't fight because she had been drugged. That was different. Brant was different –

She had told him the stars made music. He could hear them if he listened.

Brant tried. He thought he heard a faraway melody....and then somehow he knew the answer was inside him.

He called the fire. It swirled around him like lightning, deadly and uncontrollable. Afraid for himself, he let the fire go. A flash of white-hot light blinded him. An explosion rattled the world.

Brant couldn't move, barely breathed because pain made him want to curl up into unconsciousness. He only wanted to scare the muggers.

A voice: "Hang on, man, hang on."

Sirens wailed....

Brant remembered the mugging with a clarity that surprised him. Unlike the story he'd told of the woman at his cabin, he remembered the fight, the pain, and at the last, his regret at having called the fire. From some secret place, he had summoned fire that killed the two men.

The memory of the woman's face didn't come. He had listened to his voice on the recording. He felt only that he had once met her, but couldn't place her. He felt some surprise that his head did not hurt.

"What happened?" Liz said.

He stared at the now silent recorder. How could he make her understand what he himself did not?

"The fire, Brant," Liz said. "What happened?"

"I did it," he said. Guilt washed through him. "I thought the fire. It was easy…but I didn't mean for them to die."

Brant rubbed his temples, expecting the pain to start any second.

"Does your head hurt?" she said.

"No."

"Dr. Carson gave you a posthypnotic suggestion that it wouldn't hurt. It doesn't always work. Maybe this one did. Are you all right?"

He lowered his hands to his lap. They were trembling. "Is it true?" he whispered.

Brant saw only questions in her hazel eyes.

"What you said is what you believe to be true," she finally said. "There is a rational explanation." There was a strange expression on her face, a flash of something that she hid quickly. Fear?

"The police never found one," he reminded her.

"No, they didn't," she admitted.

"I still don't remember spending two weeks at the cabin. It's like something I read that happened to someone else."

"Hypnosis is like that. Sometimes you remember things only when you're in a trance. There may still be something your mind doesn't yet want to face. Dr. Carson also planted the suggestion that you would remember. It'll take a while. I hope eventually your waking mind will be able to accept what you've told me and integrate it with reality. What you said when you were under may not be exactly the truth."

He snorted. "Of course, it can't be true."

"Why?"

"Because, for chrissake, people can't think fire. Only in a Stephen King novel. It was a fairy tale."

"Good choice of words," she observed. "You said the woman called herself one of the Fair Folk. I know a little mythology and that means – "

"According to Irish mythology," Brant interrupted, "the Fair Folk arrived in Ireland by flying down from the clouds in shining ships. They were tall and fair – not Vikings – and could make magic. They lived apart from the Celts and Anglo Saxons, and by the time the Normans appeared in the middle of the Eleventh Century, there were no fairies in Ireland. Just mischievous sprites and leprechauns. My Grandda told endless stories of – "

"Fairies." Liz said.

"I don't remem – " He gaped at her. "You mean…mag – "

"Yup. Magic and all that."

He rose from the chair in a blast of nervous energy.

"You can't be serious," he said.

"Of course I don't believe it, Brant. But I think that for some reason you do."

"I *am* going nuts." A twinge of pain bored into the left side of his head. He grimaced.

"Face it, Brant," Liz said. "Something happened to you at that cabin. So far, all we know about it is what you've said under hypnosis. You've told me what you *think* is true. What you *believe* you saw. There has to be a simple explanation for all of it."

"Yeah, but how do we get to the simple explanation?"

"I'd like to continue with the hypnosis sessions. See what more we can find out."

"Okay," he said. A nebulous scheme began to form in the back of his mind. He rubbed his temples.

"The headache back?"

"What? No." He shook his head. It felt like something shifted inside his skull. "Yeah. A little."

Liz rose. "I think that's it for today. I'm sure it's been quite a drain. The sedative should help you sleep. We can take this up again tomorrow. Would 10:00 be all right?"

"Yeah," he said absently. "Okay."

"See you then?"

"Yeah. Ten tomorrow morning." He left her office.

There was something he should remember. Like an unreachable itch, it teased him, but he could not scratch it. An irrational sense of dread filled him, a sense that something momentous would happen to him. Shouldn't the sedative take away his anxiety, make him not care about anything?

He punched the elevator button.

He wished there could be real magic: a magic pill that would restore his life to normal.

22

Ceallachan entered the cottage and shook cold rain from his hair and beard. He welcomed what little warmth emanated from the peat fire. Outside the wind scratched at the corners of the wattle and daub dwelling, a chill reminder of waning autumn. He caught a fragrant whiff of rabbit stew from an iron pot cooling near the hearth. A flat board on the small table held a rounded loaf of warm soda bread.

His daughter looked up from her needlework. Her hair fell unbound down her back, a waterfall of auburn curls.

"The time is ripe, Lassariona," Ceallachan said and seated himself at the table, his back to the fire.

"What will he say, Father?" Her strong fingers picked at a mistake in her needlework. From bits of gold and silver thread she embroidered a small banner, interwoven with an earth spell of protection for her son. Murchad's son. Eoghan. Well-born in the language of the Celts.

Ceallachan heard the steady thunk, thunk of the ax as the boy chopped wood behind the dwelling. Eoghan had grown stocky and darkly handsome like Murchad. His willingness to fight with the village lads showed he had inherited his father's ready temper.

"If I knew what he would say," Ceallachan said "I would not need to talk to him, would I, Daughter? I am an Earth wizard, not a predictor of the whims of mortal men."

The young woman laughed, throaty and perverse. "But the stars speak to you, Father. You dabble in the black arts. The dark side of the Earth Mother sometimes yields what will be."

"What the stars and the Earth Mother tell me, and what men choose to do are sometimes not the same," Ceallachan reminded her.

Her green eyes were luminous. "What if Murchad refuses to acknowledge the boy?"

"How can he?" Ceallachan said. "Eoghan could be a younger version of him. His voice has much the same quality as the father. Gareth – the one who keeps Murchad's accounts. He at least has a sense of propriety. He will talk to Murchad and convince him to recognize his bastard. Your son may not be the first born, but even a bastard can inherit land."

"Gareth." Lassariona rolled the name off her tongue. "I see him when I attend the women in the fortress. The *Sidhe* witch thought she thwarted me by blocking my entrance through the gate. There is another way in. Human frailty being what it is, there are those who still admit me. Gareth is handsome. I could fancy him if it would not interfere with the plan, Father. I have heard it said his bed has been lonely all the years he has lived with the o'Ruairc."

Ceallachan glared at his daughter. "There will be time enough for amusement after the deed is done."

"Ah, well." She sighed. "I have heard it said, too, that Gareth is given to a gentleness that brands him a coward. Some say the only blood on his sword when the Northmen attacked was his own.

"Do not be hasty to judge any man, Daughter," Ceallachan shot back at her. "Judgments have a way of proving themselves wrong. There is much more to any man than what he shows the world. Do not underestimate *anyone*. I made that mistake once, and I will not do it again. Even Murchad holds surprises. All must be guided carefully, lest the plan go awry."

"When, Father?" Lassariona's voice became petulant. "It has been a long time festering. Bran and Eoghan are almost fifteen. Nearly grown men. Eoghan chafes, knowing he will someday be rewarded, but the waiting does not agree with his nature. You may find the hawk striking on his own if you do not move soon."

She held up the banner. It bore the likeness of a hawk in flight.

"Do not push me," Ceallachan said, his voice hard as the edge of a sword. "And mind the boy. If you do not control him, he could ruin everything. Another moon cycle will make no difference."

"So long?"

"The signs are not yet right. Year's end is the time. *Samhain*. Even though

Bran o'Ruairc is mortal, Siobhan is fey, and has the resources to protect her own. She used her enchantment once before against the North invaders and would have killed more if others had defied her. Her powers increase with age. We have heard only gossip about her abilities. The *Sidhe* blood in her veins may have overshadowed whatever human ancestor she had. Her powers are strong…strong…." He paused and stared into the fire. "There may be more to Siobhan than I have read."

"I will bide my time, Father," said Lassariona, "as will Eoghan. But only one more moon cycle. Then a new time will begin."

Ceallachan nodded.

Lassariona set her needlework aside, rose and ladled stew into a bowl. "Do you have the weapon?" She set the bowl on the table at Ceallachan's place.

"It arrived a few nights ago. A shard of crystallized iron from across the sea, forged by the Earth Mother when the world was young. It was brought here untouched by human hands. It has not been seen by human eyes. The man who prized it from the earth and brought it here was, by my instruction, blind. He has no tongue to tell about his mission."

Lassariona served herself a bowl of stew and set it across the table from her father. She broke the bread and handed half to Ceallachan.

"One moon," she said and sat down to eat.

Siobhan sat on a carved oak stool before a low table hewn from a hawthorn trunk. She smoothed her hair with the comb she had taken from the man's dwelling so long ago in time yet to come. Even with the longevity of her people, it seemed too far in the future to comprehend. She tried not to remember, tried keeping images from her mind. She feared the images, feared the remembering almost as much as she feared the druid. He had absented himself from the o'Ruairc dwelling for many years, and yet she feared his absence boded ill.

Lately Siobhan felt as if he were lurking about. She sighed and dismissed this thought. The druid could not penetrate her warding spells.

There was no spell to banish the memories of the only man she loved. As the years passed, her powers had grown. The memories seemed to be more insistent, too.

Reminders of the future man – a man who would not be born for a thousand years – were always in the back of her mind. She had never allowed herself to grieve. She had chosen her path long ago, the path that would protect her son. Grieving would change nothing.

She swallowed, forced the tears away, stolidly blanked her mind.

She felt the worn places on the comb that had served her well for fifteen years. She thought of the innumerable times she had combed her son's hair when he was little. His hair, thick and dark like Murchad's.

Bran resembled Murchad's looks, but not his quick temper. Bran's singing voice was not inherited from his father. In imitation of Bebhinn, Bran had a clear, mellow voice. When the men sat after supper in the Great Hall singing bawdy ballads, Bran's clear baritone lifted above the rest. The monks at the abbey had encouraged his singing, unlike his father. Since Liam had fallen from a horse and died, the holding had been without its own bard, sharing one with the Mac Carthaigh holding to the north, as their chieftain was a distant cousin of Murchad. Currently the bard was on the road gathering news far and wide. Bran and Gareth possessed the only tuneful voice in the Hall.

Siobhan missed Bebhinn. In the years since Bebhinn's death Siobhan had allowed no one else to serve her. Bebhinn's room contained nothing but her personal items and memories. Memories haunted, as surely as mortals believed ghosts did.

A movement drew Siobhan's attention. A flicker in the air near her chamber door presaged Ceallachan's appearance. She did not understand how he appeared and disappeared at will. She thought he probably worked some elaborate illusion, but would never question him. She could not see into his mind. Try as she might, there wasn't a loose chink in his mental armor.

Mist formed, obscuring the oaken door, a heavy vapor that swirled for a moment and finally coalesced into the druid. There was no odor of iron, just a faint scent of mist and dry leaves.

Feigning nonchalance, Siobhan continued combing her hair.

"Druid." She acknowledged his presence.

"*Sidhe* woman," he returned. At least he did not address her as child.

Siobhan had long ago given up waiting for the druid's banter. She did not like being defensive. "It has been a long time," she said, turning to him. She gave him a calculated smile, hoping her indifference would infuriate him.

"Five summers," the druid said, unruffled. She knew how long it had been. She, too, watched the moon and the stars, listened to their songs, counting the seasons of her life, of her son's life.

"*Samhain* is once more upon us," Ceallachan said.

More memories. Siobhan forced them back into the depths of her mind. If she thought of her time in the future as a dream, she could believe it had happened to someone else.

"Yes," she said, her voice steady. "The year's end. A time to look forward to new beginnings, Druid. A time to put your house in order for the coming year."

Ceallachan nodded, his eyes glittering in the enchanted light of Siobhan's chamber. His red hair and beard had not grayed nor faded with age. She thought of Murchad's gray-sprinkled hair, the lines in his face. She had seen the unspoken pain that often clouded his eyes when he thought nobody noticed. His bones were growing old.

Ceallachan was ageless. Perhaps he had a bit of *Sidhe* heritage. That would explain his longevity. He had lived near the Wood almost as long as Siobhan had.

She rose and gazed into the druid's eyes, consciously masking her mind and strengthening the warding spells that guarded her room.

"This will be a momentous time," Ceallachan said.

"Why?"

"It is indeed a time of endings," he said. "I have read the entrails and the earth signs." He stopped. If he expected her to ask his advice he would be disappointed.

"The signs speak of strange and wondrous events," he continued. "They hint at a world fading and another opening. And the signs tell of endings without beginnings, broken circles, and closing circles. I have seen one who loves from afar. Love unreturned is a dangerous thing, Siobhan. Dangerous indeed."

"You speak in riddles, Druid," Siobhan said with disdain.

"All the riddles of the earth and stars eventually reveal themselves and come to pass."

She snorted. "If you would spend some of your time just enjoying the stars instead of trying to wring predictions from them, you might find peace. The future is better left unplumbed. Even my people do not truck with divining what is to be. That touches the black arts."

"There are those of your kind whose predictions are known for their accuracy," Ceallachan said.

"I have never met them. You follow legends. My people leave the stars and mortals to their own wanderings, as you should."

"Heed me, Siobhan o'Ruairc," Ceallachan said. "There is more within you than you know. And perhaps more within others. The fire of your heritage can burn even the one who wields it."

"My patience wears thin," she said quietly. "My spells will repel anyone who enters this dwelling to harm me or the boy."

"I accede to your wish for privacy," he said. He bowed, then straightened and raised his arms. Mist formed around him again, swirled up his legs and writhed around his waist.

"Beware, Siobhan," his voice seemed distant. "Iron kills indiscriminately."

Siobhan blinked. The mist eddied, cloaking the druid. When the fog dissipated, he had vanished.

Perhaps he was plotting some political subterfuge against Murchad. It frustrated her that his mind was closed to her. Next summer when she and the boy went to the forest home, she would seek out one of her father's people and ask about it. Although most had retreated underground beyond the scope of humans, some still occasionally went abroad in the forest.

Siobhan would see Bran this evening at supper, and she would add to the spells that guarded him. The cloak pin had protected him all these years. It would always carry the enchantments that kept him safe.

A sword could cause Bran a fatal injury, but a scratch would heal. Even a scratch from iron could kill her. Bran was mortal. At fifteen, he was nearly a grown man, not a child like a *Sidhe* boy would be at the same age. Siobhan's spells would prevent entrance to someone carrying a weapon forged of the hated metal. No injury could befall Bran within the fortress or while he carried the brooch.

Siobhan laid the comb on the table with her other possessions, rose and strode from her chamber, closing the door against the lonely silence behind her.

23

Brant floated in that netherworld of alpha state sleep where he knew he must be asleep, and yet he was somehow hyper-aware of his surroundings. Colors seemed vibrant, even in the firelight. He smelled the faint odor of wood smoke. Felt the quilting on the comforter where his arm rested on it.

She stood at the window, her back to him. She gazed at the falling snow, loose hair like golden sunlight down her back. His flannel shirt hung to her knees. His wool socks, way too big, bunched around her ankles.

Her fingers traced patterns in the condensation on the window. There was meaning in the patterns if Brant could understand it, but the significance was beyond his grasp.

Her shape was familiar to him, as if he had known her forever. He knew the contours of her body as a lover would. Her body gave him pleasure and took pleasure from his.

How many days had Brant known her? A week, perhaps two. He had not left the cabin, had not called to let his sister know he was all right. Someone might come to the cabin to check on him. But no one had.

"Siobhan," he said, "come back to bed. It's cold."

"Not yet." Her voice only a whisper of sound.

This was not real. It was only a dream. When he opened his eyes, it would all vanish, and he would be left with fragmented images and a sense of loss that increasingly overwhelmed his thoughts.

Siobhan turned toward him, her face shadowed. A narrow band circled her neck. It glowed like one of those chemical lights kids get at carnivals. It was gold, but had no clasp.

He ached to go to her, but he was frozen in the dream state.

The dream image shifted. Siobhan's image floated above him. Her fingers touched his cheek, raised goose bumps. He wanted to wrap his arms around her, drown in her. If he held her tightly she wouldn't fade away.

The same dream for two nights, repeating, waking him with a physical need. But this time he didn't wake. This time the dream was different, more vivid. It continued.

Might he exert some power over the phantoms conceived by his sleeping mind? If he could not, the dream would become a nightmare of loss. He willed his dream-self to focus on her. The paralysis faded, and he grasped her arm, his fingers dark against her moonlight-pale skin.

Her eyes drew him in, blue depths rushing up to meet him…her features swam into focus: narrow nose, wide-set eyes, high cheekbones, soft lips. He wanted to gaze at her forever, memorize her features. This was the face he drew over and over, the face he painted in misty, fairy scenes.

She leaned down and touched his cheek.

A wave of longing washed over him.

He felt a cloying sense of *Deja vu*. The dream felt tangible, like a memory. He wanted to draw her down and kiss her. She touched his lips with a finger, shook her head, her hair made more golden by the glowing band around her neck.

Immobile, Siobhan listened to something he could not hear.

"I must go," she whispered.

"No," he groaned. "Don't – "

"I must. She calls."

Then, as dreams do, her form wavered, shimmered, and she wore a gauzy dress that outlined the slight contours of her body. Once more she leaned over him. Her lips gently brushed his, but he could not respond. His limbs were leaden, weighed down by uncertainty…or was it fear? Her hand was cool on his cheek. She whispered something so quietly he didn't hear the words.

He felt sleepy, as if a powerful drug coursed through his body. He tried to fight, struggled to keep his eyes open, but they grew heavy. He smelled flowers, flowers in a mountain meadow…. He forced his eyes open and squinted in the cabin's dimness.

Mist curled around her, intensified to a blue glow that spread to him.

For an instant he glimpsed a mirror behind her, saw his image reflected in it. There was another mirror behind his image. His face disappeared into a infinite maze of mirrors.

He tried to speak her name, but the words froze in his throat.

She whispered, "I wish there could be a returning for you."

There could never be a returning, but he didn't understand why.

She would be lost again, just as in all the other dreams, as in reality. Lost in the mirrors in his mind, a circular path of mirrors.

He must act or she would be gone forever.

He swung a clenched dream fist at a mirror. There was a satisfying impact. The mirror shattered. Shards of broken glass rained down, obliterating Siobhan in a shower of sparks. He drew his hand back, expecting blood. No blood…but behind the broken mirror, another, and another…mirrors within mirrors….reflecting his image, and beside him a shadow silvered by moonlight against the black sky and a field of stars.

Brant bolted upright. He was in bed in his hospital room. Darkness pressed down on him. But the images persisted.

It wasn't a dream. It was a memory, or perhaps many memories compressed into one dream. There were mirrors in Brant's mind, as if he had walked into a fun house of reflections and shadows. But he had broken one of the mirrors, allowing him glimpses of fragmented memories.

The fullness in his groin made him feel like an adolescent waking in the night after an erotic dream. But under the longing there was fear. Fear that he was remembering what had happened to him, and that he had done something he would regret.

The clock beside his bed said 11:12. He'd only been asleep for an hour. If it had been sleep. He threw back the covers, rose, and wearing only boxers, went to the window. He pulled back the blinds and peered into pearly fog. From his third floor vantage point he could see the ground below and vague shapes of trees maybe a couple hundred yards away.

Beyond the trees headlights pierced the mist, then were swallowed by fog that rolled and curled with a damp life of its own.

He remembered Siobhan. Not the dream woman, but the real one. She was real. Not a child, but old beyond her years. She told him that her people lived a long time. Fifty years comprised childhood. He wasn't sure what that meant. There was something else…something about her…something important he could not remember….

An ache gnawed into his head behind his left eye.

He opened the window as far as possible: only a few inches. Fog crept into his room, cold, smelling of rain. He shivered. And remembered....

She had smelled of fog and flowers. There were fireflies, long after the autumn frosts should have killed them off. He shut his eyes and opened his mind to the memories.

He loved Siobhan beyond the lust he'd felt in the dream. But he would never see her again because...because....

That idea eluded him.

Was what he'd said under hypnosis true? How could it be? Time travel wasn't possible.

But love was.

Was this love? This constant ache of loss, of wanting. Knowing he wanted to spend the rest of his life with her, grow old and die with her.

Die...that was it. Something worried at the edges of that thought. He would die, but she....

He lost the thread of memory.

Fog dampened his skin, evoking images that held him in thrall. He could not grasp a single detail and pull it into focus. So he just let the images flow, flashes out of sequence.

Questions popped into his mind. He wanted answers. Now. Where were the answers? What were the *right* questions?

All the pictures rattling around in his head begged for paper. His fingers ached to draw. Maybe that would ease the rapid-fire flow of thoughts, calm him, and allow him to focus. Help him make sense of everything.

He turned on the light beside the bed and pulled on jeans and his sweater. His mind raced. He pulled on his socks and shoes – the light hiking boots he favored – and tied them. He retrieved his sketchbook and a charcoal pencil from the bedside table and propped himself against the headboard with pillows, not caring about his feet on the bed. He opened the cover and stared at the first blank page, hoping some muse would pity him and let the pictures out.

He closed his eyes, pencil poised above the white paper. Where to start? The answer was a whisper in his mind, an echo: *Siobhan*.

That was where to begin. What had she looked like? He tried to bring back the dream images, the images he had painted. He opened his eyes and tentatively drew a line, then another, and suddenly the pictures flowed through his fingers: light, shadows and textures. He flipped the page, began another sketch. Not satisfied, he began a new page. Furiously, he tried to capture the dream woman. But she would not take shape. He left another sketch unfinished. Began another. Then another, this one different.

A slash for a tree. A few strokes for the corner of the cabin. A Douglas fir beside the porch. Turn the page. More trees. More angles. This time the drawing began to make sense. He concentrated, intent on getting it just right. Almost finished, he stopped and stared at it.

The cabin nestled among the trees. In the foreground a shadow of another cabin.

Did the cabin hold the key?

He had to talk to somebody about this. His doctor? No. To her he was just a patient. Granted, she knew him socially, but theirs was a professional relationship. The detective? No. Despite the man's insistence, Brant barely knew him. The woman who claimed to be his sister? There was something about her....

A little girl with freckled cheeks, her dark hair tangled, her eyes full of tears, that first Christmas after his mother died.

What'll we do, Brant? A girl, trying to be brave.

So maybe he did know her. He grabbed his cell phone from the beside stand and scrolled through his phone book.

SIS.

Someone's initials? Someone he knew, but had forgotten? He pressed the call button.

The phone rang three times. Four.

"H'llo?" Although thick with sleep, an unmistakable voice.

We're orphans. A little girl with tears on her cheeks. An echo of memory.

"Maeve?" he said.

"Who is this?"

"It's Brant." He could not say he was her brother. He did not remember all of it. She didn't respond, but didn't hang up. He said, "I need a favor. A big one."

"I thought you never wanted to see me again."

"I...I thought I didn't."

A protracted silence. He let it drag out.

Finally she said, "Okay. What? Are you all right?"

"Maybe not. Will you come out to the hospital? There's something I want to show you. It's really important."

"Now?"

"Please come." He willed her to come.

"It's late – "

"It's not midnight yet," he said. "I wouldn't ask if it wasn't important."

She sighed. "I'll be there in an hour. Maybe longer. It's really raining. Looks like it might even snow."

"I'll meet you at the front desk," he said. And then belatedly, "Thank you."

She had already hung up.

Brant paced and kept looking at his phone. The damned battery must be dead. It seemed to be changing too slowly. Agitation lengthened his strides, and the room seemed to be getting smaller.

He forced himself to take smaller steps, concentrating, trying to focus his thoughts. The mirror that had broken in his dream wasn't *real*, not in a physical sense; it could be a metaphor that meant something beyond empirical knowledge. Some meaning buried in his subconscious trying to emerge. Images raced through his thoughts, like a randomly organized slide show, so much out of time sequence that he wasn't sure what was long past or close to the present. Or...was it possible he was seeing the future? Could this be a precognitive experience? Some weird phenomenon that blared from the front pages of tabloids: Man's visions predict...what?

He stopped. Tendrils of fog coiled through the open window.

A memory of fog...of the woman who came from the mist...mirrors and circles....

Brant turned and picked up his key chain from the dresser. The arc of gold glowed softly within the plastic as if with an inner light.

The cabin...circles....

Some memory clicked in his mind. The gold had to be part of a larger piece, a circle....

Brant felt an ominous sense of dread, a sense that events were coming full circle, things were drawing to a close. He must be at the cabin to complete the circle.

Maeve would never believe him. She would never take for granted his sudden presentiment that the cabin was the key. He must *show* her. He dropped the keys in his jeans pocket, propped his sketchbook on his pillow and went to the lobby.

A woman talked quietly to the night security guard who sat behind the desk. Brant did not recognize him.

The man looked up. "Trouble sleeping?" he said.

He looked too young to be in charge of anything. He could be ex-military: buzzed hair, erect posture. He wore a baseball cap emblazoned with MH Security. An ID tag clipped to his uniform collar identified him as Allen Morrison, Night Security.

"No," Brant said. "Just sketching."

Morrison grinned. "You're that artist."

Brant held out his hand. "Brant Edwards."

The other man half rose and pumped Brant's hand. "Allen Morrison. Glad to meet you, sir. My wife's a great admirer of your work. She goes to that gallery at least once a week."

"Thanks," Brant said, trying to hide his impatience. The clock on the wall was the same time as his phone.

"Mr. Edwards," the woman said. Amber Singer, RN, the name tag on her cardigan identified her. "If you're having trouble sleeping I could get you a sleeping pill."

Brant caught himself before he rolled his eyes. "No," he said. "I just had a little extra energy. I guess it is late." He turned back toward the hallway and said over his shoulder. "Later."

Back in his room Brant grabbed his jacket, thankful that a pair of gloves were crammed into one of the pockets. He had seen the weather forecast earlier. It wasn't pretty. A huge system was moving in from the Pacific that would bring rain and sleet in the city and snow in the higher elevations.

Brant had a plan. Still vague, but he had to get to the cabin.

Out in the hallway he stood beside the Coke machine. The position afforded him a view of the lobby doors, but hid him from those at the desk. He heard their voices: indistinct, pleasant chatter. Above him, on the opposite wall, a security camera's red light drew his attention. It was pointed toward the soda machine, and him.

He moved to the front of the machine, as if he were trying to make a selection. Maybe whoever watched the monitors somewhere in the depths of the building wouldn't notice anything unusual until it was too late to stop him.

A car pulled up to the entrance, a boxy red SUV, somehow familiar. Lights reflecting off the windshield obscured the driver. It could be Maeve. Brant ran for the door. He hit the escape bar at a run and was in the seat beside Maeve in a couple of seconds.

"Go," he said. "Don't ask questions."

She hesitated an instant, her eyes wide, then stomped the accelerator. Brant hoped she didn't think she was making a getaway with a crazed psychiatric patient. He glanced back. The security guard barreled out the door, stopped and spoke into his radio.

As they moved away from the building, Brant turned and saw the security guard speak into his radio. Maeve leaned forward, gripping the steering wheel. She peered into the fog and rain, where streetlights delineated the road.

"Turn left here," Brant ordered. She did. He pointed. "Turn left again. Follow the signs for I-5 north."

A mile or so later Maeve turned onto the I-5 ramp, barely accelerating into the thick fog.

"All right," she said. "Rich is still at work, and I sneaked away from a rookie cop who's probably going to get fired for losing me. I feel like I've just helped you break out of jail. What the hell's going on?"

He settled back in the seat, fastening his seat belt.

"Drive to the cabin," he said.

"Why?"

"I have to be there. Don't ask me how I know that. I just do. I know something's going to happen there, and I have to be there when it does."

The rain intensified. Maeve was silent, concentrating on driving. She hugged the reflective line on the right shoulder. They passed no cars on their side – occasionally Brant glimpsed a red taillight ahead of them – nor did Brant see many lights coming south. The windshield wipers barely kept up.

They crossed the Interstate Bridge over the Columbia River into Washington. A few miles later, visibility improved slightly. The car sped up.

Maeve glanced at him. "Are you all right?"

"Yes. No. I don't know. I just know that I have to be at the cabin. Don't worry, I'm not an ax murderer."

"I know that," Maeve said. "Despite what you think, I know you're not dangerous. I just think, well…I think something happened to you, and it's causing you problems."

"I'm remembering things."

"Me?"

"Maybe."

"What –"

"No details, just scattered bits and pieces. It's like a TV in my mind that keeps flipping channels."

She drove in silence for a while.

"The cabin," she said.

"Yeah. If it doesn't work out you can go home in the morning."

"It's going to snow."

"You want me to drive?" he offered.

"No, I'm fine. What the hell. It'll be an adventure."

The car splashed on into the rainy darkness.

Brant relaxed into the seat and stretched out his legs. "Get off at Spirit Lake Highway and – "

"I know how to get there."

Maybe she did. Everybody in the Northwest knew how to get to Mount St. Helens. He sighed. "If I sleep," he said, "will you stop at the Castle Rock police station and turn me in? I won't resist."

She didn't answer.

"Well, then, will you wake me up at Seaquest Park?"

Maeve nodded. "We used to go there for picnics when I was little. Do you remember?"

"No...." He remembered huge trees and sitting at a picnic table while his father grilled hamburgers and his mom sat in the sun and...there was someone else at the table. "Well, maybe I do. Vaguely."

"That's a start."

He was tired. He closed his eyes, willed his mind into silence. The motion of the car lulled him. Maeve turned on the radio. Music played, the new age music he liked.

Confused images flooded Brant's thoughts. He changed position and tried to relax. He drifted....

A gloomy corridor vanished somewhere far away in the darkness. Every few feet on either side there was a closed door. Soft light seeped around the edges. The hallway seemed sinister with shifting shadows. Brant tried to run. Some sticky substance stuck to his feet and dragged him down. The more he tried, the slower he moved until he stopped beside a door. He put his hand on it and pushed. It swung inward, screeching on rusty hinges like a sound effect in some bad horror movie.

He was in a dimly lit room, barren of furnishings. He heard the sound of weeping. His eyes grew accustomed to the darkness. A woman cowered in a corner, her dark hair disheveled. He went to her. She looked up and raised her hands as if to fend off an attack. Maeve.

"No," she whimpered.

He recoiled, horrified by the grief on her face –

"Brant – "

"What?" He sat upright. The seat belt caught him. He forced himself to relax backward and gently worked the belt. It released.

"Sorry," Maeve said. "We just passed the Park."

He felt groggy. An hour and a half had gone by on the clock. He must have dozed. Time flew when you were having fun...*time....*

Time was running out. Where had that thought come from?

He had driven up here just three weeks ago.

Time flies....

Time tugged at him, pulling him inexorably somewhere....

It had been foggy and rainy that time. But now the rain had turned to sleet that pattered on the windshield. The road was shiny in the headlights, a harbinger of ice when the temperature fell as they gained altitude.

They passed scattered lights of the tiny towns of Silver Lake and Toutle and turned north onto what locals called the Toledo Cut-off. Within a few miles the sleet changed to large, wet snowflakes. The wipers tolled their regular rhythm, back and forth, a metronome that marked passing time in the partial circles they made on the windshield.

Time...circles closing....

"Road bad?" he said.

"A little slick. But I'm going so slow that if we slide in the ditch we won't get hurt."

He checked his seat belt. Miles passed in a white blur.

The car slowed. "Turn here?" Maeve said.

"I think so." Just as the fog had hidden things the last time, the snow made the familiar seem strange. Brant's mind wrestled with the confusion of roads and indistinct landmarks. They guessed at a few turns.

"Stop," Brant said.

She reacted so quickly the car skidded and slewed toward the edge of the road. It stopped short of the ditch.

"Are you sure this is it?" she said, wiping the side window with her coat sleeve.

"I think so. You better pull off the road a little so the snowplows don't hit you." Weyerhauser Lumber Company maintained these roads for hauling logs.

She stepped on the gas, and the tires spun. She let up, found some traction, and the car inched forward. She pulled off the road as far as the narrow shoulder allowed, put the car in Park and set the hazard lights flashing.

"I wouldn't do that," Brant said.

"Why not?"

"You don't want a dead battery."

"I'm going back as soon as the storm lets up."

"It could be awhile."

"I hope nobody runs into it," Maeve said.

"Who the hell in their right mind would be out here in this?"

She gave him a quizzical look. "We're out here." She peered out into the storm. "Maybe we should wait awhile."

He glanced at his watch. Just after 3:00.

"But I have to be there," he said. "I don't know why. We can't get lost. It's the only road."

He leaned forward and punched up the weather station on the satellite radio. Up to two feet of snow in the mountains.

Maeve groaned. "Why did I do this?"

"I don't know," he said, turning to her. "Why did you?" Her face glowed green in the soft lights of the instrument panel.

"I'm not sure," she said. "I guess because I thought you needed me. There won't be anything there, Brant."

"We'll see," he said. "You ready?"

"No, but let's go."

She fished gloves from a pocket and put them on. "Sorry, I didn't bring any for you."

"It's okay. I've got some." He pulled his gloves from his pocket and stared at them. They were a gift. A gift from someone special, but he didn't have a clue who it could be. Another gap in his memory.

Maeve reached across him into the glove box and produced a Maglite. She turned off the ignition, and they got out.

The only sound in the snowy darkness was the icy breath of the wind sighing through the Douglas firs. Maeve turned on the flashlight. It illuminated the ground a few feet ahead. The car beeped once – locked – and she pocketed the keys.

Brant lead the way up the road to the cabin.

24

Gareth Spencer faced Murchad in a rare display of anger.

"Do you not understand, my lord?" Gareth said, "what this means?"

"Of course I understand," Murchad retorted. He lurched up from the chair beside his hearth where he had been enjoying a cup of mead. He slammed the cup down on a small table beside him. The dregs splashed out and soaked into the bare wood. "But what in Christ's name am I going to do about it?"

"Invoking His name will change nothing," Gareth said. "It has been 15 years. Are you sure the child is yours?"

"You saw him. He looks just like me," Murchad thundered. "My wedding night, for God's sake. The witch seduced me on my wedding night."

Murchad rubbed his close-cropped beard, paced across his chamber and gazed out the narrow opening in the stone wall at the autumn mist. The haze seemed lighter than earlier. If it cleared, the night would be cold. The air smelled of snow. He would order some oak for his fire. Peat gave little warmth to his aging bones. He hugged a soft deerskin robe against his spare frame.

"There is only one thing to do, lord." Gareth lowered his voice. "Bran will inherit since he is the progeny of a marriage contract. But you should acknowledge the bastard and pay for his raising. Perhaps the woman would agree to send him to the abbey to be educated. It would demonstrate your Christian charity. If you admit being Eoghan's father you will appear generous, and the boy will never have a legitimate claim on your holding. The druid woman's child bed time is known. Bran is the elder."

"For God's sake, Gareth. Where did you acquire your logic? It does not matter. Even a bastard has rights. The woman will milk me for all she can. If Siobhan discovers this, I am undone."

"What do you care for the Lady Siobhan's feelings?" Gareth blurted.

Murchad whirled on him. "Siobhan is a good woman. She has been an example for the boy all these years. Because of her influence, Bran is growing into manhood with some wit between his ears. I thank you for your allegiance, but refrain from voicing what does not concern you. If I have sundered my land it is my own doing, Gareth. You will not speak of this matter to Siobhan or anyone else unless I give you leave to do so."

"I would not betray you, lord," Gareth said with a formal bow. He turned and strode to the door.

Murchad watched the other man retreat. If only….Life was full of if only. If only he had fathered an heir when he was younger, none of this would have happened. If only he had not dealt with the druid at all. The potion was responsible for the whole mess. He was certain Lassariona had slipped him something again on his wedding night. He had not been that drunk, would never have bedded the red-haired witch if he had not lost his senses.

Ah, well. The thing was done, and a boy had grown up without knowing his true father. If Murchad said nothing, Lassariona might guide her son into taking young Bran's place by force. If Murchad acknowledged the bastard, Bran would inherit the greater part of the holding.

Gareth might possess a logical mind, but he had neglected one thing. If Bran died before Murchad made a public affirmation of his bastard son, then Lassariona's boy could claim Bran's inheritance. Murchad himself went with Gareth to verify the woman's claim. The o'Ruairc features were obvious in Eoghan's face and dark hair. Gareth made it plain to Murchad that the witch's son had a legitimate lien on at least part of Murchad's holdings.

Murchad pulled the deerskin tighter around him and strode after Gareth. Gareth would watch over Bran. The boy admired the scribe. In spite of the rumors circulating among his clan, Gareth had once proved his worth with a blade.

Siobhan glided down the darkened hallway to Bran's living quarters. A shadow down the corridor whisked into a doorway. Was it the earth-brown robe of the druid? She sent her mind out, searching for danger. She felt the warding spells that protected her son.

Siobhan sensed Bran's surface thoughts: the early cold made him think of the approaching winter. He was ambivalent about hunting with his father the next day – a pastime she found morbidly distasteful – and there were unexpectedly vivid images of a girl in the kitchen, the desire and lust of an adolescent –

She broke off and quested beyond the boy's thoughts, searching for the barest hint of danger.

Ceallachan. She felt him in the darkened corner of a room adjoining Bran's. She stopped. The air around her seemed thicker.

What did the druid intend? Nobody could enter the boy's room with evil intent toward Bran, for the spells had been applied and strengthened countless times during the boy's lifetime. The cloak pin also guarded him, at least would warn her when he was in danger.

She saw nothing in Ceallachan's mind. Nothing.

Siobhan did not understand how he could hide his mind so well. No matter how much pressure she applied, he held the barrier against her intrusion. No one could get close to the boy with evil intent, so how could –

The answer rushed into her mind. Cunning he was, oh so cunning. By masking his thoughts completely, he had thwarted her. If there was truly nothing coherent in his mind, he could penetrate her defenses without raising an alarm.

She ran, knowing it was too late.

"Bran," she cried.

Her thoughts fragmented by dread, she tried to break through the druid's mind barrier. Solid resistance. When she pushed, the obstruction retreated, but she perceived no inkling of the man's thoughts.

Panic, a human emotion, overwhelmed her enchantment. Fear blinded her mind senses. Magic retreated beyond her grasp. If she could determine the extent of Ceallachan's treachery she could let go of her mind probe and gather the energy for a counter spell. Now she knew the feeling of utter hopelessness that overwhelmed mortal minds. The legacy passed to her by her human mother betrayed her. Human emotions blocked her magic

She turned the corner and slammed into Gareth. His arms went around her, and his arms tightened with badly concealed passion. His lips brushed her hair.

"Lady – "

She pulled away from him. "Gareth," she said, "you must help me. The druid – quickly. The boy's life is lost if we do not act."

"What – ?"

206   *Trilby Plants*

"Ceallachan. He got past my spells. He plans something – I cannot use my enchantment – "

The corridor and Gareth's face disappeared in a burst of crimson fog. Body-wrenching pain knifed into her left shoulder. She cried out and clung to Gareth, unable to draw a breath.

"What is it?" His voice sounded faint, as if it came from a long distance.

She thought her chest would burst. Her knees grew weak.

"Bran…come – " She grasped Gareth's arm and pulled him into the boy's chamber.

"No…." she moaned, her heart in her throat. "No…."

Too late. Bran lay in a widening pool of blood. A glittering metallic shard protruded from his left shoulder. Blood bubbled up and became pink froth. He labored for breath. Siobhan smelled burned flesh and the acrid tang of pure iron.

She rushed forward and knelt at Bran's side, heedless of the blood. A hundred thoughts vied to be recognized in her mind, but she could not grasp any of them. She wanted to withdraw the metal from Bran's wound, but its poison would kill her.

She would give her life for her child, but it was too late. Bran slipped away. How did the druid obtain such as this – crystal iron from the fires of the earth? Undiluted with a base metal and untainted by man's workings, it was beyond her enchantment. And the burning of Bran's flesh told her the truth.

Gareth appeared by her side. "It is only a minor wound, Lady. He will recover. Do not fear."

Too late….The boy was *Sidhe*. A late developer, but fey, just as Siobhan was. The trauma of the injury had precipitated his transition. Only one who was fey would be burned so and destroyed by the iron shard. The lethal poison coursed through his body.

All the years she had sacrificed her own happiness had been for naught. She could have raised Bran by herself waiting for his *Faerie* heritage to blossom. Now the child of her body lay dying. Bran could not heal himself of a mortal wound inflicted by the hated iron. If only she were a healer….

Too late….

"Oh, Bran," she whispered.

She took the boy's clenched hand, slippery with blood, and held it tight. His fingers opened. In his palm lay the cloak pin. It was little protection against the earth's cruel weapon.

"Mother." Bran's voice was barely a whisper.

"What have you done, Druid?" Gareth said, pain choking his words. "Murchad would have recognized your grandson."

Bran's dark eyes were glazed with pain. One so young should not face death like this.

She opened herself to her son's dying mind, hoping to ease his bewilderment. His gift must have been buried beyond her ability to probe. If only she had been able to go into his most secret places, she might have known....

*Mother....*A thin thought tugged at her. *I thought...he made me think it was the shank. I tried to pin it to my brat....*Darkness descended in his mind. *It hurts...burns....*

His life force dwindled. She followed, unable to grasp so thin a thread. Her mind became calm, again able to reach her magic.

"Bran. Bran. Bran o'Ruairc." Siobhan spoke his name. But her magic did not pull him back.

She reached for his fading spark, sent a spell of comfort, felt an answering pressure. His thoughts pulsed stronger for an instant. His life glow hung poised over the brink of the chasm. He hesitated, turned to her.

I am not afraid, Mother, he said. *All my life I have lived with death. It holds no terror. Bebhinn awaits me. Liam too. They call me. They welcome me. Do not weep for me. It is men's lot to die. You still have your life to live.* He turned and floated further into the void. His thought was softer, further away.

Mother...there is a...wench in the scullery...she is with child...my child...I am sorry, Mother...sorry...please care for her...she loves me...I love...her name is Slaine....

The little spark that spoke to Siobhan faded into silence. Her mind whirled back to her body. Bran's fingers closed on hers once with a burst of strength, then fell limp.

Strong arms raised her from the floor, supported her, loved her. Gareth. She leaned against him. Grief flooded over her, tried to drown her. She heard Ceallachan step closer.

What had Gareth said? *Grandson....*

Heavy footfalls rushed over the stone floor. Siobhan heard the swish of a sword being drawn from a leather scabbard. She flinched away from the loathsome metal.

"Step away from my wife, traitor." Murchad's baritone resounded in the chamber.

Siobhan felt the comforting arms withdraw, sensed the bewilderment in Gareth's mind, the angry denial, and the guilt. For one brief instant she felt Ceallachan's triumph.

A storm gathered and Siobhan stood becalmed in the center. Swaying as the world crumbled around her, she opened her eyes. Gareth held the shard. Blood dripped from it. He stared stupidly at it, unable to grasp how he came to hold it. Murchad glanced once at the body of his son sprawled on the floor, looked back at Gareth.

Murchad looked at the druid. "My son – "

"Dead," Ceallachan said.

Siobhan turned to Murchad. He would tell her the truth. It was too late for deception.

Murchad's voice was thick with rage. "I took you in, you of the *Sidhe*. You would not let me near you, not allow me to touch you all these years. And now I find you in the arms of a foreign betrayer."

Siobhan was too stunned to think. She reeled from the jealousy that raged in Murchad's mind.

Murchad struck his blade into Gareth's abdomen upward to his heart. Gareth crumpled to the floor without a word. The shard clattered on the stones. His blood spattered hot on Siobhan's upraised hands.

I did not – Gareth's fading thoughts. *I love you, Siobhan….*

"I know," Siobhan whispered. "But it was not enough."

His life bled away.

Siobhan looked up at Murchad. "How could you – ?"

Ceallachan stepped over Bran's lifeless body and stood before Murchad, a triumphant smile on his face.

"Now that the game is played," Ceallachan said, "the other child inherits." Malign satisfaction glinted in his gray eyes.

Murchad's eyes held murder. He raised his sword to point at the druid's heart.

Ceallachan threw back his head and laughed. His chest rose and fell in spasms. "You got what you bargained for, did you not, Murchad?" he finally said, gasping for breath.

Ceallachan's laughter swept away the human emotion that had betrayed Siobhan. Coldness settled in her mind and heart. She did not have to see the druid's thoughts to see his treachery with Murchad.

Bargain…bargain….

The word echoed in Siobhan's mind. Murchad must have conspired with the druid to kill Bran. This was Murchad's doing.

"Bargain?" she whispered. She saw on the confused surface of Murchad's mind the awful truth of the bastard son – the druid's grandson – how Bran had stood in the way. Murchad bargained with Bran's life –

She probed no deeper.

Coldness rose inside her, the cold dispassion of the *Sidhe*, the emotionless part of her that distanced her forever from mortals. Like a monstrous storm spilled lightning and thunder from the heavens, her magic lashed out. An indigo aura sparked around her, rose to the nearly white light of pure power.

Murchad stepped away from her. "I swear to you, Siobhan, I did not – I loved my son. You would not let me near you – "

"I could kill you," she spat. She searched for the spell.

"I have faced death more times than you imagine," Murchad said. He glanced at his son's body, then back at Siobhan. "I have lost all that is dear to me. Death is not frightening."

"Then fear this," Siobhan said. "Death is simple. A heart can cease to beat, your life can bleed away from an injury. Life brings pain. Your pain will consume you until you beg for release, Murchad, but release will never come. You will live with what you have done. You will live with it forever...*forever!*"

Murchad stepped back again. A movement drew Siobhan's attention. She raised one arm. Power crackled from her fingers, streaked to the druid, and slammed him across the room. He thudded against the stone wall with a grunt and slumped into a heap. His head lolled forward.

She clenched the cloak pin. It pricked her palm, mingling her blood with Bran's and Gareth's. She raised the brooch, held it in front of her, channeled her sorcery through it. The gold and the blood would add the impetus she needed to command the awful spell she called upon. The blood of three would more than thrice increase the power of the magic.

"Forever, Murchad," she said in a venomous whisper. "You will live forever!"

Murchad's expression changed from grief to fear. He glanced at the druid. Ceallachan raised his head groggily. He would be powerless to stop her once the spell was invoked.

All Siobhan's enchantment surged into her fingers. She released it in one blinding burst of power that thundered into Murchad's chest. He staggered back, engulfed in a blinding flash. His sword fell to the floor, and he stumbled backward. He shaded his eyes against the glare and fell to his knees, all his muscles contracting in a great spasm. His mouth opened, but no sound issued from his throat. His hands went to his chest as though to drive away a terrible pain. Down he sank until he sat upon his heels. Then the fire faded, absorbed into his body.

"Do you understand, Murchad?" Siobhan said. Her voice was barely audible. Weariness numbed her. "You will live forever. I have given all my power to do this. None can take back the spell. It is irrevocable. All you treasure, those you know, friend, kin or foe, will all grow old and die, but you shall endure. For all eternity."

Siobhan walked an unsteady course from the chamber. She did not look back. She could not bear to see her precious son's body, or Gareth's. She wanted to run, to fade away to her safe place, but she could not. The summoning had totally depleted her. She stumbled down the corridor.

Siobhan paused and steadied herself against a wall. The cold seeped into her palm. She pulled her hand away, leaving a bloody hand print. She raised her other hand and opened it. The cloak pin was sundered into two pieces.

In that awful moment of vengeance, Siobhan had used all her strength, all her enchantment – even drawing on the pin's ancient magic – to conjure the spell she had forced upon Murchad. Because of the summoning, she was doomed to a mortal life span, fated to die a mortal death, her sorcery spent in one instant of ultimate reprisal.

But Bran's child could live. Her line would continue if the babe lived. Murchad would eventually unravel the truth. The serving girls, the cousins, someone, would repeat the gossip, and Murchad would know of the *Sidhe* babe left behind. The druid would counsel him. The girl's life would be in danger. The babe would never be born.

Siobhan must find a refuge for the girl and her child. There was one who might help her.

Orghlaith.

25

Kirk Morgan's cell phone rang. He set the glass of Dom Perignon on the table beside his chair.

"Hi, Mark? Remember me?" The woman's was young and expectant. "I work at the Maywood Clinic out in Milwaukie?" Her voice evoked a memory of a sensual mouth and soft skin. He closed off that line of thought. Unproductive thinking would defeat him now when he felt the circles closing around him.

"Yes." He had given her a false name. Her name was Amber Singer.

Morgan was a man with unlimited resources. He had hired a teenage felon who claimed he could hack any computer system on the planet. Once he got Morgan into the hospital's computer records, it had taken only a few minutes in the personnel files to find someone who might be useful. A young, attractive nurse.

An accidental meeting in the parking lot as she left work the day before yesterday had netted him a dinner date – at an exclusive restaurant – and an evening of interesting sex. She was intrigued by the reward he offered her for information. She left the hotel room in the middle of the night, saying she had to get some sleep so she could go to work the following afternoon. He'd vaguely promised to call her. What he most remembered about her was how virtually everything she said came out as a question.

She had followed through on his request. All he wanted were updates on Brant Edwards. Unethical, perhaps, but not illegal.

"Well…" She hesitated. "I called to tell you something?" He waited for her to continue, his heart beating a faster rhythm. "It's about that man? Brant Edwards?"

He glanced at his Rolex. One thirty-six in the morning. A cigar and a glass of fine Champagne before bedtime had suddenly lost their appeal.

"Hello, Amber." Morgan tried to make his voice seductive, but he wished the damned woman would get to the point. Although brainless, she was good in bed. Was she stalling for more money?

"You wanted me to call you if anything developed?"

"Yes," he said, forcing patience in his voice.

"I'm sorry it's so late?"

"Not at all," he assured her. "You're doing exactly what I asked you to do."

"Well…it's kind of odd? I don't know if it means anything?"

"Tell me," he said. "I'll decide if it's important."

"I was chatting with Al? He's the night guard? And Mr. Edwards ran right past us – didn't say a word – and got in a car with someone. It was just like a jailbreak, you know? Why do you suppose he did that? Why didn't he just check himself out? Anyway, Al – the security guard? – didn't get a license. He called the police?"

Shit. Just what he didn't need. Cops had a way of snooping and eventually finding out things that were none of their business.

The woman prattled on. "Anyway, they're looking at the security tape to see who it was. It's all very strange. The police are questioning everybody who's on duty? I got away long enough to go to the bathroom and call you. What should I tell them?"

"Nothing except what you saw," Morgan said. "Do you understand?"

"Nothing? Okay?"

"When did this happen?"

"Close to midnight."

What the hell was going on? "Thank you, my dear," he said. "You did a fine job. Wasn't too difficult, was it?"

"No," she said. "But please don't tell anybody I told you? When people come to the clinic, it's supposed to be confidential."

"Oh, it is," he said. "I didn't ask you to release privileged information, did I? And I won't tell on you. I'm going to my computer right now. In the morning you'll find a substantial amount deposited into your checking account. It will be six figures."

"Oh. My. God." She sounded breathless. "How do I explain where the money came from?"

"A letter will follow with income tax information saying it is a bequest from a long-lost relative," he said.

"Geez, how can I ever thank you?"

"I'm sure you'll find a way, Amber." She did not know who he really was. And this was another in a long line of untraceable cell phones. "Don't worry. No one will know. I'll call you." He pressed the Off button and put the phone in his pants pocket. He would smash it and throw the pieces into the Columbia within hours.

Morgan sat in the darkened room with his chin in his hands and thought for a long time. Ghosts of memories flitted at the edges of his thoughts. It was obvious that something big was happening, but he couldn't grasp the pattern. The woman, Maeve might be in on whatever Edwards was planning. Or her cop husband. Maybe the whole damned situation was an elaborate con. What if it wasn't?

Shit. He should have dealt with the sister before things came to this.

The Champagne and his cigar forgotten, he went to his study where he sat at his computer and transferred money to Amber's checking account. Morgan composed the legalities required by law, ran off the forms and signed them. He put them in a Fed Ex envelope and filled out the necessary information. In the foyer he set the envelope on the marble-topped table beside his car keys – the Hummer he used when he didn't want a driver.

He picked up his personal phone and dialed.

After five rings a male voice said. "Gordon here."

"Detective, this is Kirk Morgan, from Morgan and Associates."

An instant's pause. "I know who you are."

"It's about Brant Edwards."

"Yeah?" Gordon said. "So. What the hell do you want? Make it quick. I'm driving."

"Brant has disappeared."

"I know. I'm on my way. How did you know?" Gordon's tone was suspicious. Or was Morgan just paranoid?

"Let's say I have a source, Detective. I – my firm has a vested interest in the guy, you know."

"Yeah."

"Can you do anything? Investigate?"

"I work homicide, Mr. Morgan. In the city."

"Suppose there's been a…murder?"

"Murder?" Gordon's voice rose a bit.

"Remember the story of the girl who came out of the woods?"

"Yeah."

Not given to premonitions, Morgan had a strong feeling that where Brant was, he should be. Murder. That was something to motivate Gordon.

Morgan made his voice smooth and calm. "Please find Mr. Edwards."

"That's what I'm about to do," Gordon said and cut the connection.

A few minutes later Morgan dropped the envelope in the nearest Fed-Ex box and then drove himself across town, ducking every traffic light that threatened to slow him down. Perhaps he shouldn't have called Gordon. But he might have to rely on the detective's resources to find Edwards.

Morgan arrived at the clinic in 40 minutes. The main entry doors were unlocked, guarded by two local law enforcement officers. He showed them his identification, saying he was an attorney with a client waiting. The officers let him pass, but Morgan felt them watching him as he strode to the front desk.

Behind the desk a young man sat with a cell phone hugged between his ear and shoulder. The man nodded and kept on talking. Morgan drummed his fingers on the desk for a moment, then reached over, snapped it shut and laid it on the counter none too gently.

"Hey," the man said, rising from his chair. "What the hell was that for?"

Morgan read his name tag and said, "Mr. Morrison, I understand you lost a patient."

"Lost?" The man stared at him.

"May I speak with your supervisor?" Morgan said. "There…there's been an emergency.…I must find out where he is."

The man did not respond.

"Brant Edwards," Morgan said.

Eyeing him with suspicion, Morrison picked up a phone and punched buttons. After a couple of seconds he spoke. "I've got another one here looking for Edwards." Pause. "No, he doesn't look like a cop." He listened a moment. "Okay." Looking up at Morgan, the guard said, "Just a minute."

Morgan waited impatiently, gazing at the security guard who looked away and began straightening things on his desk. Within moments a heavyset, middle-aged woman waddled from the hallway toward him.

"This is the guy," the guard said, pointing at Morgan.

"May I help you, sir?" the woman said, her tone stern and businesslike.

She wore a dark suit and a blouse that tied with a fussy bow at the neck. The bow was perfectly symmetrical.

This would require some acting skills. He tried to appear distraught and held up his ID.

"I must speak to your lost patient," he said.

She took his arm, and he allowed himself to be guided down the corridor into a tiny office. After the door closed she turned to him. "Are you referring to Mr. Edwards?"

"Yes." He handed her his business card. "I'm the law firm that handles Mr. Edwards' legal affairs. There's a family emergency. It…it's rather tragic, I'm afraid." He tried to sound upset. "His sister has had an accident. She's very bad, they don't think she's going to live…."

"Oh no," the woman said. "I'm so sorry." Her eyes registered sympathy.

Morgan put on an unctuous smile. "I came to deliver the news in person. Didn't want to inform him by phone. I believe her husband might have been here a while ago – Lt. Richard Gordon with the Portland PD." The woman nodded. "We must speak to Mr. Edwards. Someone must make a decision to turn off the machines…no hope…." That should do it.

"Well," she hesitated. "It's a matter of confidentiality…."

He wrung his hands. "I must find him. He's the only one."

The woman sighed. "After Mr. Edwards left in someone's car, Detective Gordon came here. He looked in Mr. Edwards' room and then left."

"Do you have any idea where he went?"

"The police are working on that," she said. "But I think that detective might know something. He saw a drawing that had been left on Mr. Edwards' bed, and then he just took off. Didn't say a word."

Morgan glared at the woman. "What drawing?"

She held her ground. "Mr. Edwards is an artist."

Morgan leaned toward the woman. "What kind of drawing?"

She moved back, just a tiny step. "Well, it was done with pencil, charcoal, maybe – "

"What did the drawing show?" Morgan said, his voice hoarse with anger.

Her eyes were frightened now, flicking around. "I don't – "

"What was in the fucking drawing?"

The woman's eyes held panic. "There were trees and a cabin – no there were actually two cabins, one in front of the other – and there was a light coming from the woods and – "

Morgan turned and hurried to the door.

The cabin. Edwards had gone there, like a rabbit to its hole.

"Goddamnit," he snarled, although he had stopped believing in God a long time ago. He broke into a jog and didn't stop running until he reached his car.

26

Siobhan and the girl rode all night, around loughs of black water, up and down hills. They splashed along streams and went in circles to confuse their pursuers. Near dawn heavy mist promised rain. The two horses were tiring.

Siobhan clung to the bay gelding's neck. She was slipping, but she hadn't strength to pull herself upright.

"Lady," Slaine cried.

Siobhan could not communicate with the horse's mind. Even that part of her enchantment was gone. The girl urged her horse up beside the gelding, and pushed Siobhan up on the horse's back.

Desperation clouded Siobhan's judgment. "Keep moving," she said.

Siobhan's human intuition had not failed. Murchad's men were behind them, riding hard. Murchad would want answers, and he wasn't witless. He would discover Siobhan's vulnerability and hold her to keep her from the forest. He would kill the girl to prevent another fey child.

Siobhan's had no desire to see the son of the red-haired druidess made heir in Bran's place. She could not live inside the walls, knowing what memories the stones held. Bereft of her sorcery, she was helpless, prey to the emotions that caused her such pain, and subject to the political manipulations of Murchad and his people. Strong of will even in her grief, she would not submit.

She tried to ignore her empathy for the horses' fatigue. "Keep moving," she said again and kicked her heels into the gelding's lathered sides. Gamely, he moved at a faster walk.

She was glad she could not feel the horses' thoughts. Both animals' labored breathing wrenched her heart, but pursuit was only moments behind. Saving her son's baby was all that mattered.

Siobhan's gelding slowed. This beast hadn't nearly the endurance of the Kerry mare, but that fine horse was long gone, mortal like so much in the world. Slaine kicked her horse forward, grabbed the gelding's reins and pulled him along. Finally, both horses were reduced to a shambling walk, and no urging could make them go faster. The two women rode side by side in silence.

Heavy mist turned to cold rain. The two women skirted a marshy dell and cut across a muddy field of stalks that had recently been corn. At the edge of the *Sidhe* Wood the horses stopped and stood splay-footed with their heads down. They panted streamers of breath that drifted on the still air.

Siobhan turned and studied the way they had come. No sign of pursuit, but in her heart she knew Murchad was close. He would soon enough determine she had misled him, and he would head straight for the woods.

Spent, broken by the heavy burden of sorrow, Siobhan hadn't strength to slide from the gelding's sweaty back. Slaine helped her and guided her bare feet to the ground. She had lost her slippers somewhere. Without her enchantment she felt the earth's chill. A stone dug into her heel, but she forced herself to walk. The horses were useless.

With Slaine supporting her Siobhan stumbled into the forest. Within a few paces the cold gripped her and gnawed at her like a hawk picks at a rabbit's bones.

"Lady," Slaine said. Siobhan stopped. "We cannot go further."

"Why not?" Siobhan said, not turning. She could not waste the energy it took to face the girl.

"It is a place of the *Sidhe*....The queen of *Faerie* will spirit us away, and we will not set foot on this earth again."

Slaine stood shivering. Siobhan remembered this girl from the kitchen. She was always courteous and attentive when serving, though awed by the duty of attending a lady of the *Sidhe*. Slaine was fine-boned and slight, a pretty girl. Her dark hair, once plaited neatly around her head, hung damp and unbound. Her face bore smudges and streaks where tears had run through the grime. Slaine crossed herself as Siobhan had seen Gareth do countless times.

Gareth. Thinking his name brought Siobhan a fresh pang of grief. That he had loved her unrequited all those years preyed on her guilt. If only she could have chosen a different path.

"You came this far with me, Slaine," Siobhan said quietly. "I am one of those you fear. And so was Bran. Murchad is only human. He is consumed by anger and fear."

The girl stood, indecisive, wringing her hands. The forest held its breath.

"I can offer you no protection," Siobhan said. "My powers are gone. But I believe the one who dwells here will aid us. She helped me once. She is not evil.

"Slaine, Slaine, Slaine, come." Siobhan spoke the name thrice, hoping to call up some vestige of her powers and compel the girl. "If Murchad finds you, you and your child will die. The child is one of my kind. Murchad will not give sanctuary to one like me ever again."

Slaine nodded, walked into the forest as if drawn by an invisible thread. Siobhan dared hope some part of her sorcery still remained. She probed for the girl's mind. Nothing. She held out her hand. Slaine grasped it.

"You tremble," Siobhan whispered.

"I am afraid," Slaine replied. "But more afraid of the o'Ruairc's wrath than the *Sidhe*. Perhaps the child I carry will be graced with some of the powers of your race."

"Perhaps not."

"I will love the babe no matter," Slaine said. "He will be a part of Bran." A blush spread across her face. Her lips trembled.

Siobhan brushed a wisp of dark hair from the girl's dirty face. "You loved my son."

Slaine nodded. "He…he was kind to me. I have no family. My mother died of the fever when I was very young, and my father fostered me to the o'Ruairc clan. Bran was kind to me, gentle. I loved him…he loved me, I think."

"Yes, child, he did," Siobhan said. "His last words were of you."

"Oh, lady," Slaine wailed. "God will punish me for my sins – "

"It seems to me," Siobhan said, "that you have done nothing to warrant chastisement. You loved my son, and he loved you. Surely your God can love." She dug in the fabric pouch that served as her purse, extracting the sundered pieces of the gold brooch. She felt the exposed iron core against her skin. It did not burn her. Choosing the smaller fragment, she pressed it into Slaine's hand.

"What – ?"

"It is Bran's broken brooch," Siobhan said. "Give it to the babe when he reaches the age of reason. Instruct him to pass it to his firstborn and thence down through the generations. If nothing else, it will be a talisman against evil. Someday, perhaps, it will remind the one who bears it of his heritage and give comfort or aid in time of need."

Tears flowed again from the girl's eyes. She brushed them away with nervous fingers.

Siobhan touched Slaine's cheek. "Do not be too proud to cry, child. Even the *Sidhe* weep." Tears filled her own eyes. "Perhaps a day will come when those of *Faerie* and mortals can live together in harmony. Till then, hide your babe and teach him to be good to others and true to the land that birthed him."

Slaine nodded.

"Come," Siobhan urged.

The girl followed her into the shadowy world of the *Sidhe* Wood. A breeze moved bare branches, rattling them like old bones. Fallen leaves and old needles, dry reminders of summer's verdant glory, crunched under their feet.

Siobhan shivered and pulled her *brat* around her, drew the knot tighter. Without a warming spell the keen edge of the wind cut through her clothing, gnawed at her bones. She squeezed the girl's hand, grateful for the warmth of her touch.

Siobhan followed her memory and led the girl to the center of the forest. Ancient and proud, the oak must have stood for centuries guarding the portal to the *Faerie* world. Its branches spread wide, forbidding entrance to Orghlaith's realm. Not the world of Siobhan's special place – now forever closed to her. Orghlaith's world was far more powerful and mysterious than Siobhan could fathom.

Without hesitation, swallowing her own fear lest the girl sense her uncertainty, Siobhan led Slaine to the tree. She gathered up her courage, pushed hopelessness to the back of her mind and rapped seven times on the bark.

"Orghlaith, Orghlaith, Orghlaith," she whispered. "Hear me. I have need. Great need." She sank to the ground. Slaine tried to catch her, but could not hold her. Siobhan did not feel the turf when she hit it.

"Who calls me into the mortal world?" A melodious voice.

Slaine stammered, "I – it is Lady Siobhan. She knocked on the tree. P-please help us."

"Will you come, child? You must say yes. I cannot take you against your will. Soldiers with iron ride to my wood. Iron will kill you and me. There is no defense against it."

Hesitation. Then, "Yes," Slaine said.

The darkest night enveloped Siobhan. She hoped this was the darkness of unconsciousness that she craved, oblivion that would take away the pain. A warm cloak of enchantment wrapped around her. Then there was no sight, no sound, no feeling. Numbness stole over her and robbed her mind of thoughts.

She fell a great distance, fell through the starry void of the heavens, falling and falling. She was too weary to try and stop herself. And then even the falling sensation left her, and there was nothing…nothing….

Murchad reined his horse with a vicious jerk. The other men yanked on their reins. They cursed and tried to keep their mounts from ramming each other.

Harness metal and weapons clanked as the skittish horses milled around. Murchad dismounted and stood listening at the edge of the trees. Heavy rain clouds hid the sky. Under the trees darkness reigned. A chill raced up his back.

"They came this way," Murchad said. "Their tracks go into the trees."

His men whispered to each other and cast apprehensive glances at shadows that shifted and flitted around in the forest dimness.

Finding some reason in his single-minded desire for revenge, Murchad faced his warriors.

"I will not order any of you to accompany me," he said. "But the witch has wrought great evil to my clan." The men shouted their support.

Murchad raised his sword. "We must kill the girl and the unborn witch child or we are doomed to an unlucky holding."

Did something rustle the bushes? He glanced around. Silence. Unnatural silence. The hair on the back of his neck rose.

"Who will come with me?" he said.

Hands went up slowly. Murchad pointed. "You, Niall. And you, Daire and Fioon. I will ask no others. There is something uncanny about the wood."

Murchad handed the reins of his horse to a younger man.

"Return for provisions and post a guard here," Murchad said. "Wait two dawns. No longer. If we do not return, ride home and tell them the o'Ruairc is dead. Bury my son. The druid will see his grandson installed as the proper heir." He tasted bitter gall.

"Two dawns," the man beside him said. "Farewell, my lord."

Murchad strode under the winter-bare trees. He did not wait for the chosen men. It wouldn't do for them to think he was hesitant. If they followed he would accept them. If not, well, he had faced battle alone before. He heard slow footfalls on the brittle leaves behind him.

Murchad traced the women's tracks in the disturbed leaves and broken twigs. They had not bothered to hide their trail. He would find them and kill the girl and her *faerie* child. The *Sidhe* witch he would imprison for adultery. He should have known. Dealings with witches never went well in the end. They would pay. Even the druid.

At first the way was easy, the trees spaced far enough apart to admit the men. They walked uphill a long time while the trees grew thicker, closer together. Murchad and the three men squeezed between massive trunks so close together there was hardly space for a man. Finally, they reached the edge of a clearing. Murchad raised an arm, halting the others.

In the center of the clearing loomed a massive oak whose naked branches clawed the sky as if in supplication to approaching winter. Little lights twinkled in the branches like tiny stars. Or fireflies. But the lazy evenings of summer, when fireflies hovered over the fields, were past, the fireflies were gone.

Murchad drew his sword and stalked up to the huge trunk. He waved the lights away, but they swarmed around him, avoiding his blade.

"Who comes into my wood?"

A voice had spoken from the tree. Was the oak enchanted? Evil? He crossed himself awkwardly with his free hand.

"I am Murchad o'Ruairc," he said, feeling foolish talking to a tree. He turned to his men. They stood at the edge of the clearing, swords drawn, ready to defend their lord. They seemed to be very far away, further than the few steps he had walked away from them. The fireflies grew thicker, clustering around him like spring butterflies. He swung his sword. The lights retreated.

The three who accompanied him turned and ran. He could not fault them. He would run too, but it was too late for him. He must see this through. Revenge would be his.

"What do you wish of the Lady of the Wood?" The voice compelled him to answer, drew him closer. Vapor formed and curled around his ankles. Damp tendrils of mist swirled up his legs. The forest dimmed, blurred. All around him was obscured by more then just the fog that rose from the ground.

"I wish only to find my wife," Murchad said. "And she who bears my son's child." He hoped his falseness did not show.

Laughter echoed from the air around him. "I know you would harm them, king." The woman said. "They are beyond your reach. I have taken them into my world. They are safe forever."

Murchad's fear receded, replaced by anger born of the sorrow that filled his heart. Sorrow not only for the son he had lost and the wife who had betrayed him, but for the choices he had made that could not be taken back.

"I know of you," he said putting on a boldness he did not feel. "Orghlaith, Orghlaith, Orghlaith, Queen of the Fair Folk." He spoke her name three times. Did the tales of the magical folk have some truth? If he called her thrice, could he exert any control over one such as she?

Laughter again. "You call my name thrice, mortal," she said. "It amuses me to speak to you. Will you come into my world? Your world tires me. Murchad, Murchad, Murchad, come." She turned his own ploy on him. "But not the sword. Iron may not enter my domain. Leave it and any other iron you wear."

Hearing his name spoken thus, Murchad had no choice. He lowered the sword. It clattered against a stone. If Siobhan were right, he would live forever, so what harm would it do to speak with the woman of the wood? He unpinned the brooch from his *brat* and the bronze wristlets and dropped them.

"1 will come into your world," Murchad said. "But you must give your oath you will let me return to mine."

"I promise," the woman said.

A cloak of darkness wrapped around him. He fell into a bottomless chasm. The glowing firefly lights winked on and swarmed around him.

And then he stood on a solid surface. The fireflies on his skin and clothing glowed in the gloom. His eyes adjusted to the dimness. He was in a circular room – as if he were inside the tree – a room whose walls were finished with fine wood, polished to a high luster. Beautifully crafted furniture adorned the space, a table and a chair with flowing lines. On the table rested a vase filled with spring flowers. He smelled their fragrance. The lights left his person and drifted away in a cloud. They drew together into the vague outline of a female form.

Radiance flowed from her face and blinded Murchad. He squinted against the glare. The fireflies defined themselves into a flowing gown of dazzling light. Golden hair haloed a face of such serene beauty that men would murder for a glimpse of it.

"Orghlaith," Murchad whispered.

"You know me?" He flinched from her probing eyes.

"I know of you," Murchad said. "Many a lad has come into this wood never to return to the land of the living. But some escape to tell the story."

"The others stay by choice," she said.

"Whose choice?" he said. "They may enter your kingdom by choice, but how many of them would return if given the chance?"

"I ask them," she said, "every hundred years or so."

"It is true, then, what I have heard," Murchad said. "Time passes differently in your world?"

"Time is relative, Murchad," Orghlaith said, "like it is in your world. Some of your people use their time well, others do not. I give you some of my time, but I see Siobhan has given you much." He gazed at her, questioning. She chuckled. "You doubt the possibility of immortality?"

"Is it possible?" he said, afraid to hear either answer.

"Feel your body, mortal. Does not your heart beat stronger than yesterday? Are not your muscles those of a younger man? Do not your joints flex more easily? Touch your face." He raised trembling fingers to his cheeks. "Where are the lines the years had graven into your features?"

The skin was smooth high on his cheeks where his beard did not cover. "It is true?"

"Yes, man. It is true. The one you know as Siobhan transgressed greatly when she summoned the spell that will allow you to live beyond your time. Oh, you can be killed if your head is severed. Any wound short of that, and your body will renew itself and heal as you sleep. You will not age. Enjoy what Siobhan has given you, Murchad o'Ruairc. The gift was dearly bought."

"What do you mean?"

"One such as she who is only part *Sidhe* loses all her powers invoking such a spell."

"Part – ?"

"You did not know. That was Siobhan's vulnerability: her mother was mortal. Alas, one of our kind fell in love with one of your women, and Siobhan was born. The woman chose to raise her daughter in your world. But that was before your time or your grandfather's time."

The woman floated closer to him. "You are concerned with what has happened to you. Knowing her heritage was how the druid knew her weakness. Siobhan felt the mortal emotion of anger. It was that anger that led her to grant you the spell. Anger…that is what started the whole thing, is it not? Anger at your inability to father an heir, anger at Siobhan's aloofness. Anger…." Her voice trailed off.

Murchad searched through half-formed thoughts for the words that would put his life aright. But he could think of nothing he could say that would take back the past.

"I would speak with Siobhan," he said finally.

"She is not here."

"What have you done with her?" He reached for his sword, but it was gone.

Orghlaith laughed. "Your blade avails you naught," she said. "What is done cannot be revisited."

The witch could hear his thoughts. He guarded the images in his mind. "I would speak with Siobhan," he repeated.

"She is far away, Murchad," Orghlaith said. "Far away, indeed."

"What of the girl, Slaine?"

"She is safe. You will not see her again. She will be safe and content with the babe. Those who shelter her will see to her needs. She will make no claim upon you."

Murchad's fury rose. He wanted to discover why Siobhan had dallied with Gareth, when she never let her lawful husband touch her.

"Siobhan never deceived you with Gareth." Orghlaith spoke quietly. The words branded themselves into Murchad's mind.

"Never?"

Orghlaith shook her head. Golden sparks fell from her face. "Never, even in thought. She was faithful to you and the boy."

Suddenly much became clear. "I have been a fool," Murchad moaned.

"Many more than you have admitted such," Orghlaith said.

"May I talk to Siobhan? Then I will leave."

"She is gone, Murchad. Beyond your reach."

"With you?"

"No. Much further away."

Murchad remembered an old legend, dug in his pocket for the coin Gareth had given him long ago. He held out the small, round bit of gold. He had no desire to keep a reminder of the man. "I have heard it said that for a bit of gold given by a human, you must prophesy what will come to pass."

"Ah." She chuckled. "That is true. But whether you will understand what I say, or use it wisely, is another matter."

The gold coin lifted of its own volition from Murchad's palm and flew across the room to Orghlaith's outstretched hand, and then became another gleam in her radiant garment.

"I will tell you what will be, man," Orghlaith said. "Use it as you see fit. I will not explain it. And know also that Siobhan's kind will not aid you. Siobhan was one of the last of her people: half human, half fey.

"My race has weathered many storms in the history of men, but we are few. Events will come to pass that we have no desire to see. We do not bother with the affairs of mortal men. Except for you, Murchad, your people are but leaves on the currents of time. My people will endure until the end of time.

"You wish the future revealed? Here is what will be, if you can understand. Take note of the words. They are written on this." She held up a hand, and a scroll appeared. "Hearken well. And remember that when the prophecy has come to pass, you will live long, man, almost as long as some of my people. You will see things in your lifetime that even I will not see."

Her voice took on a deep resonance that penetrated to Murchad's bones.

"Into the oak the acorn grows
And spreads its seed around it.
Death's cold seed grows too within;
The earth-forged knife has bound it.
Endless circles draw together,
Sought by three who find them.
Once made whole, the circles close.
Eternity will bind them."

She gestured, and the rolled sheet appeared in Murchad's hand. It was a parchment-like material, much finer than the monks of the abbey used for their writing. Words were graven on the sheet. Murchad recognized some of the Latin characters Bran and Gareth had taught him. The druid would decipher it.

"Now go, man," Orghlaith said. "Do not summon me again, for I seal the gates to my realm for good. I will barricade the paths to my world that none may disturb us again. Others like me do this now, taking with them those of Siobhan's kind who will accept our shelter. Hurry from the wood, man, before the storm of our leaving overtakes you. I cannot protect you if you hesitate."

Her body blazed with light. Murchad stumbled backward, shading his eyes from the sudden brilliance. He reached behind him with his free hand, expecting to fetch up against the wall.

Instead, he struck the rough bark of the oak. The dark forest spread around him. He thrust the scroll into his shirt.

A streak of lightning across the sky revealed the naked branches of the oak in stark outline. Thunder crashed an ominous warning.

Murchad grabbed his belongings from the ground and ran for the cover of the trees across the meadow. He glanced back. A bolt of lightning struck the oak, and it shattered into splinters. The boom of the thunder threw him to the ground, knocking him senseless.

When he caught his breath and was finally able to stand, he ran as fast as his younger legs would work until his breath labored in ragged gasps. Orghlaith was vindictive enough to destroy the entire forest, not just the one tree.

He ran and dodged branches that fell from the trees. Any moment a flaming bolt might impale him from behind. Finally Murchad burst from the trees. Rain slashed down in torrents. Jagged lightning tore the heavens. Half a dozen of his warriors tried to stay mounted on horses that plunged and snorted. All but two of the terrified horses bolted.

"Murchad! Lord!"

Rain streamed into his eyes, and he could not determine where the sound came from.

"Over here." It was Donall, a man who had served him faithfully over the years. The old man held the reins of Murchad's rearing stallion and his own dancing mount. The frightened beasts dragged on the man's outstretched arms. Murchad ran through the pelting rain and seized his horse's reins.

"How long?" Murchad shouted over the roar of the thunder and the rain. The man stared at him. Again he said, "How long was I gone?"

"Two days," Donall shouted above the noise. "We were afraid, lord. The storm has raged ever since you entered the wood. The other men fled. Do not blame them. They have never seen such an uncanny storm."

Murchad snorted. "Why did you few remain?"

"My grandmother claimed she was touched by the *Sidhe*, lord," Donall said. "The Fair Folk frighten me only when they are silent. Anger I understand. I have lived through many storms."

Murchad sprang to the stallion's back, waiting long enough for the older man to mount, then set his heels into the steed's sides and held on as the beast galloped toward home. Donall's mount pounded behind him.

The *faerie* woman's scroll crinkled against his skin. The druid would expect payment for deciphering it. It would be a small price for Murchad's declaration that Ceallachan's grandson would sit in his place after he was gone. Murchad smiled in satisfaction. One day he would depart. But not for the next world. There would be time enough to track down the girl and her child. He had all the time in the world. The witch queen had promised him eternity.

Murchad plunged into the teeth of the storm. By the time he and his guard reached the fortress, the cold rain had become sleet, and Murchad's plans were set in his mind.

27

Brant turned his jacket collar up and hunched his shoulders against the icy wind. Maeve trudged beside him, holding her parka hood around her face. Heavy snow swirled around them. Enormous Douglas firs and hemlocks afforded a little protection from the brunt of the wind, but snow crystals stung Brant's cheeks. The flashlight only penetrated a few feet into the wall of snow.

"Welcome to winter," Brant said, false cheerfulness that fell flat.

"Are you sure this is the right road?" Maeve said. "I haven't been here in so long – everything looks different."

"Yeah," he said. "It's the road." An invisible force drew him toward the cabin. "It's just around the next bend." Nothing seemed familiar.

"God, it's cold," Maeve said. "I wish I'd brought a thermos of coffee."

"When we get there I'll get a fire going and make some."

The trees whispered and moaned in the wind. Snow was already ankle deep. Brant's ears felt numb.

"There's plenty of firewood," Brant said. "I come up here every spring for a few days and split wood."

"I know – "

He turned to her. She had stopped, her mouth open to say more. Snowflakes clung to her eyelashes. She shook her head and continued walking.

"It's hard to believe," she said, "that just a few miles away a volcano caused so much damage. That was the year I was born."

"I was nine," Brant said. "All the places I used to go when I was a kid… all gone….Weyerhauser got rich from that little display of nature's power."

"Little display?" She turned and glared at him.

"Figure of speech."

"Mom used to tell me about the ice caves," she said. "How she took you up there in the summer to cool off when it was really warm. You had to wear winter clothes over shorts and t-shirts."

"Ice dripped from the ceiling and covered the walls…." Brant said. In high school he and his buddies hid beer inside and went sliding on the glacier with cardboard sleds. The beer stayed frosty cold. Brant shivered at a blast of wind that worked its way between the trees.

They rounded the last bend. They were no more than 50 yards from the cabin, barely visible through the snow.

"Told you this was the right road," Brant said.

"You always did have a great sense of direction."

He remembered hiking with a girl and trying to decipher a map.

We're headed east, he had said. *We should be going north.*

How do you know?

Because I just know.

He had started off on a trail that right-angled from the one they traveled. She followed him and was amazed when they arrived back at the trail head where they had started.

How'd you do that? she said.

He pointed to his temple. Magic, he had said…Magic….

"It's so beautiful in the snow." Maeve's voice drew him back to the present.

"It is, isn't it?" His grandfather had bought the land from a man who had sold 200 acres of virgin, old growth timber to the lumber company. Another friend, a carpenter, helped build the cabin, at first crude, but over the years it had become a work of carpentry art.

Brant stepped up onto the porch, Maeve close behind him. They brushed snow from their clothing and stamped it off their feet.

He fumbled for his key ring. His numb fingers almost dropped it. Finally he managed to get the key right side up and slid it into the lock. He almost cowered as the door swung open.

Nothing is wrong, he told himself.

His wet shoes squeaked on the hardwood floor. The battery-powered lantern and a fireplace lighter sat on the table beside the door, just as Brant always left them. He lifted the lantern. He flipped the switch, and a soft glow flooded the room. The cabin smelled musty. His breath puffed out in a cloud. Behind him Maeve swung the door shut.

Brant turned full circle, peering into the shadows, not knowing what he expected. His gaze stopped a moment on the sink, then on the bed with its bright quilt. He felt a momentary dizziness of *déjà vu*.

Shadows. Shadows and hints of memory. There *was* a woman here with him. One who had gone away to…somewhere….

What if he had done something to her? Wouldn't he remember that? He remembered the fire when the two men robbed him.

He called the fire that night.

"What are we looking for, Brant?" Maeve said.

He threw his hands up. "Shit, I don't know," he said, a little too loudly. "Something that makes sense, that'll tell me I'm not going nuts, that the world is still on the right track. I guess I want to know *I'm* on the right track."

She backed away, her eyes wide.

"Hey, I'm sorry," he said. "I didn't mean to sound so crazy. I'm just…I feel confused…." Brant shivered. "I'll build a fire. It's colder than hell."

"I always thought hell would be fiery," Maeve said.

He had heard that expression before. Where? He couldn't remember.

"Wood," he said, pointing to the door.

She followed him around the side of the cabin where a lean-to sheltered an enormous amount of neatly stacked, split wood. They each returned with an arm load. While he started the fire, she waded through the deepening snow to the lean-to and brought back several more loads which she piled beside the fireplace. Finally, a blazing fire's warmth permeated the room. Maeve removed her mittens and laid them on the edge of the hearth to dry.

A sealed canister on the counter held coffee. Brant measured some into an old metal coffee pot. He pumped a long time before water flowed. He hoped he'd remembered to winterize the septic system before he'd left. He filled the pot and hung it on the fireplace hook to brew.

Maybe this hadn't been such a good idea. He should have waited until he could get the electricity turned on. He flopped on the couch and motioned Maeve to join him, but she sat away from him, leaning against the sagging arm.

He traced the worn pattern in the sofa fabric.

"I'm going to tell you a story," he started. "Suppose someone came forward in time – "

"That's impossible."

"But what if, just once, it really happened? Once. A fluke."

"Magic?" She leaned forward with her hands out to the fire.

"Forget magic. Just suppose it could happen. Suppose a woman came from the past, and I just happened to be where she appeared" – he pointed downward – "at that instant."

"Pretty lucky."

"Luck or fate. But for one moment imagine it could really happen. I meet this hypothetical woman from the past and spend two weeks with her."

"Two weeks you don't remember?"

"Only glimpses," he said. "What do you know about Irish mythology?"

"As much as you do. What I've read. And Mom used to tell us stories – "

"The Fair Folk – the *Daoine Sidhe* – who came to Ireland long ago when magic was real. Not leprechauns, or sprites, or anything like that. According to the myths they were a magical race who kept apart from all the waves of people who invaded and settled Ireland. They lived in an underground realm, occasionally venturing out to fall in love with mortals or entice one into their world."

"Or to replace a baby with a changeling." She snorted softly. "The changeling stories are how superstitious people explained sickly babies."

"But suspend disbelief for a moment," he said. "Suppose that I did meet someone from the past. Don't look at me like that. I know I sound like a lunatic. But what if it's real? And what if something terrible happened, and that's why I can't remember all of it."

Brant had seen something, or been part of something that still eluded him – something *wrong*. He remembered bits and pieces, fragments glimpsed through the broken mirror in his dream. But there was more buried inside him, some convoluted secret that he could not find no matter how he searched. It scared the shit out of him. So much so, that when he tried to remember, the headache started.

"So what happened to her?" Maeve said.

"She went back to the past, the world she came from. A thousand years ago." It was paradoxical to think that she was long dead, and yet, for him, meeting her had happened only a few weeks ago. "Her name was Siobhan." He rose and took two mugs from a cupboard, poured them each a cup of coffee.

Maeve accepted a steaming mug, blew and sipped. She sat with her hands wrapped around the mug and stared into the flames. The fire crackled.

Wind-blown snow scratched at the cabin like an animal trying to get in from the cold.

Maeve shed the jacket and dug out her cell phone.

Brant's jacket joined hers on the back of the couch, and he stepped closer to the fire.

She looked at the phone's display. "Shit," she swore softly.

"No service. Remember?"

"I thought maybe someone finally built a tower somewhere nearby," she said. Sighing, she returned the phone to her pocket and met his gaze. "I don't think you could have done something awful."

"Thanks," he said. "But *something* happened to me, Maeve. Something I don't understand. There aren't such things as magic, or fairies, or time travel. None of it's possible."

"Wasn't it Sherlock Holmes who said that when you eliminate the impossible, whatever is left, no matter how improbable, is the truth?"

He nodded, but a knot of worry settled behind his eyes. The lantern had dimmed. He set his mug on the hearth and went for a fresh battery. From the darkness under the sink he pulled out a liquor bottle. Another reach netted the extra battery which he set on the counter. He held up the bottle.

"Drink?" he said. "Nothing fancy. Canadian Club. We can put in the coffee if you like." He shook the bottle. "There's a little left from when I was here before."

"Sure," she said. "But not in the coffee."

Brant opened an overhead cupboard for a glass. The storage area had been filled with packaged and dehydrated food. He brought supplies up when he came to chop wood. That way the cabin was always stocked. He could come up here anytime and only had to bring perishables. The shelves were bare except for a package of instant potatoes and an unopened box of crackers. He checked the other side of the cabinet. A few packages of freeze-dried stew. There had been enough food for a month. Two people could have eaten all of it in a couple weeks. Two people. He and Siobhan.

He grabbed two cups. When he touched them, they changed from plastic cups to shining goblets. If there had been brighter light, he was sure they would have reflected golden sparks.

"Siobhan…." he started.

"What?" Maeve came up behind him.

A memory rippled across the surface of Brant's thoughts: an image of two plastic cups that became metal goblets set with shiny stones. Two goblets that held a sparkling drink that bound a mortal to a fairy forever....

"Open the bottle," he said, handing it to Maeve. He did not trust his shaky hands. He held the stems of the cups tightly. They would have broken if they had been crystal. He remembered from somewhere that crystal was a relatively recent innovation. A thousand years ago people couldn't afford it.

Maeve must not see the cups in the dim light. That was it. The light was bad. If they really were goblets she would notice.

"What's wrong, Brant?" she said. "Are you all – ?"

"Open it," he hissed, holding the cups down by his sides.

She took the bottle. He shut his eyes and heard the cap being unscrewed, heard her say, "Hold the cups up."

Automatically, he did. The bottle clinked on the edge of one goblet. Solid. Like metal. Didn't she notice?

"Oh, God – "

Brant opened his eyes, not really wanting to see.

Blue fire splashed out of the bottle. Maeve's hand jumped and azure sparks flowed over the side of the goblet onto the floor. The sparks skittered across the wood like a Fourth of July sparkler dropped by a careless child, then winked out.

Maeve held the bottle away from her, staring at it. "What the hell – ?"

He laughed. He thought he sounded slightly manic. Deranged. He laughed until tears formed in his eyes.

"It's true," he said when he could talk. "True. Don't you see, Maeve? Something *did* happen to me. It's all true. Siobhan was here. She made a special drink, a potion, I think."

Magic. Not a parlor trick or sleight-of-hand, but honest-to-God real magic that defied natural laws.

The bottle fell from Maeve's hand and hit the floor with a clunk. Fiery liquid gurgled out and spread across the floorboards, an azure brilliance that flared and then died away until there was only a wet spot on the planks. Brant set the goblets on the sink. When he let go of them, they reverted to plastic cups. He had no doubt they would change again if he touched them.

He had the same gifts Siobhan had. Dangerous thoughts...not sleight-of-hand...not kid stuff....

Maeve's backed away from him, her eyes wide and frightened.

"They changed," she whispered. "I saw them. It's not possible – the cups changed – " *Oh God it's true it can't be true it's real it can't be –*

For a moment Brant thought she had spoken aloud. Then he realized he heard her thoughts, jumbled and broken, but he heard words, saw images in her mind, saw his own face through her eyes. Vertigo washed over him. He reeled backward. He braced himself against the counter and forced himself back to the silence of his own thoughts.

Brant knew why Maeve had come to the hospital and brought him here. He had touched her mind and influenced her thoughts.

He picked up the bottle and threw it into the sink. Glass shattered in a splash of aquamarine fire that died to indigo and then was gone. At that moment the lantern, too, died, leaving the cabin lit with flickering firelight.

"Brant?"

"What?"

"What's happening?" Maeve's voice sounded small.

Brant stepped over the wet place on the floor and put his arms awkwardly around her. She trembled, but let him hold her.

"Christ, Maeve, do you think I'm not scared?"

Maeve stood with her heels against the raised brick hearth, thinking that the fire poker would be a good weapon.

He knew answering thoughts was dangerous, but it didn't seem to matter any more. "You don't need to defend yourself." He kicked the tools into the corner. "I don't know what's going on, either."

She started to cry.

"It's all right," he said. "Let me put a new battery in the lantern. The light will help."

He changed the battery and turned the lantern on. Brighter light pushed back the encroaching gloom and created sharp shadows in the corners. He found himself looking away from the corners. He imagined all sorts of scary things lurking just beyond the light.

Ghoulies and ghosties and things that go bump in the night....

He set the lantern on the hearth, threw another log on the fire and sat on the couch. He felt better with the light. Maeve sat on the hearth, shivering. She was silent a long while. Her trembling gradually diminished.

"Now what?" she said.

"We wait," he said. "Something will happen. I know it."

"What if nothing does?"

"Then you can take me back to the clinic. I'll go quietly." He stared into the fire, pretending to be entranced with the patterns in the flames. He ran his fingers through his hair. "If nothing happens, I'll go and live in my loft and paint and see my therapist once a week and find somebody nice and stable, get married and have a couple of kids and do all the stuff any other normal man does, dammit, and nobody will ever see me do anything weird again for the rest of my life."

His stomach growled. "Are you hungry?"

She looked at him with a puzzled expression.

Brant went to the cupboard and took out a package of stew. He held it up, and she nodded.

He filled a cast iron pot with water from the hand pump at the sink and hung it from the hook over the fire. When the water was hot, he poured in two bags of freeze-dried stew and let it simmer. The only sounds were the crackling fire and the wind. The cabin filled with the fragrant odor of stew. When it was ready, he served it in plastic bowls with plastic tableware.

They ate in strained silence, finishing the whole pot and most of the stale crackers.

Then they took turns pacing the cabin.

Finally, Maeve yawned. "It's 4:30," she said. "Six o'clock, Brant. No longer. Then I'm leaving."

They wouldn't get her car out of the snow anyway. He didn't think it would matter. The premonition that had dogged him all day had grown into a sense of impending doom. He wondered whose.

He sat in the overstuffed chair beside the fire, put his feet on the hearth, and dozed. He came awake with a start. Maeve was curled up on the couch with the quilt wrapped around her. The fire had died to glowing embers.

He turned on the cell phone for the time. Five fifty-six. He should tell her they were probably stuck here at least for the day. She could have the bed, and he'd sleep on the couch.

Thunder rumbled off in the distance, rattling the windows.

Maeve sat up, stretching. "Thunder snow," she said. "You don't hear that very often."

"Strange," he agreed.

Maeve rose, and using the quilt as a cloak, went to the window. She peered into the darkness.

A flash of light lit the window. Brant counted, something his father had taught him: one hippopotamus, two – a resounding crash shook the cabin.

"Close," Brant said and rose. He snagged the lantern and opened the door. Lantern glow flooded the porch and reflected off a swirling curtain of snow.

Another flash of lightning momentarily blinded him, followed almost instantaneously by a crash of thunder. He blinked, trying to clear his vision. He thought he saw movement in the snow.

"Maeve," he said. "Look."

She edged up beside him in the doorway, squeezed against his arm. He felt her worry. She feared for his sanity, didn't want to stay alone with him. She wouldn't have to. Something was going to happen. He patted her shoulder reassuringly.

"There." He pointed. "By those two trees that are close together. Wait'll the snow blows aside. There."

She peered into the snowy darkness. "Nothing. Nothing. No – lights. Little lights. Fireflies…in the snow?"

The lights moved toward them. Brant felt Maeve's indecision. She wanted to stay, and yet the fearful part of her mind wanted to run. But she was more afraid to go into the storm without a coat. She would have to cross the room by herself to retrieve her parka.

Brant felt Maeve's unspoken fear as if she voiced it.

The lights moved closer, stopped at the end of the porch. In the center of the sparks moved a brighter luminosity. The twinkling lights faded one by one, until only the central glow was left, a radiance that dimmed and revealed a slender woman.

The specter moved closer. A face became visible: elfin features, frightened eyes, narrow nose, high cheekbones. Hair like moonlight.

"Siobhan," Brant said. And he remembered….

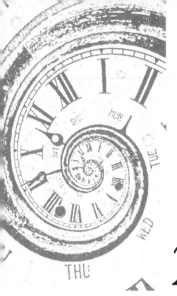

28

Brant leans into the back of the Escape. Fog encloses him and the car. He hoists the duffel and bangs his elbow on the edge of the hatch opening. Pain shoots down his arm. He straightens, forgetting he is taller than the hatch. The top of his head hits the metal. Speckles of darkness whirl in his vision, and then the fog comes back into focus, glowing with reflected light.

A figure materializes from the mist, a small, child-like woman, wearing only slippers and a dirty tunic and a triangle of wool knotted around her shoulders.

Brant wakes in the night. The fire was dead. Siobhan stands over him, ghost-like, and then she is in his mind, tampering with his thoughts. She changes things. Memories scuttle into dark corners, behind doors. He tries to find them, but sees only his reflection in a mirror. Around a corner, another mirror. Like being lost in the house of mirrors at a traveling carnival.

Siobhan cannot take away his memories because his mind is different. Why? Why can't she erase his memories of her? Brant is aware of her moving down the mazes of his thoughts, setting traps along the way. Mirrors to reflect the memories of her into places he cannot reach.

He tries to fight and keep his memories, but he is not strong enough. They seem further and further away, until he forgets what he is trying to remember....

Brant stared at the woman who stood ankle deep in snow. He desperately wanted to remember, wanted the mirrors broken. He concentrated, turned his mind inward, pictured breaking glass, one mirror at a time.

One by one the traps vanished like smoke: a memory loop reconnected, mirrors shattered, doors opened – many doors and circular paths unwound. Images flooded his mind, sounds, tastes, smells, hopes….

Fireworks exploded in his head, a blinding burst of light that left him stunned. In a single moment all of Brant's lost memories surfaced: his sister, Maeve, his childhood, Rich – everything, including Siobhan.

This was what he had feared, what he couldn't face. He had not done anything terrible. He knew who Siobhan was. He feared those memories, because he would have to face who he was. The modern world did not have room for them.

The kaleidoscope in Brant's mind slowed and stopped spinning. Cold air rushed into his lungs, snow whipped around him. Siobhan held out her hands.

He stepped forward, reeled with the ghostly touch of memories superimposed on her face. The images blended into all that he knew of his life, sorting themselves into various sequences.

His grandda–Oh Jaysus–

His father's death – Brant had stood in the ER waiting room with his mother, overwhelmed with grief, unable to speak. The sound of his mother sobbing. Her voice, near hysteria: "Oh, Brant, what are we going to do?"

Brant shouting at the county sheriff, trying to make him investigate his mother's death as more than a car accident.

"Is Mom in heaven, too?" Maeve's voice.

Millions of things he thought had never happened, suddenly restored. How could he have forgotten his sister? He felt whole again.

"Siobhan." He jumped off the porch into the snow and embraced her. "Siobhan," he whispered. Her hair smelled of fog and flowers and melting snow. "It's really you. God, if you knew – "

Her knees buckled, and he caught her. She felt light and fragile.

Not again. So close….he couldn't lose her again. Her eyes were open, but unfocused, her skin cold, so cold. Hang on, hang on….

Brant carried her inside and laid her gently on the bed. Maeve wrapped the quilt around her, straightened and stared at him, her unasked questions almost audible. Her mind could not assimilate what she was seeing. He could do nothing for her except hope his calmness would quell her panic.

"Maeve," he said, "I remember everything. I know you're my sister."

"Than why – ?"

"Not yet. There'll be time later."

"Brant." Siobhan's voice was a faint whisper, her words blurred by her accent. "I thought there could never be a returning. Orghlaith gave me you again. I am so tired…my powers are gone, traded for a curse I gave in anger."

"What happened?" Brant said.

"I went back to my own time," Siobhan said. "I had Murchad's child. The boy is dead by the druid's hand…I thought Murchad did it. It was the druid all along. All because of the druid's potion."

A shudder wracked Siobhan's body. "Orghlaith told me," she said. "That…."

Brant stared at her, uncomprehending. Siobhan sighed, the weight of her grief unmistakable.

"It is a long tale," she said. "Do we have time?"

"We have time," he said, and took her cold hands in his. "All the time in the world."

Maeve laid her coat on top of the quilt. After a moment Siobhan stopped shivering.

"What happened?" Brant said.

Siobhan spoke haltingly at first, seeming unsure of words, but as she talked, the words came more easily. She told them all that had befallen her from the time she had left him in the cabin. She included Maeve in her telling, accepted her as a natural part of Brant's world. She told them of her son, Bran, Murchad's child.

"His hair was dark as a raven's wing," Siobhan said. "Like his father's, like Murchad o'Ruairc.

"Bran was a good son. He was bright as a star in the sky. Kind and gentle." Her voice faltered, betraying her grief. She drew a deep breath. "There was a man from Brittania, a good man called Gareth who taught the boy wisdom and fairness. As Murchad grew old and put aside the other women, he was a fair and attentive father. He just never understood that Bran would never be a warrior." Her voice was wistful. "Bran was a thinker, a dreamer.

"Over the years I came to respect Murchad. He was known for his honest dealings with the farmers and villagers in his holding and those in neighboring holdings. When it seemed our son was only human, I thought my revenge on Murchad would not come to pass – that he would have a son who commanded enchantment, fey like me. There was no shame for Murchad in having a mortal son. But he must have been dissatisfied with Bran." Tears filled Siobhan's eyes.

Maeve sat at the foot of the bed.

Siobhan hugged the quilt around her. "There was a druid named Ceallachan. He had a daughter, Lassariona." Bitterness hardened her voice. "I know now that the druid must have pressed Murchad to find a place for his grandson – Lassariona's bastard. Murchad's son, conceived on the night Murchad and I were united in a marriage bond. I never saw the boy. But I thought Murchad wanted Bran dead so the druid's grandson would inherit Murchad's holdings."

"How was Bran killed?" Brant said.

"Murdered," she said, "with a piece of crystal iron, untouched by human hands, untainted by craftsmanship. My magic was foiled." Her voice was hoarse with emotion. "It was a piece of raw iron, that in the boy's deluded mind became a familiar object. He could not to resist the druid's illusion. Bran thought it was the shank of his cloak pin and participated in his own slaying. He plunged the shard into himself."

Maeve got up and poured a glass of water, then handed it to Siobhan. She drank it down in noisy gulps and handed the plastic cup back to Maeve.

Siobhan's eyes held a deep well of sorrow.

"Such a minor wound," Siobhan said. "When the iron pierced Bran's skin, it brought on the fey change. The poison spread through his body and he…he…succumbed. Murdered" – her voice betrayed raw grief – "by the clever, evil druid."

"How did the piece of iron change into something else?" Maeve said.

Siobhan turned weary eyes toward Maeve. "It…."

"How?" Maeve urged.

"It is secret," Siobhan whispered.

"Why is it secret?" Maeve persisted.

Brant knew she would not give up.

Siobhan glanced at Brant and then back at Maeve. "It is…magic."

"Where does magic come from?" Maeve said.

"I do not know where Ceallachan's magic came from," Siobhan said.

"Where does *your* magic come from, Siobhan?" Maeve said.

Siobhan spread her arms. "It comes from deep within me. A place I cannot see….Why is this important to you?"

"I'm curious," Maeve said. "I meant no disrespect."

Maeve would be curious. And skeptical. Magic was mere sleight-of-hand. Rabbits appeared from hats, lovely stage assistants were levitated, the Statue of Liberty disappeared on network television. None of it was *real*.

Siobhan's eyes filled with horror. "It was horrible," she said. "Murchad killed Gareth with his sword. Gareth was a good and faithful man, sworn for life to Murchad's service. Murchad thought Gareth helped the druid for... for love of me." Siobhan's voice fell to a faint whisper. "Gareth loved me all those years, Brant. He only spoke of it once. I could never return his affection. My heart belonged to you."

"I'm sorry," Brant began, knowing it was inadequate.

Siobhan hung her head. "I did something terrible. Something forbidden. I called up powerful magic and conferred immortality upon Murchad – "

Maeve gasped. Her mind filled with rebuttals and questions.

"It is true," Siobhan said. "I found the girl my son loved and we fled the fortress into the *Sidhe* Wood, hoping to find refuge with the *Faerie* Queen, Orghlaith. She sent me here again to you. For that I am grateful. But my son is gone. Dead. Buried for a thousand years. And somewhere Murchad still lives. He must hate me for what I did."

Brant touched her cheek. "We can be happy," he said. "You haven't lost me." Brant put his arms around her and crushed her to him.

"It just happened for you, didn't it?" he said.

"Yesterday. See...my son's blood on my dress." She pointed to a dark stain. "I should have stayed here with you. I should have found a way to break Orghlaith's spell. You would have understood about the baby...none of this would have happened...."

"Siobhan," Brant said gently, "you can't change what has been, only what will be."

"She said that...Orghlaith...how did you break free of what I did to your mind?"

"I don't know. It just happened. Things came undone." He had no other way to explain it.

"I did a terrible thing to you," Siobhan said. "Something my people must not do. Magic is secret, meant to be kept apart from others. I am truly sorry if I caused you pain. I meant only to help you, to ease your loss. I went inside your mind and rearranged your memories so you would not remember me. But for some reason I could not take away the memories. I could only hide them. I ran out of time, and it was done badly."

Brant chuckled. "I know you messed with my mind. I knew all along, but I couldn't remember." He glanced at Maeve. She looked panicky. He turned back to Siobhan. "I tried to remember. I thought I must have done something horrible and then blocked it out completely. There were parts of it, Siobhan. I remembered you bruised and scratched, and I thought I had done it. Had gotten drunk or something and beat you up and…and….”

Brant was aware of Maeve staring at him. He reached to her. “It's all right,” he said, but she backed away. Fear spilled from her mind.

“Oh, Brant,” Siobhan said. “I am eternally sorry for causing you grief. You could never do anything bad.”

But he had. He had killed two people. It was self-defense, but that did not make his action any more palatable.

“Will I lose you again?” Brant said.

“No. I must stay here. I have no way to get home.” Siobhan pointed to her neck. “See? No golden band to take me back. I am trapped here in your time for the rest of my life. And now I am mortal like you. When I cursed Murchad with eternal life, I made the mistake of reinforcing the spell with the blood of three – mine, Gareth's and Bran's – with a golden brooch made by one of the Fair Folk. I lost my power. I will die, like you, in a normal span of years.” She smiled through her tears. “It is worth it to be here with you.”

She picked up Brant's keys from the night stand beside the bed and turned them over, studying them. “What is this?”

“My lucky key chain,” he said. “I thought for a while it was nothing but bad news, but I see my luck has changed.”

“Where did you get it?” Her voice was sharp, more animated than it had been.

“My mother,” he said. “It's been in the family for generations. Only heirloom we have. Mom told me that her father gave it to her when she was young and she was to give it to me. Grandda told her it had been passed down for too many generations to count. He used to say it was a fairy's gift. The story is that the firstborn son in each generation receives this. My mother had an older brother who died in infancy, so as the only child, she got it. It's very old – ”

Siobhan fumbled in a pouch at her waist and brought forth another golden object. Part of a circle with a small gap. It gleamed in the lantern light. Brant's piece was worn smooth. Siobhan's half was decorated with interwoven designs molded into the gold.

“When I cursed Murchad,” Siobhan said, “I held this pin in my hand. When I opened my fingers it was rent in two. I gave one piece to the girl who carried my son's child. She was to guard it and give it to him when he was old enough. I impressed upon her the importance of handing it down to the firstborn son, that it would always bring the good luck of the *Sidhe*. The Fair Folks' luck, Brant.”

He stared at her. In his mind pieces of a puzzle fell into place.

"See," Siobhan said, holding the two pieces up. "They go together. Your piece fits here. They don't match perfectly. A thousand years is a long time."

Brant glanced at Maeve. She opened her mouth, but nothing came out.

"This is what linked us," Siobhan said. "Of all the people in the world, Orghlaith picked you, Brant. You and your time. You are my descendant. We are bound by a common ancestry. That is why I could not take away your memories. That is how you broke free of the blocks I put in your mind. Don't you see? When you have *Sidhe* ancestors, hidden inside you is the spark of our inheritance. Even though unused for generations, this seed is rooted within you. Your mind is like mine, with all the built-in barriers against invasion and all the potential of my father's people. That is why I could only set traps, a few circular paths in your mind, some reflections. I could not take anything from you. It is all there inside you."

His heart lurched. A rush of intuition told him the truth. Siobhan's re-patterning of his memories had somehow disturbed whatever it was that had lain dormant in his genes for generations: a blueprint for magic. Real magic. A different reality. She had released within him vast, untapped energy.

He had called the fire and incinerated the two men who attacked him. But there was more – the ability to evoke the full gamut of magic. Training and discipline could bring it to fruition, but it was there, way down deep, waiting to be unleashed.

When he was in the hospital, he'd healed fast…miraculously fast…. He'd never been sick, never had a cold or the flu. Perfect attendance through school, even college. The recent headaches. Were they a manifestation of his emerging abilities?

Power rested in the deep, secret places of his mind, waiting to be tapped. The crisis of Siobhan's tampering had acted as a catalyst for what had been within him all his life. Real magic.

Siobhan had given up her powers. She was mortal and would live and die in a normal span of years. He would not. His latent abilities would rise in spite of his efforts to keep them hidden. The magic would betray him in anger or fear or emotional stress, just as it had when he'd protected himself from the muggers. He had no conscious control of the forces. Against his will, his body would heal itself, mend from all but the gravest wounds. If this legacy hadn't given him immortality, he would at least live a very long time. Near immortality was an uneasy concept. Think of what he could do, what he would see….

A heavy tread sounded on the porch – someone stomped. Siobhan's gaze turned to the door. Brant put a hand on her shoulder.

The door burst open. A spare, middle-aged man stood in the lantern light, framed by the whiteness behind him. He was dressed in a down parka, his face hidden by the hood. He pushed the hood back. Snow sparkled in his hair. Terrible anger lit his face. Brant sensed a trim body and muscular arms beneath the coat.

Lightning illuminated the man in stark silhouette. Thunder boomed, rumbled off into nothing.

Siobhan's voice was a knife slicing through the silence.

"Murchad."

29

Maeve had listened to Siobhan's story, trying to understand. The rational part of her mind told her magic was impossible. It was one thing to talk about successful ESP experiments, quite another to accept magic – the real, supernatural kind. People didn't live forever. Not even for a thousand years. If there ever were people like Siobhan – fairies, for God's sake – they were long gone from the earth. Since it couldn't be true, then it was a con of some sort, unbelievably well executed, for reasons beyond Maeve. Why would Brant stage such an elaborate charade? No answer came to mind, except the one Maeve didn't want to face: Brant was suffering a psychotic break, and he was delusional.

Maeve knew the man in the doorway. Had known him all her life.

"Murchad!" Siobhan repeated.

Maeve was a dupe. She wracked her mind for a motive. Unless...unless it were true....But it couldn't be true –

The man's features were rugged, not quite handsome, his once dark hair graying at the temples. In the sudden brightness of the lightning, his face was weary, filled with bitterness. He opened his mouth, but thunder drowned out any sound he might have made.

Maeve turned to Brant. Something monumental, if not magical, was happening. Something had made Brant different. Raw power emanated from him in an almost visible aura. The lantern light flickered and took on a faint bluish cast.

What if it were true? If real magic were possible, then it rocked Maeve's reality to its core. It shook the reality of the universe.

The man's movement into the cabin brought an icy gust of snow into Maeve's face. Brant stepped toward him, and although he was taller than the intruder by a head, he was dwarfed by the man's anger.

"Murchad," Siobhan said.

"Morgan," Brant said.

"Our lawyer?" Meave's mind reeled with impossibilities.

Morgan's dark eyes flicked back and forth over the three in the cabin. Where before Maeve had just been an observer, she suddenly became an integral part of the tableau. Whatever followed, real or not, she was part of it, not just a spectator. Tension charged the air. The back of her neck prickled, and a shiver coursed down her back. A premonition of danger, of something beyond her understanding, brushed against her.

"I've kept track of you and your sister, Brant," Morgan said. His voice resonated low and menacing in the stillness. "A long time....I have waited a long time." He turned toward Siobhan. "A thousand years, witch woman. Orghlaith told me where you went. I gave her a bit of gold for a prophecy. Only she didn't bargain on my understanding. The druid deciphered the meaning of her prophecy in return for a declaration of his grandson's legitimacy. Something that would cause only raised eyebrows in the modern world. Lassariona made a fine wife, Siobhan. She welcomed my touch, wanted me in her bed."

Siobhan stepped back, her mouth forming a silent O.

Morgan glared at her. "All I had to do was wait for you. Orghlaith's riddle told me to seek your heir, the boy's unborn son. The son like the father, she said, the acorn that grows into the oak. Witch begets witch. It was not easy, but I found Slaine and the child, protected by means I could not thwart. I watched her for years, waited, bided my time. I made and lost fortunes while I watched Slaine's child and then her grandchildren grow and die, and always I watched the firstborn son. The first was always special. And finally, after generations, the protection wore off, and the heirs were vulnerable.

"Ceallachan didn't understand the entire verse the *faerie* woman told me. It took me a long time to see that eventually we would all come full circle."

He drew himself up straight like a preacher about to deliver the greatest sermon of his life.

"Into the oak the acorn grows

And spreads its seed around it.

Death's cold seed grows too within;
The earth-forged knife has bound it.
Endless circles draw together,
Sought by three who find them.
Once made whole, the circles close.
Eternity will bind them."

The words held power. Had they really been uttered by someone a millennia ago? A cold hand of fear closed on Maeve's heart.

"Eternity, Siobhan," Murchad said. "I've had ten centuries to understand. Do you know how many times I've been wounded? How often I lay in my own blood and that of my enemies and friends and willed myself to die, because I was tired, so tired. Do you know how many times I tried to take my own life? Do you know the pain of your bones mending? The hopelessness of your skin knitting together when you wish only to bleed to death? You do not know the agony of seeing all those I cared for grow old and die, while I lived on. Lassariona grew old in spite of her knowledge of life. Even Ceallachan died."

He glanced around. Maeve could not move. Both Brant and Siobhan seemed frozen.

"No wonder there are none of your kind left. Life held no joy so they gave up living and just withered away to nothing. Or they became like the banshee, wandering the night in search of a dying soul to give themselves a momentary illusion of life."

"No," Siobhan whispered. "They went away into Orghlaith's world. All but me."

The man glowered at Brant who stood quietly, appearing calm, but Maeve saw anger in his eyes and in the quick, nervous way he ran his fingers through his wavy hair.

"I finally understand," Morgan said. He looked back to Siobhan. "I have watched your family for all those generations. And each generation died after the first-born son became a father. A few died naturally, but most I managed to dispatch before their time. Every generation for a thousand years."

Morgan turned his murderous gaze to Brant. "Your grandfather in a bar fight: a well placed knife. Your grandmother in Spirit Lake. She struggled, but the water took her. Your father: killed as he left the bank." He nodded to Brant.

"You were right. Your mother was dead before the car hit that tree." He sneered at Maeve. "I would have gotten your sister if she hadn't married a cop.

I became your father's lawyer when your grandfather died. It was all planned. Planned a very long time."

He took a half step toward Maeve and stopped. "You," he said to her. "Your mother was the first generation of an only child. A girl at that. I thought things might be different."

He swung back to Siobhan.

"All that time I waited, Siobhan, looking for the one with the gift of magic. The one you would return to. And finally, Brant was born."

Heat crept into Brant's face. He said, "Kirk Morgan. You killed our father, our mother." His voice was devoid of emotion.

"She died easily," Morgan said. "It only took one blow to her head. I am quite adept at staging accidents. Do you know what my name means? Murchad. I changed it to Morgan somewhere along the way. It means sea warrior. It was almost prophetic that my mother named me that. Like my name, I followed your family across the sea to continue my revenge until only you and your sister were left. And now I have you both. There will be no more after you."

Morgan drew a breath and continued, "And now the *Faerie* Queen has sent the witch to you." He looked at Siobhan. "I knew if I waited I would see you again. I thought you could not lie, that your nature wouldn't allow you to deceive me. Now I see that you would lie to protect yourself and your lover." He nodded toward Brant.

"What?" Siobhan said.

Brant spread his hands and said, "It's not what you think – "

"I see now that Bran was not my son," Morgan said. Venomous hatred filled his voice, and his eyes were fiery with the madness of obsession.

"I didn't know what I was doing. The druid's potion made me crazy. I didn't use it right. After I bedded Siobhan at the *Samhain* fire the witch queen sent her away." If Morgan sought absolution from them, he didn't find it in their silence. He glanced from Brant back to Siobhan.

"You came to this time, to this man. You laid with him. I know why you named the boy Bran. He was not my son at all. All those years, I believed he was mine."

Brant started to speak, but Siobhan laid a hand gently on his arm.

"I agreed to be your wife," she said, "so you would be tormented by having fathered a fey son. It did no good. You saw him as only human, as indeed he seemed to be. He did not have time to prove himself before you had him killed."

"Killed? I? I had nothing to do – you think I – good God, woman. It was the druid. His scheming daughter put him up to it. They planned it from the beginning. The druid…all his doing…You thought I did it? How could I? I loved Bran." Morgan swallowed. "And he wasn't even mine."

"Was not love enough?" Siobhan said.

Lightning lit the windows. Thunder boomed.

"You admit your treachery?" Morgan roared in symphony with nature's rumbling. He seemed to grow taller. Brant stepped back. Brant's eyes flicked back and forth between Morgan and Siobhan. Something wild seethed beneath Brant's seemingly calm exterior.

"No, Morgan," Siobhan said. "I admit nothing that is not true." She trembled visibly. Brant grasped her arm.

Morgan raised his hand. A long, sharp splinter of metal glittered in the lantern's glow. His voice fell to a hoarse whisper. "You will pay, witch. Losing your power was not enough. Just as I agonized all those years, you will grieve for the rest of your life when your lover is dead – "

He lunged at Brant with unexpected swiftness, his body supple as an athlete's. The glittering pyrite shard slashed downward. Brant seemed frozen. Maeve could do nothing.

30

Blood filled Maeve's vision – blood to come. In her mind's eye she saw the blade penetrate –

Siobhan threw herself between the two men. At the last instant Maeve thought Morgan's thrusting hand hesitated, but it was too late. Maeve gasped at the impact as the metal splinter penetrated Siobhan's shoulder. Bright red blood flooded the front of her dress, dripped on the oaken floor. Brant grabbed Siobhan and drew out the shard before Maeve could tell him not to.

Siobhan collapsed into Brant's arms. He eased her to the floor. The pyrite clattered beside him. He stared in stupefied horror at his open hand, burned where the metal had touched him. Already blisters formed. Morgan's eyes looked dark, dead. His parka slipped off his shoulders.

Maeve's thoughts whirled. Iron. Siobhan had said that fairies were afraid of iron. It burned them. It was the only way to kill them. She stepped back in revulsion. So much blood…Siobhan's dress was red… Brant's hands were bloody.…

Bile rose in Maeve's throat.

Siobhan's lips moved, her voice low, but distinct. "There was no deception, Morgan. The boy was your son, and I did not know he was fey.…" Her eyes rolled back.

Brant bowed his head over Siobhan's still form. Tears dripped from his nose.

Morgan swayed. Pain replaced the deadness in his eyes. "Oh, Siobhan, I didn't mean…all these years.…I couldn't grieve thinking he wasn't mine…I should have loved him more…." He fell to his knees beside Siobhan and rocked back and forth.

Morgan was frozen in time. Maeve let out the breath she didn't know she was holding. Morgan leaned forward and reached out. He looked up at Brant. His fingers closed on the pyrite. Maeve knew what he would do, but her voice wouldn't work. Then it happened all over again. Morgan staggered to his feet and threw himself at Brant. Maeve imagined blood all over again, and there was nothing she could do.

Brant raised both arms. Blue-white light flashed from his hands. Morgan slammed back to the floor as if he had rebounded off an invisible barrier. He looked dazed.

"Don't. Move," Brant said. Whether he meant her or Morgan, Maeve wasn't sure. She couldn't move anyway. Fear immobilized her.

Was there nothing to be done for the woman whose life bled away? Maeve was terrified to move closer, as if by helping, she would actualize something that couldn't possibly be real.

Nothing was impossible.

Magic was impossible.

Again Brant raised his arms. Maeve saw a glitter of gold in one hand: the piece Siobhan had given him. He murmured strange words, words that gained power as they rolled off his tongue. Maeve flinched. The ominous resonance of the words hurt her head. The words would crush her, but she was powerless to stop the deep, rhythmic pounding inside her head.

Brant's voice rose. A cobalt aura like ultraviolet light gathered around him and brightened to aquamarine. All Brant's fury was directed at the man who sat on the floor, now smiling.

"I don't care anymore," Morgan said. "Do what you will."

Morgan was immortal. Maeve knew in a flash of intuition that he feared nothing Brant could mete out. Morgan had already faced and overcome every conceivable adversary in his span of centuries – both human and circumstantial. Death did not frighten him. He embraced it. Attacking Brant had been Morgan's last hope for peace. He had known Brant might have the magical strength to unravel the curse and give him a normal life. Maeve realized the attraction of immortality, but Morgan had lived far beyond his mind's ability to enjoy or endure. His discovery that the revenge he had nurtured all those years was meaningless, must be devastating.

Morgan gazed up at Brant. A peaceful smile lit up Morgan's face. He brandished the metal shard. Morgan's lips moved, but Maeve didn't hear the words.

Azure fire gathered around Brant, shrinking to encase him in a bright glow, almost white. He gritted his teeth. Energy lashed out to Morgan. For an instant Morgan glowed an eerie blue. Maeve was transfixed by the pain that crossed his face. His features wrinkled, wizened, and his hair turned snowy white. His cheeks took on the hollow appearance of old age, and his skin stretched taut and transparent across the planes of his face and skull. His hair fell out in clumps until only a few wisps remained.

Morgan raised the pyrite and stared at it. The veins in his hands became prominent, and the skin developed liver spots and wrinkles. He aged decades in a few moments. Maeve marked the physical effects, the loss of muscle tone, paper-thin skin. Morgan appeared a hundred years old, two hundred, and still he aged, the effects accelerating as she gazed, unable to look away.

This was not natural. Maeve's rational mind could only dredge up one name for it – *magic*.

Brant lowered his hands. The blue fire faded to a soft radiance. His eyes widened and his lips formed a single word. "No…."

Still Morgan aged. He crumpled in upon himself until he was half a millennium old. And still he degenerated. Maeve opened her mouth. All that came out was a strangled gurgle. Morgan aged more and more rapidly until Maeve's eyes couldn't follow the changes.

He couldn't possibly still be alive, and yet he moved feebly. There was a horrible stench of something long dead. Flesh fell in strips from his bones. Finally, when it seemed he was older than time, the blue fire flared brighter and engulfed him. Blinding flames consumed him, and he writhed and collapsed inward. The fire burned brighter and fed upon itself until there was nothing left to burn.

The brightness dwindled to a tiny sapphire spark. Finally the speck of light winked out like the last tiny dot in a television screen. The pyrite glinted on the floor. Where Morgan had been, there was an emptiness, terrible in its implication. The blue incandescence around Brant deepened to indigo and then faded until only the feeble glow of the lantern was left.

Maeve's mind fumbled to grasp what she had seen. A blue afterimage burned in her eyes. Blinking cleared her vision and brought into focus Siobhan's body sprawled across Brant's knees, cradled gently in his arms. He stroked her hair, leaving bloody streaks, but he didn't seem to notice. There was blood on his shirt and face. So much blood.

He looked up. "I didn't mean to kill him." His voice was low and distant. "I just used the pin to…to take away the spell. Siobhan showed me how…I went into her mind. He would have killed me and you…I didn't know…."

Brant's eyes lost their focus. She knew he didn't see her. Tears made tracks in the blood on his face.

Siobhan barely breathed. She was dying. Maeve had to do something. She knelt, her knees striking the floor with bruising force, but it didn't matter. All that mattered was the blood. They had to stop the bleeding.

Maeve tore a strip of fabric from the hem of Siobhan's dress. The loose-woven fabric parted easily. The sound of ripping cloth seemed loud. Maeve didn't look up at Brant. She was afraid to, afraid to let him see defeat in her eyes. Siobhan had already lost a great amount of dark blood. A major vessel must have been pierced, and they were miles and a blizzard away from medical help.

Maeve wadded the bit of fabric so the cleanest part was exposed. She tore the neckline of Siobhan's dress. Blood flowed in a stream from a hole just below Siobhan's left collarbone. Maeve wished miracles could be summoned.

She pressed the wadded cloth tightly against the injury and only then looked at Brant. Never had she seen such fury on his face. She was shocked by the strength of it, drew back, nearly lost her courage.

"Brant?" No response. She grasped his arm with her free hand and shook him. "Brant."

He looked at her, but his eyes seemed unfocused.

"Brant," Maeve said. "Listen. Put your hand on this. Hard. We've got to stop the blood. She'll bleed to death if you don't help."

"I –"

"Do it."

His fingers opened, and the golden brooch fell to the floor. Maeve guided Brant's hands to the makeshift compress. She put her hands on top of his, pressing down.

"Hard," she said. "Hard."

With one hand on Brant's, Maeve took Siobhan's pulse: rapid, weak. Her skin was cool and clammy, her fingertips bluish.

"Brant," she said. "We've got to get her out of here." How? Going into the blizzard was suicidal.

Brant leaned close to Siobhan. "Help us," he said. "I can't find the way without you. Help me."

Hopelessness tasted bitter. Siobhan was dying, and they were trapped.

Brant grasped Maeve's arm. With a suddenness that pressed her breath from her lungs, a giant hand slapped her. The light went out, and tremendous pressure squeezed her chest. She couldn't breathe.

The pressure eased abruptly, and Maeve drew a shuddering breath. She fell a few inches, striking a solid surface hard enough to jar her knees again. She pulled away from Brant's grasp and caught herself on the surface beneath her.

The floor felt different, not the polished wood planks of the cabin. Her palms stung.

"It's all right, Maeve," Brant said. "It's safe here."

Siobhan lay across Brant's knees, unmoving, covered with blood. Brant still pressed the makeshift dressing over her wound.

Maeve shook her head, searching for a logical explanation. There was none. Her mind whispered, *magic*. She was afraid she was losing her mind, more afraid she was not, that this was indeed reality.

Maeve blinked, looked around. Smooth, gray walls enclosed a small room. The air was blossom-fresh.

"What...what...." Maeve said, her voice no more than a squeak.

"It's a place I found in Siobhan's mind," Brant said. "She goes here when she wants to be alone. She made it. It's a place out of time...something like that. I took us here. But she's dying, Maeve. Her mind is slipping away, getting dark."

Maeve crawled toward him.

"There has to be something we can do," he said. His eyes were all pupil and glittery. He looked at his hands on the bloody rag that held in Siobhan's life. His face grew rigid, his eyes lost their sparkle and became vague as he forced all his attention toward Siobhan, to what purpose, Maeve couldn't fathom. Did he think he could bring her back? Siobhan's skin already held the pallor of death.

Again Brant mumbled unrecognizable words, guttural sounds that made Maeve shiver. She felt a formless dread, knew the words held power that scared the shit out of her.

The tension in Maeve's neck grew unbearable. She stood up on unsteady legs, looked around for something that might help them.

The room had neither windows nor doors. The gray material of the walls formed shelves, a table and a streamlined chair. Each object blended into a single surface. A gray pitcher and a cup occupied the table, looking as if they grew from the flat surface.

She made her way across the room and lifted the pitcher, poured a cup of what appeared to be water. She splashed water on her face, poured another cup and rinsed her hands. A third cup. Took a long drink.

Maeve set the pitcher down. It wasn't large enough to hold three cups of anything. She peered into its interior. Empty. She lifted it and poured into the cup. Water splashed out. She looked into the pitcher. Empty. She poured into the cup again. Water.

She poured until the cup was full, overflowed, and still water issued from an empty container.

She dropped it. The pitcher landed on its side, water still pouring, running over the table and onto the floor. The pitcher righted itself, and the water stopped flowing. The spilled liquid disappeared into the gray surface.

"Oh, God," she whispered. It was true. All of it was true. This was really happening.

"Maeve." Brant's voice was hoarse, exhausted. She whirled, her heart in her mouth. "I can't do it," he said. "I can't bring her back. I'm not strong enough."

31

Sorrow and helplessness overwhelmed Brant. He was losing the woman he loved. Siobhan's mind had shown him an incredible truth.

Buried deep inside Brant, held in check for so many generations his humanness overshadowed it, was power – *magic*. Siobhan's tampering with his memories had nudged it up out of the secret places in his mind, making him susceptible to the poison of iron. The burn on his hand proved it. Power tantalized him, just beyond his reach.

He did not know how to summon the magic. His body healed itself without his intervention. If he could find a way to access the magic, could he heal Siobhan?

Brant summoned fire and destroyed the muggers. What if he called on the magic to heal her, and it backfired? What he did – or did not do – might kill her. Might kill them all.

Siobhan lay across his knees. He brushed a damp strand of hair off her face and probed her mind for answers. He sank into her thoughts. Darkness swirled around him, tangible like fog. Something brushed sinuously against his leg, cat-like, but when he looked, there was only darkness.

"Siobhan," he called. He strained to hear her answer. But no sound came back to him, not even echoes.

"Siobhan," he called louder. "Siobhan."

Here. Her voice, thin and faraway.

He reached out for her essence. "Siobhan."

Brant…too late…no time…

She hovered, poised on the edge of an abyss that roiled with deeper currents of chaotic darkness. A calling beckoned her into the emptiness, pulled her away from him. He felt the tug at his mind, like a puppy pulling on his pant leg. He saw her outline, but there were no features on her face... his dream...but this wasn't a dream....

"Siobhan, what can I do?"

Despair slammed into the center of Brant's chest. He knew from some deep memory that once she started on the journey across the darkness, there would be no returning.

Too late...

If only he could stave off death. But Death was dispassionate and stronger than Brant. Only the healing power would pull her back.

A shadowy form began to coalesce near her. The murk gathered into the graceful arch of an equine neck, a mane that flowed with star-sprinkled darkness. Mighty hooves stamped impatiently. Nostrils flared crimson. Siobhan moved toward the ghostly horse and put her hand on its neck. It quieted instantly.

"Siobhan," Brant said.

She turned and gazed at him for a long moment, then looked away.

"Siobhan, take my hand. Hold on." He grabbed at her, felt something insubstantial slide between his fingers. Then, wavery as in a dream, she was astride the dark horse, her hands pale against its neck. The horse snorted thunder. Lightning flared from its hoofs and illuminated the darkness for an instant.

"Siobhan," Brant called.

She reached for him, but the shadow-horse danced away.

You have power." Siobhan's voice spoke in his mind, a faint whisper. "*You have called me thrice, holding me here. You must let me go or I will be trapped between the worlds, neither alive nor dead.*

"What can I do?" he shouted into the darkness.

Go back...the brooch...it has power...you can fix this...you have power....

"I love you," he said.

A faint answer whispered, *I love –*

Brant was in the gray room once more, holding Siobhan across his knees. Her face pale as snow. He could not feel her breathe.

"There's nothing you can do, Brant," Maeve said. "She's gone."

Anger welled up inside him. Rage was strong, stronger than defeat. Maybe stronger than death. He could use his anger, channel it through the brooch. If Siobhan was right.

"Come here, dammit," he said. He hadn't meant to sound so sharp.

Maeve stared at him and started to speak, but he held up a conciliatory hand. "We've got to get out of here, Maeve. Now. Before it's too late. You have to come closer. I can't take you with me unless I'm touching you."

She moved toward him until she stood just within arm's reach. She clasped her hands together, kneading her thumbs.

"Don't fall apart on me," he said through clenched teeth. "We've come this far. I can do it. I know I can."

Brant grabbed Maeve's hand. He closed his eyes and searched for the way home. In the darkness of the void a shining thread stretched before him. He followed it, willing the three of them back to the cabin.

Maeve stumbled and almost fell. Brant held a motionless Siobhan close to him. How long had it been? An eye blink? Hours?

Sunlight streamed through the windows giving everything inside sharply delineated edges. The brilliance was surreal after the bland grayness of the world they had left. A small fire burned in the fireplace. Blue flames cast an azure tint into the room. Brant picked Siobhan up and laid her on the bed.

"The pin, Maeve," he demanded. "The gold pieces." Time was running out. He leaned over and lifted up the corner of the quilt.

"Brant," Maeve said, "it's too late. Let her go."

He ignored her and scanned the room. There. Under the table by the bed, glinting in the sunlight. When he touched the gold, his hand tingled. He opened his fingers. The encasing plastic of his piece had vanished, and the fragments had somehow joined together. The golden pin was shiny and new and untouched by time. His keys, still on their metal ring, dropped to the floor.

Some corner of Brant's mind pushed away the thought that this was unnatural. If he dwelt on it, he would stop believing. Disbelief would mean Siobhan's death.

An electric shock of energy flowed up his arm, working along his muscles to find the right pathways to the secret places of his brain. His mind blazed with blue fire, flames that didn't burn, but cleansed and strengthened. He saw Siobhan's image in his thoughts, surrounded by fire, and he hugged her to him. He channeled all his will, all his yearning, toward her. Every fiber of his being ached with the effort, and then he gave more, more and a little more, until there was nothing left to give. He struggled to give his all. His strength began to fail.

Maeve was right. It wasn't enough. He couldn't reach her. If only...if only....

A glimmer at the edge of his consciousness. Brant shut out every thought, hope, dream, even doubt, and reached out for the tiny spark. Touched it –

Power flooded into him from somewhere outside himself, and he understood the awe Siobhan had meant at the *Faerie* Queen's superior abilities. A sense of indestructibility and confidence washed over him. Strength flowed into him, a dangerous flood. Raw energy filled him.

He embraced the power. Pure white radiance expanded until he was only an infinitesimal spark at the center. The light carried him into Siobhan's mind to the very edge of the great chasm.

He saw her in bold detail. Small and frightened, she sat astride the dark horse, grasping its neck. The horse gathered itself to plunge into the darkness.

"Siobhan," Brant shouted.

The steed hesitated, turned a baleful eye toward him. Tears wet Siobhan's face, and she trembled. But she held onto the horse with a fierceness that Brant knew took strength.

The horse's ears pricked, and for an instant, it stood still, listening. The darkness flowed away from it. Its form wavered. It grew insubstantial as its matter seeped back into the void that had spawned it.

Siobhan stood before him. He held out his hand. She took it, and Brant's brightness encompassed her. The light filled and strengthened her and drew her back from the edge of the precipice.

He wanted to call her name again, but found himself so caught up in holding the energies in check he was unable to speak. Instead, he drew her mind into the light until a sweet, white incandescence surrounded them.

"Love is enough," Siobhan said, looking up at him. "There is a returning for both of us."

Brightness exploded. Something pounded in Brant's head...pounded.... Brant's muscles trembled, his heart beat in time to the rhythm of some enormous drum.

He found himself prone on a hard surface, panting, unable to take in enough air. His heart hammered as if it would burst. He couldn't focus.

"Brant? Maeve?" A man's voice came through the door. "You there?"

Pounding filled Brant's head.

"Coming," Maeve said, her voice hoarse. She cleared her throat. "Just a minute," she said, stronger. Her course to the door wavered. Her legs were shaky. She fumbled with the lock and finally turned it. Rich pushed the door open.

"Maeve," he said. "Are you all right?" He stepped into the cabin and steadied Maeve as she swayed. Melting snow slipped from his shoulders and knit hat.

Cold air hit Brant in the face, bringing him out of his torpor.

He wanted to say something, but his throat did not obey.

"It's light," Maeve said.

Brant looked up at the icy blue sky that filled the doorway behind Rich. A snowmobile was parked beside the front step. Its tracks disappeared down the cut between the tall trees that marked the road.

"What's going on?" Brant finally managed.

"Going on?" Rich echoed. "I've been looking for both of you. The storm was so bad nobody could get up here. I finally commandeered some of Weyerhauser's equipment. I've got a battalion of trucks out on the logging road."

"Storm's over?" Brant's head hurt. He didn't understand. The storm had just begun.

"A blizzard," Rich said. "It finally let up this morning. Brant, are you all right?"

Brant tried to smile. "Both my sister and I are all right."

Maeve looked startled. "You remember me?"

"I don't know how I could have forgotten you."

Rich hugged Maeve against him and kicked the door shut behind him. "All right. What the hell's going on here?" Rich said. "You two have led me on a merry chase all over half the goddamned state of Washington. I had to convince Cowlitz County's finest that I had a reason to get up here in a hurry. The local sheriff didn't take too kindly to being dragged out of his Saturday poker game. It's been three days, Maeve."

"How did you know we were here?" Maeve said.

"The drawing."

"What drawing?" Maeve said.

"I left a sketch," Brant said.

"It didn't make sense at first," Rich said to Brant. "You drew the cabin, but the trees weren't right. And there were *two* cabins – the real one and another, like a shadow in the foreground."

"You figured it out," Brant said.

"Figured out what?" Maeve said.

"When I was missing," Brant said. "When Rich came up here, what he saw wasn't really the cabin. There was a duplicate – a shadow of the real cabin. It was empty."

Maeve said, "You — "

"Were here all that time," Rich finished. "Two weeks."

"In plain sight," Brant said. "If you had known where to look." He pointed to Siobhan where she lay on the bed.

"Who is she?" Rich said. "Is she all right?"

Siobhan wasn't going to fade into the night as she had before. Her eyes fluttered open. Her lips moved. Brant put a finger on them and hushed her tenderly. A tiny smile quirked at the corners of her mouth. Brant peeled back the bloody dressing from her shoulder. Her fair skin was unblemished. The wound was gone. The only evidence was the dressing and blood on her dress. Even the blood on the floor had vanished.

Maeve leaned against Rich. "Magic," she whispered.

Rich looked from Maeve to Brant. He seemed to be about to say something.

"It must not have been as bad as it looked," Maeve said. "There was just a lot of blood...."

Siobhan opened her mouth, but only a whisper came out, so quiet Brant had to lean close to hear it.

"Morgan," she said. "Where is Morgan?"

Rich stepped forward. "Yeah, Brant, where is Morgan? His car's stuck in the snow out on the road."

"Not here." Brant said.

Siobhan raised up on an elbow. "Where — ?"

Brant put a hand on her arm. "He's gone, Siobhan."

"How?" she said.

Simple question. Brant was aware of Rich waiting for him. Maybe it was best just to say it. Catharsis was sometimes necessary for sanity.

"The pin, Siobhan," Brant said. "Somehow I used its power. I took away the spell you used on Morgan. He aged in seconds. I didn't mean to hurt him." He turned to Rich. "I used the magic once before. When I called the fire — the two men who attacked me. I was afraid to admit that I had really done it."

"Even benevolent power can harm," Siobhan said. "I cannot hear your thoughts. Can you hear mine?"

"No." Nothing rattled around inside Brant's mind but his own thoughts.

"Perhaps it is a blessing," she mused. "The *Faerie* Queen told me I lost all my powers because of that terrible spell. You have lost yours, too. The pin has made us equal."

"Equals?" he said.

"Orghlaith said the pin had a part to play. It harbors ancient magic. It made my power great enough to curse Morgan. It added to your strength, and you healed me. But it also took away something from both of us." She reached down, picked up the discarded shard of pyrite and offered it to Brant.

The blood that had stained it was gone, seared away by the magic fire. He hesitated.

"Take it," she urged. "It will not harm you, either."

He reached for it, faltered. His hand throbbed where the iron burned it before. The blisters were still visible. Healing Siobhan hadn't helped his wound. He raised his other hand and gingerly closed his fingers on the splinter, wincing in expectation. Nothing happened. The metal felt cool and neutral.

"Does it burn?" she said.

"No," he said, turning the shard over. "No. It doesn't."

"Don't you see?" Siobhan said. "What you found, you also lost. The healing was strengthened by the pin and drained by it."

"Yes," he said. "But there was something else, another power beyond mine that helped me. I almost had it...." He trailed off, thinking of what he had glimpsed in his mind. Magic. True magic. For a few moments he had controlled power.

He looked inward and he saw nothing but his own thoughts. No surge of energy at the edges of his awareness. The *faerie* heritage that had blossomed only briefly, that had allowed him to call the fire, to hear others' thoughts, burn his hand on the metal, and heal himself and Siobhan had evaporated.

The pin had given all its inherent power to recall Siobhan from the brink of death. Brant had joined his ability with the ancient magic and lost it all. There was nothing in his mind but a deep well of kaleidoscopic memories.

"Gone," he said.

Siobhan touched the spot just below her collarbone where the metal had penetrated. "You gave my life back to me. That is the greatest of all gifts. I am sorry."

"Don't be sorry," he said. "I'd do it again, knowing what I would lose, to get you back. I owe you my life, too. If you hadn't jumped between us, Morgan would have killed me. I guess that makes us even." He grinned, an honest affirmation. He rose and helped Siobhan to her feet, put his arm around her and held her steady.

Brant turned to Rich. "Thank you," he said.

Rich's expression betrayed bewilderment. There would need to be a long and truthful explanation before he would be satisfied.

"I wouldn't have come if Morgan hadn't called me in the middle of the night," Rich said. "He wanted me to hightail it over to the clinic because you'd left – escaped, was how he put it. He said there'd been a murder. Said he had proof."

Rich turned to Maeve. "You were gone. I head the word murder and was really worried."

"I left you a message," Maeve put in. "I called your cell when I got in the car, but it wasn't turned on. I was going to call again from the hospital, and then, well, I guess I got distracted by helping Brant escape."

Rich hugged her too him. "I have to admit, Babe, that I was slightly frantic when I found you gone. And I didn't realize my phone wasn't on till I got to the clinic. Dead battery. I forgot to plug it in." He looked at Brant. "When I saw your drawings, I figured you came here."

He kissed the top of Maeve's head. "And another thing, Brant. I thought there was something fishy about Morgan. He has no birth records, no parents. And he should be 80 years old, but he doesn't look a day over 40.

"I couldn't come up here on a whim in a blizzard with the SWAT team," Rich went on. "The county sheriff thinks I'm a nutcase. So I called a guy I know who works for Weyerhauser, and he got some of his buddies to clear the roads." He glanced at Maeve. "They're digging your car out." He looked around the cabin. His gaze settled on the fireplace. "Pretty cozy in here. There's more to this, isn't there?"

Brant nodded. The blue glow in the fireplace did not emanate from burning logs. The ashes were long dead, the grate empty. A knot of sapphire flames hovered just above the grate.

Rich approached the hearth and gingerly put his hand out. "It's not hot up close."

Maeve peered around him. "What is it?"

Brant had not created the tiny ball of fire. He looked at Siobhan. She shook her head.

Rich leaned over and reached behind the glowing sphere. It moved out of the fireplace and hung in the air above the brick hearth. He rose upright and backed a step.

"Brant," he said, "for chrissake, what is it?"

Maeve retreated to the door.

Brant shot Siobhan a question with his eyes. They would have to explain this, too.

"Orghlaith," Siobhan whispered so softly Brant was sure Rich didn't hear.

"Brant, where's Morgan?" Rich said.

"I could say he went out into the storm for help," Brant offered.

"That's not true, is it?" Rich moved around the blue ball of fire and studied it. As he did, it shrank perceptibly. "What the hell is this thing?"

The truth. "Would you believe it's magic?" Brant said.

"Magic? Shit," Rich said.

Brant sighed. "It's a long story." The azure fire dimmed, faded and was gone. The cold crept in.

"You know, Brant," Rich said, not unkindly, "I always thought you were sort of strange – creative strange. But this – " He swallowed. "Maeve told me about all the paintings you don't remember doing. What the hell's going on?"

Brant held up his hands, but Maeve spoke first. "Don't judge, Rich, before you know the whole story. We'll all swear Morgan went for help – "

"Is this a crime scene?" Rich interrupted.

"No," Brant said.

"Sort of," Maeve said. Then, "No."

"He went for help," Brant said. "Nobody will ever prove anything else. We'll explain on the way home." His mind searched for a way to tell the story without revealing the magic. But he knew Rich would want nothing short of the absolute truth. He was his sister's husband, and he deserved honesty. Even that would not set everything right. There were some things that could not be spoken. Perhaps that was what Brant had tried to capture in his latest paintings.

Beside him Siobhan shivered. Brant nodded toward her. "Can she change into some of my clothes?"

For the first time Rich really looked at Siobhan. "Who are you?" His voice was gentler than when he spoke to Brant.

"I am Siobhan o'Ruairc," she said without hesitation. "Once I was Siobhan of the forest. In my other life long ago I was *Daoine Sidhe,* those you call the Fair Folk. I made magic, but alas, the power is gone."

Rich's eyes widened. "This is going to be a goddamned good story," he said. "Isn't it?"

"It is," Brant said.

"I'll say it is," Maeve echoed. "I was here. I don't understand all of it myself."

Siobhan pulled some of Brant's clothes from the closet. She changed and cleaned up in the tiny bathroom while Maeve found the first aid kit and applied antiseptic to Brant's blistered hand and wrapped a gauze bandage around it.

Siobhan emerged, dressed in jeans and a wool shirt – much too large – and on her feet a pair of Brant's old boots. She managed to walk without losing the footwear. Brant helped her into his jacket, put an arm around her shoulder and guided her toward the door.

"It's been a rough night," Brant said. He leaned toward Maeve and kissed her cheek. "Come on, Sis."

There were untold questions in Maeve's eyes, but she said nothing and zipped her jacket. Brant grabbed an old barn coat from the peg beside the door and put it on as he went into the cold morning.

They slogged through knee deep snow, following Rich on the snowmobile. Siobhan kept glancing ahead, apprehensive at the roar, but seemed to accept Brant's gentle assurances that it was not a monster that might capriciously turn and devour them.

At the end of the road the snowmobile coughed and died. Silence seemed loud. The snowplow had cleared a space in the road. A black Hummer, Morgan's car, was almost buried in a drift, but Maeve's red Rav4 had been dug free. A small crew of men huddled around the snowplow and two trucks, drinking coffee from steaming mugs. One of the men poured from a large Thermos into a foam cup which Maeve accepted with thanks. Siobhan turned her nose up at the coffee, and Brant didn't have the stomach for anything.

Maeve handed Rich her car keys.

"I can't drive," she said.

"I'll get someone to drive your car back to Portland after they haul out the Hummer," Rich said.

Maeve was shaken, but strong.

Brant could have been truly strong. He could have had magic. Unlimited power.

There was no use thinking about it. It was gone.

It took Brant several minutes to coax Siobhan into the backseat of one of the trucks, but she finally understood that the metal would not harm her. They settled in with Rich at the wheel, Maeve beside him, and Brant in the back with Siobhan.

Brant turned and looked back. All he saw was a narrow, snowy canyon between the trees. The cabin was hidden by the forest. He and Siobhan would come back in the spring. Life would go on. He turned around, bumped his knees on the front seat, and leaned back and closed his eyes.

"If you think you're going to sleep, Brant," Rich said as he started the truck, "you're wrong. I need to hear what happened in there."

"Well," Brant began, "it didn't *all* happen there...."

Brant thought a moment. There was so much to tell. Where should he start? There would have to be an official story about Morgan's disappearance. Going into the night for help seemed plausible. Siobhan and Maeve would back him up. He was certain there was no other way to explain it. Siobhan's presence would have to be accounted for. People didn't just pop in from the past. She would need a life: birth records, immigration records, citizenship papers, a Social Security card, documents that would substantiate her existence in the modern world. She needed a history. Rich would help. He would understand once Brant told the story. Rich had seen the magic. Brant could point out that small shred of proof. The story would go no further than the four of them.

Magic. Real magic. He would never watch a magician perform without remembering, knowing that somewhere it could be real.

He squeezed Siobhan's hand, but she was busy watching the trees go by with what must seem dizzying speed. It reminded Brant of an old movie where the hero rides off into the forest. But, unlike a movie, his story and Siobhan's would continue. At least for whatever life span Fate allotted them.

He put a hand into his jacket pocket and felt the golden brooch. That was real. He traced its shape. A circle with an opening. The *Faerie* Queen's prophecy had spoken of an eternal circle....

"Well," Brant said, "a woman came out of the fog, from the past, from a thousand years ago."

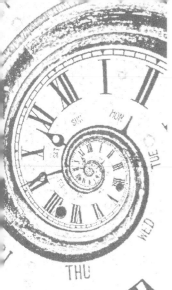

EPILOGUE

A knock on Brant's studio door drew him away from his painting. He glanced at the clock. Just after eleven. Siobhan usually brought lunch in after one so he could have five or six uninterrupted hours of work time.

He'd been painting since dawn, struggling with a large canvas in which he hoped to capture the Olympic rain forest with ethereal faces hiding in the shadows. Dozens of photos littered the counter beside him. Photos he and Siobhan had taken a few weeks ago on a reconnaissance to the area. He almost had what he wanted.

Again Siobhan knocked, louder.

"Come on," he called. He rose from his stool and stretched the kinks from his back.

The door opened and Brant was immediately drawn from the images in the painting to the reality of his pregnant wife. He set his palette and brush on the counter and went to her.

"You all right?" he said. The baby was due in a week. He needed to finish the painting. With an infant in the loft there would be little sleep for some time.

"I'm fine," Siobhan said, using her newly acquired ability to use contractions.

Brant placed a tender hand on Siobhan's distended belly. Their son moved.

"How you doing, Brandon Matthew Edwards?" he said.

"He is strong."

She extended a open envelope and two sheets: one looked like stationary, the other was a page ripped from a magazine.

"What's this?" Siobhan's face wore a strange expression.

"It came in the mail," she said, "with this note."

Brant took the sheet of paper and read.

Thought you might be interested in this. Feminine handwriting. *Don't worry, it won't go any further.* A signature was scrawled at the bottom: Jess Thomas.

Brant scanned the envelope. It was addressed to Brant and Siobhan Edwards. He skimmed the article about a recent archaeological dig in Ireland and then focused on a paragraph highlighted with a bright yellow marker.

"Oh, baby." He put an arm around Siobhan. "This can't hurt us. There's no way to connect this to us."

"Brant," she said, "she has connected it. She sent this to us."

"Honey, don't worry." He hugged her as close as her belly allowed. "If Jessica were going to use this, she would have already."

Siobhan grunted. Brant felt the baby's kick.

"Active today," he said.

Siobhan nodded. "My back hurts."

She so seldom complained that Brant looked at her closely.

"And," she continued, "there's a puddle on the kitchen floor. I was making lunch, but my back started to hurt and then my water broke – "

"Call the doula and get your bag and – "

"I already did." Siobhan laughed. "You're going to be a daddy."

Excitement, terror and tenderness warred in Brant's mind. He hugged her tighter, crumpled the note and the article into a little ball and dropped it in the trash basket by the door.

"Ouch," she said. "I need to sit. It's starting again." She held her belly.

Brant guided her into the living area and helped her sit on the couch.

Siobhan took his hand. "Don't be afraid," she said. "Rich is coming to take us to the hospital, and my bag is by the door. We will be a family by this time tomorrow."

Brant kissed her and rubbed her shoulders as they had learned in the childbirth class. He never gave the letter another thought.

Archeology International, May 2012 Issue

Orley, County Cork, Ireland –

…on a hill where an 10th to 11th Century fortress once stood. Official excavation began at the site in 2005. Recent digging has uncovered a treasure trove of artifacts that have provided valuable information about the Celtic people who occupied the area.

Two curious artifacts have been found. An English coin, dated to the late 10th Century indicates either a foreign visitor at the fortress, or possible trade with the Anglo-Saxons who inhabited Britain. Another find that has been dismissed as a hoax – either deliberate or accidental – was the finding of a plastic comb in a layer of debris dated to the late 900s. Tests indicate it was manufactured in the early 21th Century. Dr. Rufus Sweeney of the University of Dublin, in charge of the dig, dismisses the artifact as accidental contamination from one of the many volunteers who participate in excavating such sites.

Trilby Plants won a blue ribbon at the State Fair for her first story when she was in fifth grade. That began her love of storytelling and all things fantastical. Plants lives and writes in Murrells Inlet, SC.

TrilbyMPlants.blogspot.com

Facebook: Trilby Plants
Twitter: @TrilbyPlants

Made in the USA
Charleston, SC
11 October 2012